TRIP

Zoe

Thank you for joining me on the 'Olivia Swift' Journey.

All my best wishes,

Freddie P Peters.

Also by Freddie P Peters

River Swift Vigilante Thrillers

KILL SWITCH
SAVAGE PEACE

Henry Crowne Paying the Price Thrillers

INSURGENT
COLLAPSE
BREAKING POINT
NO TURNING BACK
SPY SHADOWS
IMPOSTOR IN CHIEF
RED RENEGADE

Nancy Wu Smart Woman Crime Thrillers

BLOOD DRAGON
SON AND CRUSADER
SAVAGED INNOCENCE

TRIP WIRE

A River Swift Vigilante Thriller

FREDDIE P PETERS

Shadow Network Press

London

Print ISBN: 978-1-7394253-26
E-book ISBN: 978-1-0686722-93

Cover design by Lizzie Gardiner
Typesetting by Danny Lyle

Chapter 1

The men were running down the steep slopes of the valley, guns in the air, shooting their AK-47s to announce their presence, when Matondo slapped Kruger's shoulder.

"No one will stand in the way of my men. I told you. I control the whole of this valley—the one after that and the one after that, too," Matondo said in his heavy French accent. "The richest regions around North Kivu are mine—gold, diamond, cobalt, and . . . coltan."

The big man exploded into laughter. It made his large belly jump and accentuated the slash that ran across his left cheek. His shaved head glimmered in the sun. He adjusted his Ray-Bans and eyed Kruger's response—keen, it seemed, to impress.

Kruger crossed his arms over his chest, feet planted apart, and surveyed the scene of devastation with a critical eye. He needed Matondo, so he turned and gave him one of his rare smiles.

"Impressive. How many villages have you burned down this week?"

Matondo grew serious, appreciating the compliment. He came to stand alongside Kruger, imitating him and crossing his arms over his chest. The villagers hiding in their houses would have seen two men dressed in jungle fatigues and khaki T-shirts, one black, one white, one distinctly shorter than the other, surveying without emotion the massacre of innocent people.

"We've only ransacked three this week," Matondo said as he lifted his head toward Kruger. "They don't call me Dr. Death for nothing. I have a reputation to maintain."

Kruger dropped his chin to his chest. "As long as it improves the production of coltan, and as long as the armaments flow unchecked through this region, you do whatever it takes."

The temperature had started to rise, even at 9:00 a.m., and Kruger could feel sweat gathering on his forehead and starting to run down his back. He hated this sort of humid heat; it sapped his energy. South Africa's drier heat was what he liked best. It was perfect for tracking and hunting—animals and men. Kruger ran a hand over his buzz-cut gray hair and blinked a few times. His steel-blue eyes could always take the morning light, so he'd left his Oakleys in one of the side pockets of his pants. For him, wearing glasses was a necessity, not a showing-off exercise, as it was for Matondo.

Matondo's men, who'd run ahead of the pack, had slowed down as they approached the outskirts of the village. They were in the open, and it would have been easy for a sniper to take them down. But none of the villagers had the money to purchase guns or the training to handle them. Still, perhaps a little caution was warranted.

"Progressez. Allez . . . progressez," Matondo shouted. He started running in the direction of his scouts, and the rest of his militiamen accelerated to run alongside him.

The few houses bunched together at the bottom of the valley were now surrounded. Built of red bricks with white tin roofs and no more than two stories high, the houses didn't look expensive or grand, but they stood on valuable land. Villagers of Katuba, in the Democratic Republic of the Congo, had sought to capitalize on its generous stores of coltan (a short cut to Columbite and Tantalite, the two minerals constituents of coltan). This ore had become essential to the production of cell phones and computer hard drives.

Kruger didn't join Matondo's men. He knew what would happen next. Women in the village would be raped, some of the men would be killed, and the surviving men would be forced to use machetes to chop the bodies of the dead. Kruger despised that sort of violence. It wasn't the sort of sport he liked. He had no problem killing a man, but it had to be done after a serious hunt or a battle of equals at least. Still, Matondo was the rising star in the region, more ruthless than most, and his methods suited Kruger's international business model.

Certain corporations in the United States and the rest of the world paid him to find what no one else could find—the sources of rare minerals and markets for armaments. The business he'd started to build some fourteen years ago was stronger than ever in central and southern Africa. He had become the unavoidable go-between until recently.

He took a few steps forward and winced. He was still recovering from a shot to the leg he'd sustained in Washington, DC, five months ago, the result of a setup he hadn't seen coming—and neither had his DC lobbyist contact, Chuck Clery. Clery had been duly made to pay for his mistake and crudely eliminated. All the evidence that linked Kruger to Clery via a case involving the former Navy SEAL Jason Wayne had been destroyed, too. Wayne had been nosing around a little too closely for Kruger and Clery's liking into the impact of heavy use of weapons by Special Forces personnel. Wayne was supposed to be framed for murder, and down he should have gone. Instead, his badass girlfriend, River Swift, had gotten involved, and now Clery was dead and Kruger had to flee DC.

The uncanny link between River Swift and the couple Kruger had had murdered in the DRC some fourteen years previously had rattled him. He was now certain that the couple, who worked for Doctors Without Borders, was related to the woman who'd caused Kruger so much grief. He wasn't sure yet how much River Swift knew. And Matondo, who'd been the executioner at the time, had assured him that no evidence could link Kruger to the murder apart from Matondo himself. Kruger wasn't taking any chances, and he intended to find out how much River Swift knew.

He'd called on a couple of his assets to find out more about the Swift girl. They'd been active for more than two months now and had informed him that Ms. Swift had been asking questions of former colleagues of her parents still working for Doctors Without Borders. That had answered his question as to the links between River and John and Beverly Swift. Now that she was inquiring into an elimination that should have been carried out in a much tidier way, Kruger needed to take care of her, too. Following the principle that if you want something done well you should do it yourself, he would be the one putting an end to River Swift's life.

Kruger couldn't go back to the United States, though, and his CIA contact had been very clear that Swift couldn't be eliminated on US soil, either—too messy. He'd have to lay a plan that attracted the woman to Africa, and then . . .

The thought angered Kruger. He would have to call in more favors from his US contacts, favors he thought he'd never need. He was also locked out of the States for the foreseeable future. He was safe enough in South Africa, his native country, but he needed to keep connecting with his DC circle of influence. He recalled Matondo's axiom: *Loin des yeux, loin du coeur.* Out of sight, out of mind. Although there was very little heart or mind involved in the business of armaments and rare minerals, DC was a place where men and women were continually jostling for position. He needed to keep his place atop the very shadowy pyramid of true power he had climbed so successfully, and the offer of more coltan to the tech industry might just do the trick, ensuring that the incident with Jason Wayne might be conveniently forgotten.

Matondo's voice brought Kruger back to Katuba. Dr. Death was yelling, almost certainly keen to offer Kruger one of the young girls before his men took their share. Kruger wasn't into rape, either—or at least not the rape of a simple village girl. He needed resistance from a more spirited woman in order to enjoy her subjugation.

Kruger's progress was made slow by his wound and the slippery slopes of the grassy hill. He stopped for a moment, unhurried. Matondo's men would have to wait for him before they could satisfy their lust.

Katuba was surrounded by lush hills and rainforest on one side. Land became drier toward the north, and the pit where minerals could be extracted was visible in the distance. It should have been a good place to live—but for men like Matondo and Kruger, its pull was undeniable.

Matondo yelled again, and Kruger resumed his progress. He wasn't in the mood to indulge Matondo, but perhaps he could choose one of the girls and then let her go. The idea of robbing Matondo's thugs of one woman pleased him. Kruger heard raised voices, and he quickened his pace.

As he drew closer, he saw that Matondo's men were surrounding a young boy holding a knife. The boy must have been ten years old, no more. He was bravely standing at the front door of his house, knife trembling in his hand. The men were lunging forward, daring the boy to strike, calling him names Kruger didn't understand—not that he needed to.

Instead of joining the crowd and making fun of the boy, Kruger walked straight up to him. His assurance surprised the youth, and Kruger sent the knife flying with a precise flick of his hand. The men protested. He'd just spoiled their fun.

"Who's inside?" Kruger asked as he held the young boy by the arm, almost lifting him from the ground. The boy looked at Kruger with a mix of anger and fear. Kruger shook him and asked again. This time, in French.

"*Qui est a l'intérieur?*"

A young girl appeared on the doorstep. She was perhaps twelve, but you could already tell she was going to become a beautiful woman—high cheekbones, big almond eyes, and a delicate oval face that matched a delicate, yet sensuous body.

"*Moi,*" she simply said.

Her brother turned to her, and his face dropped. He hadn't managed to protect her, and he knew what would come next.

"She's mine," Kruger said.

Matondo grinned, pleased, it seemed, that his business contact was about to join his men. He left Kruger to it and started looking for a woman who captured his own fancy. The girl disappeared inside, and Kruger walked into the small house, still holding the boy. He looked around the small space. The furniture was sparse, but the room was clean and well-kept. Kruger pulled a chair away from the table, sat down, and let go of the boy.

"What's your name?" He asked the girl first.

"Masika."

"And you?" he said with a small jerk of his head toward the boy.

"Antoine."

They both stood in the center of the small space, close to each other. In the soft light that came from the single window in the room, Kruger noticed that they were both shaking. Screams had started to come from inside some of the houses. Kruger looked around and spotted a small door that must lead to the back of their dwelling.

"Where is your mother?"

"Gone to the next village, bringing remedies for the people there," Masika said.

"And your father?"

"Dead."

"Where does this door go?"

Masika and Antoine looked at each other. Surely this must be a trick question.

"Down to the bottom of the valley?" Kruger continued.

This time, Antoine nodded.

Kruger pointed to the door. "Off you go. Find your mother. Don't come back until nightfall."

Both children remained frozen in silence.

Kruger stood up abruptly. "Go on before I change my mind."

Antoine was the first to move. He grabbed Masika's hand, and they both ran out through the back door.

The files that River had pulled together were open on her small kitchen table. She had hoped that they would be bulging with information by now, but they remained unhealthily slim. She sighed, stood up, and went to the kitchen to prepare a fresh pot of coffee. She had inherited two important traits from her mother: her unusual blue eyes—light-blue irises surrounded by a darker outer rim—and the ability to drink gallons of coffee with little or no effect.

River poured some water into the kettle, placed it on the burner, and lit the flame underneath it. She ran her hand through her shoulder-length blond hair, pulled the scrunchie from her wrist, and tied her hair into a loose ponytail. The kettle started humming, and River opened the cabinet door. She was tall enough to reach the top shelf easily and took down the jar of coffee she'd bought on the way back from visiting her brother, Luke, in Utah.

When she opened the jar, a distinct aroma rose to her nostrils—a complex blend of toasty, nutty, and perhaps even earthy notes. She scooped two large helpings of grounds, dropped them into the coffeemaker, and poured the boiling water over them. River checked her watch—9:03 a.m. Her close friend Karen, an Inupiat, would be ringing the bell of River's one-bedroom apartment any moment now.

River took two mugs and a sugar bowl out of the cabinet and placed them on the table between her open laptop and her files. The freshly brewed coffee was slowly dripping into the pot. The doorbell rang. River walked to the diminutive entrance hall and pressed the Release button for the door to the building without asking who wanted access. She left her front door ajar and returned to the kitchen.

The coffee was ready; she brought the pot to the table and sat down.

"Seriously, Riv. Do you ever ask who wants to get into your condo?" Karen said as she unfastened the strap of her shoes and took them off before entering River's apartment. "I could be Jack the Ripper for all you know." She'd arranged her thick brown hair into traditional Inuit hair loops that accentuated her oval face. Her brown eyes glinted with a mix of strength and humor—the first thing River had noticed about her friend.

"So what? I'd deal with him fine if he ever showed up," River replied with a smug smile that was meant to rattle Karen a little.

"You were a field medic with the Air Force, deployed alongside Special Forces," Karen replied, not taking the bait. "You weren't one of the bad boys."

River pursed her lips. "Very true. But at nine o'clock in the morning, it's not Jack the Ripper who's at my door but rather Karen Robinson—because she can smell my coffee from all the way across Kotzebue."

Karen gave River a quick hug before she said, "And I have to admit no one is as good at making coffee as you are."

"I learned from the best. Mom could always find the best beans wherever we went around the world, and—" River's voice wobbled.

Karen laid a friendly hand on her shoulder. "It's tough to reopen old wounds. Especially when there was no closure in the first place."

"At least my brother and I have been talking through email," River said as she poured Karen a mug.

"Wow . . . you mean he's stopped being an ass about your disturbing his well-ordered life to save his own town from a drug cartel?" Karen picked up the sugar bowl and helped herself.

River shook her head. "That's a little unkind to Luke, uuma. I didn't realize how much Luke had suffered from the life we led with

Mom and Dad. He was desperate for a home he could call his own." River poured herself some coffee and continued. "And then there is this business of not going to visit our parents in the DRC when he thought they might be in danger. He and Dad had an argument about that, and Luke caved in. That decision will haunt him for the rest of his life."

Karen went to the refrigerator to get some milk, returned to the table, and poured a generous helping into her mug. "I hear you, but did he really have to hide some of the items that had been returned from the DRC after their death?"

Her friend had hit a nerve, and River took a sip of coffee before she replied. "That was crappy of him, and he knows it. I guess he's trying to mend fences."

They both sat down, sipping their coffee in silence for a moment, until Karen asked, "Any news from the woman at Doctors Without Borders? Can't recall her name."

"Angela Graham," River said. "Nothing yet. I only got her name from Luke a couple of days ago."

"Where is she deployed?" Karen asked.

River smiled at the question. "You and I *deployed* because we were with the Air Force. I don't think the doctors of DWB see themselves as being *deployed*."

"You know what I mean . . . So where is she working her butt off to make sure people survive epidemics, malnutrition, armed conflicts, and AIDS?"

"I called Doctors Without Borders headquarters in New York, but they wouldn't say. Although they did say she was in Africa."

"How generous of them to be that precise. And when is she due back?"

"In the next couple of weeks," River said before finishing her cup. "But I managed to get another little nugget out of them."

Karen leaned forward with interest. "Don't keep this little nugget to yourself."

"I told the guy on the phone to wish her my best and good luck. He then replied that she would need it and sounded really frazzled."

Karen tipped her head to one side, thinking. "There is no massive pandemic at the moment—like Ebola—in Africa. So she's gone to a war zone."

River nodded. "And the worst at the moment is near Goma, in the DRC."

"I recall reading an article about what women and girls go through there. It's terrifying—and I've seen what the Taliban can do to women," Karen said, shaking her head.

"Ethnic tension combined with rare minerals and arms trafficking," River said. "The perfect storm."

Karen remained silent for a moment and then said, "We've been to some bad places, you and I, right?"

"We have."

"At the end of the day, the guy you want to bring to justice is Karl Kruger, and it's very likely he's back in South Africa."

"He might not be," River said, wary of where Karen was heading. "He has connections with the DRC. In any case, the man who calls himself Dr. Death is there, and I'll be damned if I'll let him get away with"—River braced herself and then said—"my parents' murder."

"Okay. Just checking," Karen said as she stood and picked up the half-empty coffeepot. Her solid frame made the room feel a little smaller and yet more secure. "Tell me when you're going, and I'll pack my bags."

River sat back in her chair. "It's a solo mission. Washington, DC, was bad enough, but this is a whole different ball game."

Karen poured more coffee into their cups. "Yep, and that's why you need a team. Didn't they teach you anything in the Air Force?"

"I've been taught plenty," River said. "I can also assess the level of danger of an operation—"

"Nonnegotiable," Karen said, returning the coffeepot to its stand, then sitting back down. "You're just not going on your own. I repeat, you need backup, and I need the action. I never realized until DC how much I miss the buzz of being in theater." Karen rolled her shoulders at the thought of what they'd accomplished five months ago and grinned.

"I'm serious," River said, pushing back. "I don't want to have to tell your father that I got you hurt or, even worse, killed in Africa when you managed to come back from several tours in Iraq and Afghanistan unharmed."

"Do we ever come back from these places unscathed?" Karen asked, thoughtful.

"That's not the point. You're alive and doing good for the community here in Alaska."

"You mean training my father's dogs to win the next musher competition?"

River's hands flew up in mock anger. "You are your father's daughter—pigheaded and unyielding."

"Yep. That's what it takes to be chief of police in these parts," Karen responded. "And you forgot to add that I'm as resilient as his best husky dog."

"What will it take to make you reconsider?" River asked.

Karen sat back for a moment, eyes to the ceiling. She then leaned forward and said, "Have you spoken to Jason about your mission to Africa yet?"

"There is no way I am telling Jase about this," River said with irritation.

Karen remained calm. She knew she had a point. "He, too, got framed by Kruger, and he almost spent the rest of his life in jail because of it."

River stood up abruptly. "Please—you don't need to remind me that I'm the one who got him out of that mess."

Karen cocked her head.

"Okay . . . *we* were the ones who got him out of that mess," River said, rearranging a pile of documents that looked perfectly well in order.

"It's not the getting out of the mess that rankles you. It's the fact that you still haven't figured out what it is that you want out of your relationship with him."

River paced the small kitchen a couple of times. "Not true. I know what I *don't* want. I did chicken out of getting married to him only a couple of months before we were due to commit."

"But the minute Jase needed you, you ran back to DC to help."

"He is one of my best friends, too," River conceded as she sat back down.

"Now we're getting somewhere," Karen said, extending her hand across the table and squeezing River's arm.

River briefly closed her eyes, and when she opened them again, she looked straight at Karen. "If I tell Jason I'm going to Africa to challenge Kruger and bring him to justice, he will of course want to come. I can't ask a former Navy SEAL to sit on his hands while I'm tackling a man as dangerous as Karl Kruger, but you know why he can't come with me."

Karen took a short breath and said, "His injury makes him vulnerable."

"He will never stop limping. He'll never run, climb, kick the way he was trained to. So no, I don't want him to know where I'm going because he will want to do what he used to best—take the fight to the bad guys. But this time, it will get him killed."

Chapter 2

The streets of Kotzebue were still packed with ice, although the temperature during the day was hovering around thirty degrees Fahrenheit, announcing that the May thaw would be coming soon. River had managed to fit in a few runs since the weather started to turn a little warmer. She was trained to run on frozen ground, cautious of its reduced traction. Away from the center of town, though, she'd spotted a few trails where the ground was of better quality, and she wouldn't be so likely to fall.

She slowed down to a brisk walk and then stopped altogether near a copse of bare trees. Her muscles were still reluctant to be subjected to a long run after a month of treadmill activity. Nothing could replace the outdoors. River stretched thoroughly, found a fallen tree trunk, and sat down to indulge in some of the ginger tea with lemon and honey that she'd made and brought along in her backpack. A plume of steam rose in the cold air when she unscrewed the top of the flask. She poured the liquid into the cap and enjoyed a few sips.

Her cell phone hadn't buzzed during her run, so, curious, she mechanically took out the phone from her jacket pocket and started to scroll through her emails. No matter how careful she was, her account still seemed to be bombarded by spam. She grumbled a few insults at the junk mail clogging her inbox, but then stopped on a message that stood out. She rose slowly as she started reading.

Hello, River,

I hear from my colleagues at DWB in NY that you'd like to

speak with me. I will be in the DRC for a while longer and don't always have access to the internet. I believe you'll remember what it's like. But I am in Goma today and tomorrow, so I could speak to you via Zoom then. Let me know.

Angela Graham

River was about to reply, but then stopped after typing the first few words of her message. She recalled that the time difference between Alaska and the DRC is ten hours and that Goma is ahead of Kotzebue. She resumed typing and offered to call Angela in an hour, at 10:00 p.m. Goma time. If Angela was anything like her parents, she would be working until late and going to bed late, too.

River jogged carefully back to the main road and made her way to her apartment. As soon as she was in, she checked her emails, but Angela had been silent.

She opened the refrigerator and half-heartedly surveyed its contents. There was enough to make an omelet. She checked her emails once more before taking the eggs out, but by that time Angela had replied, sending a Zoom link. They'd be talking in less than ten minutes, and River forgot about food.

Finally, a small breakthrough. She booted up her laptop, took the flask out of her backpack, and poured the rest of the tea into a fresh cup. The laptop was ready. She went to her email inbox and opened Angela's message, ready to activate the Zoom link at the top of the hour.

At 12:00 p.m. exactly—10:00 p.m. Goma time—she opened the link and waited for Angela to join the call. River wondered whether she'd ever met Angela, but she couldn't remember. The screen suddenly came to life, and an image of a woman in her late fifties materialized. Her light brown hair was short, and her eyes were framed by some heavy-rimmed glasses. She looked tanned from years spent in hot climates, and wrinkles had formed around her eyes from squinting in the sun. She smiled as soon as River's face appeared on the screen.

"You probably don't remember me. We met a long time ago when your parents were in Rwanda."

"I'm sorry, Angela. I'm afraid I don't."

Angela's laugh seemed to echo around her room. She'd blurred her background so River couldn't tell exactly where she was calling from. "I'm not surprised," she said. "You and your brother, Luke, were very young. Perhaps seven and ten or thereabouts."

"I only remember a few bits from our stay in Rwanda."

"I tell you what you *will* almost certainly recall, though," Angela continued. "You and Luke rescued a spotted hyena cub, and your father almost had a fit."

"Oh, wow, I do remember that!" River could hardly believe it. This was one happy memory Luke and she had been reminiscing about only a month ago.

"Well, I was the one who persuaded him to let you keep her."

River snapped her fingers. "Now I recall. Luke and I were worried when you left. We thought Dad would throw her back in the wild, but we kept her until we had to move again.

"I heard that he almost cried when you had to surrender her to an animal sanctuary."

"That's right. None of us could believe it." River tried to hide her surprise. Angela seemed to be well informed about what happened in the Swift family after she'd left Rwanda.

Angela must have picked up on it and added, "Your mom and I stayed in contact for a while after I left. I'm so sorry for what happened to them. The DRC is an unpredictable and unforgiving place."

"Thank you," River said, her throat tightening. "I hope you don't mind if I ask you a few questions about what you remember around that time."

Angela nodded, took a moment, and then said, "I should have reached out earlier. I'm sorry I didn't."

River thought she'd detected a little anxiety in Angela's voice. Although her face remained open and engaged, her expression grew serious.

"Were you in the DRC, too, when my parents moved to Katuba?"

Angela shifted in her chair. "I was, but I remained in Kinshasa to help with some medication shipments. I'm a surgeon, but when there is a shortage of staff and a big delivery arrives, it's all hands on deck."

River drew a pad that was lying on the kitchen table to her and said, "Do you mind if I take notes?"

Angela nodded, lowering her voice. "Fine but let me know if you ever need to quote me. Some of what I'll tell you isn't public knowledge."

River felt herself lowering her voice, too, as she asked, "I recall one instance in which a man visited our parents. I shouldn't have seen him—I was supposed to be in bed—but I did. He had a gun with him, and he was showing documents to Mom and Dad."

Angela's eyes widened, and she moved closer to the screen. "Have you spoken to anyone about this?"

River shook her head. "You're the first person. I haven't even mentioned it to Luke."

"Then you must keep it that way," Angela replied, looking relieved.

She went silent for a moment, then added, "What I'm about to tell you can't be discussed with anyone else. Do I have your word?"

River hesitated. "I can't promise that. But what I can promise is that if I need to disclose it to someone, I will let you know who that person is, and then you can tell me whether you agree."

Angela seemed to think about it. She then said, "All right. I can see that if you're trying to find out more about your parents' death and who's responsible, you may need to discuss what I'm about to tell you with people you trust."

River hadn't yet divulged what her ultimate goal was, and she was taken aback.

"I wondered whether this was what you were after when the head office in New York told me you wanted to chat. After so long, it seemed to be the only valid reason for a conversation," Angela said, sensing River's surprise.

River considered her next statement carefully. After all, she didn't know Angela. But then again, why pull back now?

"Since you've anticipated what I wanted to talk to you about, I'm going to be frank with you," River said. "I suspect—actually, no, I *know*—my parents were murdered. It wasn't a random attack by one of the militia groups that roam around the DRC. It was an elimination by someone who didn't like what my parents were doing and decided to shut them up."

Angela's mouth opened, and she slumped back in her chair. "How can you be so sure?"

River made an apologetic face. "I'm sorry, Angela. Unless you divulge more information, I'll be keeping some of my powder dry. The truth is rather shocking if what I suspect is confirmed."

Angela started to fiddle with a piece of jewelry that hung from her neck, a small silver cross.

"You're right. I need to give you more before you can trust me," Angela said. She moved closer to the screen again and started to relay her story in a low, unsteady voice. "Doctors who work with international organizations are sometimes approached by government agencies."

She paused, perhaps to let the information sink in or to gather her thoughts. "We see a lot of things in this job . . . civil wars and border conflicts, arms smuggling, drug trafficking, jostling for economic supremacy. The world comes to Africa and tries to play the game of influence. We see them offer weapons that move around between various warring factions and among nations involved in the conflict between the West and countries like Russia and China. Contracts for exploitation of natural resources are signed by governments and big corporations, and the ones who benefit aren't the locals but the people who wield power. We see war crimes and asylum seekers. We see big companies wreaking havoc with the environment and with people's lives."

Angela's expression had turned grim, and River felt as though this lovely woman had seen it all during her long career with DWB.

"So agencies approach us. Sometimes they are part of our own government, sometimes not," Angela said. She was no longer looking at the screen; her gaze had settled in the distance, as though she was reliving some of the events she was about to relay.

"The FBI approached me. I didn't know they operated abroad at the time, but they were pursuing a fugitive. A serial killer who was suspected of murdering old people. As it turned out, this man was also a doctor, and the FBI had found out he was hiding in the medical community under an assumed name."

"They asked you to help catch him?" River asked.

Angela suddenly refocused on the screen and said, "They've got a program called Project Welcome Home."

Both women couldn't help but chuckle. "Did you get the guy?" River asked.

"We did." Angela sighed, her gaze again drifting off in the distance. "And then I was hooked. It wasn't enough to save lives. I had to help catch the bad guys, too. I've often wondered why I got so into it. Perhaps, for once, I could see the SOBs who've hurt innocent people being brought to justice."

"That must have felt good." River said.

Angela looked up, and the fierceness of her eyes startled River. "All these corrupt, greedy, selfish politicians and business executives who don't care a fig about other people or the environment. For them, it's about money, clean or dirty. It's about power at all costs. So few of them get what they deserve."

"You sound just like my mom," River said. She could almost hear her mother's voice, berating this government or that politician. The memory made her shudder, and her throat tightened.

"That's why she and I got along so well." Angela's voice had become softer, and then she brought a hand to her face to muffle a sob. "I should never have introduced your parents to them."

River's eyes widened. "The FBI?"

Angela shook her head, finding it hard to carry on. "No. The CIA."

The information blew River's mind. She slumped into her chair, unable to utter a word. Angela was weeping softly, and River fought the urge to kill the call, shocked and angry at the news. It took both women a moment before they regained composure and resumed their conversation.

"You need to tell me all you know," River said crisply.

Angela grabbed a tissue, dried her eyes, and then said, "My FBI contact introduced me to this guy. I was in South Africa then. He was looking for people in the DRC and said that the violence was only going to get worse unless the militia groups were brought under control by a stable government. I wasn't sure I bought all that to start with, but then I spoke to your mom, and she said something similar, so I thought perhaps the guy was right."

Angela stopped and moved away from the screen to fetch a tumbler that she brought back with her. She drank a few sips. River still couldn't absorb the idea that her parents might have worked for the CIA. This seemed so far from the people she knew them to be—or perhaps thought they were.

"Do you remember what this guy looked like?" River asked.

"Of course. How could I forget?" Angela said. "But you're going to be disappointed. He looked very bland, medium height, brown mousy hair. He had a slight southern drawl. He called himself Dexter Law, but I very much doubt that's his real name."

Angela stopped and frowned, trying to remember anything that might be more helpful. River went back to the night she'd been sitting at the top of the stairs, listening to what her parents and the stranger were saying. She'd briefly seen the man enter her parents' living room.

"Do you know why he wanted my parents' help?"

Angela shook her head. "Your mom wouldn't say much. But I got the impression it was all about bringing increased economic prosperity to the region of the DRC near Goma, in which they were working. In retrospect, I think it was all about the exploitation of coltan; the ore that's used in microchips and cell phones."

"I read about this in a magazine. The DRC is very rich in coltan, but there are some constraints with its export because of the way it's exploited—murder of civilians, rape, and the use of boy soldiers to carry out terrifying crimes," River said, a shudder running down her spine.

"The level of cruelty is unimaginable," Angela replied. "Even after all these years working in war zones, I get scared when I go to this part of the DRC."

Both women fell silent, and then River asked, "Why talk to me now? Why not keep all this hidden?" It'd taken fourteen years for Angela to speak. Was she simply waiting for someone to ask the right questions?

"I've come to the same conclusion as you," Angela said. "It's taken time for me to face the truth, but I, too, know your parents were murdered. Now that I have awakened the past, I fear it will soon catch up with me."

The sound of voices shouting and the rattling of a door startled River. Angela's face turned white, and she stammered, "They're coming for me. I need to go."

She left the Zoom session open and disappeared from the screen. Because Angela had blurred the background at the beginning of the session, River could only see out-of-focus movements. She heard gunshots, a door banging open, more shouts and screams. Then someone's face materialized in front of River—black, heavy jaws, and a scar running across his left cheek. River disconnected the Zoom call immediately and then sprang out of her chair. She'd looked straight into the eyes of a ruthless killer.

The aircraft PA system crackled, and for a moment River wasn't sure where she was. She opened her eyes, looked around, and it came back to her. The flight she'd boarded the day before from Anchorage at 8:16 p.m. was heading to New York. The first officer announced that they were going to be on time, arriving at Newark at 7:16 a.m., in around forty-five minutes' time. The sound of a trolley coming down the aisle made River sit up. The woman sitting next to her had already woken up—a small woman, Mary, who'd been chatting about her husky dogs all through the flight. It was a good thing that River was interested in dog mushing and that Karen's father, Chief Robinson, had taught River about it.

"Did you manage to get some sleep?" Mary asked.

She looked perky and ready for the day. River nodded and stifled a yawn. She had been glad of the conversation with Mary, taking her mind off the reason she was on her way to New York. After River had closed the Zoom session, she'd immediately called Doctors Without Borders headquarters in New York. They hadn't been able to raise Angela, and she hadn't been in contact since. Angela wasn't in one of the remote locations doctors sometimes visited in the DRC but in Goma, a big enough city, and DWB should have been able to get hold of her.

But what prompted River to make the trip, was the reaction of the man she'd spoken to to report Angela's abduction. She'd insisted on a zoom call and he'd been guarded to start with but then had become more forthcoming. River had spoken about her parents—not to reveal their tragic end but to establish trust, and it worked.

Mike Wilson had been in the field for years, too—around forty years. He'd witnessed a lot of difficult situations, and Angela's kidnapping rattled him. It wasn't, unfortunately, uncommon—two Spanish doctors had been kidnapped at the border of Kenya and Somalia in 2011, and five workers snatched in Cameroon at the border with Nigeria just a few months ago, in early 2023. He knew some of the DWB staff who'd gone through this ordeal, but what seemed to have surprised and worried Mike even more were the circumstances surrounding Angela's disappearance.

"Our people are snatched from refugee camps near the border and then traded for medicine or food. DWB is a nonprofit, so it doesn't have enough money to deliver a large cash ransom," Mike had said.

"Goma is near the border with Rwanda, though," River had suggested.

"But Angela was in a small hostel we use when doctors are between assignments. She wasn't dealing with patients or refugees. This isn't the way kidnapping usually happens," Mike had replied. "I'm sorry—I make it sound as though it's something that happens all the time. But with Angela . . ."

River had picked up on the additional worry—something personal.

"That's okay. I know that working for Doctors Without Borders can be dangerous. My parents were perhaps more cautious when we were with them as kids. They didn't choose the worst assignments, and yet I saw a lot of tragedy."

Mike had gone silent, and then River had taken the chance.

"I'm visiting New York in a couple of days' time. Perhaps we can meet for coffee?"

"Good idea. Call me when you're in town, and I'll make myself available," Mike had replied. "I'll call you if I hear from Angela."

She hadn't told Mike that she'd only decided to make the trip a second beforehand. She left her email address and phone number with him and spent the day preparing for the journey—the first leg of a much longer excursion that was taking her out of the country altogether.

The flight attendant offered the two women food before Mary could ask about the nature of River's visit to New York. River decided on pancakes with syrup and coffee. The two women fell silent as they ate their breakfast, and River was grateful. She needed to focus on the days ahead.

As soon as she finished her food, River went to freshen up and returned to her seat just as the SEAT BELT sign went on. The landing was smooth, and as soon as the SEAT BELT sign went off, River and Mary stood up. River collected her old duffel bag, bade Mary goodbye, and made her way out of the airport. She bought a ticket for the New Jersey Transit train to Penn Station. It took twenty-five minutes to get to Manhattan. River disembarked and was immediately assailed by the noise and the dense crowds that filled the station during rush hour.

People kept bumping into her without apologizing, and she made a few gruff comments before realizing that each commuter seemed to be in his or her own world, just eager to get to the next destination. She took a moment to orient herself, then boarded the subway bound for Times Square. She'd found a hotel not very far from there that offered a good discount for veterans. She had a little time before her meeting with Mike at ten thirty. It would only take fifteen minutes to get from the hotel to the DWB headquarters, on Rector Street, and she wanted to take a shower and think once more about what she needed from Mike and how she would get it.

The Buzz Cut Hotel was easy to find. The building was rather small and old-looking. The entrance was a little bland, but she wasn't interested in luxury—simple and clean would do.

The man lifted his head and waited without showing much interest. River got to his desk, dropped her duffel bag to the floor, and said, "River Swift. I have a reservation for two nights, please."

"Military discount, right?"

"Yes. That's right."

"Still in service?" he said as he handed over a pad with a form to fill in.

River took the pen that he handed her and replied, "No. Former Air Force medic." She still felt embarrassed at the thought of having left the service for something she imagined would be a blissful married life.

The old man nodded. "With the 24th Special Operations Wing–Hurlburt?"

River's eyes widened. "How did you know?"

"My son—Colonel Billy B. Jones—is still in the Air Force and was involved with the creation of that unit," the old man said, then smiled.

"That's incredible," River said, shaking her head in disbelief. "I met him a few times when I joined the Air Force. He came to talk to us about why the new unit would be better at saving lives. Were you in the military yourself?"

The old man shook his head. "A and E for a very long time. Retired, and then I got bored with retirement after my wife passed, so I got this job. We have a lot of military personnel because of our good discount and our central location."

He extended a hand and said, "Bob."

River shook his hand in return. "Very nice to meet you, Bob." An expert in Ammunition and Explosives—always a good connection to have.

"Anything you need," Bob said, "give me a shout. I do the morning shift."

River picked up her key from Bob and made her way to the elevators, one of which arrived quickly. She got off on the seventh floor, turned right, and found her room. She was pleasantly surprised by what she saw. The room was small but looked fresh. She dropped her duffel bag and flopped back onto the comfortable bed for a moment.

She'd packed for more days than the two she intended to spend in New York. Karen had been suspicious, but she'd let River go on the assumption that River wouldn't be stupid enough to go after Kruger without backup. Or would she? She might have given a different answer a few days ago, but the encounter with the man River was now convinced was Angela's abductor had shattered her resolve. Going solo, seeking justice for her parents' murder, was looking more like an impossible mission. But was she prepared to risk the life of her best friend?

River closed her eyes and thought of Jason, her ex-fiancé. He, too, had a vested interest in finding Kruger. His Navy SEAL training would have been a priceless asset to her operation, but she knew he would want to be in on the action—impossible with his life-changing injury. Their abrupt separation made it awkward to be with him, and she still wasn't sure how she felt about it.

River opened her eyes and sat up. This indecisiveness wasn't like her, and she felt irritated. She checked her watch—9:41 a.m. She had a few more minutes before she needed to be on her way. River zipped open her duffel bag and took out the laptop she brought with her. She sat cross-legged on the bed and booted up the device. A moment later she was perusing her emails, looking for a response to a question she'd sent to a contact in DC a few days previously.

If she couldn't speak to Jason about her African trip, she could share the idea with Reggie Cameron, the young lawyer who'd helped her free Jason. He had proved resourceful and daring. He'd been handed the case with the hope he would fail, but he'd surprised everyone at Thompson & Meyer. Now, instead of being on the short list for dismissal, Reggie had his own office and a long list of high-profile clients. River had wondered whether he might be too busy to answer, but gratitude was another of his qualities. He'd sent her a return email the same day she contacted him.

Reggie had agreed to send out feelers in an effort to find out whether the FBI—perhaps the Welcome Home Program—and Detective Parker, the man who'd investigated Jason, had made any progress in finding Kruger. She went through her recent emails twice. She sighed—unlike the last time, there was nothing from Reggie. River closed her laptop and returned it to her duffel bag. She took out her old backpack and loaded it with a few essentials—water bottle, wallet, the passport she didn't want to lose and wasn't comfortable leaving in the room, and a scarf in case the weather turned chilly.

She zipped the duffel bag shut, showered quickly and changed, shouldered the backpack, and then made her way to the first floor. In the elevator, she checked her jacket to confirm that her cell phone was there. When she got to the lobby, Bob was busy with another customer, but he nodded when he spotted her, and she returned his nod with a short salute. River got to the street and took a moment to adjust again.

The noise of a big city took time to get used to. DC had been easier, because some of it felt like a network of small villages coexisting closely together. New York was different: the cars, the delivery trucks, the horns, the people talking, yelling, the hum of all things electric—all this blunted River's sharp sense of observation.

The Times Square subway station was only a block away. When she got there, she boarded the number 1 train and sat in one of the free seats.

The palms of her hands had turned moist. River couldn't figure out why she was suddenly nervous. Mike sounded like a nice enough guy, but perhaps too much was riding on this meeting. She rubbed her hands on her jeans and thought about the questions she wanted to ask him, including the most important one: whether she could help him find Angela.

The train arrived at the Rector Street station. River disembarked and walked to the Doctors Without Borders offices. When she turned a corner, she spotted Mike. He was waiting for her on the pavement, pacing. She started to jog toward him, slowing down as she was approaching. Mike saw her and seemed to hesitate at the sight of a woman running toward him. But as soon as he recognized River, he waved. River waved back.

"River Swift," Mike said. The face that looked so amiable on their Zoom call now looked drawn.

"Good to meet you," River said, extending a hand.

They shook briefly, and then Mike started walking. "Let's find a place for a coffee away from the office."

They walked west on Rector Street, crossed West Street, and remained silent. Mike was walking fast for a small, pudgy man. He couldn't get away from the DWB offices fast enough, it seemed. River didn't ask why. She just followed as they turned right on South End Avenue, arriving at the North Cove Yacht Harbor. Mike kept going until they reached a little café next to the water.

He finally turned to River and said, a bit breathless, "Few people from the office come here. It's more expensive, but the coffee is the best in the area."

Mike chose a table away from the front window and settled in a small booth. River sat opposite him, and a smiling waitress came to take their order.

"I haven't seen you for a while," she said to Mike.

"I've been traveling and only got back a couple of days ago," he said, returning her smile.

"Coffee, please; black, no sugar," River said.

The waitress smiled at River and then turned to Mike. "Same as usual?"

"That's right."

River waited for her to leave and then asked, "Any news from Angela?"

Mike's face dropped, and he shook his head. He took a moment and then said, "It's really bad. When DWB came to Angela's address in Goma, the room was empty, and there was blood everywhere."

Chapter 3

The coffees arrived quickly. Mike added sugar and cream to his. He wrapped his hands around the cup for a moment and then, unprompted, told River what he knew.

"Angela and I go a long way back. We joined Doctors Without Borders in the same month twenty years ago. We're both surgeons. She was one of the first female surgeons to join her male colleagues in war zones."

Mike stopped to take a sip of his coffee. His eyes were riveted to the table, perhaps seeing images he couldn't share with River.

"She's always been very progressive in her ideas—and vocal about them, too," he continued.

"You mean politically engaged?"

"It's complicated with Angela. She doesn't trust politicians or political parties, but she keenly follows worldwide developments. I think she just wants to make the world a better place."

River nodded. It tallied with the impression she'd formed of Angela and with her stated justification for helping the FBI find fugitives who'd escaped the law.

"Do you think she's been abducted for money?" River regretted putting it so bluntly.

Mike averted River's gaze and said, "That might be the most optimistic of outcomes."

"She hadn't sworn me to secrecy, although she might have wanted to vet what I'm about to divulge to you. However, under the circumstances, you need to know that Angela was working with the FBI."

Mike's reaction was instantaneous. He looked amazed and stammered, "She told you that?"

"She said she'd been doing it for years."

"The truth is, she told me about it, too, and I tried then to convince her that saving lives the way we do should be enough, but she never seemed satisfied with what she did. There was always more to do."

River thought how similar Angela was to her mother. She shuddered at the thought that Angela might have met the same tragic end.

They sat in silence for a moment and sipped their coffee. But then it was time for River to tell Mike the reasons why she'd been in touch with Angela in the first place.

"I'm not sure Angela told you why she thought I wanted to talk to her."

"She mentioned that it was about your parents and what happened to them in the DRC."

That Angela had spoken to Mike about her impending conversation with River could only mean one of two things—either that Angela trusted Mike with her life or that Mike had eavesdropped on her. River discarded the latter as soon as she thought it. Mike's grief was genuine, and she wondered how intimate these two had or hadn't been. She wouldn't ask. Experience told her that the inquiry wasn't necessary and might even alienate Mike.

"I guess the news of my parents' demise spread through the entire DWB at the time," River said before drinking a little more coffee.

"We were all shocked. Angela was devastated as I was, although I didn't know your parents as well as she did."

River now understood why Angela would have been upset if she'd linked her parents' death to their work with the CIA. But it meant that even back then, Angela was suspicious about the story that had circulated in the papers and had been accepted by the authorities. Her parents were supposed to have been caught in the crossfire between two warring factions and been murdered along with the villagers because they simply stood in the way.

"Do you believe the story that surrounded my parents' death?" River asked as calmly as she could.

Mike's eyebrows shot up. "What do you mean?"

"Did Angela express doubt at the time?" River asked.

Mike ran a weary hand over his face. "She was very upset, as I said, but she didn't say anything to me that would lead me to become suspicious."

Then Mike's face dropped. "She also kept saying that it shouldn't have happened." He paused. "At the time I would reply, 'Of course it shouldn't,' and that used to irritate her, as though my answer wasn't what she expected."

Mike was looking at her quizzically. River took a deep breath and said, "I think—no, I know—that my parents were murdered."

Mike didn't react. River continued. "Angela told me she suspected it wasn't an accident, but more important, she told me she'd indirectly introduced my parents to the CIA."

Mike slumped in his seat. River could see it on his face. He was no longer sure he knew Angela as well as he thought he did.

The waitress came back with the offer of a refill. They both shook their heads, trying to remain courteous despite the interruption.

"Do you think the CIA was involved with your parents' murder?" Mike said, his face animated by a new desire to understand.

"I'm not sure. But I know some of the people behind the hit. They may not have been the only ones wishing my parents gone."

"Who are they?" Mike asked, leaning forward and lowering his voice.

River leaned forward, too. "I hope you won't mind, Mike, but these people are dangerous and well connected. Perhaps it's better if you don't know their names."

Mike thought for a moment. "I also accept that you may not want to trust me just yet. After all, we've only known each other a month or so. But I can't help thinking that there is a link between what happened to Angela yesterday and your parents' murder. And I want to help find Angela and find the people you suspect."

The outcome of their conversation couldn't have been better, but River now hesitated. Mike was right. There must be a link between Angela's abduction and her parents' fate. Nothing had happened for the past fourteen years, though, and this also meant that it was River's questions and Angela's willingness to answer that had set things in motion.

"I see you hesitate," Mike said. "And I thank you for being honest and not wanting me to take more risks, but I think it's too late. I've already contacted people here internally to find Angela and secure her release, and I've spoken about my concern that she was a specific target. DWB is very good at this. Our staff gets kidnapped regularly, unfortunately. There will be an inquiry into this incident, and I'll make sure we get to the bottom of it. Angela wasn't in a war zone or in a border refugee camp. She should have been secure. We can't afford to have our people hunted down like animals when they are simply doing their jobs."

"You mean whoever is taking an interest in Angela will know you won't rest until you've gotten your answer."

"People think I'm just a nice guy. And most of the time I am, but I also don't let go when I feel I'm fighting for what's right."

"That's why you and Angela got along," River said.

Mike blushed a little and asked, "What do you need from me?"

River waited a moment and then said, "I need to see any information DWB has on what happened in Katuba fourteen years ago. As you say, the organization has a good reputation for protecting its staff, so I'd like to get hold of the report that was submitted after the incident and anything else you come across that you think may help. You said it yourself: DWB is good at this, so they must have at least opened a file on my parents' death."

"I'm on it," Mike said.

"I suggest we communicate through burner phones from now on," River said.

Mike gave her a faint smile. "Done this before, have you?"

River returned the smile and said, "Perhaps more than I expected I would when I left the military."

"Will you buy the burners?"

"Yes. Let me buy the phones, set them up, and I'll drop one for you at your reception desk. I'll give it a call without leaving a message. The number that'll show will be mine."

River raised her hand, signaling that she'd like to settle the bill. Mike took cash out of his pocket, but River stopped him. "It's on me."

She paid as soon as the waitress came along. She left a tip and stood up. Mike stood up, too, and they walked to the door. They retraced their steps in silence. When they came to West Street, River and he shook hands.

"I'll take care of the phones now," River said.

"Good. I'll tell reception I'm expecting a package and to call me as soon as it's delivered."

Mike and River stood at the pedestrian crossing. The light turned green, and Mike stepped into the street in front of the waiting cars. River spotted the motorbike just in time. The rider was weaving through traffic, but she could tell he had no intention of stopping from the way he pitched himself forward on the bike. He should have been sitting up straight, ready to rest his foot on the ground to hold the bike steady at the light.

"Watch out," she yelled as she ran across the street. The biker accelerated even more, and River lunged forward, desperate to push Mike out of the way. They both tumbled to the ground. The bike grazed River's leg. The rider revved the engine and disappeared down West Street. The traffic light changed, and drivers at the back started honking furiously. A couple of drivers got out of their cars and helped River and Mike, shouting at the others to be quiet. They both thanked the good Samaritans and, shaken by the incident, walked to the safety of the DWB lobby. Neither River nor Mike were hurt except for a few scratches and bruises. They both collapsed on a couple of chairs.

"Did the guy not pay attention?" Mike asked, his voice shaking.

River shook her head. "I saw him coming from way back. He was gunning his bike, ready to run you over."

Mike stood up slowly, offered his hand to River to help her stand, and said, "If they're trying to intimidate me, it's not gonna work." He continued before River could interrupt. "I don't want to hear you telling me I should think it over. I've made up my mind. I want to know who's behind this, and I want them to pay."

Back in her hotel room, River sat on her bed to take stock of the morning. After the missed hit on Mike, she'd bought two burner phones and had one of them delivered to his office. She wasn't expecting him to call immediately, but she couldn't shake the doubt in her mind. His bravery may well vanish once he had time to think about what just happened.

The speed at which Kruger had figured out her next move surprised her. She knew he was well connected at the most senior level, but she had underestimated the breadth of his reach. She couldn't make the same mistake twice and hoped she would surprise him once she was in Africa. River went to fetch her laptop from her duffel bag. She booted it up and checked her emails. Still nothing from Reggie. Doubt knotted her stomach. Reggie had been directly involved in Kruger's attempted arrest. He needed to know he might be the next in line for a hit-and-run.

She fetched her cell phone from her jacket pocket and dialed his number. He picked up on the second ring.

"I'll call you back in a second." Reggie killed the call, and River waited for him to call back. At least he was alive, and from the way he spoke he didn't seem to have been rattled by threats.

A moment later her phone rang, and she picked up.

"I was getting a little bored, not being involved in a case that deals with hardcore criminals and high-profile people—and here you are again," Reggie said with a smile in his voice.

River imagined the young man sitting at his new desk, surrounded by stacks of papers that would dwarf his small frame. She couldn't help but smile in turn. "Reggie, so glad you missed me."

"And I'm not the only one missing you. Kruger, or at least someone close to him, seems to be asking a lot of questions about you, me, and Jason."

That piece of news wiped the smile off her face. "How do you know?"

"I've built a good network of sources. You won't believe how popular you become once you've had a case like Jason's dismissed. I've been dealing with a few less-than-savory individuals who need my legal expertise, and I've amassed several contacts in the process. Some of these people I wouldn't wanna meet in a dark alley late at night, but they are good to know when you need intelligence."

"Where is Kruger?"

"As far as I can tell—and my sources agree—still in Africa and almost certainly in South Africa."

"Doesn't the FBI have a program to bring SOBs like him back into the country?" River thought she might tell Reggie about the program Angela worked for.

"I presume you're referring to the Welcome Home Program?"

"That's the one."

"And may I ask how you managed to come across it? Don't tell me they tried to recruit you."

"No—I'll get to that later. But what else did you learn about Kruger?"

"Yes, Kruger." Reggie paused. He seemed to be moving around but then stopped and continued. "Sorry—I'm in the basement of the building, in the archives room. It's very secluded, and I'm sure there will be no eavesdropping here. Back to your question. I felt as though I'd been followed a few days ago, and since this seemed to coincide with your calling me to tell me about your next move with Kruger, I put my own feelers out."

"So Kruger had you followed?"

"I didn't say that exactly. *Someone* had me followed, but I got a couple of old pals to intercept that guy. There is surprising advantage in coming from a rough DC neighborhood. Anyway, the guy talked to them. Well, maybe I should say he was incentivized to talk to them. This guy has apparently never met his boss before, and my pals got the impression that whoever employed him hadn't asked him to be discreet anyway."

The information made River pause. Kruger wasn't the sort of man who wouldn't meticulously plan his moves. She'd not dealt with him directly and only met his lobbyist puppet, Chuck Clery. But Kruger had been clever enough to outsmart the police and border control when he was wanted for questioning and escaped from the United States.

"Either Kruger or whoever that other person is wants us to know he's on to us," River said slowly.

"I think so, too." Reggie seemed to be thinking it through. "Unless . . ."

River waited until she couldn't any longer. "Is this for effect? Or are you genuinely hesitating?"

"I am hesitating, Riv," Reggie said, his voice unusually sharp, "because if I'm right, it means someone is laying a trap."

River was stunned. "You mean that person knows I'll take the bait if they threaten people around me? So they're not trying to put me off but are pushing me to engage?"

"Look what you did for Jason," Reggie said. "You'd never dealt with a murder case before, but you came back to DC to help your ex-fiancé, with whom you hadn't spoken for almost a year, and then tackled some of the most connected men on Capitol Hill. I bet that has impressed a lot of people in a weird way, but they might also be challenging you."

"What? Like a 'Come and get me if you dare' sort of challenge?"

"Something like that. If it's Kruger, he's gonna be on his turf in South Africa with a lot of resources and fewer constraints."

"Constraints?" River said, amazed. "He didn't seem to be that constrained when he got Clery's house burned to the ground with Clery in it—and all that in the middle of Kalorama Heights, one of the most affluent parts of DC."

"That's my point exactly. If that's what constraint looks like to him, then can you imagine what will happen without it?"

River mulled it over for a moment. "But you assume he's got free rein in South Africa. He might not."

"Are you out of your mind?" Reggie said in disbelief. "Okay, maybe you don't want to speak ill of a country you and your parents visited often and really enjoyed, but let me say it for you, since I am the black guy here. South Africa is a country that's currently descending into hell—corruption everywhere; the far right is having a field day spreading misinformation; gun violence is rising; there's an energy crisis and a power blackout every day . . . I could go on and on."

"And how do you know all this?" River asked with a mix of surprise and irritation.

"First, I don't only read law, I also read the news. Plus, I have family in Limpopo Province, near the border with Zimbabwe—close cousins, in fact. We're in touch regularly, and what they describe is freaking terrible—no electricity, bribery everywhere, apartheid in reverse."

River ran a hand over her face. "Okay, so Kruger thinks he's gonna lure me into South Africa and then settle a score."

"You bet. He's probably still limping after you got one of Clery's men to shoot him in the leg. I'd be seriously fucked off if I were him."

"But he doesn't know I've been planning to go to South Africa anyway," River said.

"So what? Whether you've been planning it for months or you've taken the bait, same result. He wants you on his turf, right?"

River was about to counter Reggie but then stopped. No point in being in denial. Kruger wanted her in South Africa, and she wanted to oblige, but now she had to play it smarter.

"Fine. So we're going to tell Kruger what he wants to hear. I'm going to South Africa, and I think Limpopo is a great place, near the country's largest national park. We lived there for a while with Mom and Dad. They were running an AIDS program for Doctors Without Borders."

The line was silent, and River thought she and Reggie might have lost the connection.

"Are you still there?"

"I am, and for once I'm lost for words."

"That's not encouraging. Are you trying to tell me this is a very stupid idea?"

"I'm not sure it's stupid—it's more like suicidal."

"But what if Kruger thinks I'm coming to South Africa on my own, without backup?"

"Go on," Reggie said with renewed interest.

"But in fact, I'll have a team with me, and we'll have a well-thought-through plan to take him on."

"Who's on the team?"

"Not sure yet," River replied.

"You need the A team," Reggie said without hesitation. "Karen and me for starters, and—"

"Hang on a minute. Karen is former military and has been to a war zone, but you haven't—"

Reggie took his turn at interrupting. "I think you'll find that the rough neighborhoods of DC are a good introduction to what a war zone might look like. Plus, I have a lot of contacts in South Africa, and these guys can help beef up the team. My cousins are rangers. They know their way around the African bush."

"Haven't you got a raft of new clients to defend? A new intern to take under your wing? I mean, we might be gone for a while," River said, hoping Reggie would come back to his senses and remember that he was working for one of the best law firms in DC.

"Just got a couple of clients acquitted—who deserved to be, before you ask. It'd be excellent training for my intern if she holds the fort on her own for a while. Besides, I am due for a vacation."

"Vacation? I thought you lawyers never took a vacation for the first twenty years of your careers."

"True, but I ain't the usual DC lawyer. I'm the guy who got Jason Wayne, former Navy SEAL, cleared of all accusations, and helped unravel a seedy conspiracy in DC that was meant to hide the impact of high-intensity weaponry exposure on Special Forces," Reggie said with mock arrogance.

"So the law of gravity doesn't apply to you," River joked. "Is that it?"

"Not quite, but I can take a few days off."

River couldn't deny that. She racked her brain to find a reason why all bets could still be off.

"I'll bet Karen has already packed her bags," Reggie added.

"There is one condition, though. And that one is nonnegotiable."

"I don't speak one word about this to Jason," Reggie said, now serious.

"How did you know?" River said, not hiding her amazement.

"'Know thy client' is the motto of all lawyers," Reggie replied. "You and I know I'm good at it and that I do care about you both."

"If I say one word about this to Jase, he will try to talk me out of it."

"I know," Reggie said.

"And then, because I insist I'm going, he'll want to come to Africa to tackle Kruger himself."

"I know."

"But his injury is still not fully healed, and it would be madness to think he can go back to combat and . . ." River felt herself grow emotional about Jason's dramatic story.

"Riv, I know all that," Reggie said softly. "Who are you trying to convince you should keep him in the dark?"

River bit her lip and took a moment to answer. "It's hard for me to lie to him. I did a lot of that until I couldn't lie about what I truly felt anymore. I should have been honest with him right away when we talked about getting married rather than waiting until the very last moment. He doesn't deserve that sort of treatment."

"No one disputes that," Reggie said, "but you're right. I've seen him recently for a beer, and his limp hasn't improved. I can see he's still in pain when he walks, although he won't talk about it. At least not to me."

"Thanks, Reggie. It helps to know that. Although I wish the case for his not being involved wasn't that clear-cut. It would mean he's in much better shape physically."

They both fell silent until Reggie asked, "What else have you got for me?"

River went through what she'd discovered in the past twenty-four hours, including the aborted hit-and-run on Mike Wilson. Reggie listened without interrupting until she was done.

"Just confirming what I told you earlier: Kruger is on the warpath and means business."

"But what worries me is that he seems to know my every move—and fast," River added.

"True, but it sounds like so far you've been discreet, but not careful."

"That's a fair assessment," River said, "but Kruger can't be that well informed simply by employing his own team of thugs and spooks. He's got access to intelligence from inside one of the big agencies."

"You mean he's protected and someone is helping him here, in the United States?"

"Exactly," River said.

"That could be," Reggie said. "But does this mean that the agency backing Kruger doesn't want to get involved directly?"

"Perhaps that agency doesn't want to deal with me stateside, but that might very well change the moment I'm abroad."

Reggie grunted and then added, "And maybe it's not an entire agency that's behind Kruger but one person or a group of individuals."

"That's an interesting thought. Someone's gone rogue and is partaking in Kruger's lucrative business," River said.

She could feel a surge of anger at the thought that whoever was helping Kruger escape the law might also have helped him with her parents' murder just for the money. Suddenly the task felt daunting. Even if Karen and Reggie joined her, they would have to outsmart a well-resourced agency, and if that agency was the CIA, the most powerful intelligence service in the world . . .

Reggie must have picked up on her hesitation. "Sometimes it's okay to admit that the task in front of you looks impossible. And sometimes it's also okay to let go."

River shook her head as though Reggie could see her. "And sometimes it's okay to keep going because the task looks impossible. What did John F. Kennedy say about going to the moon in 1962? We choose to go to the moon not because it is easy but because it is hard."

"I, for one, am happy with a hard task," Reggie replied.

Chapter 4

River stood in the middle of the room, thinking about what to do next. Reggie had a plan he was following, and she needed to use her day as best she could while waiting for him to contact her again.

She'd been successful at fooling Chuck Clery five months ago by transforming her appearance. She wondered whether she could use the same trick to lose any tail Kruger had set on her. She'd brought the fake ID she'd obtained in DC at the time, but it wouldn't do her any good if she wasn't prepared to change her appearance to match that of her brunette alias.

Her backpack lay on the floor next to her duffel bag, which she still hadn't unpacked. She unzipped the bag and got out a dressier T-shirt and a smart leather jacket. The change of clothes would help. Once she was done, River twisted her hair into a tight bun. She shouldered the pack and, this time, decided to use the room safe to store her laptop. A professional would almost certainly have no problem getting to it, but why make his life easy? She left the room, called the elevator, and arrived at reception just as Bob was ending his shift and another receptionist was coming on duty.

Bob waved, and she went to the desk.

"This is Al," Bob said. "He's been manning the desk here for almost eighteen years."

River smiled. "Nice to meet you, Al."

The old man smiled back and said, "Bob tells me that I need to look after you on account of you knowing his son, Colonel Billy B. Jones."

"I'm very grateful to Bob here, but I'm not gonna be any trouble or ask for any favors."

Bob shrugged. "I don't know. New York can be a tough city, and having a friendly to talk to is always good."

River nodded and then decided to jump on the opportunity. "Since you're so kindly offering to help, I was wondering whether there is a back door to this building I could use."

Bob took the request in stride. "Yep, there is. It's the way I'm planning to leave."

"Mind if I follow you?"

Bob gave a quick jerk of his chin toward a corridor that led to the back of the building. Al waved again, not perturbed by the request. Bob and River found themselves in an alley that was kept clean despite the presence of several large dumpsters.

"I'm going to Macy's. Any idea which bus or subway I need to take?"

"Take the 1 train to 34th Street from Times Square. As it turns out, I'm taking that train, too," Bob replied. Bob started walking toward the top of the alley. He looked back to make sure River was following. She did and hoped that together with the change of clothes, she might lose any trail Kruger might have put on her.

"I'm not gonna ask why you want to leave by the back door, but if it's a guy problem, you can let me or Al know," Bob said without looking at her.

It's a guy problem, all right.

"That's very kind of you, and I'll bear that in mind," River said. Bob didn't belabor the point, and they chitchatted until they reached Times Square subway.

They walked down the stairs that led to the platforms and jumped on the next 1 train. River only had to take it one stop. She waved at Bob when she disembarked and climbed the stairs toward the exit. The crowd moved dizzyingly fast around her, and she couldn't tell whether she'd been followed. The thought that Kruger's men were already on to her irritated her more than it scared her. She left the subway and walked to Macy's.

The place hadn't changed at all since she'd visited with her mom many years ago. The thought brought back some fond memories—ones she wanted to hang on to. She couldn't help but take a moment to admire the architecture and the merchandise in the windows. The Empire State Building stood as impressive as ever in the distance. River would have liked to spend more time leisurely wandering around, but lingering was a bad idea, and she entered the store promptly.

She found a set of escalators and took one to the second floor. She wasn't sure what she would find there, but her idea was to keep moving and then find a place within the store where she could stop and observe. She had a list of items she'd like to purchase, but she would only do that once she knew she was in the clear.

She wove through the passageways that connected one brand of women's clothes to another, and then she found the perfect corner. The clothes she stopped to take an interest in looked expensive, and from the racks on which they were displayed she could see a large chunk of the sales floor. Nothing seemed amiss. She was about to move on but then stopped. Perhaps she shouldn't be looking for a man.

The women around her looked as though they were all doing the same thing—stopping in front of a display, lifting a jacket or a pair of pants to check them out. Then they would move on and repeat the process a little farther down the aisle. Then River noticed something different. Most of these women were smartly dressed. They were alone or with friends, enjoying the process of hunting for the perfect outfit or for a bargain.

River wasn't hunting for the perfect outfit in her jeans and leather jacket, and neither was a small woman who'd stopped only a few displays away. She was dressed for walking and merging into the crowd, but here, in her dirty running shoes, dark pants, and hoodie, she looked out of place. River considered her options and cursed. She could confront the woman and tell her to stop following her, but then Kruger would know she'd sussed him out.

River figured she was there to shop, and she figured she might as well do what she'd set out to do. She walked the floor hunting for an attractive suit that would further change her appearance. She spotted a light-gray spring pantsuit that was elegantly tailored and yet didn't cost a fortune. She then ventured to another part of the store where she bought a simple white shirt.

The woman was still following her, but her rather bedraggled appearance started to attract disapproving looks from some of the customers. River kept going and went to the handbag department. Her old backpack could do with replacing. She didn't care so much about labels and would have been content with a military-issue substitute, but the plan she'd just hatched required something a little more upmarket. She chose a gray Tumi rolltop backpack. The price tag made her cough, but she convinced herself that it was the right choice for the right cause.

The cash registers were only a few paces away, and River joined the line of people waiting to pay. After she paid, she finally proceeded to the cosmetics department. She quickly chose some blue eye shadow, a dark mascara, and a soft lip gloss. She paid for the items, then found a corner of the store where she could stop and observe her pursuer. The woman was checking the offerings at one of the counters. A clerk was trying to persuade her to try some lipstick, and River saw an opportunity.

She hid her old backpack in the shopping bag she'd been given, took out the new backpack, and undid the bun in her hair. After fishing out a scrunchie from her old backpack, she gathered her locks into a neat ponytail, and applied some of her new makeup using the small mirror inside the eye-shadow compact. She then made her way to the store's sixth floor.

The trattoria was busy when she arrived. At the entrance, the hostess gave River a disapproving look. River ignored her and smiled.

"I'd like a table for one please, and would you mind if I used the restrooms to change? I don't want to wait to get into the dressing rooms. That takes forever."

The hostess took a second look at River. She seemed to approve of the tastefully applied makeup and the Tumi bag. River held open the shopping bag that held her suit.

"I can't wait to wear it," she said with a chuckle.

The hostess relented. "The restrooms are immediately to your right. I'll seat you as soon as you've changed."

"That's very kind," River said as she took a quick look over her shoulder. Her pursuer had stopped in the distance. Unless Kruger had given her a budget that involved updating her wardrobe, she wouldn't be following River into the restaurant.

River walked into the ladies' room, chose the first stall, and changed quickly. She took her hair out of the ponytail and combed it, applied a little more lipstick, and went back to the restaurant. The woman who'd been waiting for her gave her an approving smile and led her to a small table near a long window overlooking Manhattan. River sat down and perused the menu. Her eyes watered at the price of a simple plate of pasta. But she hardly ate out in Kotzebue, and when she did, it was for a burger or a pizza at Little Louie's. She chose pasta Bolognese and a green salad on the side with some sparkling water. The wine list looked inviting, but she had to stay sharp.

A small, plump waiter came to take her order, and she was left alone. River took her cell phone out of her new bag and checked her emails. Nothing from Reggie yet, but she had to give the guy a chance. She then noticed she had a couple of text messages. Karen had been trying to get in touch.

Do you need me yet?

River checked the time. It had been sent at 11:47 a.m. But then another message had followed at 1:14 p.m.

It's no longer a question—I'm coming to NY.

River dialed Karen's number, and she answered almost instantly.

"Before you say anything," River said, "I'd like to know whether you still have the burner you bought in DC."

Karen didn't ask why and instead said, "What's your new burner number?"

River gave her number to Karen. "Call me back."

She dropped her cell phone into her bag, retrieved her burner phone, and switched it to silent mode so the ringtone wouldn't attract attention. The burner vibrated, and River answered. "What's up?"

Karen sounded serious. "A guy who thinks he's really clever is asking questions about you in town."

"Why do you say he thinks he's clever?" River asked, surprised.

"He arrived a few weeks ago. He found employment at the seafood processing plant. Gets along with the guys there, apparently. Looks all friendly, but then he started asking questions."

"How do you know that?"

River could imagine Karen rolling her eyes. "I ain't the daughter of Chief of Police Robinson for nothing."

River took a moment to absorb the information. Kruger was sparing no effort to get to her. She wondered why he hadn't tried to terminate her already, but perhaps it was because of what Reggie and she had discussed: It would be easier for River to have an unfortunate accident abroad than here in the United States.

"Are you still there?"

"Sorry, Karen. I had a conversation with Reggie and with this guy Mike Wilson."

"Wilson. The doctor from DWB who'd given you Angela's details in the first place?"

"That's the one."

River spotted the waiter making his way to her table. "Hang on a moment. My lunch is arriving."

Karen picked up on the remark. "You mean you are in a *proper* restaurant?"

River smiled to the waiter, who arranged the plate of pasta and the green salad in front of her.

"Would you like some Parmesan?" he offered, opening a small bowl containing grated cheese.

"That would be wonderful."

The man dusted the pasta with two generous helpings. River nodded her thanks, and the waiter left her to it.

"That was the only way to get rid of the woman who was following me," River said when the man was out of earshot.

Karen whistled. "You need to fill me in on what you've learned so far."

Between mouthfuls of pasta, River told Karen all she knew and suspected.

Karen waited until River had finished. "I agree with two things you said—Kruger is baiting you. He must by now have realized you're the daughter of the couple he . . ." Karen hesitated but then said, "Had murdered. And he is also settling a score. He's badly hurt, because of you, and he won't be setting foot in the United States anytime soon, so, he is good and mad."

River took a sip of water. Karen was right to call it what it was—murder—but it still hurt to think that two generous and bright people had been killed to protect mere business interests.

"Still, he won't get to me here in the States, it seems. Perhaps whoever is protecting him has told him to stay under the radar to avoid attention from the US media," River added.

"Reggie's got to be right. It would be suspicious to say the least if you got bumped only a few months after helping with Jason's release. Whatever agency is covering Kruger's ass needs to be a little more careful here at home. Abroad, it's going to be a free-for-all, as you and I have witnessed in the Middle East."

River thought for a moment. "Just one thing occurred to me. Kruger must have been useful to some very powerful people if he was allowed to run his business with such impunity. But what about now?"

"That's a good point," Karen said. "Still, that doesn't change the fact that Kruger is after you, and that you are after Kruger."

Both women remained silent for a moment, and then Karen asked, "What's the plan? And don't tell me you're gonna go on your own to face this SOB."

"I'm not gonna go on my own, *but*," River said, anticipating Karen's protests, "I want him to *think* I am."

"So you need the A team," Karen said, excitement in her voice.

River frowned. "Have you and Reggie been talking?"

"Nope, never. Wouldn't dream of it."

"Pinocchio," River said, torn between a little anger and a warm feeling of friendship—they cared about her.

Karen chuckled. "My nose isn't growing any longer, so, I must be telling the truth."

River ate more food. It was a shame she didn't have time to savor the pasta, but she needed Karen to start coming up with a plan for flying to Africa undetected.

"You and Danny seem to have hit it off since you came back from DC," River said. She could imagine Karen half closing her eyes, trying to suss out why River was asking.

"Mmmm . . . Do I sense a need for his ATR 42 cargo plane?"

"Depends on whether he can fly that thing across the Atlantic," River replied.

"That *thing* flies all over the world," Karen said. "Would I be reading your mind accurately if I suggested a pit stop in DC to pick up Reggie and then a trip across the ocean to Africa?"

River wiped her mouth with her napkin, took as sip of water, and said, "Your mind reading is scarily accurate."

"What if Kruger has got informants in whatever country we're supposed to be landing in?"

"He almost certainly has. But Africa is a big continent. South Africa is a big country, too, and he can't have people in every airport. Besides, you won't be arriving on a commercial airline flight but on a cargo flight."

"So we don't land in Johannesburg but somewhere more discreet?"

"That's the plan, and since the final target is Limpopo Province—"

A buzzing tone interrupted River. Someone else was trying to get hold of her—Mike Wilson was waiting for her to pick up.

"Sorry, Karen. Gotta go; Mike Wilson is calling."

River killed the call and caught Mike just before he went to voicemail.

"Thanks for calling me back," River said by way of greeting.

"I managed to find some additional information," Mike said. His voice sounded echoey. "But the file I found is very slim. There are only a few witness statements, mainly from the people who arrived at the village afterward and described the massacre. No one who was at Katuba that day made it out alive."

Mike paused, and River felt a surge of anger rise inside her. Kruger couldn't have been the only one who needed to cover his tracks if the casualties were that extensive.

"But then I went through the file again, and something struck me. The story was very disjointed. Surely some of the villagers had been away on that day—working the fields, tending their animals, or getting supplies. These villages aren't static or self-sufficient. But no mention of anyone who survived. The police carried out a very perfunctory inquiry. So DWB did a lot more digging—or so a document says—but then I can't find any evidence of it." Mike stopped, sounding out of breath by the marathon explanation.

"You think the file has been redacted?" River asked.

"Worse than that. A redacted file tells you that it has been edited because some details are blacked out. Here, the documents are just missing."

"How easy is it to get a file like this?"

"You mean to access DWB files? Obviously, the organization is very careful, but we're not a match for the likes of the FBI or the CIA. And anyway, we shouldn't have anything to hide."

The waiter came to remove River's plates. She was surprised to find that she'd managed to finish her meal. He softly asked whether she'd like to see the dessert menu. She nodded. Even if she didn't select anything, it would give her a few more minutes before it was time to pay and go.

"It's confirming what we suspect: The people we are after are connected and efficient," River said.

"The one thing I haven't had time to do is to check whether Angela herself has left any form of information that might help."

"It's a very long shot. It was fourteen years ago. Why would she have suspected foul play then and not speak to you about it?"

"I think she tried to," Mike replied. "But perhaps she rightly felt I didn't want to hear it at the time."

"I need to get to Africa," River said after a short silence.

"I thought you might suggest that. In which case, you need some help. I'll send you the contact details of my brother, Orson Wilson. He's been living in Africa for more than two decades."

"Is he a medic, too?" River asked.

"No. He's a priest."

"Oh." River was taken aback for a moment and then said, "Is he a missionary?"

Mike's voice became a little lighter, cheered by memories of his brother. "Not his style. He's there to help, and he doesn't really care whether people believe or not. He talks to the communities he serves about his faith, but he's not forcing it onto them. He is also a very good biologist."

"Does he carry out some sort of scientific research?" River asked. She recalled one instance in which her parents had been collaborating with a Jesuit priest on a matter concerning immunology.

"He spends a lot of time researching how plants we know little about could help in developing new medications, mostly targeting cancer and AIDS."

"I presume he knows Angela?" River asked.

River noticed the slight delay in Mike's response. "He does, and you can be open with Orson. He's the sort of person people trust. For all I know, Angela might have confided a lot more in him than she might have in me. Angela and he were close when they were teenagers."

Another pause, a sigh, and then Mike added, perhaps not wanting to elaborate on the nature of Orson and Angela's closeness, "He's a much better listener. I guess that's part of the job, if you can call it that."

Hearing confession must be quite a skill.

"Do you know where Orson is at the moment?"

"He was in South Africa last time we spoke, but that was a couple of months ago. He'd just landed in Jo'burg, but we didn't speak about where he was going next."

"That's very helpful. Thank you. Hang on a moment," River said.

The waiter approached to take her dessert order. She smiled but declined and asked for the check.

"When do you think you'll be heading to Africa?" Mike asked.

"I'm not sure yet."

She was certain it would be within the next couple of days, but not certain she was prepared to reveal this even to Mike.

"Haven't you got friends who can help you?"

"Not really. I don't want them involved in this."

Her response was only half a lie. She wished she could have dealt with Kruger on her own. A mission to take down a man like him needed trained people if it was to succeed. And she had no intention of failing. Her parents deserved justice, and so did Jason, and so did all the villagers Kruger had massacred fourteen years ago.

"I'll keep digging," Mike said. "If there is something material, I'll contact you ASAP."

"As long as it doesn't put you in Kruger's crosshairs."

"That time has come and gone, I'm afraid. I'll just have to be careful when I cross the street." Mike tried to laugh, but it stuck in his throat.

"Good luck."

"Same to you."

Mike hung up. The check arrived, and she paid it, wondering whether the woman with the hoodie was still waiting for her. River returned to the restroom to reapply makeup and give herself a chance to leave the restaurant unnoticed.

A couple of women were there, too, when she walked in. They gave River a quick look, and both seemed to approve of the suit and Tumi backpack. River started to touch up her lipstick. One of the women took a scarf out of a small bag. It looked like a new purchase.

"Such a good color on you," her friend said.

"Absolutely," River gushed. "Perfect with your eyes."

"Thank you," the scarf woman said, turning to River. "So kind. People don't bother with compliments these days."

"That's so important," River added. She admired the scarf and then asked, sounding a little shy, "Did you buy it here? I'm looking for something to brighten up my suit."

The two women looked at each other, smiled, and said, talking over each other, "It *is* from Macy's. They have a fabulous accessories department—happy to show you."

"That would be very nice."

River finished with her makeup, and the three of them left the restroom, making small talk about the department store and what they liked the most about it. They walked out together—three girlfriends having enjoyed a good meal and a shop. River thought she recognized the woman in the dark hoodie, but by the time River left the sixth floor, the woman was still waiting for her to leave the trattoria.

There's something to be said for shopping with girlfriends.

Chapter 5

The water was cool enough for Kruger to enjoy his evening swim. The Olympic-size swimming pool he had had built at his luxurious house in Johannesburg was hidden from public view, as was the rest of his property. Kruger had chosen to live in one of the high-end suburbs of the city, not because of its profile but because he could build fortifications around his home without anyone asking questions. Morningside was renowned for its gated estates, beautiful homes, and private hospitals, and it all suited Kruger's need for military-grade security.

He wrapped the towel he'd left on a chaise longue around his waist, letting the water run down his back and his chest. He looked up at the second floor, where he detected movement. The maid appeared, and Kruger relaxed. She was finishing turning down his bed and would soon be leaving. Unlike most of his neighbors, Kruger didn't have a lot of personnel weighing him down. The maid and cook arrived in the morning and left in the late afternoon. The people on twenty-four-hour duty were his security detail—men he'd known for a very long time, whom he remunerated handsomely.

Kruger walked across the terrace that surrounded the west side of the property and into the dining room. The place could have easily housed a family of ten, but Kruger liked his space. His security team lived on the east side of the building, and they interacted with him during the day. Kruger liked eating his evening meal on his own, though. The cook had laid his dinner out for him. She was still in the kitchen, making sure the food was to his liking. Kruger ignored the food, moved farther inside the house, and climbed to the second floor two steps at a time.

He entered his bedroom and changed into a pair of jeans and a dark T-shirt. The habit of living in camo clothing for years had left its mark. For example, he would never consider wearing a white shirt at night, which would turn him into a highly visible target. The thought elicited a bitter smile. Despite all his Special Forces training, Kruger had gone down in DC and was still feeling the pain coursing through his leg when he exercised.

Perhaps his SADF training was wearing thin. He'd joined the South African Army right after he turned twenty and been taught by some of the best and most able officers he'd ever known. The South African Defence Force was dealing at the time with border wars with Nambia, as well as counterinsurgency. Kruger was born during apartheid in South Africa, and the SADF had been extensively used to quash insurrection. This had meant acquiring sophisticated equipment and providing highly skilled training. Kruger proved good at it, and he joined the Special Forces. He'd also proved adept at helping circumvent the UN sanctions that had put an embargo on the sale of armaments to his country—where there is a will, there is a way, one of his commanders told him. Kruger had never looked back after that, and when apartheid ended, in 1994, Kruger retired from the army and began his own "facilitator" business.

It had been quite a journey from the family farm where his parents toiled using black laborers and brought up their ten children to the rich suburbs of Jo'burg. Some of his siblings hadn't lived to reach adulthood. He sometimes saw one of them who did, although her marriage to a Zulu man with whom she ran the farm had put an end to his visits.

Kruger returned to the dining room. He lifted with mild interest the silver cover of the dish the cook had left on a hot plate for him. It looked like pork cooked in a light mushroom sauce surrounded by vegetables. She'd made sure there wasn't any eggplant in the mix. She had forgotten once, and he made sure she'd never forget again. The green salad she prepared was covered with a net that prevented insects from landing on the food. It looked suitably good, yet Kruger couldn't care less. He'd rather eat what he killed on a hunt in the bush and roasted over an open fire.

The cook appeared at the door, and Kruger waved her off. "You can go for the evening."

She curtsied and left. It was late enough, and he wanted to be left alone. He helped himself to a pork cutlet and vegetables, removed the net from the salad, and started eating. He should be hearing from DC soon. The thought stopped him for a moment. He'd since found out a lot about River Swift. She had been trained by the US Air Force as a field medic in a new unit that intervened when troops were in theater. She'd seen action in Iraq and Afghanistan, but she wasn't Special Forces, although she'd worked alongside them. She was surprisingly impressive for someone who wasn't either a Marine or a SEAL, and she was resourceful.

Kruger resumed eating. He'd almost finished when his cell phone rang. He dropped his fork and answered the call.

"She slipped away" was all the woman said.

Kruger stood up in a single motion, sending his chair flying. "How the fuck did this happen?"

"I don't know. She walked into one of the restaurants at Macy's, and I didn't see her coming out. Perhaps she used the staff exit."

"Which means that she must have clocked you," Kruger said through gritted teeth.

"Something else happened that put her on her guard. She'd already left the hotel through the staff door, and I almost lost her then."

Kruger swallowed his anger. The woman he was employing was good, and her calm told him that she was certain she'd been made because River had become suspicious and therefore careful.

"Be on standby. I might still need you," Kruger said before he killed the call.

He paced the length of his oversize dining room, then went upstairs to his office. The door was locked, and he opened it by entering a code on the keypad to its right. The door clicked open, he went in, and the door clicked shut automatically behind him.

He went to his desk, opened the top drawer, and retrieved a burner phone. Something had happened in New York that he wasn't aware of and that had spooked the Swift woman. He had an inkling of what it might be, and he needed to stop Davis from interfering—if indeed he had.

The burner rang twice, and CIA agent Dexter Davis answered. "I'll call you back." Davis was at his office in Langley and perhaps ready to go to lunch.

Kruger grunted. The burner went dead, and he waited for Davis. The burner rang a minute or so later.

"What?" Davis asked.

"Did you get involved with Swift?"

"I've been involved with her ever since I made sure you could leave the States without being arrested," Davis replied tersely.

Kruger made a fist. Davis wasn't wrong to remind him of that, but this didn't mean he had to be a jerk and keep being involved.

"You don't need to remind me every time we speak, but I need to know whether you've been following her."

"We agreed I wouldn't, and I stuck to that."

Kruger believed Davis. But the reply felt a little too certain, as though rehearsed. How else could Swift realize she was being followed?

Davis interrupted Kruger's thinking. "Anything else?"

"Have you been tailing anybody close to her?"

The slight delay in Davis's response told Kruger he'd asked the right question.

"Why do you want to know?"

"Because she's become suspicious, and I'm certain that something has spooked her."

Davis cleared his throat. "I had to give a warning to a certain person at Doctors Without Borders."

"Which consisted of what?" Kruger asked, knowing he'd regained the upper hand.

"You don't need to know that," Davis shot back.

"Yes, I do," Kruger replied. "You and I know that I need to stop Swift from digging any further into what happened to her parents fourteen years ago."

"And I need to make sure that DWB doesn't help her discover why the Swifts had to be eliminated," Davis said, a little less confident.

Kruger ran a weary hand over his face. Davis had always been a burden, ever since he'd started doing business with him. But Kruger also knew that having a willing CIA agent on his side was crucial to his business. He just would have to make do with Davis and persuade him to let *him* deal with the situation.

"Look," Kruger said. "I get that you do not want me to eliminate the Swift girl on US soil, but let me do what I do best—track people and bring them to me. She needs to come to South Africa thinking that no one is aware she's here. Clery underestimated her, and that miscalculation got him killed. I will not make the same mistake."

"What are you telling me?" Davis said, genuinely uncertain. "That I should lay off completely?"

"Whatever you did has put her on the defensive. So yes, lay off the man or woman you almost got run over. Let them think it was just a careless driver, but make sure there are no documents left at DWB that can help Swift in her quest."

"There is nothing left in the Swift file. I took care of that a long time ago," Davis retorted. "But how did you know—"

"About the failed hit-and-run?" Kruger said after a smile. "New York is the ideal place for that—a lot of traffic not always abiding by the rules, and, if you're on a bike, the rider can disappear in a moment."

Davis didn't seem ready to terminate the call, and Kruger waited.

Something else has gone wrong.

"Have you spoken to Matondo recently?" Davis asked.

Kruger straightened up. It was one thing to cook up an intimidation attempt in the middle of New York City, and another thing altogether to involve Matondo in any form of operation, which would almost always end in bloodshed.

"I was in the DRC with him three weeks ago." Kruger wouldn't volunteer more.

"Someone else at DWB needed to be persuaded to keep quiet."

Kruger bit his lip in anger and tried to remain calm as he said, "Then that person is almost certainly dead."

Davis seemed stunned at the thought. "Those weren't my instructions."

"Matondo doesn't do 'instructions' when it comes to dealing with people. The only way to control him is to be looking over his shoulder, and even then . . ."

Images of the onslaught that had followed Matondo's intrusion into the village flashed in front of Kruger's eyes. He truly despised the man.

"Who was that person, anyway?" Kruger asked.

Davis hesitated but then said, "Angela Graham. She was a friend and colleague of Beverly Swift."

"Why focus on her?" Kruger asked. "She can't be the only DWB staff member who worked with Beverly Swift."

Kruger could hear it in Davis's silence. The woman was important in her own right. He'd learned that the CIA, like every other intelligence agency, kept its contractors at bay, even when knowledge might have made it easier for them to deliver their services. The intelligence community kept its operations well under wraps.

"Is she a CIA asset, just like the Swifts were?" Kruger kept prodding.

"She isn't my asset," Davis volunteered.

Kruger concluded that she must be as asset for another agency altogether. Davis wouldn't have dared manhandle the asset of another CIA handler. "But again, why the interest?"

"She's been contacted by River Swift," Davis finally volunteered.

Kruger exploded. "When were you going to tell me? Now, we may never know how much this woman knew and how much she told Swift."

"That's why I called Matondo," Davis replied, on the defensive.

"And has he come back to you with an answer?"

Davis stayed silent.

"Then we know for sure that this woman is dead. He's an executioner of the worst sort, and I have seen my fair share."

Kruger leaned against his desk, head bowed. This was a mess and not of his doing.

"You need to let me have all the intelligence you gathered on the Swifts that I don't already have. I also need to know how much their daughter, River, has accumulated. I want the intel sent after this call."

His voice had acquired the sharpness he knew scared others.

Davis knew that voice, too, and he grumbled, "I'll send you what I have today."

"You will send it now. I need to plan." Kruger had tonight and the next day ahead of him to work out a way to bring River to South Africa . . . alone.

The reception area of the Marriott Marquis on Broadway was what you would expect from a four-star hotel—spacious, pleasant, and perhaps a little predictable.

River crossed the lobby and walked into the bar, a cozy space that exuded good taste and abundance. She scanned the room and saw Reggie sitting in a far corner, waiting. He wasn't wearing a suit but rather jeans and a white shirt, which made him look far younger than he was. His tight, curly dark hair had been freshly cut, and it suited him well.

He'd gotten in touch with her just as she left Macy's and announced he was on his way to New York on the next flight. He would be landing at LaGuardia at 4:19 p.m. and reckoned he'd be at the Marriott by 5:30 p.m. She'd tried to question him about the reason for the trip, but he simply said he would explain when they met.

River had warned him that she might look a little different from what he expected, and he chuckled. The last time she changed her appearance to that of a dark-haired, suit-wearing executive, it had worked wonders. And this time, the disguise was even more successful, since the two women she met at Macy's had helped her choose.

River crossed the room confidently and plunked herself in the seat opposite Reggie. He arched his eyebrows and then said, "Suit-wearing brunette. You're predictably on the warpath."

"But I saw it in your eyes. You hesitated for a moment."

Reggie pursed his lips. "A second—no more." And then he smiled, stood up, and gave River a brief hug. "So nice to see you again."

River returned the hug and waited for Reggie to settle again. He lifted his hand confidently and waved at the waiter. River smiled at the way Reggie's self-assurance had grown—firm and yet respectful. River ordered an iced tea and Reggie a Diet Coke.

"I'm pleased to see you in person, Reg, but why not call?" River asked as soon as the waiter was out of earshot.

"Because in one hour we're meeting a contact of mine in Harlem," Reggie said. "She works for Homeland Security, and I think we want the same thing as she does."

River couldn't hide her surprise. For someone who came from DC's tough neighborhoods, Reggie was doing well at creating a network. They both fell silent as the waiter delivered their drinks. River waited again and then asked, "I'm intrigued to find out how you know her and what it is she wants."

"Ariana, too, decided that she could beat the odds against her and get a decent job, although she's a little older than I am. She was in my older brother's year in high school," Reggie said before he took a sip. "And she, too, is interested in Karl Kruger."

River took a sip of her own drink and sat back. "That's a hell of a coincidence," she said.

Reggie shook his head. "I know you and I don't like or believe in coincidences. But it isn't one, really. Ariana and her team have been trying to catch Kruger red-handed for years. When he fled to Africa after Clery's death, every agency got wind of his escape. It was linked to Jason's case. She looked up who was defending Jase . . ."

"And there you were," River concluded.

Reggie grinned and nodded.

"Why Harlem?" River asked.

"Because she's got good contacts there, and if we're followed, it's easier to spot our pursuers, assuming they're white."

"Don't you think Kruger employs black guys, too?"

"Perhaps in Africa, but here in the States I don't think so. He'll favor the white community of thieves and thugs, and that suits me just fine."

River wouldn't contradict Reggie. She knew her stuff when it came to medical and military matters. He knew his stuff when it came to gangsters, dealers, and moles in DC.

They fell into a comfortable silence. Reggie finished his Diet Coke, she her iced tea. He got up, and they made their way to the subway. River fought the urge to look over her shoulder. They stopped in front of a shop window, using the reflection in the glass to spot any tail. They resumed their walk, but then Reggie motioned River to stop. He knelt and feigned tying one of his shoelaces. He stood up and said, "I think we're in the clear."

They walked to Times Square and got onto an uptown number 2 train. The car was full, but they managed to cram themselves in. River squeezed her backpack against her chest, and Reggie transferred his cell phone from his back pants pocket to his inside jacket pocket. River's possessions were all stuck in her bag, away from wandering fingers. They remained silent until Reggie said, "We're getting out at the next stop."

River checked the sign on the station wall—135th Street. When the train stopped, they made their way to the door, apologizing as they squeezed through the crowd. Reggie took the lead again, and they emerged in Harlem, at the intersection of 135th Street and Malcolm X Boulevard.

"We're just a couple of blocks away," Reggie said as they waited to cross the street.

The light turned green, and they walked west. When they turned south onto Adam Clayton Powell Jr. Boulevard, a pink neon sign shone in the distance, brightly visible now that daylight was dwindling: RENAISSANCE.

Reggie took the burner phone out of his jacket pocket and called a number.

"We're almost there."

He listened to what the person at the end of the line said and nodded.

"Fine. We'll see you in a moment."

River gave Reggie a quizzical look.

"Ariana is a little delayed. Only by a few minutes."

River didn't ask whether he was sure she'd be coming. No point now. Reggie pushed the restaurant door open. A buzz of voices and the scent of roasted meat welcomed them. A tall woman dressed in black trousers and a black shirt greeted them as they entered.

"We have a booking under the name of Pettit," Reggie said.

The woman checked her iPad, smiled, and led them to a table at the back of the long room. It overlooked the entire restaurant and made it easy to survey the comings and goings of the patrons.

River took her jacket off and hung it on the back of her chair. She sat down and took in the decor and the mood—dark wood paneling and translucent glass globes; brass at the long bar, where the bartender was preparing cocktails that looked very festive. Waiters and waitresses busied themselves with the clientele.

"This looks like a gem of a restaurant," River said.

"It's run by two chefs who were born in Senegal and who've worked with the well-known French chef Daniel Boulud. Wait until you see the menu—it's mouthwatering."

River hadn't heard of Boulud, but then she hadn't spent much time in New York, even when her parents were alive. Although she felt a pang of regret at the thought, her mom would have loved the place.

"How do you know?" River asked, surprised that Reggie seemed familiar with the place.

Reggie chuckled. "I checked it on the internet."

River chuckled back. "You almost had me convinced you were a regular."

"I'm glad I became a lawyer," Reggie said, "otherwise I might have become a con artist."

River shook her head. "Not you, Reggie. It can't have been easy to get into law school, and then to secure a spot at one of the top law firms in DC. You don't choose what's easy. You choose what's right."

Reggie got a little shy and looked away. "Some people will tell you I got there because of DEI rules imposed on law firms."

"That's a lot of BS, and I hope you know it," River replied with feeling. As far as she was concerned, organizations should hire the best people for the job. It doesn't matter who they are, as long as they're honest and hardworking.

The door of the restaurant opened, and Reggie's attention turned to the person who entered—tall, slim, wearing a light-blue suit and a small, colorful scarf knotted around her long neck. River guessed that Ariana Pettit had just arrived. The hostess welcomed her with warmth, and this time, River was certain that Ariana was a regular. The women chatted for a moment, and then Ariana looked in their direction.

Her face lit up as she saw Reggie stand up. She waved and made her way to the table. Ariana's delicate face, high cheekbones, and sensuous lips reminded River of the beautiful women she'd met in Kenya—the Maasai women had always impressed her with their graceful features, colorful dresses, and intricate beaded jewelry.

Ariana hesitated when she reached the table, but chose to give Reggie a hug and then extended a hand toward River. River stood up, and they shook hands.

"I'm Ariana. You must be River. Very nice to meet you," Ariana said. She followed with a smile, and yet River could sense that Ariana was already observing her closely.

"The pleasure is mine," River replied.

They sat down, and the hostess brought menus and the wine list. Reggie had suddenly gone quiet, and River could tell he was impressed by Ariana—but then who wouldn't be?

"Shall we order? And then we can talk," Ariana offered.

"That's a very good idea. Anything you recommend, since you seem to know the restaurant well," River said.

Ariana took it as a compliment and grinned. "There are so many good dishes here—but I'd say the Renaissance burger, the mussels in white wine, and the truffle mushroom risotto are my favorites."

"Then I'll go for the mussels," River said, closing her menu.

"I'll join you," Ariana replied.

Both women turned to Reggie. He took a few seconds to realize he had to make his choice and then said, "The Renaissance burger for me."

Ariana's friend returned to take their order and offered to select a wine that would suit the food they were having. Everybody agreed, and she disappeared toward the kitchen, passing the order to a waiter.

"Thank you for meeting me," River said to get the conversation going.

Ariana's lightheartedness evaporated, and her expression turned serious. "Reggie told me about the person you are pursuing." She took a moment to find the right words. "It's more than gutsy on your part but also necessary. We can't let the likes of Kruger run his business with impunity in America."

"How much do you know about his business?" River asked, leaning forward so that she could lower her voice and still be heard. "He's involved in armaments for certain, but my research indicates there is more to his enterprise."

"He deals on both sides of the fence. Legal and illegal military-grade weapons. He's prominent not only in Africa but also elsewhere. He's now using his well-structured network in Africa to provide weapons to countries that are on embargo lists."

"Such as?" River asked.

"Russia, Syria, Iran . . . he doesn't care."

"And in Africa?"

"The DRC, South Sudan, Somalia—and Yemen."

River shook her head. "He is a busy guy."

"Because he's incredibly well-connected and always good at detecting the next best deal," Ariana said.

She stopped as the waiter who'd taken their order returned with three glasses of wine. They all took a sip, made the appropriate chirps of approval, and were left alone again.

"Have you heard of coltan?" Ariana asked.

River shook her head, and Reggie finally butted in. "Isn't it a type of ore that's used in cell phones?"

"Well done," Ariana said, sounding suitably impressed. "It is. And all the tech companies are tripping over one another to get some. The issue with coltan is that its production is concentrated in a few countries only—the DRC is at the top of the list."

"I don't recall any being found in South Africa," River said with a frown.

"If there is, it's nothing in comparison to what the DRC contains," Ariana said before taking another sip of wine. "The DRC supplies more than 40 percent of the world's coltan. Most importantly, the production is concentrated around the Kivu-Goma area."

"You mean the part of the DRC where militiamen wreak havoc?" River said, feeling her stomach knotting.

"I believe so, although I don't know Africa well at all. But that's the information I got," Ariana said.

"How long has Kruger been after coltan?" River asked.

"More than ten years, but it's hard to put a date on something that is not always legal. It's only noticeable when it becomes a big enough business."

The timing seemed to coincide with River's parents' assassination, and the thought made her shudder, although she couldn't imagine why they would have gotten involved.

"What's in it for Homeland Security?" Reggie asked.

"Kruger is feeding armaments to terrorists indirectly, but his involvement in the coltan trade could endanger the export of key minerals to the United States," Ariana said.

"And yet he's been extending his influence in DC, and no one seems in great hurry to stop him," River said.

"That's the problem with a guy like Kruger. He's got his finger in several pies, and he's more helpful to several US agencies than he is a hindrance. So they keep him free to roam as long as he serves them."

"Which agencies are we talking about?" River asked. "CIA, FBI, NSA? Or even your own agency?"

Ariana waited, as food was brought to the table. The aroma that rose from the dishes made River's mouth water. The three of them looked at one another and without saying a word tucked into their food. Ariana expertly picked a couple of mussels from their shells with a fork and then returned to the topic of Kruger.

"We know the CIA uses him a lot, although we don't know who his handler is."

"You've been told to back off?" Reggie said before he bit into his burger hungrily.

"In no uncertain terms," Ariana said. "But we are still keeping tabs on him."

River enjoyed the seafood, too, savoring a bite of steamed clams before she asked, "Are you waiting for the right opportunity to catch him? Wait for him to make a mistake that even the CIA won't be able to ignore?"

Ariana gave her a crooked smile. "Something like that."

River found the answer strange. Was Ariana flying solo? Looking for a big case that might advance her career?

"What does your boss think about it?" River asked, returning to her food.

She picked up a small movement that Ariana made with her cutlery. An involuntary reaction that indicated surprise and perhaps annoyance.

"He's fine with the idea," Ariana said as she lay down her fork. "I would welcome a little more enthusiasm from him, though."

River and Reggie nodded, and River was grateful that Ariana hadn't tried to sidestep the question or even simply lied.

"It's tough to make an enemy of the CIA, I imagine," Reggie said.

Ariana agreed. "At best, it's career-limiting and means getting the sack. At worst, it's ending up swimming with the fishes at the bottom of the Potomac."

"What's in it for you?" River asked before she took a sip of wine.

Reggie gave River a quick look. He squinted, and River got the message that he didn't like the directness of the question.

"It's the right thing to do," Ariana said with feeling. She looked at Reggie as she answered, yet avoided River. Reggie gave her an approving smile.

Wrapped around her little finger.

That Reggie thought so much of Ariana wouldn't be an issue, until River stopped believing that Ariana was on their side. Then she would have to convince Reggie, and that might prove complicated.

"I'm going to need a little more than just that," River finally said. "I'm planning to go to Africa. Kruger is hiding there, and the only way he's going to make the mistake you're hoping for is if he feels he's being hunted down. It's good to know that Kruger is protected and by whom, but I need an address, and I need the names of some of his contacts."

"You're going on your own?" Ariana asked, genuinely surprised.

Reggie was about to answer but River kicked his shin under the table. He controlled a wince, and River added, "It's easier to be undetected on my own. If I find Kruger and enough evidence about his dirty business, I'll call for backup."

Ariana finished the last mussel on her plate, picked up her spoon, and scooped some white wine sauce before saying, "I understand from Reggie that you were in the Air Force, but I didn't think you were Special Forces."

She'd delivered her question without aggression, and yet she was driving home a point—River was going up against a trained operative.

"If you're asking whether I've got the training to carry out an assault on Kruger's compound, one of which I imagine he has, the answer is no. But spending time in Iraq and Afghanistan with the Special Forces you mentioned has taught me a thing or two—including perseverance and resourcefulness."

Ariana laid her spoon across her plate. She then locked eyes with River. "I, too, am putting my neck on the line here. So I'm sorry if I come at it a little too strongly."

"No need to apologize," River said. "We're all taking a lot of risks in tackling Kruger. But perhaps the good thing about us is that, either he won't know who we are or he'll dismiss us as amateurs."

Ariana seemed to think about River's assessment. River had to hand it to her. The woman was together. Whether she was after Kruger because she wanted a promotion or because he deserved to be put behind bars, she had the determination to see the mission through.

"Okay," Ariana said, glancing at River and then Reggie. "Let's do this. I have some intel I've been gathering under the radar. I'll send you Kruger's address in Johannesburg. It's a mansion in a rich part of the city, but it's not the only place he owns in South Africa. I'll see whether I can find out more. I reckon a man like him has a base for training his men and storing the weapons he helps smuggle."

River gave Ariana a smile. "And I'd be glad to take a trip to the bush to find out where his compound is. Kruger may be surprised by how much I know about Africa for someone who wasn't born there."

Chapter 6

Ariana had already left. They agreed it was better if the three of them weren't seen together outside the restaurant.

The restaurant was now full to the rafters, but River and Reggie weren't pressured to vacate their table. River ordered a coffee, and Reggie a fresh ginger tea.

"You're suspicious," was the first thing Reggie said as soon as they were on their own.

"I'm suspicious of everyone at the moment." River tried to make it sound as though it wasn't a big deal. "Kruger is a dangerous guy, and we don't know yet how far his connections go in DC. I suppose it's different for you and Ariana. You've known her a long time."

"It's not only that," Reggie said as he stirred some honey into his tea. "I've seen how good she's been with my brother over the years. They were best friends at school, and she still asks about him and visits whenever she's around."

River remembered Reggie mentioning that his older brother had had his struggles, but she'd never belabored the point. She didn't even know what Reggie's older brother's name was.

"I get it," she said. "She's proved faithful to your family."

"But—" Reggie started.

"Ambition does funny things to people." River lifted her hand before Reggie could continue. "I'm not saying she can't be trusted. I'm just saying that we must be careful—or, rather, that I have to be careful. She may be protective of you, but I get the feeling she won't be so considerate with someone she's only just met."

Reggie opened his mouth, but then closed it. He ran a hand over his face. "You might be right. Ariana is tough. She's had to be in order to get where she is at Homeland Security."

"Still, if she comes up with Kruger's address, it'll be more than enough to get us started," River said.

Reggie poured a little more honey into his tea and stirred. "What if Ariana wants to join us?"

River straightened up. "You mean go to Africa?"

Reggie shrugged. "She might want to be part of the plan."

"Can she handle a gun?" River shot back, grappling with the unwanted suggestion.

"Are you serious, Riv? We were born in the poorest area of DC. Everyone has handled a gun there by the age of ten."

"How good will she be surrounded by wild animals in the bush or the jungle?"

"I don't know about that. And that goes for me, too."

"I can cope with one person fainting at the sight of a snake but not two."

Reggie shook his head. "The snake might dissuade her," he said and then got closer to River to ask, "Are there lots of them?"

"What? Snakes?" River couldn't help but chuckle. "It's the wild, Reggie. It's full of poisonous snakes, hungry lions, big elephants . . . but you know what? I'll take the animals over some of the people anytime. And anyway, you've got family in Limpopo Province, haven't you?"

Reggie whispered, "You're not selling this to me very well, Riv. I couldn't handle cockroaches whenever we had them at home. And I've never visited my cousins in Africa."

"Have I found a way of dissuading you to come along?"

Reggie straightened up and cleared his throat. "Nope. I'm still joining your gig."

"In that case, we need to plan how you and Karen will get there. But I presume you've spoken with her," River said, hoping Reggie would confirm her suspicions.

He kept a poker face and said, "What makes you think that?"

"Because you're my friends, and I know you well."

Reggie still wasn't falling for it.

"Never mind," River said. "The one thing we need to do is to ensure that Kruger thinks I'm on my own."

"You mean vulnerable and an easy target?"

"That's right," River said. "He had me followed again this afternoon. This time, the woman was much more discreet."

"Don't you think it's odd?" Reggie asked.

River took a sip of coffee and then said, "You might be right. Why try to scare Mike and even me in the morning and then follow me discreetly in the afternoon?"

"I don't think Kruger wants to scare you," Reggie said. "I think he wants you out of the country so that he can settle a score. He wants you to come to South Africa alone."

They both fell silent, each giving the matter further consideration.

"The other actor we haven't seen evidence of yet is the CIA," River said. "And since they were the ones my parents got involved with—"

"And the ones protecting Kruger," Reggie added.

"But why scare me off? If Kruger is trying to make me feel as though it'll be easy to pursue him, surely, they wouldn't interfere."

"Perhaps Kruger didn't know. Or the CIA guy is following his own agenda," Reggie said.

"What does that mean? The guy at the CIA no longer trusts Kruger?" River asked. "If that's the case, why help him escape the country?"

"Because Kruger's handler needs to clean up around him before"—Reggie hesitated—"he cuts Kruger loose."

"That's a thought," River said before finishing her coffee.

"Could we perhaps be on the same side as the agency?" Reggie asked.

"I don't think we'll ever be on the same side, despite the fact that we may want the same thing."

"It's the A team against the world again," Reggie said with a grin.

"I sincerely hope I'll get more people to join the A team if we are to tackle Kruger *and* the CIA," River said.

"You're good at persuading people to do the right thing, Riv. I'm sure we'll find help along the way."

The compliment was honest, and River didn't quite know how to respond. She squeezed Reggie's shoulder and then said, "Speaking of persuading people to do something for us, Karen is working on making Danny's ATR 42 plane available for a trip to the African continent."

"What sort of plane is that?" Reggie asked.

"Wings, engine . . . it's a cargo plane. It's big."

"And with zero comforts, like the Marines," Reggie said. "I like it."

River was about to contradict Reggie, but he wasn't far wrong. Comfort wasn't what the military was all about. "Perhaps a little less impressive," River said.

"So we're all going to Africa incognito?"

"You and Karen are. I'm not. I'll be flying in on a commercial airline."

"You're not getting soft, are you?" Reggie said, feigning shock.

"Never. I'm being noticed, and I'm being noticed on my own."

"But will Kruger think you've fallen into his trap?"

"He isn't the sort of guy I'm gonna fool that easily—I agree. But it's a good start. He'll eventually figure out I'm not alone. The later, the better, though."

Reggie thought for a moment and then said, "Change of plan. I'm gonna throw a sickie rather than a vacation and claim I've got the flu. I'll have my sister come in every couple of days and check on my empty apartment."

"Good thinking." River nodded. "I'll see what Karen can come up with on her side."

"What's our move once we reach South Africa?" Reggie asked.

"I still have to think about that—it will depend on what Ariana says. I'd rather you and Karen fly to Kruger's training compound without our meeting beforehand. That's where we can find the evidence we need to get this SOB locked up for good."

"I suppose a cargo plane can fly anywhere."

"It's a question of how long the runway is rather than whether there is a terminal to welcome passengers."

"Has Karen been to Africa?" Reggie asked.

"She has. It was before we met, though, and I think it was in Niger, but we never spoke much about it."

Reggie seemed to get lost in thought, then suddenly checked his watch.

"Shit. I've got to be on my way to Newark to catch the last plane to DC."

He waved to the waiter and added, "I'll be ready to go as soon as you say so."

"I'm all packed, so I don't have to get back to Kotzebue, and Karen was packed the day I left for New York."

"That figures," Reggie said with a grin.

The bill arrived. They split it down the middle and paid. Reggie and River stood up to hug briefly, then Reggie left on his own, and River sat back for a moment. It wasn't late, and no one had come to claim the table. Perhaps she could indulge in a final cup of coffee and try to plan for the days ahead. She'd said it to Reggie, but it felt truer than it had ever been—she'd taken on Clery and his men, and a Mexican cartel in Utah, but was she now biting off a lot more than she could chew?

The hot water ran over River's hair, face, and body. She'd left Harlem with a clear plan, but no plan was good enough until it had been scrutinized by people who could give it some tough love. Karen would take her call no matter how busy she was, and she needed the no-BS clearheadedness of her friend.

River stepped out of the shower and towel-dried herself. She wrapped a smaller towel around her head, put the hotel bathrobe on, and went into the bedroom. She took the burner phone out of her jacket pocket and dialed Karen's number.

"Danny's up for it," Karen said as soon as she picked up.

"When has Danny ever said no to anything you suggested?" River said, teasing.

"You make me sound manipulative," Karen replied in mock offense.

"He shares your spirit of adventure. It just happens that you're the one who tells him where that adventure leads."

Karen chuckled and then said, "The idea is to stop for refueling in DC, because it'll take around twelve hours to get there from Kotzebue. We pick up Reggie, then continue on to Cape Town. That will take around fourteen and a half hours."

"That's a lot of time in the air."

"Agreed, but Danny will have two copilots with him, so they'll take turns in the cockpit."

"A little more than a day," River said, thinking. "I just met Reggie and Ariana, one of his contacts at Homeland Security."

Karen gave a low whistle. "Our boy is going places."

River laughed. "I'm not sure he would appreciate being called a boy, and apparently Ariana is an old school friend."

"Do I detect a little romance there?"

"You might be right. In any case, I think Reggie is perhaps a little too trusting and, yes, even smitten."

Karen grew serious. "Ariana hasn't struck a chord with you, though."

"You're right. She's very eager, and I can't figure out why."

"Then she's not coming," Karen said bluntly.

"But we need some of her intel."

"Look, I get that she's gotta be a tough girl if she comes from the same neighborhood as Reggie. But Africa, arms dealing, and the CIA are on a different level, even if she can handle a gun, which I presume she can."

"We still need her intel," River said.

"Have a frank conversation with her," Karen said with heat. Perhaps she might have liked to have that conversation with Ariana herself. "You can tell her that if she's after a promotion and a leg up the ladder, that's fine by you, but the crucial point in this operation is that we need to win the battle *and* the war. No half measures here. We need to get Kruger and the guy who covers his ass, and that's a tall order."

"That's a good idea, uuma, and a good way to flush her out. She doesn't need to know the details of the plan as long as she can be counted on when it comes to nailing Kruger. On the other hand, if she insists on a step-by-step description of what we're planning . . ."

River let it hang, and Karen remained silent. They'd agreed on how to deal with the newcomer to the team.

"Danny is trying to find a commercial load he can pick up from DC and fly to Cape Town. He's got some good contacts in commercial aviation, and he doesn't want to make lots of money—just break even. He was talking to a pal last night. I've got the feeling we could be ready to roll as soon as tomorrow."

"I've been thinking about the timing, too," River said. "I reckon Kruger will be focusing on me more than you guys, and then when he knows I've gone, he'll be checking on you and Reggie."

"You think we go at the same time as you and make our next move shortly after you do?"

"That's the idea, and then we travel separately to Kruger's compound."

"What? You already know where that is?" Karen asked, genuinely surprised.

"It's complete guesswork, but I've been spending time poring over maps of South Africa, southern Africa, and the DRC. I'll bet you a bottle of the best French wine that Kruger's compound is at the border of South Africa, Mozambique, and Zim."

"Zim?"

"Sorry—I mean Zimbabwe. The country is ideally placed for access to the rest of Africa through countries where bribery is widespread or where there are border-control problems. And with Mozambique, it gives Kruger access to the coastline all the way to Somalia and Yemen."

Karen thought for a moment and then said, "So a bunch of perfect routes through Zimbabwe to central Africa, then more routes through Zambia to the DRC, and more through Mozambique, trafficking arms to paramilitary or terrorist groups along the coast right up to Yemen."

"That's what I assume."

"What do you think Kruger uses to transport the weapons? Trucks?"

"Maybe," River said. "But the distances are vast in Africa. Africa is three times the size of the United States, so I think he'll be using small aircraft."

"In that case, we're looking for a place that has a landing strip nearby," Karen said.

"My thinking, too, but planes do land on strips of savanna, so they may not be very visible, even using satellite imagery."

"Reggie has family living in South Africa," Karen said. "Surely they can help with identifying landing strips in the region where they live."

"His ranger cousins should be the perfect contacts for that, although I'm not sure I'm ready to explain to them why I need the information."

Karen's attention seemed to wander for a moment. Then she said, "Just got a text from Danny. We'll be on our way to Cape Town tomorrow night."

"Then I need to get Reggie ready and get Ariana to spill the beans," River said. "Kruger will also be eager to know what my next move is. So I'll book a flight to Johannesburg leaving tomorrow evening. I'll arrive in the late afternoon the day after with the time difference. I don't know yet how I'll advertise that, but I'll try to focus Kruger on Johannesburg, away from Cape Town."

"Very well," Karen said, sounding satisfied. "We'll arrive in Cape Town a day after you. That's got to work. Danny's made sure that the two other pilots he's hiring are trustworthy. The news that he's flying to Africa will take a bit of time to process."

"And when we're there, we must get to Kruger fast," River said. "We've gotta rely on the element of surprise. If we delay and Kruger finds out we're the A team and that we have a few more supporters, he'll get organized, call on some of the mercenaries he knows, and that will be game over for us."

"Unless we get some mercenaries of our own," Karen said.

River shook her head. "No—I'm not mounting a special op. We're not trained for that, but we can access Kruger's evidence and collect enough to incriminate him and his CIA pal. So we must play it smart."

Karen stayed silent, and River wondered whether she was thinking of another way of getting to Kruger. She wouldn't have mentioned mercenaries without a reason. But then River suddenly understood what her friend meant.

"I'm not talking to Jase about this. I need to do this on my own. I mean it." River could hear her voice trembling, and Karen must have heard it, too.

"I know you don't want to, and I think you might be right. He would want to get involved in the action, but it's still a shame we can't use him to help with the logistics."

"It's a shame, but we still agree. We're leaving Jason out of it."

"Okay," Karen said, relenting. "We're leaving Jase out of it."

River remained silent for a moment. She needed to control the mix of anger and regret building up inside her. Jason would never be an operative again. Every time she thought about it, the idea brought sadness to her heart. And then there was the tricky issue of how she felt about him. She'd concluded that it was complicated and had, so far, left it at that.

"Ground control to Major Tom," Karen said in a grating synthetic voice. "Are you still with me?"

"Sorry, Karen," River said after clearing her throat. "I'll get in touch with Reggie and Ariana."

"And I'll confirm with Danny that we're 100 percent on. I'm also thinking about bringing a few bits and pieces."

"Such as?"

"Stuff you won't have time to buy yourself—sunscreen, mosquito repellent, emergency medical kit, Glock, SIG, plenty of ammo, and a few night-vision goggles. You know, the basics when going abroad."

"Seriously, do you think the South African authorities are going to let you bring that in?"

"I'm not gonna tell them, and that'll be one box among many. I'll even use a little bribery if need be. Danny reckons I'll be fine."

"Your call," River said. "I would have thought it's not that difficult to buy a gun in South Africa, but why not start with something we know works?"

"Let's touch base tomorrow morning with news," Karen said.

"Speak then."

River hung up. She sat still for a moment. The fear of biting off more than she could chew nudged her again. She untied the small towel she'd wrapped around her hair, ran a hand through it to loosen it, and then sat down on the bed. She was proud of knowing courageous people like Karen and Reggie, but she couldn't shake the feeling that the fight for justice was hers and perhaps hers alone.

Restless, she stood up and went to the bathroom to comb her hair and brush her teeth. It was after 10:30 p.m.—too late, perhaps, to call Mike for a final recap of the day. She checked for text messages on her burner one last time and noticed she'd missed one.

Just received mail from Angela. Call me anytime. Mike

River dialed his number, and he picked up almost instantly.

"Angela sent me a package through the mail. It arrived this morning, so I got it when I arrived home late this evening. I spent time at the office and couldn't find any other files, but then this package was waiting for me at my neighbor's."

"What is it?" River's stomach tightened. Could it be that Angela was still alive?

"A memory card from a camera. It's old but in good enough condition for some of the images to still be viewed and printed."

River shuddered at the thought of what these might be.

"Some of them are . . . terrifying," Mike said, his throat running dry. "But they are helpful, if you can call them that."

"You mean Kruger is in these photos?"

"Only a few of them, and it looks as though he's arrived toward the end of the . . . massacre. But there is another man—and these images are from Katuba, fourteen years ago."

River felt bile rise to her mouth, and for a moment she thought she might be sick.

"From the massacre?" she forced herself to repeat.

"Your parents aren't in the photos," Mike added quickly. "Apologies. I should have said that right away. But you can see the main man, and you can see his soldiers slaughtering the villagers."

"How come this didn't surface fourteen years ago?"

"According to the note Angela included in the package, the person who took the pictures was a young woman who hasn't said anything until now."

"She had a camera that long ago and used it then?"

"Angela went back to Katuba recently, in the past few days—before she was kidnapped. She started talking to people who told her that the village had been once more targeted. She then came across this woman, who's now in her late thirties and who spoke about a man called Dr. Death. She said she'd witnessed the same horrors fourteen years ago and was only spared because she'd gone out to the fields to take pictures of nature and wildlife. She'd always wanted to become a photographer, ever since she'd seen journalists taking photos, so she borrowed a camera and tried her hand at it."

"Someone lent her a camera, and she happened to be away from Katuba, where my parents died on that day?"

"Thar's the story as far as Angela is concerned." Mike seemed to hesitate and then said, "The part that's most disturbing it that it seems that one of your parents lent her the camera."

River was lost for words. For a moment she couldn't recall whether her mom or dad owned such a thing. But then she recalled the old Kodak. They weren't very good with it, but they seemed to think that some special occasions deserved a picture, and so the camera usually came out for birthdays, Christmases, and the occasional party. But what were the chances? Or perhaps her parents' generosity was paying off in a strange and unexpected way.

"I know it sounds mad, but Angela seems to believe that the woman is genuine, and I can tell you that the images are bad enough. I, too, don't think this young woman is lying."

"We have a witness, and we have photos," River said, almost to herself.

"I'm in way over my head here, but I'd say we do."

River's mind raced ahead. "We need to preserve the evidence and then find the woman."

"Tell me how I can help," Mike replied.

"I'll give you another email address. Could you please send the images to it? And then send whatever Angela has sent to you to an address in Alaska?"

"Alaska?"

"Yes," River said. "The person you'll be sending it to is the chief of police in a town called Kotzebue. He'll know what to do with it."

"I'll do that tomorrow," Mike said.

River thought for a moment. "How well do you know your neighbor?"

"The one who picked up the package is very helpful. She works from home and doesn't mind. Why?"

"Perhaps you should repackage what Angela sent you tonight and give it to her to mail tomorrow. You can buy the postage online."

"You're right," Mike said. "I'll do it as soon as I have the address in Kotzebue. My neighbor works until late, so she won't mind my calling her now."

"I'll send you the details right after we hang up," River said. "And Mike . . . thanks for doing all this."

"We both want these SOBs behind bars."

River hung up and immediately sent Mike an old email address she barely used and the mailing address of Chief Robinson in Kotzebue. She texted Karen as soon as she sent Mike the details so she could warn her father that a package coming from New York addressed to him was carrying crucial evidence.

Incriminating, very graphic evidence sent to your dad by Mike Wilson.

Are you okay?

He says my parents aren't in the images, but I won't look at them until I'm in SA.

I understand. Will text Dad right away.

River closed her eyes for a moment to prevent the room from spinning around. She grabbed the back of a chair and dug her fingers into the soft material. She finally opened her eyes and slowly finished preparing for the night.

When she slid between the sheets of her hotel bed, she was wide awake. She couldn't get the memories of the old camera her parents owned out of her mind. It had brought them close again, and the thought of their untimely and violent death was made vivid once more.

River lay awake for a while, trying without success to find sleep. She eventually got out of bed, took the laptop out of the safe, and booted it up. If she wasn't going to rest, then she might as well use her time to further her quest for justice. She braced herself for what she was about to discover when she opened Mike's email.

Chapter 7

The pot of coffee Kruger had prepared a couple of hours ago was almost empty, and the rest had gone cold. He stretched and decided on something a little stronger. He opened a small cabinet at the far end of his office and got a simple tumbler out of it. He chose a bottle of single-malt Scotch and poured himself a generous helping. Kruger brought the drink back to his desk, sat down, and took a sip.

The warmth of the alcohol hit his tongue and then his throat. He grunted in pleasure. Nothing could compare to a good Macallan. Kruger sat back and thought about what he'd learned so far and what it all meant for his next move.

River Swift had been a busy girl, getting in touch with DWB, finding Angela Graham, and then, when Angela disappeared, she'd contacted Mike Wilson. She might have been spooked when this idiot Davis had tried a hit-and-run on Wilson, but all would be calm around her now.

Kruger would get her followed from afar, and he hoped that Angela's disappearance, together with the lack of information in her parents' file, would prompt River to come to Africa. He had never met her—or so he thought. Her face on the couple of images he'd been sent looked somehow familiar, but perhaps it was just because she resembled her mother. From what he surmised, though, she was a resourceful, gritty thing. He was certain she would take the bait. She might even know she was being baited and still fly to South Africa or the DRC. The thought made him pause. If she somehow was looking forward to the hunt, he sure would relish the pleasure of giving her what she wanted.

The taste of Macallan felt a little less sweet on his tongue, and he cursed the woman who was spoiling his drink. She'd gone to New York on her own. Kruger's man in Kotzebue had told him that one of her friends, a certain Karen Robinson, was still there. Kruger hadn't checked on Jason Wayne, River's former fiancé, or Reggie Cameron, Jason's lawyer. Perhaps it was time to call upon some of his best surveillance people and start tailing Swift's close contacts.

Kruger picked up a pen and added Jason and Reggie to the list of people he needed intel on. Karen was already being followed, but he'd made sure the man he was employing doubled his efforts. He also toyed with the idea of getting Davis followed, but although he thought Davis was incompetent, he might prove a more difficult target. Kruger couldn't afford to find out whether he was right about this, at least for the time being.

A yawn interrupted his thinking, and he checked his watch—1:37 a.m. His men would be waking up in a couple of hours' time, readying a small convoy of cars for their journey to Kruger's compound, toward the east of the country. It would take six hours to get to Masisi, near the Zimbabwean border, and then another forty minutes or so to get to the compound, which only lay an hour away from the Mozambique border. He could have flown, but Kruger wanted the use of more armored vehicles, and he needed to bring the latest models of Humvees to the compound. He'd take a quick nap in the car while his head of security, Arno Botha, drove.

The late hour didn't dissuade Kruger from calling his main contact in the DRC. Matondo would still be up. The man liked to party—with willing or unwilling participants. He would still be at it, and Kruger vaguely hoped Angela Graham might be part of the fun. At least it would mean she was alive, although he wasn't sure that being alive in the conditions offered by Matondo was much of a perk.

Kruger selected the burner phone dedicated to Dr. Death and pressed Redial. Kruger would ditch the phone after this call. The burner rang a few times, and Matondo finally picked up. Kruger was greeted with a mix of hard rock music, laughter, and screams before Matondo spoke.

"Kruger!" Then Matondo sounded like he turned around to speak to someone in the strange French dialect the DRC used. Back on the phone, he said, "You're still awake? I thought an old guy like you would be in bed by now." Matondo burst out laughing.

Kruger didn't bother with a reply. He had a question to ask. "Where is Angela Graham?"

The phone remained silent for a moment. Then: "You mean the old DWB woman I took care of in Goma?"

"That's the one," Kruger said.

"*Une dure à cuire*," Matondo replied. "I thought she was never gonna talk."

For a man whose English was almost nonexistent fifteen years ago, Matondo had done well in adopting American English, interlaced with French, as his main language.

"Did she talk? And is she alive?"

"Of course she talked." Matondo sounded offended at the thought that anyone could withstand one of his interrogations. "I wasn't told she had to be kept alive."

"So she's dead and you have information about what she knew about the Swifts."

"She's not quite dead yet, and I got her to tell us why she went back to Katuba."

Kruger attention perked up. "And why was that?"

"She wanted to check whether anyone recalled the incident. You know . . ." Matondo sounded appropriately embarrassed. The idea had been to eliminate the Swifts and make it look like a robbery as they drove between villages. Matondo, then a keen up-and-coming warlord, had been eager to show his dedication and effectiveness and had his men take down the entire village. In retrospect, Kruger wished he'd eliminated the idiot, but Matondo was now a feared and wealthy man in the DRC, one with political ambitions.

"Did she find anyone?"

"No. There was no one left, as I said to you all these years ago," Matondo said, irritated.

Kruger took a moment to consider the information. "Keep her alive; patch her up. I have a couple of questions I want to ask her myself."

"I could ask her for you," Matondo said, gleeful.

"I said I want to ask the questions myself. Make sure she's alive when I turn up."

"Fine," Matondo grumbled.

"I'll let you know when."

Kruger hung up, took a sip of Macallan, and wondered whether Matondo was right. Was it true that no one had ever witnessed the killings? He'd been sure then. He wasn't so sure now.

The alarm had rung at 7:00 a.m. River had gotten up and gone for a run around New York. Her night had been restless. She'd only glanced at a few of the images in the series Mike Wilson had sent, but what she saw remained seared in her mind. She'd seen plenty of atrocities in her deployments, but the DRC killings were the worst.

She forced herself to stick to her initial plan that morning and hadn't bothered to use the hotel's back door. She no longer cared whether she was being followed. Bob was back manning the reception desk when she returned from her jog, and she'd stopped to chat with him for a few minutes. Nothing heavy, just telling him she was moving out today and catching a flight to Africa. Bob had frowned, but she assured him that she knew South Africa well and that she would be safe. He allowed her to stay a little longer in her room after the checkout time of 12:00 p.m.—something she appreciated.

Her flight to Johannesburg on United was due to take off at 8:50 p.m. from Newark Liberty International Airport, and she was asked to get there a good three hours in advance. Normally, she might have grumbled, but today she didn't mind. She would leave the hotel at 4:40 p.m. and have plenty of time to make more calls, coordinate her people, and perhaps shop for a few essentials while thinking about her next move. She'd booked a couple of nights at the Holiday Inn at Tambo International Airport. It was clean, safe by Jo'burg standards, and cheap.

River got to her room, showered, and dressed in faded cargo pants and a moss-green T-shirt. She then made herself a cup of coffee and took the bagel with smoked salmon and cream cheese that she'd bought earlier out of her jacket pocket and placed it on a small, laminated table. She took her time eating, checking her emails and texts as she did. Keeping busy was a good way to push away the memory of the Katuba images she'd seen the night before.

Karen had sent a text to River's burner confirming that she and Danny were good to go to DC and would be leaving Kotzebue that evening. The trip was as discussed: Karen and Danny would be arriving in DC on his ATR 42 cargo plane twelve hours later, making it by 9:00 a.m. Danny had allotted four hours to turn the plane around and load the cargo. They would depart DC at 1:30 p.m., arriving in Cape Town at 4:00 a.m. DC time and 11:00 a.m. local time the following day.

Their schedule would give River an extra day before they arrived to decide where they would meet next. She replied to Karen that it was all fine and that she would let Reggie know he was expected at Newark at around 12:00 p.m. He'd need to get in touch with Karen for more details, but River suspected the two had spoken anyway to mount a coordinated effort—River needed a team, and they were it. The thought gave River comfort.

She checked the time and decided that at 9:30 a.m. Reggie needed a coffee break. She dialed the old burner phone number—the one she'd purchased when the three had teamed up to free Jason.

"News?" Reggie said as he picked up.

"Good morning," River replied with mock offense.

"Morning. Have you slept well? Are you feeling positive? Is there anything else I need to add to make your day a better day?" Reggie said.

"Do I detect a hint of annoyance?" River asked.

"My boss is insisting I take on this very large case, a high-profile job . . . and for obvious reasons, I'd rather not."

River turned serious. "I don't want you to jeopardize your career for this trip—"

"It's not a trip," Reggie said. "It's an expedition. And I want to be there when you nail Kruger. Law doesn't always provide justice, but now I have a chance to feel as though I've closed Jason's case properly."

"What if your boss gets wind of the *expedition*, as you call it?"

"Well, I'll be testing my ability to defend a client on him, but this time, it'll be me I'm defending," Reggie said, sounding almost eager to be put to the test.

River was about to push back, but then she relented. Reggie had made up his mind, and he wasn't going to change it. He would be hitching a ride with Karen and Danny to South Africa whether she liked it or not.

"Then you need to get yourself ready for tomorrow. Call Karen for the details. She'll tell you where to meet at Newark, since you're flying cargo."

"Can't wait. I've never flown cargo before."

"Brace yourself. It's not business class and not even military standard," River said.

"If you'd asked me before we met yesterday in New York, I would have told you this was my first time in the air."

River hesitated to tell Reggie that crossing the Atlantic might be a little less comfortable than flying between DC and New York, but she chose a softer approach. "It'll take fourteen and a bit to get to Cape Town. Speak to Karen, and she'll give you some tips about how to make the long trip more comfortable."

"Will do, but what about you?"

"I'm flying out tonight and will be landing in Johannesburg the day after. You guys will be landing a day after me."

"And then what? Have a nice braai with my family near the Limpopo?" Reggie asked, referring to the traditional cookout where meat was grilled over an open flame.

"I haven't spoken to Ariana yet. I'm still in the dark when it comes to Kruger's compound, although I do have an idea," River said.

Reggie was taken aback. "Oh. I thought you would have—"

"I will, but I'd rather keep the momentum going. Kruger needs to think I'm on my own, and the more we wait, the more he's going to suspect I'm putting a team together."

"What if Ariana wants to join us?"

"We spoke about this before, Reggie. I don't want to have someone join us who hasn't seen action before. I know you from our efforts to free Jason, and I trust you. I don't know enough about your friend to judge how she's gonna react under the sort of pressure we're likely to face once we decide to take Kruger on."

Reggie took a moment and then mumbled, "I see where you're coming from, but she can be trusted."

"I'm not saying she can't," River lied. "But this trip is unlike anything you or she has been through before. I don't want to get you or her killed."

This time, River was being honest. There was no getting around it. Engaging Kruger and his men, even if River and her team took them by surprise and extracted information without their noticing, was going to be high-risk, with little room for error. She needed people who'd been trained a certain way—which Reggie and Ariana hadn't been.

Reggie was silent, and River detected hesitation.

"I know you mean well, and I don't want to be a burden, either, but I can pull my weight in other ways," Reggie said.

"You can, and that's why you're on the team. I'll speak to Ariana after our call and will find a way to give her what she wants." River let it hang. She wasn't committing to what that might be and didn't want Reggie to hold her to whatever she might promise.

"That's okay," Reggie said. "But you need to keep her on-site. She's our best source of intel on Kruger."

"That's true, and I appreciate it," River said. She was hoping she might find out more when she spoke to Mike Wilson or even his brother, Orson.

"I guess I'll see you in Africa, then," Reggie said after a short silence.

"That's the plan," River replied. "Be safe—and see you in a couple of days."

River hung up and realized that her coffee was cold, so she brewed another cup. Reggie's strong bond with Ariana was an unexpected complication. She hadn't anticipated this and hoped it wouldn't cause problems when they were on the ground in South Africa.

River returned to her bed and sat cross-legged on it. She ate her bagel, drank some fresh coffee, and just tried to enjoy her food. In a day's time, she would be back in an environment that felt like a war zone—the weapons and rare-minerals trades were brutal and unforgiving. It was war, just of a different type.

River finished her coffee, found Ariana's number, and dialed it. The phone rang a couple of times, and then Ariana answered.

"Ariana Pettit."

Her voice was formal and noncommittal. She was expecting her interlocutor to get right down to business.

"River Swift here. Can you talk?"

Her tome changed instantly as she said, "I'll call you back right away."

The phone went dead, and River waited. A few minutes later, Ariana called back.

"I found a place where I can speak to you without being heard," she said.

"Have you found out anything about Kruger?"

"I have, but I need more time to validate the information."

River swallowed her sudden impatience. "I've been thinking about where Kruger might want to set up his compound and have come up with an idea, so any details you have would give me a good leg up."

"South Africa is a big place," Ariana said with a mix of wariness and surprise.

"But for an arms dealer like Kruger, there are very few locations that are as well situated as the country's border with Zimbabwe and Mozambique. He needs access to central Africa and to the coast for smuggling weapons with maximum efficiency," River said with confidence.

The silence that followed told her she'd just hit the bull's-eye. Now, the ball was in her court, and she needed to capitalize on her advantage.

"Kruger will also want a place that has an airstrip or at least enough flat land for a plane to land."

"That's very impressive," Ariana conceded. "But I might be able to narrow the search for you."

"That would be much appreciated," River said, "and I'll be happy to share the results of what we find out about Kruger with you."

"Perhaps I could see whatever evidence you collect for myself?"

Here we go . . .

"That means entering Kruger's compound and extracting the intel from there," River said, seeking to raise the stakes as high as she could.

"I'm not pretending I'll be the right person for that job, but I sure can help you make sense of the intelligence you gather once you get hold of it."

The silence that followed felt uncomfortable.

"Look," River finally said, "I'd rather you stay out of it until we're back in the United States. I worry that I won't be able to keep you safe in South Africa, and I need someone in DC who can help with intelligence as we track down Kruger."

All that made sense to River. She hoped it would be a good enough argument and that Ariana wouldn't suspect River's lack of trust.

"I see," Ariana said. Her mind must have been racing to find a counterargument to River's, but one didn't seem forthcoming. "Then what I'd like to have is an idea of what you plan to do and where you plan to go. I might be able to help with the logistics."

"Sure," River said, knowing she wouldn't tell Ariana anything. "I'll keep you updated."

"Or I can speak to Reggie," Ariana said.

"Why not?" River tried to sound agreeable. "It might be a good way for you to get a regular brief. And now that we have agreed on how you get the intel you need from us, perhaps you can tell me where your sources tell you Kruger's compound is."

"The compound is near a town called Masisi, in the northeastern part of the country. It takes six hours from Johannesburg. The drive is due north up the N1 for around 490 kilometers and then another hundred kilometers across the R525. Then the maintained roads stop, and there are just dirt roads to the borders," Ariana said with assurance.

"But that can't be where the compound is," River replied. "If I recall correctly, Masisi is around forty kilometers from the border with Mozambique, although it is only fifteen kilometers or so from the Limpopo River."

Ariana hesitated, and then River explained. "The Limpopo delineates the border with Zimbabwe, and forty kilometers on dirt roads or even the bush is a pain if you want to cross a border quickly."

"But that gives you a good idea of where Kruger is, right?" Ariana said, a little on the defensive. "South Africa isn't a small country. It's around twice the size of Texas—"

"But somewhat smaller than Alaska—I know," River said. "Don't get me wrong: I'm grateful you reduced my search perimeter to four hundred square kilometers, but I don't have much time, so if you could find out more and help narrow the search further, that would be great."

"I'll see what I can do. I don't want to alert anyone I'm looking into Kruger. As I said when we met in New York, this is very much under the radar. But I'll go back to his file and see whether I can get more."

So the DHS has a file on Kruger.

River pushed her luck a little. "The one thing I don't get is why the DHS has a file on Kruger. I have the impression that he was never stopped from conducting his arms-dealing business out in the open."

"Kruger is very well-connected politically. He has friends in high places, and that includes large corporations in the arms and defense industries. Also, Kruger plays both sides of the fence. He's helpful to agencies around the world, to the military, and to unsavory agents that represent pariah states like Iran and Russia."

"In short, he is untouchable," River said. "If you're trying to take him down through conventional routes, that is."

"That's right," Ariana said, "but then we're not trying to get the guy the conventional way. Are we?"

For the first time, River felt as though Ariana had let her see her hand. Perhaps she, too, was guarded about trusting River.

"Agreed, and therefore speed is essential. The moment Kruger suspects anything is afoot, he'll call in reinforcements. He'll shred all the evidence he's keeping hidden, and we won't get close to any of it. Without mentioning the cost we'll have to pay for trying to stop him. This is a one-way trip in more ways than one."

"No one at the office knows I'm on to him—the only two people who do are Reggie and you," Ariana said, her voice dropping as though she meant to be even more cautious.

"Then let's keep it that way," River said. "I'm traveling today and will be reachable until eight o'clock tonight. After that, I'll be in the air for around fourteen hours. Leave a message or text, and I'll call back as soon as I can."

"Safe travels," Ariana said.

"You stay safe, too."

River hung up and flopped on her bed. The margin of error on this mission, as she'd now decided to call it, was somewhere between slim and nonexistent. For the first time since she decided to go after her parents' killer, she wished she could talk with Jason about the way to mount that operation. Karen would tut-tut at her and say I told you so, and River would respond that she still wouldn't involve him. Jason had spent too much time being a Navy SEAL before his injury robbed him of the job he loved doing. She didn't want to remind him of all he'd lost.

The convoy left the outskirts of Johannesburg at 5:30 a.m. Kruger settled in the back seat of the Humvee. The compound he'd built more than twenty years ago near the Limpopo River had been at the center of his empire ever since. He'd made it an impregnable structure that only his men and a smattering of additional personnel knew about. His head of security, Arno Botha, had been with him since the beginning, and Kruger knew that their shared Special Forces training gave them a bond he could rely on.

Kruger had never shied away from the front line, always willing to pave the way when he was with the SADF, and he didn't see why that should change now. His Humvee, as usual, was in the lead, and Botha was driving the vehicle. Kruger closed his eyes as soon as the houses became fewer and farther between, and he knew they'd left the city behind.

He didn't fear confrontation, but he was continually on the lookout for an ambush. He'd been successful so far in life because he took nothing for granted—ever. The memory of Chuck Clery made him open his eyes. Clery had become complacent and arrogant. Kruger had once remarked on this, and Clery seemed to have taken note, but it hadn't sunk in. The thought that he, too, might have become smug irritated him. Kruger could still not fully accept that he'd been defeated in DC by a woman like River Swift—a young medic, perhaps military but certainly not Special Forces. And yet a woman with grit.

Pain shot up his leg, a harsh reminder of the shot he'd taken. He slowly massaged the scar, which was still giving him grief, hoping he would soon be able to return the favor. River may find that she'd bitten off more than she could chew.

One of Kruger's burner phones rang, and he picked up.

"She's on her way to Jo'burg," the woman said. "I stayed for a while at the airport and checked whether she might not have boarded, but I'm almost certain she's on the 8:50 p.m. United flight."

"Almost?" Kruger said. He wasn't paying for uncertainty.

"I am certain," the woman said. There wasn't a wobble in her voice or even a hint of doubt. She knew what it would mean if she wasn't right.

"When will she be landing?" Kruger asked.

"At 5:45 p.m. local time. She's booked a room at the Holiday Inn at the airport."

Kruger closed his eyes again. River Swift wasn't planning to stay long in Johannesburg, or she would have chosen another hotel. "Let me know if you learn anything else. I now have another assignment for you. I'll send you the details by text after we finish the call. I need you to get to DC and start following someone called Reginald Cameron, a lawyer."

"Okay. As soon as I have the details, I'll make my way to DC."

Kruger hung up and sat up in his seat. He liked dealing with Monica. She never groveled and always delivered. He sent her the details he'd amassed on Cameron—background, home address, work address, family members. Enough to get her going. Monica was resourceful. She'd find out more, and he'd see where the intel she gathered would take him. He was concerned, though, about River's friend Karen, also ex-military. The intel he'd received was that she was still in Kotzebue, but things could change, and River might decide to call her as backup, just as she'd done five months ago in DC.

The thought that River was on her way to Africa made him smile. He was very much looking forward to having a conversation with her. If she wanted to understand why her parents had to be eliminated, he was more than willing to enlighten her: Never get in the way of an arms dealer's business, not ever.

Kruger checked the satnav device that had been plugged in between the two seats in the back of the Humvee. He'd mapped the route to Masisi but would never enter the coordinates of the compound in any navigation tool, just in case it might be hacked. He and Arno knew the road by heart, but the system would alert him to any problems that arose on the journey, even on the N1.

"It's all clear at the moment," Arno Botha said as he glanced in the rearview mirror. His strong Afrikaner accent reminded Kruger that he had almost entirely lost his. Too many years mixing with people around the world.

The price of good and lucrative business . . .

Kruger nodded his thanks and settled again in his seat for a well-earned nap. He had worked until after 3:00 a.m. to organize one of the largest arms deals he'd put together in a long time. Warmongering showed no sign of abating in central Africa, as well as in Yemen, and other Middle Eastern countries. He'd be sending arms to these places via land, air, and sea. More of his men would be busy trafficking the cargo across borders in Africa, but he should be able to maintain a good enough contingent at the compound to defend against any attack or intrusion.

And then there was coltan, the ore every tech company in the world was vying for—and willing to purchase, legally or not, as long as the price was low enough. The United Nations had sought to control the illegal mining of coltan, but it had only made the price more attractive and the purchasers more eager.

Matondo maintained control over production with an iron fist. The absurd amount of money he earned from that trade had fueled his political ambitions. The time would soon come when a replacement needed to be found, and Kruger knew that candidates would be easy to find. Kruger thought about it and relaxed a little. The plan looked sound, and he could now enjoy a few more hours' rest.

But then another burner phone buzzed. This time, it was a text message.

RS knows the compound is near Masisi.

Kruger gave the text one of his rare smiles. Matters were going the way he wanted them to, and the net was closing in.

Chapter 8

The plane banked right over the northern suburbs of Johannesburg. River lifted the shade on the window. Her neighbors, a young couple on their honeymoon, didn't mind. It was their first time in South Africa, and they were on their way to the country's best-known game reserve for two weeks, the Kruger National Park. They'd been picking her brain about local attractions, and River had indulged them. It was good to take a break from thinking about Kruger—the man, not the national park—and what lay ahead. Besides, she was cooped up in an aircraft cabin, unable to do very much about the mission.

River had never spent much time in Jo'burg when she was a child. The city had always been the place where she and her parents entered South Africa on their way to another destination. The northern part of the city was affluent, she recalled. Even from the air, River could tell that the houses were widely spread apart, and she spotted a few areas of lush greenery that announced the terrain and the climate.

The seat-belt sign chimed, and the captain made the usual announcement on the intercom. River leaned farther toward the window and enjoyed the movement of the plane as it banked a few times, lining up with the runway for landing. The aircraft made smooth contact with the tarmac and came to a slow crawl toward its assigned gate. They'd landed dead on time—5:45 p.m.

As soon as the plane stopped, her neighbors jumped out of their seats, wished her a safe trip, and lined up for the exit. River took her time. She wasn't going anywhere for the next couple of days and didn't mind letting other people go first. They'd all be waiting around the baggage carousel anyway, and she wasn't in a hurry to fight that crowd.

River eventually shouldered her backpack and was among the last to disembark. She then made her way to customs and was let in by a dour-looking woman who scrutinized her passport and then delivered the required stamp. River had stated that the purpose of her visit was a vacation so she wouldn't need a visa for the first ninety days of her stay. If she wasn't finished in fewer days than that, she wouldn't be coming out of the country at all.

Her duffel bag arrived at baggage claim quickly enough, and she picked it up, walked onto the airport concourse, ignored the taxi line, and went to rent a car. Johannesburg was a large city of six million people with a rather haphazard public transportation system, rough road conditions, and a high crime rate. If she needed to get anywhere, a car was a must. She toyed with the idea of renting a motorcycle, but the risk of smash-and-grab at intersections or being rammed by an out-of-control truck were too high.

River was handed the keys to a Jeep. When she reached the parking lot, she checked it out. It looked in good enough condition, but she opened the driver's-side door and found no steering wheel. She then laughed. South Africa was a former British colony, and the driver's seat was on the right. She'd be driving on the left side of the road, just the way they did in the UK.

River opened the door on the correct side and settled in. She plugged the address of the Holiday Inn into her GPS, then nosed the car onto the airport's main circular road and was immediately reminded of what it felt like to drive in a city like Johannesburg—there were no rules, so you had to rely instead on grit and the liberal use of the horn.

River found herself in her Holiday Inn bedroom within one hour of her arrival. She secured her laptop and passport in the room safe and left to carry out a quick reconnaissance of the hotel—security staff, emergency exits, and adjacent streets. The place was situated at the corner of two main roads on the south and west and a side street that ran along the east flank of the building. There was only one main entrance and a service entrance at the back, but it looked secure enough, although River was sure that a determined assailant would have no difficulty getting in.

The sun had already set when she returned to the hotel. The temperature had dropped, and she shivered. South Africa was coming into its fall season, and it would get chilly at night. River took a detour to the hotel restaurant on her way back to her room. She found the kitchen, pretended to be lost, and saw what she was after. The service entrance, which opened onto the street, was visible from where she stood. As she suspected, a serious opponent would have no problem entering the hotel through the back.

When she returned to her room, she took her laptop out of the safe and her burner phone out of her jacket pocket. She checked her emails—nothing there. She then turned to her burner phone and found the number Mike Wilson promised he would send. He'd warned her that his brother, Orson, was often out of reach but that she could give him a try and leave a message if necessary. Orson checked his messages as often as he could and responded whenever he had cell-phone coverage.

Her thumb hovered over the number. She'd prepared what she wanted to say, but she suddenly felt odd about the call.

Calling to ask for help catching a notorious arms dealer. That might sound like a good introductory line, but she was reluctant to immediately talk about Kruger.

On the trail of my parents' murderer felt awkward and unsavory.

But perhaps she should go with what she'd decided was a possible option—*Angela Graham has disappeared, and I know why.*

River's mouth ran suddenly dry. The couple of images she'd seen from the series Angela had sent to Mike Wilson made her shiver. She hadn't yet had the courage to look at them all and hoped she would be spared the ordeal. River went to the small refrigerator in her room, removed a bottle of water, and took a few sips. She returned to her bed, sat on it, and pressed the Call button. The phone only rang once, and a gravelly voice answered. River hesitated and then asked, "Orson Wilson?"

"Speaking."

"My name is River Swift, and your brother—"

"How nice. I spoke to Mikey this morning. He told me you would call. I'm in Jo'burg at the moment. If you're not doing anything for dinner, let's meet up."

River immediately felt at ease with this man. Mike had told her that Orson had a way with people that made them feel relaxed around him. "Let me know where. I have a car," she said.

"Mike said you've lived in Africa with your parents, but do you know Jo'burg well?"

"I don't. We never spent much time here. It was more of a transit hub for us, but I've got GPS."

River could almost see the man shaking his head. "Not a good idea. You need to know which areas to avoid. Carjacking is unfortunately rather common. I'll come and pick you up, and I can choose a safe place where we can eat."

"I'm not sure how much Mike has told you, but I'd rather avoid people knowing that we've made contact."

Orson remained silent for a moment, and River hoped she hadn't spooked him.

"You mean you might be followed."

"I almost certainly will be followed."

Another silence, and then Orson said, "In that case, I'll give you an address in Auckland Park and a way to get there that is safe. If there is anything stopping you from taking the route I'm indicating, go back. Do not try to find an alternative even if there are detour signs on the road. Do we agree?"

"Sure," River said. "I'll get back to the Holiday Inn if I can't follow your route."

"The address I have in mind is a shopping center on Kingsway Avenue. You can easily park your car and then text me as soon as you've arrived. I'll find a way to lose a tail if someone's following you."

River's eyebrows went up. She'd known quite a few priests when she was deployed, but none that seemed so on the ball. "I'll call you when I'm in the center. What time shall we meet? I just need half an hour to get ready."

"Let's meet at eight thirty. I'll text you the route right now."

Orson hung up, and River stared at her phone for a moment, not able to reconcile the conversation she'd just had with the fact that Orson was a priest. Her parents had worked with a few of them. They'd been helpful with vaccination programs and building health centers to combat malnutrition and AIDS, but she couldn't quite recall having met someone as together as Orson. The fact that she might be followed hadn't thrown him a bit.

River got a change of clothes out of her bag, took a quick shower, and made herself ready. She had one more thing to do before she left for her meeting. Laura Crain, the alias she'd used so successfully in DC to deceive Clery, had another part to play in the new mission. River had booked a bedroom in her name at the Holiday Inn, but now needed to let the hotel know that Laura might be late. She dialed reception from her burner phone. A man answered, and she gave him the information. No issue, he said. The hotel would be holding Ms. Crain's room until late.

Satisfied with his answer, River left the Holiday Inn half an hour after her call with Orson, armed with a precise set of directions. She got into the Jeep, locked herself inside, and started her journey. Traffic was busy, and no one—trucks, buses, or cars—seemed to bother with speed limit, but she was grateful that she hadn't encountered any roadblocks or detours. River parked her car along Kingsway Avenue, spotted the shopping center immediately, and made her way there.

The place was buzzing with late-evening shoppers, and she almost felt she was back in one of the large malls typical of major US cities. River walked into a women's clothing store, found a quiet spot between two racks, and sent a text to Orson.

> **Just arrived. Found a good hiding spot in a women's clothing store on the first floor.**

He responded quickly.

> **I know the one. There is a second door toward the rear of the store. Take the elevator to the third floor and walk toward the restaurant called the House of Ribs.**
>
> **On my way.**

River took a moment to survey the store. She couldn't identify anyone who might be following her, but that didn't mean anything. One of the salesclerks came to talk to her, and River declined her help with a smile. She cursed silently, because the interaction had made her more visible. Still, she walked to the back of the store and found the elevators. Shoppers were piling into one. She squeezed in and watched as the doors closed. Someone had tried to get in, but was too late.

All the buttons were illuminated, so the elevator would stop where she needed it to. People got in and out. She stepped to the back of the car, melting into the crowd. When the door pinged open on the third floor, she walked out. No one could miss the House of Ribs. The neon sign hanging over the main entrance was large, looking more like a flying saucer than a piece of meat. Customers were coming out, looking satisfied, and more were waiting to be seated. The aroma of cooked beef made River's mouth water. Airline food hadn't been particularly tasty, and it hadn't been plentiful, either.

She didn't notice the tall man walking alongside her until she almost reached the restaurant. She glanced at him, and he smiled. She hesitated.

Flirt—friend or foe?

There was something in his smile that stopped her from telling the man in no uncertain terms that she wasn't in the mood.

"Keep walking past the restaurant and toward the next set of stores," Orson said.

River didn't acknowledge him but kept walking as he took the lead. They arrived in another part of the mall that felt a little like a bazaar—small shops with open fronts, vendors displaying their goods on the walkway. Customers were haggling over the price of goods on display.

River followed Orson into the crowd. He would be difficult to lose—tall, thick brown hair clasped into a ponytail, trimmed beard. She noticed he was wearing a pair of jeans and a black shirt. No clerical collar and certainly no cassock, but then what was she thinking? It was Africa, and he was working among people who cared about his deeds rather than his clothes.

Orson slowed down to let her catch up with him. He went into a bookstore, walked straight to the back, and stopped in front of a shelf. River stopped alongside him and took a book out at random.

"You've been followed," he said by way of introduction.

"Have we lost them?"

"We'll know in a moment or so."

Orson moved to her right, hiding her from view. He, too, chose a book, opened it, and turned toward the entrance of the store. River couldn't see anything now, except Orson's impressive back. Mike hadn't told her at what point Orson had decided to become a priest, but she was sure he must have made the American football team when he was in college.

"She's walked past," Orson said, his attention still seemingly on the book he was holding.

"You're pretty sharp for a man of the cloth, Father," River replied without hiding her surprise.

He turned around and smiled. "I've acquired many skills since I moved to Africa. I am not always welcome when I go to help people in need. I disturb men who try to exploit them, enslave them, or even traffic in them, so I learned to watch my back and that of others."

"What do we do next?"

"We're going for a meal," he said as he replaced the book. "And you don't need to call me Father unless you'd rather. Orson will be just fine. You're a friend of Mike and Angela."

River nodded. She dropped her backpack to the floor, opened it, and took out a black cap and a sleeveless black T shirt. She quickly put on a T-shirt over the white one she was wearing and stuffed her hair into the cap. Orson raised an eyebrow.

"I see that you're not a complete novice when it comes to deception, either."

"I've had a crash course in the past few months, but I'm happy to improve my skill set."

Orson chuckled and went to speak with the shopkeeper, a small black woman with graying hair and thick glasses. River couldn't quite catch what they were saying, but she recognized that they were speaking Afrikaans. After a moment, the woman smiled at Orson and then at

River and let them use the emergency exit. They walked alongside each other without talking, left the shopping center, and turned onto another large avenue. A restaurant called Piza e Vino stood at the corner of the next intersection. They crossed the road and went in.

The atmosphere felt vibrant yet cozy. A waitress dressed in black with a small Italian flag sewn on her shirt found them a table at the back of the restaurant, and River and Orson sat down.

"I think we're in the clear," he said.

"At least from where we're sitting, we'll see who's coming in."

The waitress brought them menus and took their drinks order—a ginger beer for River and a Diet Coke for Orson. They chose their pizzas quickly, both eager to talk about what was bringing River to South Africa.

"How much did Mike tell you?" River asked after they'd placed their order.

"He told me about Angela—the entire story," Orson said as his expression turned somber and his eyes seemed to grow misty.

"So you know about her involvement with the FBI?" River asked. There was no point in shying away from the truth.

Orson nodded. "Mike also told me about your parents. I'm very sorry to hear about what happened."

Their drinks arrived, and River used the occasion to take a sip before she answered.

"It had never felt right—the story about warring factions taking them down—but I guess they were always taking risks with the places they visited. I was deployed at the time it happened. It was hard to take a step back and think about it rationally. I felt as though I was swapping one war zone for another . . . and somehow, I guess I was."

Orson's eyes rested gently on her, and River felt strangely at ease discussing the harsh subject of her parents' murder with him. He didn't seem eager to know more, but simply was receptive to what she had to say—he displayed no morbid curiosity but gave her space to speak and room to go as far as she felt she could.

"My brother suspected something was amiss, but at the time didn't say anything. In his defense, we weren't on speaking terms then," River said before taking another sip of her ginger beer. Her throat felt tight, and the memory of her brother's deceit roused her anger. He hadn't told her of his suspicions, and she was no longer sure that not being on speaking terms was a good enough excuse. And then later he'd neglected to tell her that he had received their parents' effects, which had been sent from the DRC. He'd also hidden a letter addressed to her by her mother—a letter that told River her parents knew they were in mortal danger.

River cleared her throat and continued. "I've come across details that now make me believe their death wasn't part of a village massacre but that they were targeted. Unfortunately, the village paid the price and gave their executioners a cover-up story."

Orson shook his head. "I love Africa, but to me it is a place of extremes, and sometimes, it's hard to comprehend how this could be."

"My parents enjoyed their work and felt at ease here as well. They wanted to help make it a better place. Perhaps help is not always wanted or even possible," River said.

"You're right. It's hard to find the right balance." Orson waited. He wasn't going to debate the rights or wrongs of the help he and DWB provided.

The food arrived, smelling delicious, and this gave River an opportunity to decide how much she wanted to reveal—Kruger, the CIA, and the team that was coming to join her in South Africa.

They took a couple of mouthfuls, enjoying the food and sharing their appreciation.

Then Orson asked, "You must have more than strong suspicions if you're coming all the way to Jo'burg."

"I know who ordered their killing, and I know where he is," River said. If she couldn't trust Orson, then she was doomed anyway. She might as well find out now, before she revealed the names of the people who were working with her and put them in harm's way.

Orson chewed on the thought. "That's what I gathered from Mike, but he wasn't sure how much you wanted to say about the man or men you suspect."

"It's time I spoke about it. I wasn't sure what my course of action would be when I met Mike, but I'm here now, in South Africa, and I'm here to make sure that they pay."

Orson didn't seem to react to the thought of River bringing direct justice to her parents' killers. Perhaps he'd seen enough terrible things to empathize with her point of view.

"I would understand if you weren't happy with the idea," she continued, "but human justice doesn't seem to apply to these people, and I've not seen a lot of God's justice, either." There, she'd said it. She had found some comfort in reading Scripture but wasn't yet sure about what to expect from a God who often felt far away from the battlefield.

"We could debate what the founder of my order—Saint Ignatius of Loyola—would do in your situation. But to many people's amazement, Ignatius was a soldier and possibly a bit of a ladies' man, too. Then a terrible injury stopped his military career, and during the ordeal of recovery, he underwent his spiritual transformation. Perhaps a story for another time," Orson said with kindness.

River gave Orson a smile and then said, "You're going to tell me that God is within?"

Orson smiled back. "That's a good start for what we need to achieve—finding God in all things."

"Father—I mean Orson—there is no *we* here. I'm not putting your life in danger."

Orson's smile broadened. "There is one thing that the people of my order aren't frightened of, and that is a good and just fight."

River shook her head. "Why are people insisting they want to help and put themselves in danger in the process?"

Her question was genuine. She was grateful but still puzzled that Reggie, Mike, and now Orson wanted to support her in her quest.

"Good people will know, sometimes through reflection but often through intuition, that your fight is right and that you're only asking for justice," Orson said. "And I mean justice, not revenge. Revenge is death and rarely brings closure. Justice is right and will give you the relief you're looking for."

River pondered that thought for a moment, taking a few more mouthfuls of her pizza. Orson returned to his food, too, and they both fell into an easy silence.

"The man who murdered my parents is called Karl Kruger.

He's a notorious arms dealer who benefits from unimaginably tight protection back in the United States," River finally said.

"The name isn't familiar," Orson replied as he cast his eyes to the ceiling, thinking. He shook his head and confirmed. "No. Not a name I've heard of."

River put her cutlery down and wiped her mouth on her paper napkin. "Then there is another name that I haven't spoken about to anyone, but that also was mentioned alongside Kruger's. The name is Dr. Death."

This time, Orson's expression darkened. "Now, that is a name I unfortunately know only too well. He's a butcher back in the DRC. The man has no soul."

River's eyes widened, and Orson shook his head. "I apologize. I should never say that of anyone."

He closed his eyes for a moment; his face transformed into a mask of pain. "I have seen what this man and his troops do to women and children. I sincerely hope Angela hasn't ended up in his clutches."

River hadn't thought about that. Dr. Death, a ridiculous and yet far too evocative name, had only been that—a name on a piece of paper she'd collected in Chuck Clery's office. Now, it was clear that the man was a monster, and she recalled the face on the Zoom call she had with Angela. The man had killed the connection fast, but she thought she might recognize him if she saw him again.

"Do you have his name? I mean his real name? And any chance of a picture?"

The request surprised Orson. "Do you think you've seen him already?"

"Perhaps."

"He's called Dominic Matondo, and he isn't camera-shy, either," Orson said as he fished his cell phone out of his jeans pocket. He accessed the internet and started scrolling. Then he stopped and turned the screen toward River. "This is Matondo."

River could feel herself growing cold, and the expression on her face must have said it all.

"You've seen him before?"

A shiver ran down her spine, and she nodded. "I saw him on a

Zoom call I made to Angela. Men broke into her room, and they took her away. I heard more than I saw. But then one man approached the laptop, so I only saw his face briefly, but I'm almost certain it was Matondo."

Orson's head dropped to his chest, and he clasped his hands tight. He then shook his head and said in a trembling voice, "I know that Angela isn't religious, but may God help her soul. She will need it."

They both fell silent for a moment, but then River asked, "Do you know where in the DRC she's likely to be held?"

"Matondo has numerous encampments in the Kivu region. She could be anywhere."

River took another moment and then said, "The only person who would know where she is, is Kruger. This is all connected—my inquiry into my parents' death, Angela contacting me with information, and her abduction."

Orson frowned. "What do you have in mind?"

"We find Kruger, and we ask him—not necessarily nicely—where Angela is, and we go and get her out."

Orson's eyes widened. "Are you serious?"

"Never been so serious in my life."

Orson dropped his head to his chest once more, and when he finally faced River, he said, "I'm in. Tell me how I can help. You can't do this on your own, as I expect you know."

"I am gathering a team," River said.

Orson took a sip of the Diet Coke he hadn't previously touched. "You also mentioned you knew where to find Kruger."

"I'm after the compound he uses for his trafficking. He probably has another place, something more like a home, somewhere in South Africa, but the place where he stores the weapons he sells is the place I'd like to find. I have a name—Masisi, at the border of Zim and Mozambique."

Orson took another sip and seemed to think about it for a moment. "I guess it makes sense. A place in Masisi gives him access to central Africa, in particular the DRC, across Zimbabwe's border, and then access to the sea through Mozambique."

"You're pretty clued in when it comes to trafficking," River said, hoping she didn't sound suspicious.

"Trafficking and diseases are the greatest killers in the villages I work with. Disease we can try to do something about by bringing medication and education to the villagers, but trafficking has stayed the same for years, and that is frustrating to me."

"I understand. I've just returned from Utah, where my brother lives, and had to deal with the aftermath of a gang of drug traffickers running their business through his town. It was devastating to the community."

"Different continent, same fight," Orson said.

"Surprising but so true. And what I plan to do is to make sure I gather so much evidence against Kruger that whoever is protecting him in Washington will have to cut him loose."

"Hence the reason you want to get to his compound in Masisi," Orson said. "That's a good plan, but I can't imagine a guy like Kruger not having top military-grade security there. And when it comes to asking about Angela, you might be better served by finding information in the same way you want to find evidence. People like Kruger, traffickers of his type, are often ex-military, and if he is ex-SADF, you have a Special Forces man to contend with."

"I gathered as much, and that is an issue I've been thinking about. I need him to think that I am alone, and I need a diversion."

Orson dropped the piece of pizza he was about to eat. "Hang on. Are you telling me Kruger knows you're after him?"

"He does, but I also believe he thinks I'm coming on my own."

"Does he think you're mad or that you want revenge at all costs?"

"I'm not quite sure what he thinks about me, but he's concerned enough to get me followed in the States and now here."

"You're going to have to tell me more about how you came across Kruger himself."

River hesitated. This would involve telling him about Jason and the murder accusation in DC. It would also involve talking about her failed engagement to him. Even if she kept it to a minimum, Orson would know. She considered telling him about Clery only, but if she needed Orson's help, she needed to make sure he trusted her. A little honesty now could go a long way.

She took a breath and then said, "My ex-fiancé, Jason Wayne, was wrongly accused of murder, and I went to DC to help."

River unspooled the rest of the story: that Kruger and Clery had tried and failed to silence former Navy SEALs in their search for the truth about what affected their health in later years after a life of service. Clery had died in the process, a casualty of Kruger's ruthless business tactics, and Kruger himself had to flee America for his native South Africa. Now it was time for Kruger to pay the price of years of manipulation, murder, and deceit.

Chapter 9

Orson insisted he would follow River with his own car until she reached her hotel. She argued with him, telling him she was sure she'd manage to get back fine, but he wouldn't relent. He didn't seem the kind of person who would overprotect, so she took his advice. She hadn't left the United States for almost three years, and it felt like an eternity.

They agreed that they wouldn't signal each other once she got to the Holiday Inn. Orson would simply drive on, ensuring that anyone tailing River wouldn't know of their meeting. She watched as Orson's old and battered SUV drove off.

Once she parked her vehicle and got into the hotel, and then her room, it was 10:21 p.m. She found a text from Karen, which she'd sent just a moment previously.

Reggie on board. We've been allocated a departure slot in 20 minutes' time. South Africa, here we come!

River pressed the Call button and hardly waited a second before Karen picked up.

"We're all set," she said. "How about you?"

"I arrived on time and met a contact—Orson Wilson, Mike's brother."

"Any good?"

"He knows Angela and is familiar with the man who abducted her. I told him about Kruger, and he's eager to join the team. He's also worked in Africa for years."

"I have a couple of questions about this Orson guy. First, how well does he know Angela? Are we talking in the biblical way?"

River couldn't hold back a chuckle. "If you want to talk Bible with him, he's your man. Orson is a priest—a Jesuit, to be precise."

"The kind who wears a dog collar? Father Hopkins back in DC doesn't."

"Not a collar in sight. Jeans, black shirt, ponytail, and beard."

The description silenced Karen. Then she asked, "Why do you trust him? Apart from the fact that he's a priest?"

"I liked what I saw when we met. He feels and sounds genuine, and he doesn't have the lifestyle of a man who's after wealth or power. I also trust my instincts. More important, though, he doesn't yet know of you guys, at least by name. He knows I've got a team, period. So I'll see what happens in the next twenty-four hours."

"Offering yourself as bait isn't a good idea. You don't even have a gun," Karen said, sounding concerned.

"But I have a strategy and a fake ID."

"What? Laura Crain has been traveling to Africa, too? I never thought you'd enjoy fitting into the brunette role so much."

"It worked well in DC and in New York. I don't see why I shouldn't play that game again here."

"What's the plan?"

"I've booked another room under the name of Laura Crain at the Holiday Inn. I'm about to go and check in, collect my key, and move into that room for the night. And I don't even need to dye my hair: I got a wig."

Karen whistled. "You're turning into a pro."

Someone interrupted Karen, and then she said, "Reggie wants to talk to you."

Reggie came on the line and said, "Hey, just to let you know, I sent a note to my department telling them I had COVID and that I didn't want to give it to anyone at the office. They'll freak out and leave me alone for a while. I've asked my sister to come to my apartment every couple of days with a small amount of food. If someone is surveilling the place, they should buy the fact that I'm unwell and being looked after by family. Anything else you can think of? Karen couldn't, but that doesn't mean there isn't."

River heard Karen's protestations in the background.

"Sounds good, Reggie. Have you spoken to Ariana?"

"Should I have?"

Reggie's answer sounded a little defensive, and River wondered how much he'd told Ariana before he decided to go to South Africa.

"No, and it might be a good idea to leave it that way until we decide what we do next."

"Okay. I'll bear that in mind," Reggie replied a little stiffly.

Karen came back on. "We're about to take off in less than ten minutes. I guess it's over and out until we reach Cape Town. Although I might persuade Danny to let me use the aircraft's in-flight Wi-Fi to check my messages. Anything urgent, send me a text."

"Understood," River said, lowering her voice. "And Karen, find out how much Reggie's told Ariana."

"You got it," Karen said.

"Safe flight."

"Safe night."

River hung up and took a moment to consider her next move. She took the Tumi backpack she'd bought at Macy's out of her duffel bag and chose a different pair of pants and a shirt. They looked more upmarket, in keeping with the backpack. The shirt was a little rumpled, but it was the end of the day, so it wouldn't look out of place. The brunette wig she bought at Macy's came out of the backpack, too. It and the pants and shirt were appropriate for Laura Crain's personality—stylish yet understated. Finally, she pulled out an additional burner phone.

The device was already set up and fully charged. She looked around for the best place to hide it and selected her duffel bag. Then she called her cell phone with the new device and answered the call. Once the two phones were connected, she laid the burner, still connected, inside her duffel bag, zipped the bag shut, and secured it with the small padlock she used for traveling. She moved a chair around, checking that she could still hear the sound from her other cell phone—all loud and clear. She'd be able to track any sound an intruder might make inside her room.

She then quickly freshened up and got dressed, worked at settling the wig on her own hair, and applied a little makeup. She considered the result in the full-length mirror and nodded. She went to the safe, took out her laptop and Laura Crain Driver license, stuffed them in her Tumi backpack, shouldered it, and made her way to reception.

The receptionists were not the same as the ones who were on duty when she first checked in that evening, and she selected a young woman who looked friendly.

"I made a reservation for a couple of nights and called to let you know I would be arriving late," River said with a smile as she stood at the reception desk.

The woman smiled in return. "Of course—let me check you in. What is your name, please?"

"Laura Crain," River said.

The receptionist stepped to one of the computer screens behind the long desk, scrolled down, and found River's alias. She slid a form toward River. River picked it up and filled it in.

"I'll be paying cash, if that's okay," River said. "I can settle up front if you'd rather."

"It would be much appreciated."

River nodded, handed the form she'd just filled out back to the woman, and took a roll of bills out of her bag. She had already gathered the right amount and unfolded the rands, giving them to the receptionist. The woman hesitated a fraction of a second, took the money, and proceeded to count it. River smiled. She hoped there would be no further questions and that the driver's license she'd listed as an official document—rather than a passport—would be sufficient, too.

"All in order," the young woman declared.

River tried not to look relieved and then asked, "Any chance of getting a room on the third floor?"

The receptionist nodded, returned to her keyboard, and said, "Room 344." She handed the key card to River and gave her one last smile. "Enjoy your stay with us."

"I'm sure I will."

So far so incredibly good . . . but it can't last forever.

River took the elevator to the third floor, walked past her old room, and headed to room 344. It was a little farther away from her old room than she wanted, but close enough for her to react if there was any disturbance. She got in, locked the door behind her, and sat on the bed. As far as she could tell, the room was the same as her old one—same bed, same carpet, same image on the wall.

She sat down on the bed and waited a moment. Jet lag was wreaking havoc with her sleep patterns. She'd always taken a few days to adjust when she was deployed and eventually got used to the shift in time zones, but tonight she felt wide awake. She would give herself another hour, until midnight, and then would go to bed no matter what.

The laptop was charged and ready to use. Perhaps it was time she got acquainted with Masisi and the terrain around it. River booted up the device and went through the security protocols. She'd asked advice from Karen's father, Chief of Police Robinson, and had installed enough software to ensure that it wouldn't be easy to hack. A photograph of huskies running in front of a sled greeted her as the computer came to life. She needed to change the background to something more appropriate—perhaps a pack of lionesses going in for the kill.

River opened Google Maps. She typed in "Masisi" and waited for an image to pop up. When it did, the place she saw was smaller than she anticipated—two hundred houses, if that, plus one restaurant, a clinic, an emergency health station, a police station, and a church. She stood up from the bed and went to the dresser, on which a TV stood. She found the standard hotel pen and paper there and brought them back to the bed. She started making notes and noticed that the church was UAAC—a United African Apostolic Church. She'd recalled her parents working alongside some of its members. It was sometimes difficult to combine faith and science, but somehow her parents always managed.

The memory shook her. She had been thinking about her parents a lot in the past few months, but back in the States, they had felt somehow remote. Here, in South Africa, so close to places River and her family had lived, the emotions suddenly became much stronger. She'd reconnected with a land that had meant something to her and to her parents. If she adhered to some of the ancient beliefs among the African people, she might have thought her parents' spirits were talking to her.

A sob she wasn't expecting rose to her throat and shook her entire body. She let her sorrow take over, tears flowing freely. River hadn't cried this hard for a very long time, perhaps not even on the day she learned of her parents' death. She rummaged through her backpack, found a tissue, and wiped her eyes and nose. The unfairness of their death had been made crueler by the memories of their goodness and dedication to others. They'd been good parents, good practitioners. They were good people, even if River and they had disagreed on a few matters.

River drank a little water from the bottle she'd brought with her and returned to the map, which was still displayed on the screen of her laptop. Letting her emotions spill out openly had brought her more resolve. She would find Kruger and Matondo and bring them to justice.

She focused again on the terrain and recognized that Masisi was surrounded by bush—vast areas of trees, shrubs, and grassland.

Dangerous animals would be running wild in the immensity of the savanna and the bush. She tried to compare it to the American wilderness—parts of which were home to bears and cougars, and parts of which were home to snakes and alligators. But the concentration of animals in the plains of South Africa meant that people felt the pressure of nature every day. She'd only felt the same intensity in Alaska, where polar bears were a constant threat.

Being close to nature that powerful had given River a strong respect for it. Competing with lions, hyenas, wild dogs, elephants, rhinos, and buffalo—not to mention snakes on land, and crocodiles and hippos in the water—was a tall order. The chances of survival without a gun or a car in the bush were negligible if you weren't born there.

River paused for a moment. She wondered whether all the men whom Kruger employed were from the African continent. Kruger himself would be comfortable in the bush. When she met him, even though their meeting was brief, she recognized the response of a trained operator. She couldn't imagine him making the mistake of employing people who didn't understand the terrain.

River started to search methodically around the map, looking for structures that might be Kruger's compound. The military was good at concealing its encampments, but Kruger would need a solid building, as well as a perimeter wall, and perhaps watchtowers if he used the place to traffic weapons.

She scrutinized a large area of bush before she stopped. There was nothing so far, and she wondered whether Kruger might have found a way of wiping the image of his compound off Google Maps.

He had resources, and keeping his activities secret was desirable. His connection at the CIA might have been able to help with that, too.

River opened another tab and researched the question on Google. Yes, it was possible to get an image of a building blurred for privacy reasons. Kruger didn't even need the CIA's help to do it. A blurred image would make finding Kruger's compound extremely challenging, if not impossible. River ran a tired hand over her face.

Her cell phone, linked to the burner phone in her old room, had remained silent. Perhaps Kruger wouldn't try to search her room at the Holiday Inn. She switched the cell's speakerphone off and brought the phone to her ear, paying extra attention—still nothing.

Just as she did when she was deployed, she needed get her rest whenever she could, knowing there would be long periods of time when she wouldn't be able to. River took the wig off with a dejected gesture, undressed to her underpants and bra, slid into bed, and set the alarm on her cell for 6:00 a.m. She stared at the ceiling for a while until a scratching sound coming from her cell phone made her sit up. Someone had just entered her old room and was moving around.

River threw the covers off and slid into her pants and T-shirt. She yanked the black hoodie she'd brought with her over her head and slung the hood over her blond hair. She wouldn't bother with the wig. There was no time.

River picked up her backpack and tiptoed to the door; the cell phone stuck to her ear. She cracked the door open and risked a quick glance down the corridor. It was still empty; the intruder was taking his—or her—time.

River went back inside her room, walked to the bedside table, and dialed room service. When a sleepy voice answered, River gave the man the number of the room being searched and ordered a hot chocolate. She returned to the door and cracked it open again. Within a few minutes, a young man carrying a tray appeared. He knocked at the door of River's old room, announcing, "Room service," and stood back so that he could be seen from the peephole.

River pocketed her phone, took the hood away from her face, and stepped into the corridor.

"I'm sorry," she said. "I got the room number wrong."

The waiter tried to be polite and made a "these things happen" gesture. River took the tray from him, thanking him again, and after tipping him, closed the door.

The knock at the other door seemed to have had the desired effect. All activity had ceased in the old room. River cracked the door of her new room open and chanced a quick look. She only had to wait a moment before the door opened and a small figure clad in black pants and a black T-shirt emerged. River pulled back to remain unnoticed, but she had guessed right. The silhouette of the intruder indicated that it was a woman.

She turned left into the corridor, away from the bank of elevators and toward the stairs. She'd be using the back door to leave the building.

River opened the door again and cast an eye down the corridor. She waited for the woman to round the corner, then left the room and ran to the elevators. She pressed the Call button a few times. Thankfully, at 2:00 a.m., an elevator was quick to come. She dashed in, pressed the button for the lobby, and dashed out as soon as the doors opened again. The receptionist started to stand up, ready to assist, but River ignored him and ran outside.

She slowed down as she approached the service entrance. The woman was now crossing the side street, hunched forward. The headlights of a car flashed twice. The intruder had just unlocked a black SUV. River backtracked and speed-walked to the parking lot, found her car, and got in. She started it but didn't switch on the headlights. The SUV drove past the Holiday Inn, ignored a red light, and sped off into the distance. River turned into the road, ignored the same red light, and followed.

The streets were a lot busier than River expected. Still, the woman seemed to be oblivious to any traffic signs and signals. She drove through red lights as though they weren't there. River tried to keep track of where they were going, but it was hard to remember the number of rights and lefts they'd taken. It then dawned on River that the woman might be following a route that would help her shake a tail. She hadn't managed to do it yet, though, and River wondered whether she'd been noticed and was being led deeper into Johannesburg on purpose.

A sign pointing the way to Sandton sent a shiver down River's spine. She realized that if she followed in that direction, she'd be entering Alexandra, also known as Alex, an area known for its high level of poverty and crime-ridden slums.

Shit . . . she must have clocked me.

Suddenly, the SUV slowed down, creating a bottleneck for the couple of cars that were behind her. The light turned red, and the woman finally stopped. River swore. She knew what was coming next. A man got out of the car that had just stopped behind hers, a big, bulky guy who didn't bother to hide the gun he'd stuffed in his waistband. River braced herself. She followed his every move in the rearview mirror—the swagger, the confidence . . . the mistake.

River unlocked the door on the driver's side and released the catch. The man casually took the gun out of his belt as he reached River's car door. But she rammed the door open into him with vicious force. He wasn't prepared for the impact. The blow winded him and sent the gun flying. River jumped out of her car and slammed a hard back kick into his stomach. The man dropped to his knees, gasping for air.

River ran to pick up the gun and racked it, chambering a bullet.

"You son of a bitch want my car?" she shouted. "Or you wanna put a bullet through my head?"

The man raised his hands up, his eyes darting around, but the cars that had stopped had left, and the cars that were driving past wouldn't stop.

"Just the car," he whimpered, "just the car."

River didn't have time to interrogate him. The woman, who'd called in reinforcements, would call others, and they would soon be on their way.

"Start running before I change my mind. And don't look back or I'll shoot your sorry ass."

The man stumbled back up and took a few steps back, still looking at River. He then turned and ran. River got into her car, closed the door, and managed a tight U-turn. She drove back the way she'd come, ignoring red lights, and finally found a sign for the airport. She recognized the main road that led to it and the Holiday Inn.

She had to get rid of the gun before reaching the hotel. Keeping it would be a mistake. For all she knew, it had been used in a murder, and anyway, she didn't relish having to smuggle it to Masisi. She slowed down and spotted an open drainpipe along the road. She wiped off her fingerprints with the bottom of her T-shirt, stopped, and lowered the window. She dropped the gun into the drain and took off again.

River finally reached the hotel parking lot and found a spot near the main entrance. She parked, killed the engine, and sat for a moment. Her hands were still clutching the wheel, knuckles white, palms sweaty.

She let go, inhaled deeply, and let her head roll back against the headrest.

That was very close . . . just as Orson had warned her. She wouldn't make the same mistake again.

River left the car and went back into the hotel. The receptionist ignored her. She took the elevator to the third floor and walked back to her original room. The room felt different as soon as she entered. A sense of violation drifted over her, and she wondered whether the woman had installed any listening devices. River checked that the safe hadn't been opened. She didn't think the woman would have had enough time, but it was good to make sure.

Her River Swift passport and other documents were still there. River closed the safe again and surveyed the room. Everything looked untouched. River picked up her duffel bag, and she noticed that the woman had tried to open the lock but didn't have time to complete the job. River entered the combination, unlocked it, and retrieved the burner phone. She locked the padlock again, looked around once more, and left the room. She wouldn't sleep there tonight. Laura Crain's room felt so much more appealing.

The sun was setting when they arrived at the compound. Kruger had dozed off for a few hours during the journey and then gotten down to business as soon as they arrived. He'd received emails from his armaments suppliers on an encrypted and secure communications channel announcing that the shipments he was expecting were on their way. Kruger had sworn copiously at the news. He didn't want to have to divert too many men for the delivery of supplies to his African clients. And then he reconsidered. What was he worried about—River coming to challenge him in South Africa, his domain? He shrugged the worry off and resumed responding to emails—delivery would be fine as planned.

Kruger stood up and stretched. He'd been working nonstop and was ready to retire to a more welcoming part of the compound. The structure he'd built was made of ultra-high-performance military-grade concrete and consisted of three separate buildings. Two of them were reserved for weapons and munitions. He didn't want to keep all the armaments in one place—too easy to eliminate with one well-aimed strike. The third building housed his team, their communications, and the intelligence he'd gathered over the years. A necessary insurance policy for the business he was in.

The compound was surrounded by a wall and a barbed-wire fence. Four low towers completed the structure. The whole was suitably hidden by trees and shrubs so that it wasn't visible from afar. The roofs had camouflage spread over them, and Kruger was confident that the compound would be difficult to spot from above unless the intruders knew what they were looking for. He'd taken the additional precaution of asking Google Maps to blur the site under the terms of its privacy policy. No need to get Davis involved. Kruger believed in self-reliance, and it had always served him well.

Kruger went into the part of the building that served as a home. The place had a large kitchen and a refectory-type dining room alongside it. He'd added TV rooms and a pool room with a bar where his men could relax. Their rooms were spread out on the first floor, but Kruger had carved a small enclave for himself on the north side of the edifice—a bedroom with an en suite bathroom and a small veranda that allowed him to see the sun setting. He'd arrived too late today but looked forward to tomorrow, when he would enjoy his first sunset in the wild in a few months.

The men who were part of today's convoy were having dinner. The compound's cook was busy kindling a fire that looked perfect. He had organized a braai and was tending a wood fire, ready for the men's meat of choice. Kruger rarely allowed braais. The smoke might give away the compound's position, but he liked to treat his men once in a while when he knew hard work was ahead.

Some of the men who were not on duty were drinking beer and chatting animatedly, no doubt exchanging stories about their acts of bravery and most spectacular kills—whether of animals or people. A braai wasn't just about food; it was also about bonding, and Kruger needed these men to have one another's backs, as well as his own. The braai master spotted Kruger, picked up a plate from the sideboard behind him, and got his tongs ready to pick a selection for him.

Nothing tasted as good as boerewors—a spicy beef sausage—and sosaties, lamb kebabs cooked over a wood fire. Then there were sirloin steaks, pork chops, and marinated chicken on the grill with corn on the side. The aroma of the herbs and spices made Kruger's mouth water. He pointed to a piece of boerewors and a couple of pork chops. The braai master arranged the meat on the plate, slapped on a good helping of chakalaka, a spicy vegetable relish, and handed over the food to Kruger.

Arno Botha came to meet Kruger with a plate still half full. "I checked the perimeter. It's all looking good, boss." He then picked up a lamb chop by the bone and started chewing on it.

Kruger nodded and followed his lead. He picked up a piece of boerewors with his fingers and bit a large chunk out of it. It was a little too hot, but he didn't mind the combination of a slight burn and the hit of spices. He swallowed before saying, "How many men have we got now?"

"Ten," Botha replied. "But we'll get a couple more with deliveries as they arrive."

"You mean the planes' pilots?"

"That's right. These guys are ex-military. They'll know what to do. Hannes and Gerrie will come to the airstrip with me to take control of the shipment."

"Then we have two days to build the teams—the DRC first and then Mozambique on the way to Yemen."

Matondo had called again to make sure he had priority. Kruger had relented only because he needed him to keep Angela Graham alive. Matondo had become more unpredictable as his fame grew in the Kivu region. Kruger also suspected that Matondo, like his troops, indulged in the consumption of khat, a powerful stimulant. He might even indulge in some white powder, too, and Kruger couldn't imagine what the combination might do to Matondo's psychopathic brain.

"Matondo is getting a little too cocky for my liking," Botha said after finishing his lamb chop.

"I know, but I need him for a little while longer," Kruger replied. He'd grabbed a beer and would allow himself one drink. He was about to make the rounds and talk to his men, and nothing was better than a bottle of Lion Lager when it came to starting a conversation.

"You mean the Graham woman?"

Kruger nodded. He hadn't expanded much on the reason why and had only mentioned the name River Swift as a mere annoyance without elaborating who River was or why the two women were linked. Someone who'd become too nosy for her own good. But now, he needed to know what Angela Graham had told River about her parents' murder. Even though Botha was his most trusted man, it wouldn't do to admit he'd been fooled by a woman, ex-military or not.

"You could offer an exchange. A case or so of extra ammunition for Graham," Botha suggested.

"Matondo will think she's of more interest than she really is to me," Kruger replied. "I don't want to give him more than he's asked for already."

Botha thought for a moment. "I could ask Hannes to take a few more men and bring her back."

The thought hadn't occurred to Kruger, but it was a possibility he needed to consider. "I'll think about it. I have a day to decide."

Some of the men had noticed Kruger's presence, but no one would disturb him until he'd finished his conversation with Botha. There was a pecking order, and they all knew where they stood. Kruger returned to the braai master and selected a couple of sosaties and a piece of spicy chicken. He pointed to some appetizing potato salad, was served a generous helping, and turned toward the gathering. It was time to do what he enjoyed least—socialize with men he didn't care about and who were only here because he paid them way more than anybody else would.

Botha stopped him on his way. "Is this woman River Swift going to become a problem?"

Kruger squeezed his beer bottle but didn't push back on his number two's question. He'd selected him for that reason. Arno Botha had had as much experience as Kruger in the SADF, and he didn't shy away from danger or from asking the right questions.

"She shouldn't. I'm keeping an eye on her, and as far as I can tell, she's arrived on her own in South Africa."

Botha raised an eyebrow, and Kruger saw the interrogation in his eyes. It all sounded strange. If she was on her own, there was nothing to worry about, so why keep tabs on her unless she had the means to raise more people on the ground?

"Is she connected in South Africa?"

"Only to Doctors Without Borders," Kruger said.

Botha picked up another piece of meat with his fingers and started eating, focused again on the food, but Kruger could tell he wasn't satisfied with the answer. It wasn't the end of that conversation. Botha was the only man who could challenge Kruger because he never abused the privilege. Kruger gave a quick jerk of his head toward the men who were waiting for him to mingle. He'd delay a further discussion about River Swift until the morning.

Chapter 10

The sun hadn't risen yet when River woke up. To her surprise, after the events of the early morning, she'd managed to pack in almost five hours of sleep and woke up at six. She could fool her body clock for another couple of hours before it started telling her it was time to go to bed. It was 8:00 p.m. in Kotzebue and midnight in DC.

River got dressed quickly and cracked open the door of her room. The corridor was silent, and she sneaked out to her old room, the one she occupied under the name of River Swift. She didn't anticipate another visit from the intruder, but it was important to be careful.

She opened the door slowly and stood there. Nothing seemed to have changed since last night. She closed the door and meticulously screened the entire room, checking for audio or video recording devices. She spotted the intruder's attempt to install a bug near her bed. One of the screws from the electrical socket on the wall was on the carpet, and another one was sticking out. The woman hadn't had time to finish the job.

When River was satisfied the room was clear, she returned to her second room, grabbed her backpack and laptop, and went back to the first room.

She sat on the bed for a moment, dropping the backpack to the floor and the laptop near her. She still felt rattled, but she also knew Kruger's influence would only grow now that she was on his territory. She ran her hand through her hair. She'd better get used to this. Things were unlikely to get better.

The breakfast menu lay on a chest of drawers opposite her bed. She picked it up, ordered an American breakfast, and opened Google Maps on her laptop. She spent some time focused again on the area surrounding Masisi, just as she'd done the day before. A knock at the door interrupted her. She walked quietly to it, checked through the peephole that it was one of the hotel staff, and then cracked the door open.

"Your breakfast, ma'am," the young woman announced.

River let her in. The waitress laid the tray on a low table next to the window and stepped away with a smile. River tipped her, and closed and locked the door once more. Then she poured herself a cup of coffee and returned to her laptop.

She gave up on Masisi and the Limpopo River and began examining the area surrounding one of the most renowned nature reserves in South Africa—Kruger National Park. She sighed at the thought that this most spectacular animal sanctuary should bear the same name as a man she loathed—a trafficker and a murderer. She hoped Reggie had been in touch with his two cousins who were rangers there.

The map confirmed what she recalled. The northern part of the park was on Masisi's doorstep. She returned to her breakfast tray and removed the lid from a plate of eggs, bacon, and pancakes. She brought the plate with her and sat down on the bed, going over the map while she ate. Zooming in, she discovered a promising area with a lodge that welcomed tourists on safari. She pulled her notepad from her backpack and jotted the name down. This was what she needed—a place where she and the team could be in close proximity and yet hidden among international visitors. Few people would question her American accent or Karen's Inupiat looks.

River finished the bland food on her plate. It was fuel for the coming day, and she would eat every single bite of it. She'd been trained to eat meals whenever she could, not knowing where the next would come from.

She checked her personal and burner phones. She wasn't expecting anything from Karen yet—Danny's cargo plane wouldn't be landing for another hour—but she was surprised by the text on her cell. Ariana needed a chat.

News I need to share ASAP. Call anytime.

It was almost 1:00 a.m. in DC, but River dialed Ariana's number.

"Who's that?" Ariana's sleepy voice asked.

"It's River. You said to call anytime."

"And I meant it," Ariana replied, suddenly sounding fully awake. "I've got news about armaments moving from the States to South Africa, and the recipient is Kruger."

"He's going to be busy," River said, focusing on the opportunity this might present.

"He's going to be very busy. I gather it's a double delivery, and he'll need all hands on deck to turn it around fast and get it to its final destination."

"Any idea where that might be?"

"Unfortunately, no," Ariana replied, "but I can tell you that the merchandise is on the move and will be arriving his way within the next couple of days."

"That's very specific," River said, not hiding her surprise. "How did you manage to get that close to the intel?"

Ariana seemed to hesitate and then said, "I didn't ask permission to see the details, if you know what I mean."

"But you know who's gathering intel on Kruger and why."

More silence, then, "Look. You don't want to disclose everything you're gonna do to get to Kruger. I understand. You've got to be careful. But so do I."

"That's a fair point," River admitted. "But I need to understand who it is that I am either competing with to get to Kruger or fighting with if that person wants to help cover Kruger's butt."

River's suspicion that she might be privy to information that was collected, not to catch Kruger, but to save him, seemed to surprise Ariana. "That's a point," she said after a moment.

"So what sort of file do you have access to?"

"The file on Kruger has been growing, and yet I don't know why no one at the DHS is acting on it or even who the ultimate owner of that file is. It's a group file," she explained. "Accredited people contribute to it when they gather information they deem relevant. I joined the group a year ago, so I don't always understand the dynamics and who the people who make some of these decisions are."

"How much risk are you taking?"

"Probably less than you are," Ariana said. "I can look after myself, though."

"I'm not trying to patronize you," River said, keeping her cool. "I've seen what people like Kruger and his associates can do. The moment you think you're in danger, you've got to let me know."

"You're fourteen hours away from me, and so is your team," Ariana said, skeptical.

"I'll find a way," River said. "In the meantime, let me know if you find out more about the deliveries."

"Will do. I'll keep chipping away at the file and see what else I can find," Ariana said.

River hung up, her mind buzzing with what she'd just learned. A delivery created the perfect opportunity to try to get into Kruger's compound, but two deliveries created a perfect storm—fewer than a handful of men on the premises, Kruger busy with the dispatch. The man couldn't have survived in the world of arms dealing without being precise and delivering exactly what he said he would. To River, that meant checking the quality of what was arriving and matching it with what he'd promised to supply—some clients deserved more attention than others. River had seen it in Iraq and Afghanistan. Whether he liked it or not, Kruger would be busy in the next two to three days.

Another text coming in on her burner phone interrupted her thoughts.

Landed at Cape Town . . . we're all still alive, barely.

River felt herself go cold. Had Kruger discovered they were coming? She immediately dialed Karen's burner phone.

"Shit," Karen said by way of greeting. "It was the worst flight I've ever been on—*ever*."

"You mean turbulence?" River asked, relieved.

"Six hours of being tossed around like a single sock in a dryer. I just about managed to keep the contents of my stomach to myself. Reggie wasn't so lucky, though."

"Ouch. That sounds painful."

"You bet, and then Danny took it badly when I suggested we divert to avoid the storm."

"That sounded like a good idea to me," River said, puzzled. Even military pilots, who were not known for worrying about the comfort of their passengers, sought to avoid bad weather that could compromise an aircraft's safety.

"I'm being a tad unfair," Karen admitted. "This freaking storm was everywhere."

"But you guys are in one piece—"

River was interrupted by Reggie shouting in the distance. "I don't care how long it takes. I'm walking back to America."

"That boy doesn't have an understanding of the geography of the world," Karen said with a harrumph.

"I'm not a boy," Reggie shouted back.

"Well. He seems to have recovered fast," River said, a smile on her lips.

"Wait until we get on our next flight," Karen said, loudly enough for Reggie to hear. "Speaking of which, have you decided on the next leg of our journey?"

"I've been thinking about it, and I got some intel from Ariana."

Karen seemed to instantly focus on what River said and dropped her voice. "Reliable intel?"

"I believe so," River said. "According to her, Kruger is receiving two shipments that will arrive at his compound within the next two to three days."

"He's gonna be a busy guy. That's an opportunity for us, right?" Karen asked.

"My thought exactly. I also have some intel on where the compound is, again, courtesy of Ariana. She says it's close to Masisi, near the Limpopo River and the border with Zimbabwe and Mozambique."

"Right," Karen said. "And what's her game plan? Because she must be taking a lot of risk if she's nosing around a file she's not supposed to have full access to."

"I made that point, and she almost bit my head off," River said. "Underneath all her bravado I guess she's scared and won't admit it. I told her to let me know if she feels under threat."

Karen dropped her voice a little more. "Reggie has been too busy being sick to talk about her, but the unconditional trust is deep-rooted, so we need to be aware of that."

"Understood," River said, making a mental note. "You mentioned our next move, and we need Reggie for that. I found a safari lodge that's at the border of the Kruger National Park and Masisi. I need him to speak to his cousins and ask whether they can get us in."

"Hang on. You mentioned the name Kruger again," Karen said, suspicious.

"It's unfortunate, but the most staggeringly beautiful game reserve in South Africa is called Kruger National Park."

"Perhaps they should rename it."

"Well, if we get rid of Kruger, then there is no issue."

"Good way of solving that dilemma. Anyway, will all of us be staying at the lodge?" Karen asked.

"That's the ideal place to get us dispersed among different rooms and the ideal place for us to mix as though we were tourists. With only one exception."

Karen took a moment and then said, "Give me the name of the place, and I'll get Reggie on it."

"It's called the Outpost."

"And then you mentioned an exception."

"Orson Wilson, the priest I met last evening."

"Don't those guys take holidays?"

"I'm not sure they do. Father Hopkins back in DC never seemed to, but even if they do, Orson has been around Africa for a while. It would look odd if he joined us at the lodge. He's more a local than a tourist."

"What's the plan for him?"

"A visit to a parish that's near Masisi, although he doesn't know it yet."

"But how can he help?"

"I'm not sure," River said, "but he knows the area well, and he's frequently come across traffickers, so he knows how they operate. He also knows Angela well, and that might come in handy."

"Are we trying to free Angela as well as catch Kruger?"

"I hope we can do that, yes."

"I like it when you keep raising the bar, Riv," Karen said. "You almost make it sound like rescuing the special ops guys was easy."

"That's a little unfair," River protested.

"Tell me that again when we're back in Kotzebue," Karen replied. "Then we'll compare notes between this mission and the ones we've been on in the Middle East."

River was glad Karen had chosen to call the quest for justice a mission, too, but it reminded her of the danger they were all preparing to face. Despite Orson's telling her that she inspired people because she fought for what was right, River hesitated. Was it fair to ask all these people to help, even if they were willing?

Karen must have picked up on River's thoughts and said, "We all want to do this for our own reasons, Riv, and we know what the danger is."

"That's true of you and me and almost certainly Orson, in a strange way. But I keep worrying about Reggie and Ariana. Yes, they come from a rough DC neighborhood, but that's different."

"Still, they know how to spot danger, and they know how not to lose their cool. I saw that in Reggie when he handled Jason's case. He was in control in a low-key sort of way, which in my book is the best way."

"Granted. Reggie is calm under pressure. But he was in an environment he knew well. DC is his hometown."

"But the snooty law firm he works for isn't on his home turf. I'm sure he must have thought he'd landed on the moon the first time he set foot in the offices of Thompson & Meyer."

River sighed. "Maybe. But if you ever are in doubt, you must tell me. If I need to pull someone out, you need to say."

"Always. I won't let him or anybody else get in harm's way." The tone of Karen's voice comforted River. Her friend would speak up.

"Then talk to Reggie. I'll speak to Orson and investigate the best way to get to the lodge. Let's circle back in a couple of hours."

The small plane looked like a matchbox with wings sitting on the tarmac next to its more imposing neighbor, a Boeing 737, at Johannesburg's Tambo International Airport. Orson had proved to be more surprising than she expected. He could fly small aircraft. He wouldn't be flying the Cessna Grand Caravan EX that was about to take off, but a friend of his would.

Orson looked at his watch and said, "We'll be landing at Mutele-Masisi Airfield in about two hours, just before dark."

"We never had time to discuss how you got this ride," River said as she fastened her seat belt for takeoff.

"After I dropped you off and returned to the Jesuit community center, I started looking for airstrips around the Masisi area. And I found a few. South Africa doesn't have good infrastructure outside its big cities. So without trains and buses, the best means of transportation are cars and planes, which is the reason I learned to fly. It helps when we're trying to serve communities in remote areas."

River shook her head. "I never thought about it, but that's very similar to the United States. Vast distances mean more private aircraft. And more places to land them. How many airfields did you spot near Masisi?"

Orson was about to answer when the pilot turned around. He pushed his headphones away from his ear and said, "Takeoff in a couple of minutes. Get ready."

Orson gave him a thumbs-up, and River nodded. The pilot settled his headphones back into place, spoke to the tower, and began taxiing to the top of the runway. He took a sharp turn to the left, settled the plane for an instant, then pushed the throttles as far as they would go. The plane rushed forward and pressed River and Orson back into their seats. The aircraft gained momentum, and suddenly it was airborne.

The plane rose for a couple of minutes and then banked right, toward the north. They stayed silent for a while, enjoying the ride. River watched as the number of houses dwindled and gave way to huge expanses of flat land covered in shrubs. She knew how dry the earth could become in Africa, and she felt a mix of joy and regret—the joy of being in nature again, and the regret that she couldn't share the moment with her parents.

"Harsh but beautiful," Orson said as he leaned toward her.

"That's what I like about this place," River replied. "Nature reminds me exactly where I stand in life's pecking order."

"It's humbling, and that's a good thing."

They remained silent for a while longer, and then River turned to Orson and asked, "You said you researched airfields in the region around Masisi. What did you find?"

"I found a small airstrip that's just big enough for one of these to land," Orson said as he pointed to the inside of the Cessna.

"Don't keep me guessing. I get the feeling it's an interesting find."

"Well, it is. It's closer to the Limpopo River than Masisi, and closer toward the Mozambique border."

River opened her eyes wide and then sat back. "You've found the airstrip Kruger is using," she whispered.

Orson shrugged. "It's possible. I've been thinking about it, and my take on it is that he might use that place to receive the bulk of the armaments he's trafficking but then use another airstrip to deliver the arms around Africa—an airstrip that accommodates smaller planes."

"You must be right. The aircraft that carries the armaments needs solid tarmac for landing because of the weight it carries, but when Kruger dispatches the rest of the weapons around Africa, he can use smaller planes that can land virtually anywhere."

"Or he can use the roads into Mozambique to reach the sea and then send the stuff by boat to wherever."

"I think he's shipping to Yemen and Somalia."

"Terrorists?" Orson said. "I wonder how he's able to get away with it."

"That's a very good question, and the only answer I've found is that he must deliver a lot of intel back to his handlers in Washington, DC, which must be of great help to very large players in the States."

"But who? The gun lobby? The firearms industry? Do they really need him?"

"Perhaps he facilitates the negotiation of large contracts between countries. I figure he's been in this game for a while. He can bribe them if need be to get the contracts signed, and no one will know. The way he gets remunerated is by being allowed to sell weapons with a hefty markup."

"That sounds very plausible," Orson said with a sigh.

"And then there's coltan," River added.

Orson frowned. "Isn't that the ore used in cell phones?"

"That's right," River said. "Angela Graham had a theory about this. She thought that people like Kruger would have gotten in on the action at the beginning, fifteen years ago or so, when they realized that the DRC held a vast reserve of it. Apparently the country produces more than 40 percent of the world's coltan. The problem now is that the DRC's lack of political stability means that buying some of the coltan produced there has become illegal."

"So now the tech sector needs to access it illegally if it wants cheap coltan," Orson said.

"That's what I understand."

"How did Angela manage to put two and two together?"

"I don't know," River said, glancing out the window to hide her emotions. "We didn't have time to talk about it."

Orson sat back in his seat. He, too, was distraught at the thought of what Angela must be going through. They stayed quiet for a moment, and then River asked, "You said you'd arranged for your accommodations."

"I'll help the volunteers distribute the supplies we're carrying, and then one of them will put me up."

River nodded. "I'd forgotten how it works here."

She recalled her parents welcoming prefect strangers who'd come to deliver medical equipment and medication to their clinic. It was a way of life. You helped people who helped you. That had sounded very fair to her, and she always enjoyed listening to these men and women's stories as they traveled up and down the country to make sure that vital drugs reached remote areas.

"But then I had another idea," Orson said.

River arched her eyebrows. "I'm already worried about it."

"I don't take unnecessary risks," Orson replied with a straight face.

"But you *do* take risks."

Orson gave a dismissive wave of the hand. "Think about early Christians. Now, those guys used to take risks—nailed to the cross, devoured by lions, burned alive."

River was about to take the Lord's name in vain, but she stopped herself in time, and that made Orson grin. "I won't take offense."

"You're rather liberal, you know. I was expecting the Jesuits to be more . . ." River was looking for the right word.

"Rigorous?"

"That's the word."

"Well, rigor is good when applied to oneself. Then you learn to be more tolerant with others when you see your own failures."

"I like that, too. But what's this idea of yours?"

"The second airstrip I mentioned is right outside a lodge called the Exodus Guesthouse. I might decide to spend a couple of days there."

"And do what—check what planes come and go?"

"Why not? I'll tell them I'm there to distribute supplies and that I work for a charity. Tell them I'm a priest. That usually helps, although not always."

River couldn't hide a grin. "So you've become a spy overnight?"

"I'm sure I'm not the first priest to become a spy."

"That's a revelation."

"And one of my superiors may not agree with it."

"You're a little bit of a rebel, then?"

"That's a very nice way of putting it."

The banter was interrupted by the pilot, who again pushed his headphones aside and said, "We're making good progress. Should be landing ten minutes early."

River nodded her thanks, and Orson asked her, "Who's waiting for you at the airstrip?"

"A couple of rangers related to a guy on my team, Reggie."

"Are they with the national park?"

"They are, and they've secured accommodations and a car for me. I would love to ride a motorbike, but I'll be noticed in these parts, and it might not be practical."

"I thought you wanted Kruger to notice you."

"I do, but I also don't want him to think I'm overdoing it, otherwise he might become suspicious. I can't look too confident. But how about you?"

"I'll hitch a ride," Orson said, nodding his head toward the pilot.

"Fletcher isn't flying back until the morning. He's got a room at Masisi's only boardinghouse. I'll crash there for the night and then make my way to the Exodus Guesthouse in the morning."

River took a moment and then said, "Promise me you'll pull out if this is too risky."

"Nope," Orson said, shaking his head. "I'm not going to make a promise I can't keep. And anyway, you and I might have different definitions of risk."

River turned toward him so she could look him in the face. "Are you serious? Iraq and Afghanistan were not exactly a piece of cake."

"I'm sure they weren't, but Africa isn't a piece of cake, either. In the end, I decided to help you, hoping we can save Angela. I'm dedicated to what I do, which is trying to save as many souls as possible, but if I can also help save a human being's life here on earth, then that is just as good."

River didn't push further and respected his point of view. It sat rather well with her own take on life.

She changed the subject and said, "I'm going to introduce you to the rangers as someone I just met on the flight. I hope we'll be able to trust these guys, but I won't know until I've spoken with them. I'll give them the same story you're using for moving to the Exodus Guesthouse . . . I'm here to deliver supplies and help."

"I've been very vague with Fletcher, too," Orson said, lowering his voice. "I just said you were a friend of a friend who needed a ride."

They hadn't noticed, but the plane had gradually been lowering its altitude. River looked out the window and guessed they must be very close to landing. Fletcher flew over the airstrip once. Three cars were waiting on the side of the runway. He then lined up the plane and slowly touched down with a small bump.

The Cessna came to a stop at the end of the runway, close to where the cars were waiting. Fletcher killed the engines and took his headphones off. He turned around, and both River and Orson clapped—a perfect landing. He grinned back, his strong jaw looking even stronger, and said, "Welcome to Mutele-Masisi International Airport. The toilets are in the bush, and customs has gone missing."

He then released his five-point seat belt and stood up. River and Orson followed suit. Fletcher dropped the door open and lowered a small set of steps down. He went out first and walked to the cars that were waiting.

Orson disembarked, and River followed. She could see that Orson was enjoying being back in the middle of nature. She stood for a moment, close to the steps, memories of her past flooding in—the clinics her parents worked with, the people always curious about her blond hair, the animals fascinating and yet dangerous.

Two men dressed in khaki ranger gear stepped out of two different cars—two old Ford Ranger pickups, one black, one in a jungle camo pattern—that almost certainly didn't have air-conditioning and had definitely seen better days. One of the vehicles looked a little cleaner than the other, and River wondered whether it was to be her ride. The third driver was a short woman who welcomed Fletcher with a smile and an outstretched hand.

Orson turned to River and said, "I'd better follow Fletch and introduce myself to the woman who's here to collect the cargo he's transporting. Let's shake hands as though we'd only met."

River smiled, stretched out her hand, and said, "We've only just met, but it's been a pleasure."

Orson chuckled and squeezed her hand. "If you're not sure of something, it's probably because you need to be," he said, now serious. "But I think you know that."

She nodded and watched as he turned around and strolled away. The two men were making their way toward her, and she waited near the aircraft.

The taller of the two reached her first, and he stretched a hand out, smiling. "I'm Dioko, and this is Eric," he said, pointing a thumb toward the other man. "You must be River."

River shook his hand. "Thanks for taking the time to pick me up."

"Reggie said you needed help," Dioko said.

Eric stood next to him and nodded. He was much beefier than Dioko, and he wore the sleeves of his shirt rolled up above his elbows. River could see scars along his arms, and she tried not to ogle.

"I'm visiting the Outpost lodge and need a car to get me there, but if you could show me the way, that would be very helpful, too."

"Is this your first time in Africa?" Eric asked.

River appreciated the fact that Reggie had said little about her. It allowed her to release only the type of information she thought would fit the mission's purpose.

"It's been a while. My parents worked for Doctors Without Borders, and we spent time in South Africa."

Both men looked at each other and nodded in appreciation. Then Fletcher and Orson approached, and Fletcher said, "We're going to start unloading the cargo. I'll get your bag first, though."

He climbed back into the Cessna and returned a moment later with River's backpack and duffel bag. She shook hands with Fletcher and said, "Thanks for the ride. It's been a great help."

"Anytime," he replied, squeezing her hand a little longer than necessary.

Orson said, "Enjoy your stay in Africa."

"I intend to make it a memorable one," River replied.

Dioko and Eric were already ahead, and she caught up with them.

"We tidied the vehicle a little," Eric said.

"As long as it works, I don't care about any mess," she replied.

Eric handed over the keys as soon as they reached the black pickup. He opened the back door, stuffed the duffel bag and the backpack on the seat, and closed the door.

"How far are we from the Outpost?" River asked.

"About ten miles. The trails are pretty good. It hasn't rained heavily yet, so it's an easy ride. It should take us twenty minutes or so."

"And if you're lucky, you might see some animal activity," Dioko added. "The sun is about to set, and the big cats are about to go out hunting."

"I haven't seen a lion for more than fifteen years," River said.

"Mufasa may come out tonight for you, then," Dioko said with a cheeky smile.

River smiled back. She could think of other predators who may be on the prowl for her, but they walked on two legs.

She opened the front door of the pickup and got into the driver's seat. She adjusted it and stuck the key in the ignition. The two men had taken their seats in the other pickup. She gave them a thumbs-up through the open window, and they started driving slowly down the trail that ran along the runway.

River looked in the rearview mirror. Orson and Fletcher were off-loading boxes from the side of the plane. She fought the desire to wave. She needed to keep to the script she'd written. As far as some people knew, she was leaving behind strangers, not allies.

They picked up speed, and soon the plane receded in the distance until it disappeared. Eric was right. The trails were better than she anticipated. Although she rocked from left to right from time to time, the drive wasn't uncomfortable. She'd learned to drive on these trails when she was fourteen. It hadn't even been a debate between her parents. It was a matter of practicality. They sometimes lived in remote communities, and being able to drive could be a lifesaver.

The memory burst like a bubble when Eric shouted through the open window of his truck. "Look to your right."

The sun was setting fast. River glanced in the rearview mirror again to see that its orb had settled on the earth. She scanned the landscape to her right. She couldn't see them to start with, but then a clan of spotted hyenas appeared.

"I can see them," River shouted. She waved and then kept shouting through the open window. "Are they hunting?"

"Or they have smelled a kill," he shouted back.

River followed the rangers' truck, keeping an eye on the hyenas. They ran almost parallel to her for a short while and then veered to one side. The shape of their bodies and heads had always impressed her: They had massive shoulders, so they could drag their prey a long distance, and formidable jaws, stronger than those of lions, jaws that could crush through any bone. Hunting in clans, they'd happily try to steal a kill from lions—and often succeeded.

The animals disappeared just as the sun was almost set. Eric waved again through the window, but this time, it was to indicate to River that they were almost at the Outpost. The brake lights of the rangers' truck flashed red, indicating they'd slowed down. River applied the brakes, too. They were about to cross a brook where a little water was flowing. The ground sloped gently, and River guessed that it must be a popular crossing point. They were at the end of the wet season, and she suspected that the brook would soon swell to become a small river. She managed the crossing easily, her pickup only shaking a little in the process.

Dioko accelerated up a steep slope and then slowed again as they reached the flat part of the terrain. In the distance, the cabins appeared, peppered along a rock ridge overlooking the brook. Dioko stopped the pickup at the main entrance. River drove alongside his vehicle so she could speak to Eric.

"Thanks a lot for guiding me here and for the truck. I'll go in alone, if you don't mind. The less the people who run the lodge see us together, the better. I believe Reggie has explained."

"He has, although he didn't tell us exactly why," Eric replied.

River could hear it in his voice. He wanted to know more but was prepared to trust his cousin for a little while longer. Then he said, "Reggie and his friends are arriving tomorrow at midday. They're flying out of Cape Town on the first flight to Jo'burg and then flying to Masisi in a smaller plane. ETA around twelve thirty. We'll pick them up as well."

"That's good news," River said, suddenly glad that her team was arriving soon. She'd have to make introductions to Orson, but for now she wanted to settle in and check out the surrounding area. From experience, she knew that walking in the bush after sunset was dangerous. That's when the big predators woke up and started hunting, when the temperature was cooler. She had perhaps half an hour left and needed to make the most of it.

"Thanks again," she said as she waved to Eric, and then bent forward so that she could wave to Dioko. "I'll see you tomorrow."

They waved back, and she drove the pickup inside the reception area of the lodge. River stopped right in front of a set of steps that led to a large wooden desk. The building that housed the reception desk and the lobby was open on two sides, and so was the adjacent building, which housed the dining area and a much bigger room that overlooked the savanna in the distance and the brook and trees that grew alongside it.

A young woman dressed in beige slacks and a beige shirt with SARAH and THE OUTPOST embroidered over the left breast pocket stood up. As River parked her vehicle, took her duffel bag and backpack out, and climbed the steps to the desk, Sarah said, "Welcome to the Outpost, Ms. Swift. I was worried that you might have gotten lost."

River smiled. "I don't know this part of South Africa well, but it isn't my first time in your beautiful country."

The answer seemed to both reassure and please her hostess, and she gave River a set of documents to fill out. River glanced through them quickly and signed them, then she picked up her backpack and duffel bag again, and followed Sarah along a gravel path that connected each cabin on the property.

"You're free to walk around on your own during the day, although I advise caution because animals regularly wander in and out. But at dinnertime, a ranger will come to fetch you from your cabin and will bring you back when you're ready."

River nodded and followed Sarah until they arrived at cabin 11, which stood farthest away from the main building.

"This is our best cabin," Sarah said as she opened the door. "It's overlooking the gorge below and has a view of the entire savanna."

It was true. River walked in and was immediately taken by the place—dark furniture of ebony wood, beautifully carved, a bed surrounded by light gauze curtains to keep the insects out, and then a living room that gave way onto a balcony that hung several meters above the ground.

"This is amazing," River said, genuinely pleased.

"If you need anything, just call. There is always someone on duty who will answer the phone," Sarah said as she pointed toward an old-fashioned phone that sat on a low table in the middle of the living room. Then she left and closed the door behind her.

River immediately opened her duffel bag and found what she was looking for—a camo-patterned shirt that she'd packed when she left Alaska. River slid it over her cream-colored T-shirt. She fetched her burner phone from her backpack, opened the door, and left the room. The sun had now completely disappeared, and she stood for a moment where she was, listening for any sound that would alert her to animal activity. She couldn't hear anything, although she knew she almost certainly wouldn't hear a lion coming until it was too late.

A winding dirt path snaked below her cabin, and she quickly followed it down to the brook and the gorge below. The distinct sound of hippopotamuses jostling for position in the water, grunting as they did, made her smile. A hippo wasn't the friendly, lumbering creature people assumed it was but rather a fierce, territorial beast—approach it at your peril.

River hurried along the trail. Each cabin had its own path that led to the brook. She could use these paths to visit Reggie and Karen or to escape from her room without being noticed.

The sound of another vehicle arriving attracted River's attention, and she climbed back up toward the lodge and what must have been cabin 9. There wasn't any light on, and she stopped as soon as she reached the front door and the little veranda that surrounded it. River was too far away to hear what was being said by the two men who'd gotten out of the Jeep that had just arrived, but River could tell they weren't rangers employed by the lodge. There was something a little too bulky, too assertive about their posture. The path to the main building was open, surrounded by low grass, and guests could see whether anything stood between them and their destination. River crouched and waited to find out what these people wanted.

The conversation became animated and then turned into an argument. River heard Sarah yelp, and River was about to run toward the reception area when she saw one of the men holding Sarah by the arm and walking her toward the cabins. He was so tall that she found it hard to walk alongside him. The second man had what looked like a Glock, which was drawn but pointing downward. This type of sidearm wasn't the sort of weapon a ranger would use to defend himself against wildlife.

River duckwalked backward toward cabin 9 and disappeared in its shadow. She looked around for a makeshift weapon and found a heavy cast-iron doorstop that she figured the cleaners must use to keep the door open when they made up the room. She flattened her body against the wall of the cabin, slid down to pick up the doorstop, and let Sarah and the two men walk past her. The man carrying the Glock stood back, glancing around for activity. The two men looked focused on reaching River's cabin and seemed eager to get there fast. River waited for a moment and then followed them from the shadows.

She'd left the light on, yet it wasn't easy to see inside her room. The two men stopped a few paces away from River's door. The thug who held Sarah said in a voice that River could hardly hear, "Knock at the door and call for her."

Sarah stiffened and wouldn't move, but he shook her a few times, pointing a threatening finger at her. She knocked at the door and called a weak "Ms. Swift?"

The man shook her harder, and Sarah almost cried when she said again, "Ms. Swift?"

River was now right at the back of the second man, the one with the Glock. She lifted the doorstop and crashed it with all her might against the side of the man's head. He collapsed on the wooden veranda like a sack of garbage. River caught the Glock before it hit the ground and chambered a round.

The first man turned around, still holding Sarah by the arm. He would need to drop his grip to reach the gun on his right hip.

"Don't even think about it," River said, aiming the Glock straight at his face. "I'll kill you without the slightest hesitation."

They locked eyes for an instant, and then he knew she would do exactly as she said.

"Let her go," River said as she jerked her head toward Sarah.

He released Sarah, who stood stock-still, and instinctively raised his hands in the air.

"Who sent you?"

Chapter 11

The man shook his head. "If I talk, I'm dead."

"If you don't talk, you're dead," River replied with as much determination as she could muster, knowing it would be impossible for her to kill a man who had his hands up in the air.

He gave her a faint smile. "A minute ago, you would have pulled the trigger. Now, I'm not so sure."

"If it's Kruger who sent you, I won't have a choice," River said, looking for a reaction.

She got what she wanted—the bat of an eyelid and a slight clenching of the jaw. He was one of Kruger's men.

A low groan surprised River. It came from behind her, and she knew the man on the ground was coming around. She stepped back, gun still pointed toward the standing man, but she stumbled slightly on the uneven path.

The man went for the gun at his hip, but River found her balance again and discharged the Glock at his right shoulder and leg. The man yelled. Sarah screamed. He fell to the floor of the veranda, holding his arm, grunting in pain.

Sarah was pressing her hands over her mouth, trying to control another scream. River turned to her and said, "We need to secure the man on the ground and then deal with the wounded one."

Sarah looked at River with a mix of fear and relief. She then nodded and said, shaking, "I can tie this man's hands behind his back with a rope. We've got ropes in the main building."

"Do it," River said.

Sarah ran toward the main building. River was expecting some of lodge's guests to be coming out to see what was happening. But no one did.

Sarah returned a minute later. She looked scared as she approached the man still on the ground.

"He won't fully wake up just yet. But we need to secure his hands quickly," River said. The man she had shot was still on the ground, curled up in a ball of pain. He wasn't going anywhere, either. He'd dropped his gun as he fell, and River could see that it had slid toward her. She crouched, picked it up, and tucked it in her waistband, behind her back.

"Where is everybody?" River asked as Sarah stood up after tying the other man's hands.

"The rangers are out with a couple of visitors. Most people left three days ago. It's getting a little late in the season. Besides, we're expecting some rain in the next week or so."

"When are the rangers coming back?"

"After 9:00 p.m.," Sarah said. She seemed to have recovered her equilibrium and now directed her attention to the wounded man. "What do we do with this one?"

River picked up her burner phone from her pants pocket and dialed Eric's number. "I'm calling for help."

He answered after a couple of rings and said, "Problem?"

"That's a good way of summing it up. I need your help—now."

River told him about the two men and what had happened. Eric listened carefully and then said, "We're coming, but you need to tell us why these men are after you."

"I know I do, and I will," River said. She hung up and turned toward Sarah. "Help is coming. But I need to tend to this man's shoulder and leg wounds."

Sarah nodded. She looked around and said, "There was a cackle of hyenas hunting near the top cabins last night. We need to keep an eye out for them. If they're still around, they will have smelled his blood."

"I don't want to shoot them," River said.

Sarah then frowned, fear flashing in her eyes.

"I mean the hyenas," River added.

"I agree with that," Sarah said, sounding relieved. "That's not what we're here for, but then . . ." She gestured at the two men.

River sighed. "I'm a former Air Force medic. I usually mend people after rescuing them."

"Too bad for the hyenas," Sarah said. "They could have dined on a couple of bad people."

"Still not an option," River said. "And yes, they are very bad people."

"What did they want with you?"

"I'm here because of the man who's employing them. I guess he knows I've arrived and wants to have a word."

"It seems to be more than a word," Sarah said with a frown.

"Still, if you have a first aid kit, I could use it right now," River said. Sarah wouldn't get more out of her, at least not yet.

Sarah took a moment to think about it but then walked to the veranda, staying well clear of the man lying there, and opened River's door. She went in and returned a minute later with a small backpack that had a red cross printed on its front.

"Each room has one," she said as she handed it to River.

River took out the gun she'd stashed in her waistband. "Do you know how to use one of these?"

"I can shoot a rifle," Sarah said. "I live in the bush, and I look after visitors here. I need to be able to protect them, so it's a requirement."

River handed the Glock to Sarah and gave her a crash course.

"I need you to shoot if he tries anything."

Sarah nodded without a word, and then River said, "A nod is not enough. I need you to say it."

River was still holding the weapon, not ready to release it yet.

Sarah nodded again as she extended her hand and said, "I'll shoot him if he tries to jump you the way he did me."

River handed over the gun and walked close to the man, the backpack over her shoulder. She stopped a couple of feet away and said, "I'm going to attempt to stop the bleeding. If you try anything, Sarah will shoot you, and we'll let the hyenas do the rest."

She heard a grunt and said, "Is that a yes?"

The man grunted louder and attempted to move his head, although the move must have caused a great deal of pain, because his head hardly budged. He'd lost quite a bit of blood and would start feeling weak. River hardly needed to look: She knew that most of the shoulder blade was shattered, and that the exit wound was a mess of blood and torn flesh.

She opened the first aid kit and found some rubbing alcohol, antibiotic cream, bandages, and dressings. She used a pair of scissors she'd found in the backpack to cut open the back of the man's shirt, then splashed some rubbing alcohol on the wound, eliciting yells and loud moans from the man on the veranda. She then applied the cream and the dressing as best she could and said, "It'll have to do until you're at the clinic." She repeated the same process with his leg. Although the bullet hadn't shattered a bone, it had caused serious muscle injury. It would be months before he would be able to walk.

She rummaged through the backpack again. She didn't find what she wanted, but then again, the painkillers she had in mind required a syringe, and she could understand why one of those wouldn't be freely provided. River thought a little more and decided to forget about an analgesic. Pain was a way to control the wounded man. He wouldn't think about escaping or inflicting retaliatory damage if he was unable to use his arm and leg.

Sarah turned around suddenly. She took a small flashlight out of her pants pocket, switched it on, and directed the beam into the far distance, toward the top of the hill on which the lodge was set.

"Shit," she said. "You got your wish. I think there is a hyena coming our way."

"Only one?" River asked as she stood up.

"That I can see. But it's dark, and it's no longer easy to spot them."

"Show me where," River said.

Sarah pointed in the far distance toward the part of the property where grass had been allowed to grow long. River noticed the squat shape of an animal. It was still, but she could tell from its stance that it was focused, its senses on high alert, smelling the air.

"Last time I had to shoo away a wild animal," River said, "it was a bull elephant who wasn't happy with our Jeep coming around the corner of a path he was walking on. He sort of mock-charged us. The medic who was driving stopped. We got out and waved our hands in the air and shouted, trying to look bigger than he was. That did the trick."

"Animals are getting increasingly more frightened by human voices, even more so than gunshots. And that includes lions, leopards, and hyenas."

River looked around, found a suitable stone, and took a short run in the direction of the hyena, shouting and waving her arms before she eventually threw the stone in its direction. The animal backed off, but it was still there, sniffing the air. River repeated the process, and this time, the hyena disappeared.

"It'll be back," Sarah said. "And not alone."

"I know, but with a bit of luck the two rangers I called will have arrived by then."

Both women fell silent. The two men were still on the ground, although the one who been knocked unconscious by River was starting to come around. Sarah kept scanning the far side of the property with her flashlight. The beam of light started attracting some insects, and she chased away a couple of large moths.

They heard the pickup truck before they saw its lights. The beams of the headlights scanned the reception area of the lodge before it stopped in front of it. Sarah rushed toward the two men who'd just stepped out, waving at them. "This way."

The three of them walked toward cabin 11, where River stood waiting for them. She hadn't had time to consider how much she was prepared to disclose, but she still needed to gain their trust. She'd been relying so far on goodwill. It was time to give them a reason to want to help.

Eric was the first to reach River. He saw the men on the ground, stopped, and looked at River, then dropped his gaze to the gun stuck in her waistband.

"Did you do that?" he asked.

River shrugged. "I'm a former United States Air Force medic who worked directly on the battlefield. I've been deployed in Afghanistan and Iraq."

Eric scratched his short hair and gave a low whistle. "Reggie told us you were a very capable woman. I though he was just overstating it, but perhaps he was understating it."

Dioko arrived next. He heard River's reply and asked, "How bad are they?"

"The one with the gunshot wounds needs immediate attention. He's been bleeding quite a bit. The other one needs time to come around, but he should be fine."

"Why did they want to bring a couple of guns to the party?" Dioko continued.

"To have a chat with me," River said.

The two men looked at each other. "Why? And who are they?" Eric asked.

Sarah had joined the men, and although she was standing a little farther away, she was listening. River took a moment to consider her answer. She couldn't disclose the entire story around her mission yet, but she could perhaps talk about weapons smuggling.

"I am after an arms dealer," she said, "and—"

"It's back with some of its clan this time," Sarah said.

Eric and Dioko immediately knew what she meant, and Dioko said, "We must move these two men now, before the hyenas try to attack."

He stepped toward the man who was coming around and tried to shake him awake. The man moaned, but his eyes fluttered, and Sarah came to help Dioko. They got him to stand up and started to drag him toward the main building.

Eric and River moved cautiously around the wounded man, and Eric told him, "Hyenas are coming. We need to move you."

He then knelt behind him. The man tried to get up. River came around the front, and both worked together to move him to his knees and then to a standing position. They followed Dioko and Sarah. When they got to the main building, Sarah switched on all the lights, which would keep the animals at bay for a little longer.

"The clinic is forty minutes away," Eric said. "We need to get this one there as soon as possible."

"And the other to the cops," Dioko added.

"I'll come with you," River said. "We can talk on the way."

The four of them placed the two men in the pickup bed on top of old blankets Eric had thrown there. The wounded man was pushed against the side. The other one was still dazed, and they would have to keep an eye on him.

River opened the back door and climbed in. Sarah shut the door for her, saying through the open window, "I, too, need to understand."

River nodded. "You will. I'll be back as soon as I can. But for the time being, keep this from the rangers—*please*."

Sarah nodded slowly, and River hoped she'd be back in time to have a chat with her before the guests and the rangers returned.

Dioko climbed behind the wheel, and Eric sat in the passenger seat. Dioko reversed once and then maneuvered the truck toward the exit. River checked on the two men in the bed, then gave Dioko a thumbs-up. They were on their way.

Eric turned in his seat so that he could face River and asked, "Why chase an arms dealer? And why in South Africa?"

"This dealer and some of his accomplices tried to frame a good man, someone I care a lot about—a man named Jason Wayne."

River told them that Kruger and Clery had tried to frame Jason for murder in order to discredit him and stop him from investigating the suicides of operatives in the US Special Forces. She spoke about the way Karen, Reggie, and she banded together to defeat people who thought themselves unassailable. Both men listened hard, without interruption.

"Reggie was incredibly professional and astute for such a young lawyer, but he also knew how to take sides when he needed to," River said. "It's rare to find someone who's that dedicated to his clients."

Eric nodded, and Dioko and he exchanged a glance. They then broke into a smile, and Eric said, "We don't know him all that well, only through video calls and emails, but he's got a good reputation in the family. He's the first one of us to go to college."

"How did you guys become rangers?" River asked.

"It's a tradition in our family," Dioko said proudly. "The park was created a long time ago but was named Kruger National Park in 1926. The Cameron family, our family, has always had rangers working in the park, including female rangers."

"So you must know the area like the back of your hand," River said.

"Even better than that," Eric replied.

River took a moment to check on the two passengers at the back of the truck. They were still lying down, and she turned back toward Eric.

"I know this isn't the park, but do you know the area close to the Limpopo River where it meets the border with Mozambique?"

"I know it well enough," Dioko said. "Poachers use the Limpopo to cross into Zimbabwe and traffic the parts of the animals they've taken once they've made a kill."

River thought again before asking her next question and then said, "I presume you try to secure the park first and then you hunt the poachers once you've spotted an animal that has been illegally killed."

"Exactly," Eric said. "The border with Zim and with Mozambique is very long, so we have our work cut out for us, but at least on the Zim side, we're helped by the San people."

"You mean Bushmen?" River asked. "The name San wasn't used that much when I left South Africa."

"That word sums it up—it means hunter-gatherers. They kill what they eat and live off the land. They've been around for as long as three hundred thousand years. No one knows the land the way they do, and they don't like killing for any reason other than food."

"I know who they are," River said. "My dad and I followed some of the younger hunters who were tracking a large baboon once."

Dioko couldn't help but turn around to look at River. He quickly returned his attention to the trail as the pickup swerved precariously.

Eric raised his eyebrows. "That's unusual."

"My parents enjoyed mixing with various kinds of people, and it made their job easier when they understood the culture of the individuals they were trying to treat."

River turned around again to check on their passengers at the back of the truck. Eric gave a dismissive wave of the hand. "No one is going to jump out of the truck. It's dark, and we're in the middle of the bush. It would be life-threatening for someone who's wounded or has his hands tied up."

"What's the name of the man you're chasing?" Dioko asked.

"Karl Kruger," River said. "He's South African but spends a lot of time in the United States."

The two men looked at each other and then shook their heads. "We don't know a Karl Kruger."

"And you think he's hiding somewhere between the Limpopo River and the Mozambique border?"

Eric picked up on River's surprise. "You asked whether we know the area, so it's not difficult to guess why."

"Well, yes. I think he's got more than a hiding place. I think he has a well-guarded compound. Somewhere where the arms shipments are prepared for transit. Perhaps a place with an improvised landing strip."

"Then the place can't be too close to the river because of the trees that grow there."

"That's a good point," River said, "but could they cut the trees to keep the landing strip free?"

"The San people would know," Eric said, shaking his head. "Trees are essential for them. That's where game live, and that's where they hunt."

River stuck her head through the divide between the two front seats. "That's given me an idea. Do you think the San would know of Kruger's compound? As you say, they hunt and gather food, so that means they travel along the land all the time. They may not have spoken about it if the compound hasn't caused them problems, but they still may know."

Eric thought for a moment. "That *is* an idea."

"How big do you think this compound is?" Dioko asked.

"I don't know," River said, "but if it's used for trafficking, it's got to have a defined perimeter that can't be breached. It has to be big enough to house more people when the shipments arrive and have storage space for the armaments themselves."

"So between six and twelve people?" Eric said.

"Plus a cook," Dioko added, index finger in the air.

"Now, that has given me *another* idea," River said, her elbows resting on the side of each front seat. "Kruger's men are going to need provisions—a lot of them—if they have to feed twelve people. And they're not going to have a bunch of white men who look like Special Forces personnel go and buy them at the market."

"So we need to track down a black guy who's a cook and buys in bulk on a regular basis," Eric said.

River smiled at the use of the word "we." Being brave and determined seemed to run in the Cameron family.

"I'm very grateful you feel you want to help, but Kruger's men are, as you said, highly trained—former special ops or mercenaries. They will shoot to kill."

"And so will poachers," Dioko said. "A rhinoceros horn is worth more than gold or cocaine."

"We've been shot at too many times to count," Eric said. "Poachers know the land as well as we do. Sometimes even better."

"But my fight is not your fight," River said. She needed them on board, but the thought of putting their lives on the line to fight for her parents' justice seemed unfair.

"People who traffic weapons are bad people. These weapons end up on the black market, and that's where poachers find their guns. They don't use hunting guns anymore but machine guns and AK-47s. They're not here for the tracking, the chase, or the hunt. They're here to butcher and steal the parts of the animals they're after—the quicker the better."

"That's a good enough reason for me," River said in agreement. "If it helps you save the animals, I'll be grateful for your assistance."

"Deal," Eric said, extending a hand.

River shook it. "Deal."

Dioko lifted one hand from the wheel and waited for River to shake it.

"Deal," they both said.

In the distance, the lights of Masisi had started to come on, one after the other.

"We're almost there," Eric said. "We'll stop at the emergency medical station first. Just let us handle this."

The dirt trail had become a little wider and smoother without River noticing. Dioko accelerated, and they joined a paved road that led straight to the small town. He drove for another five minutes and then took a sharp left onto another paved road that was unexpectedly wide and smooth. He parked in front of a well-lit building that looked new and had a hospital feel to it—solid white walls, a clean-looking entrance, and a well-tended reception area that River could see through panes of glass.

Dioko switched off the ignition, and both he and Eric left the truck and walked to the main desk. They spoke to the man in attendance, and a gurney soon appeared. River sat back in the pickup, squeezing into one of its corners. A young female medic appeared with another man. River saw them walk to the back of the truck. She heard the wounded man cry again, and she surmised that they must be sliding him onto the stretcher. The gurney pushed by the two medics went past her and disappeared. Dioko waved. Eric and he exchanged a few words, and then they got back inside the pickup.

"What did you tell them?" River asked.

"The truth," Eric said with a straight face.

River frowned. "You're kidding."

Eric burst into a honking laughter. "Got you there." He recovered and then said, "We told them we found him shot in the bush."

"We said it was a possible poaching accident," Dioko added. He started the truck again, left the clinic, turned right, and stopped immediately in front of another building.

"This is the police station," Eric said. "We'll handle this, too."

Dioko stopped the pickup in front of a smaller and less modern building. The brickwork wasn't painted, and the front door looked dusty. This time Eric entered on his own, and Dioko waited at the back of the truck. A few moments later, a tall, thin man dressed in a dark blue uniform walked out with Eric. He was wearing a holstered gun, and a pair of handcuffs hung from his belt.

He and Eric disappeared behind the pickup, and then there were shouts of anger rather than pain. The man was resisting being moved to the police station. Eric and Dioko joined in, and the three of them hauled the man through the doors of the building. River was again hiding in the back of the truck and wondered what would happen to Kruger's men. Judging by what had happened to Clery, she thought they might not last the night.

She had to wait a little longer for the two rangers to emerge from the police station. They got back into the truck, and River asked, "What's the story this time?"

"Same as before," Eric said. "Suspected poacher."

Dioko started the truck again, reversed, and made his way up the paved road, then turned left onto the main road and pointed to a sign a block away.

"The only decent grocery store for a hundred miles. The owner knows everyone."

They stopped opposite the place. Dioko left the pickup and jogged across the road.

"Do you think this guy will talk?"

"Yeah," Eric said. "He's dating our sister. She'd get upset if she knew he wasn't being helpful."

"Wow, I'm impressed. Is she that fierce?"

Eric gave a long whistle and shook his head. "I'd rather face a pride of lions than get on the wrong side of her."

"And does the lion lady have a name?"

"Grace," Eric said with a chuckle.

River chuckled, too. "Saving Grace is taking on a whole different meaning."

A couple of customers walked out of the market. River and Eric waited for a while, until River became restless. "He's been in there a long time."

"Let's give him another five minutes, and if he doesn't return by then I'll go inside and check it out."

Five minutes went, and Eric was about to leave the truck when Dioko emerged from the market. He jogged across the street again and came to sit back in the pickup. He lay his hands on the steering wheel and clenched it hard but said nothing.

"Something's up," he eventually said. "I got to chatting with Ike and asked why the shelves were emptier than usual. I asked if he had a bulk purchaser."

River leaned forward. "And what did he say?"

"Not much to start with. He said that supplies hadn't arrived. Dismissing it. But when I insisted, he got aggressive," Dioko said. "Ike is such a cool guy. He goes out with my sister, Grace."

"I told River about Grace," Eric said. "And yes, Ike never gets annoyed."

"No one has ever asked until now, I presume," River said. "Do you think Ike will tell whoever is buying in bulk from him that you've asked questions?"

Dioko shook his head. "Unlikely. He almost certainly doesn't want the buyer to know that his habits have attracted interest."

"Shame we can't follow that guy," Eric said.

"He would probably spot you quickly," River said. "This place isn't that busy."

Eric turned toward River with a grin. "This isn't New York or Washington, DC. You don't follow with your car. In Africa, you track. You learn to recognize the trail people and animals leave behind. Each is unique—man, truck, beast. And then you find them."

River slapped her forehead with the palm of her hand. "How silly of me. I should know better, but it means having someone watch the store all day without being noticed and then spotting the right customer."

"I reckon this guy who buys for the compound won't take delivery through the front but from the back, and he'll shop very early in the morning or late at night, just before or after the store has closed," Dioko said.

Eric nodded. "That's a good point. So he comes in before 8:00 a.m., when the store opens, or after 9:00 p.m., when it closes. By the way, there is a house under construction at the back of the market."

"Except that no one is working on it at the moment," Dioko added.

"So someone could keep watch and tell us if there is very early or late activity?" River asked.

"But it means working with someone we can trust, someone who has plenty of time on his hands," Eric said.

River sat back for a moment and then leaned between the two front seats so she could see the two men's faces.

"I have someone in mind, and I think it'll work."

Chapter 12

The river looked sluggish and silty from where he sat. Kruger needed space to think, and nothing helped as much as being alone in nature.

He'd driven his Jeep to the Limpopo and arrived as the sun was setting. He remained motionless and waited to see which animals would turn up that evening to drink. The river was just deep enough at this point to accommodate hippos. Their loud grunts told Kruger that they were jostling for position, the strongest of the lot vying for the best spot in the mud—not so dissimilar to what happened in DC. Different mud, same struggle.

Kruger had been working all day on the arrival of the next shipment and hadn't yet managed to get hold of Davis. The idea of combining two large shipments together was madness. He suspected that Davis knew it, but it must have suited his agenda, and Kruger was now wondering whether that agenda still had him as the CIA's key contact in Africa.

Movement on the right side of the truck attracted Kruger's attention. Something was advancing in the tall grass, heading for the riverbank—alone. Kruger looked through the night-vision binoculars he'd brought with him and saw that the leopard was moving slowly, almost certainly stalking a prey. He took a moment to follow the feline until he couldn't see him anymore and then put down his binoculars.

He checked his watch—7:30 p.m. The two men he'd sent out to the Outpost lodge should have called him by now. Kruger never took calls outside the compound unless there was an emergency, and he never went into Masisi. It had been bad enough that the woman he'd used to follow River in Johannesburg and then check on her room at the Holiday Inn had been interrupted by room service, but now, he wanted to have a conversation with Swift himself and do away with her. A storm was brewing, and he needed to give it his full attention. He turned the Jeep around and made his way back. Even in the dark, he knew the way to his compound, so he didn't need to switch the vehicle's headlights on.

The satellite phone started to vibrate in its holder. Kruger accelerated and picked it up.

"Two of our men are in trouble," Botha said. "One ended up in the Masisi emergency medical station. The other is in jail, although not for long."

Kruger slammed the wheel of the car hard. "Fuck. When were you told?"

"A few minutes ago. One of the police guys called me."

"And the medical station?"

"The police guy told me. Our man will know he needs to shut up."

"They'll think he's a poacher," Kruger said. "How bad is the injury?"

"According to my source, his right shoulder is completely shattered, and his left leg is bad. It'll take months for him to walk again."

"I'm ten minutes away. We'll talk then."

I should have known better.

Kruger muttered profanities all the way back to the compound. He was starting to see why Clery had found it hard to control the woman. River Swift was the gift that keeps on giving. Perhaps being deployed had sharpened her wits and made her able to stay one step ahead of him. The two men he'd sent were good, and it shouldn't have been a problem collecting her from the Outpost.

On the approach to the gates of his compound, Kruger flashed his lights once. He'd chosen a good location, hidden inside a large stand of evergreen trees, facing some flatlands from which you could see a plane for miles. The gate opened, and he rushed the Jeep in. He parked in a spot reserved for his vehicle and walked straight into his office.

Botha was already waiting for him there. He had a look on his face that told Kruger they were in for a disagreement. "Who's the woman they tried to abduct?" Botha asked.

Kruger knew there was no point in pretending she wasn't a problem or hiding her identity. "Jason Wayne's former girlfriend."

"The reason why we had to terminate Clery?"

Kruger ran his hand over his buzz cut and nodded.

"What the fuck is she doing in South Africa? And in Masisi?" Botha asked.

"Looking for answers, I believe. She knows about her parents," Kruger said.

Botha gave Kruger a dirty look. "You should have said. This is a fuckup of the first order. We've got two bloody shipments arriving from this moron who thinks he runs the CIA."

"I'm not a complete idiot, and I know she's a pain in the ass," Kruger said, trading an equally venomous look with Botha. "I don't have to tell you about all I do to keep this operation afloat."

"You do when it creates a security shitstorm," Botha replied through gritted teeth.

"She wasn't supposed to escape tonight's kidnapping."

"Then you underestimated her," Botha spat.

Kruger clenched his fist and resisted the urge to throw a punch. Botha was right, and Kruger had chosen him as his number two for that reason. He never shied away from speaking his mind, no matter how tough the message was.

"She's a former Air Force medic, right?" Botha continued.

"She was deployed three times."

Botha took a short breath, then exhaled. "We need her out of the way. Why would you want to speak to her?"

"I need to know who else is aware of the botched assassination in the DRC."

Botha thought for a moment. "So what? It was a long time ago. Matondo is now known for the maniac he is."

"Don't you think the CIA will want to keep a hand in this?" Kruger asked.

"I've been thinking about the CIA," Botha said. "I don't like how reckless Davis is becoming. This double shipment business feels like a last order to me."

"You mean he wants to sever ties with us?"

Botha nodded. "Davis has no loyalty. He probably thinks he can handle Matondo on his own."

"That's a stupid assumption," Kruger said.

"When has stupidity ever trumped greed?"

"You mean that he wants more out of the armament trade? That's not possible."

"He's got his eyes on the rare minerals that the DRC produces. He knows which tech companies are willing do anything to get their hands on cheap coltan, and he sees this as a way to make more money fast," Botha said, disgust in his voice.

"We need to know what Swift knows," Kruger insisted. "I want the list of all the people she's spoken to. If it's true that Davis wants us out of the way, then he might use them or even her to leak compromising information."

Botha sat down on one of Kruger's office chairs, head bowed, thinking. "That's a good point," he said after a moment. "He could argue that we're burned out and need to be let go."

"Davis had one of the Doctors Without Borders staff followed and then intimidated. Swift was there, too. I got pissed off with Davis, and he said he wanted to stop this guy from talking, but I now wonder whether that was true."

Botha frowned.

"It could have been a way of warning her that I had people with eyes on her. He needs her to be careful enough that I don't surprise her, yet confident enough that she is ahead of me. If she succeeds in bringing me down, it's a neat way of not engaging the CIA."

"He would have to route information to her in a way that she wouldn't find suspicious," Botha said as he leaned forward, his elbows on his knees.

"Someone told her this compound is in Masisi. Even the locals don't know about it," Kruger said.

"The Bushmen know."

"The Bushmen don't talk. They don't care about our world as long as we don't interfere with their way of life."

Botha thought for a moment and then said, "You're right. It's taken her too little time to find out that we run our operation from here. There are so few people who know our location. The leak comes from the United States, not South Africa."

Both men fell silent. The only sound was the light buzz of the ceiling fan.

"We need to let her come to us and show us her hand," Botha said. "We don't try to kidnap her again. We just observe and see who she's working with."

Kruger eventually nodded. Botha was right. Now that they'd agreed that someone was leaking information to River, they needed to sit tight and wait. Sending his men to get her had been premature. Kruger cursed inwardly. He should have been more patient.

Botha got up, since Kruger didn't seem to have any more to say. He went to the door and said over his shoulder before leaving the room, "I'll deal with the guy in the medical station. Shame. We could have done with one more man."

"And the other one?" Kruger asked.

"He should be out of jail and on his way. I'll speak to him so that I know exactly what happened."

Botha left, closing the office door behind him. They hadn't argued as aggressively as they sometimes did, and that was a warning. Botha was concerned and had cut through his anger to get to what mattered—preserving their position in the shadowy world of trafficking.

A faint knock at the door stopped Kruger from going to his desk.

"Enter," he said.

The door half opened, and the compound's cook stuck his head through the opening.

"You told me to alert you when I go to town, and I'm alerting you. I need to go and fetch more supplies."

"Do you have to?" Kruger grunted.

"More men are arriving in the next couple of days. So yes, I do."

"Can you avoid going to your usual supplier?" Kruger asked.

The cook didn't ask why. He never questioned Kruger.

"For some of the dry supplies I can. But when it comes to meat, I don't have a big enough refrigeration unit in the truck."

He would have to feed a dozen men who liked their meat and who were expecting to be treated well in the compound. Although most of them had been in the military, they weren't on a mission yet and couldn't be expected to survive on rations.

"I always go very late. After the shop's closed and there are few people on the road."

"The guy expects you?"

The cook hesitated but then said, "I order a day or so before."

"Change your pattern," Kruger said. "Go there early, before he opens his shop. Call him tonight."

The cook nodded his assent, and then Kruger waved him off, reflecting on how little it might take to bring down the well-oiled machine that was his organization. Davis was untouchable in the United States, at least for the time being, or until Kruger had more solid proof that Davis had started to play a double game. But Swift was only a few miles away, and he intended to get her to talk when she showed up. She'd tell them all she knew, and then she'd be glad when the final bullet came.

A string of Jeeps and SUVs was parked near the main entrance of the Outpost when River arrived. She loosened her shirt and covered the two guns she'd been carrying since she relieved Kruger's men of them. Dioko and Eric dropped her near the gate, and Eric got out of the pickup to walk the last few yards with her.

"I'll call you tomorrow morning," River said.

Eric smiled. "And I'll get the supplies we talked about a few moments ago."

He waved as he got into the truck, and the vehicle disappeared into the night.

Just then, Sarah approached River from the main building. "We now have a full house," she said. "The rangers are back, and so are all our visitors."

"Should I go and meet everyone?"

"It's up to you," Sarah said. "They've had some food already, and we have a buffet going."

River looked past Sarah toward the building adjacent to the reception area, where people were gathered and chatting. "I realize that we need to talk."

Sarah looked toward the crowd and said, "I haven't had any food, so perhaps we can grab a plate and find a quiet corner."

"Let's go," River said, moving farther inside the spacious building.

Sarah introduced River to the lodge rangers. They made small talk with them for a moment and then went to the buffet. They helped themselves to food and found a quiet place to sit, away from a group of visitors who were still amazed at witnessing a pride of lions on the hunt.

"What did these men want with you?" Sarah asked before she touched her dinner.

River took a couple of mouthfuls before she said, "I am after an arms dealer who tried to hurt someone I care about a lot."

But this time, River didn't give Sarah the full story. She didn't know whom she could trust. She could perhaps take a gamble on Reggie's cousins Dioko and Eric, but not on Sarah. Sarah seemed to buy River's much edited version of the story, but her eyes seemed to indicate that she also believed it was mad.

"Do you know the two rangers who came to help?" Sarah asked.

"Not really," River said as she finished her meal. "They picked me up at the airfield and said I could call if I needed help."

"But then why go with them to the clinic and police station?"

"I thought the police would want to know what happened," River said.

"Did they?"

"They didn't want the details," River said, a little ashamed at the lie.

Sarah shrugged. "I'm not entirely surprised."

River had noticed that one of the rangers had been eyeing her for a while. He finished the conversation he was having with one of the visitors and started to head her way. Walking with a confident swagger, he grinned as River made eye contact with him briefly.

River turned to Sarah and said, "How about you lead me to my room? I don't want to have to tell one of your star rangers to get lost."

Sarah rolled her eyes. "I should have known. Let's get you to your cabin. We've had enough drama for one night."

Both women got up and walked out of the main building toward cabin 11. Sarah led the way with her flashlight, but the sky was clear, and the moon helped with its glow.

"The hyenas must have gone," River said.

"One of the rangers said that they saw the clan near the stream below. They'll be waiting for small animals to come and drink."

They arrived in front of River's room. River noticed that the bloodstain left by the wounded man had disappeared. Sarah explained, "I cleaned it right away with bleach. That covers the smell of blood and won't attract any unwanted guests."

"Thanks for that and for being discreet."

Sarah let herself into River's room to check that the net surrounding the main balcony was shut and that the ceiling fans were working. "You need anything, you call me."

She pointed to a walkie-talkie that stood on the bedside table. "I'm on channel 6. Don't call reception."

"Will do," River said.

Sarah left. River went to lock her bedroom door and sat on the bed for a moment. The room was impressive—dark wood, cream-colored linens, cream and dark-brown rugs. A large sofa with matching armchairs occupied a sitting room overlooking the savanna and the bush. Multicolored cushions had been thrown on the bed, the sofa, and the chairs, giving the place a sense of deep comfort. African masks and embroidered pieces of cloth hung on the wooden walls. River loved it. Her heart tightened unexpectedly. Her parents would have loved the place, too. She pushed the sadness away to concentrate on what she needed to do next—call Orson.

She fished her burner phone from her pants pocket, then unzipped the canvas that sealed the balcony during the night and slid outside. The air was cool and pleasant. In the distance she could hear hippos' rubbery grunts and groans. She walked right to the edge of the balcony and leaned against the railing. She found Orson's number and pressed the Call button.

The phone rang a few times, and Orson picked up. "I'm glad you called," he said. "I've got some news."

"Already?"

"I may like to pray and meditate, but it doesn't mean I'm not efficient," Orson said with mock vexation.

"Unfair assumption," River said with a smile in her voice. "I was in fact about to ask you to help me with something rather difficult."

"Now my interest is piqued. Ask away."

"You go first," River said. "What you tell me may change my request."

"I've settled into the Exodus Guesthouse's best cabin. The owner insisted, and I'm glad he did, because I am in full view of the Exodus airstrip nearby. I asked him about incoming aircraft, and he told me they are expecting two planes the day after tomorrow or a day later—the biggest planes the airfield can accommodate."

"You think it's the arms shipment Kruger is expecting?"

"I'm obviously not a betting man, but if I were, I'd say yes."

"That's not very clever to be sending two planes that will be noticeable by their size and number."

"Agreed. That intrigued me, too. So I asked the owner the question. He said it's never happened before."

"How long has this guy owned the guesthouse?"

"Years, by the sound of it. He's lived there ever since the place was built."

River frowned and walked a few paces along the balcony.

"That's got to be significant," River said. "Kruger might be ready to pack it in and move the compound somewhere else."

"Possible," Orson mused, "but I wonder who decides when shipments are sent and therefore arrive."

"That's a good question," River said. "Kruger is protected back in DC, and I'm certain the CIA has something to do with it."

"The CIA? Well, that would make sense. Maybe his handler helped him flee the United States and prevented him from getting Interpol's red notice slapped on him."

"As long as Kruger is useful to the CIA, he'll get away with murder—literally, unfortunately."

"But there must be a point of no return, right?"

River stopped pacing. "I haven't been able to find anything on Kruger's handler, but Angela gave me a name."

Orson fell silent, then his voice trembled when he asked, "What did Angela say?"

"Someone called Dexter Law came to visit my parents."

River could feel the change in mood on the other end of the line. Orson was struggling. "Did he ask for help on a specific project?" he managed to say.

"Angela didn't know for sure, but I'm guessing coltan was involved."

River resumed her pacing. An unmistakable sound rolled over the plain and stopped her in her tracks—a lion was roaring his preeminence. A deep rumble that echoed along the savanna for miles.

"Are you still there?" Orson asked.

"Sorry," River said, refocusing on her conversation. "I was listening to the sound of the wild. It always gets to me."

"I know. It gets to me, too, whenever I come back to Africa after a trip away."

"Still, distraction, even if warranted, isn't a good idea. I need to focus on this mission."

She heard a slight hesitation in Orson's silence. Perhaps the word "mission" sounded odd or had a different meaning for him. "Maybe Kruger's CIA handler is in it for himself," she added.

"But why make the deliveries so noticeable?" Orson said slowly.

"You're right. Why attract the attention to trades that you'd normally like to keep hidden?" River couldn't quite get her head around it. "I need to sleep on that one," she admitted.

"So do I," Orson said. "Now, what is it you wanted to ask of me?"

River told Orson about the two men who'd come to the lodge and how the rangers got involved. She told him about the grocery store. Orson let her finish, then asked, "How trustworthy are the medics and the police?"

"Dioko and Eric didn't say, but I think it's fair to assume that Kruger already knows that his men have failed to catch me and that he knows where they are."

"So now he is two men down," Orson said.

"At least one," River replied. "The guy with the shoulder and leg injuries won't be using his right arm anytime soon."

"But how many men do you think Kruger has?"

"I really don't know, but what I do know is that with two shipments arriving at the same time, he needs all his team around him and perhaps a few more. That in turn means looking after these men, and that means—"

"More supplies," Orson said.

"Exactly right. There is only one grocery store in Masisi, and if Dioko is correct, the shopkeeper is nervous. It's worth keeping an eye on that store. Someone will soon be collecting a large order of food."

"I can do that," Orson volunteered without River's having to ask. "I'll find a Jeep or a pickup truck I can rent for a day and squat in the store's vicinity."

"I couldn't check this out, but Dioko said there is a small building under construction at the back of the store, except that no one is working on it."

"I'll find a way and let you know if I spot anyone. What time does the shop open, by the way?"

"Opens at 8:00 a.m. and closes around 9:00 p.m."

"I'll get there in the morning," Orson said.

"Thanks for joining the team."

"I've done very little so far, and I have my motivations, too. I want to find Angela."

Orson hung up, and River stayed a little longer outside on the balcony. Clouds had now gathered in the sky. Rain and perhaps thunder would soon come. She returned to the safety of her room and closed the canvas that was protecting the balcony tightly.

She checked the room thoroughly, including the cabinets and the bathroom, for unwanted visitors. River didn't fear snakes, but she'd acquired a healthy respect for them. Her mother had taught her how to handle a snake as well as the dos and don'ts of living in harmony with wildlife. River's mom once let a file snake live around their property because the large beast was not only nonvenomous but also hunted venomous snakes, including cobras and puff adders. The thought made River smile. Her father and brother hadn't been impressed with their new pet, but no one dared admit they were scared.

The room was clear, and she was starting to unpack her duffel bag when her burner phone rang. Eric was calling.

"Is everything all right?" she asked.

"Depends on what you mean by 'all right.' Dioko and I are fine, but the same can't be said about the guy we brought to the medical station. Someone walked in without being spotted and put a bullet through his head. The guy who was supposed to be in jail has escaped."

River sat on the bed, taking it in. "Now, hostilities have truly started," she said. "There is still time for you both to pull out."

"Dioko and I talked it through. We're in. It's time we stood up to people who are selling weapons like AK-47s to poachers."

River nodded. "Okay. Then get ready. I might have news by tomorrow about who's buying from the grocery store to feed these men."

Chapter 13

The ringing of one of her burner phones forced River to wake from a deep sleep. She felt for the device on the bedside table and sat up abruptly.

"I know I woke you up, but you need to hear this," Orson said in a low voice.

"Where are you?" River asked, now fully awake.

"At the back of the grocery store we talked about. And guess what?"

"Someone has come early to purchase a lot of food?"

"And I mean a lot of food," Orson whispered.

"When will they be done loading?"

"Not sure—maybe another ten minutes or so."

"Okay, I need to make a call. Call me back when the guy leaves."

River took a quick drink of water from the bottle she'd placed on the bedside table and dialed Eric's number. She was expecting to get his voicemail, but he answered after only two rings.

"You've got news already?" he said, alert.

"A truck has come to the grocery store and has started loading a lot of food."

"It's before opening—it's got to be one of Kruger's men."

"Got to be," River said. "What do you want to do?"

"Dioko is here. There are only two ways of getting out of Masisi if you're going toward the Limpopo River. We'll split up and then follow his tracks."

River was about to ask how they'd do that, but the question could wait. "I'll call you as soon as I know the truck is on the move."

"Sounds good." Eric hung up, and River waited, her eyes riveted to her phone. Ten minutes went by, but nothing happened. She checked her watch a couple of times, got out of bed, and went to the heavy canvas that sealed off the balcony. She unzipped it and stepped outside. The sky was still clear with a smattering of clouds.

Twenty minutes went by, and River started to worry. She didn't want to call and reveal Orson's presence. She was about to call Eric and report the worrisome lack of news when Orson called back.

His voice was still low as he said, "The truck has just left. I'll wait a while before I leave."

He hung up, and River called Eric. "The truck has just left."

"We're on it," he said, then hung up.

River pushed the canvas all the way out to open the entire balcony. She hadn't had time to take in the view. The balcony stretched several feet over the cliff edge. Below, in the gorge, the brook had swollen after an unexpected downpour and meandered among large trees and shrubs. She went to the edge, leaned against the railing, and spotted the small gravel path she'd taken the night before to surprise the men sent by Kruger. Just as she suspected, the path followed the rim of the cliff and led to River's cabin.

Her burner phone rang again, bringing a smile to her lips. Karen was calling.

"You made it to Jo'burg?" River asked.

"Even better than that," Karen said with the sound of engines in the background. "Danny rented a Cessna, and we are on our way. Be with you in a couple of hours, maybe a little more. Reggie's cousins are picking us up, and—" The rest of the sentence was lost in the roar of an engine.

"I wish I could be there, too," River shouted, not certain Karen could hear her. The line went dead, and River went back inside. She chose a pair of camo-patterned slacks and a neutral beige T-shirt, took a quick shower, and got dressed. The burner phone rang just as she was about to make a cup of coffee.

"Dioko got lucky," Eric said. "He's the one who picked up the trail of this guy's truck."

"Where are you?"

"I'm pulling back. Too many vehicles and the guy will spot us. In any case, I'm picking up Reggie and the rest of your crew in a couple of hours."

"I wonder how far Kruger's compound is," River couldn't help but ask, suspecting it was an impossible question to answer.

"I've been thinking about that. My guess is that the place can't be too close to the river because it would be too close to animal activity. The San people might complain if the compound encroached on their hunting territory. On the other hand, some vegetation will be good because it'll help hide the building."

"How far is the Mozambique border from Masisi?"

"Around thirty miles, but with a lot of lodges and settlements along the small river that flows just below the Outpost. So the ideal area is closer to Masisi than you would expect. Maybe ten miles."

"Dioko will call back as soon as he's spotted the place?" River asked.

"That's the idea. Why?"

"It's only five thirty in the morning," River said. "Daylight will break in an hour. I wouldn't mind taking a look at the place before the entire Kruger contingent arrives. I understand two aircraft loaded with weapons are arriving in the next couple of days."

There was a short silence, and then Eric said, "I see your point. I've got a tracker on Dioko's truck. I'll come and pick you up, and we can follow at a distance. But we're not moving closer unless Dioko tells me it's okay."

"I'll be waiting at reception."

River made coffee in the kitchenette at one side of her cabin. She helped herself to some small bananas from the fruit basket that had been left in her room and relished their taste. She then picked up her backpack and made her way to the reception area just as Eric pulled in. Sarah wasn't around, and another young woman was manning the desk. River got into Eric's truck as unobtrusively as she could, then they drove off. Eric's attention was focused on his cell phone, watching the tracker on Dioko's truck.

"Dioko's truck hasn't moved for a few minutes," he said.

"How far is he from Masisi?"

Eric smiled and then said, "Eleven miles."

River returned the smile and said, "And no one has ever noticed this place?"

"As I said, it's in a zone of little interest, and I can see from the tracker that it's close to a large bunch of trees. This guy Kruger knows what he's doing."

"I'm sure of that."

"Is he going to come after you again?" Eric said, serious.

"I'm counting on it."

Eric glanced at her without hiding his surprise. "You recall what happened to the guy we brought to the emergency medical station, right?"

"You mean a bullet to the head?" River said. "How can I forget? I've seen what he had his people do to someone who didn't deliver for him in DC, and that was far worse."

Eric looked dubious.

"Kruger had the guy tied to a chair in his office, and Kruger's thugs set fire to the man's house. In my book, that is worse."

"Shit. That's gruesome."

"I know," River said, her heart starting to pound in her chest. She couldn't now avoid wondering what had happened to her parents. She hadn't thought about the images Angela had sent, either. River opened the window fully and turned toward the outside, breathing deeply to control the bile that had risen to her throat.

Eric slowed down a little but didn't ask. River settled back in her seat after a moment. It wasn't yet time to speak to Eric about her parents' murder. Eric's cell rang, and he put it on speakerphone. Dioko started speaking in a language River didn't recognize.

"I'm with River," Eric said.

"I was saying that I've gotten as close as I can. The place is well hidden, and the only reason I spotted it is because the food truck went into it."

"Why can't you get closer?" River asked.

"It's grassland all around. I'd be happy to get closer at night but not as daylight is about to break. I'm guessing this guy Kruger must have some of his men watching the perimeter."

"We're not very far away," Eric said. "River wants to have a look at the place."

"Then stop your truck now. I need to turn around anyway and will meet you where you are. We can get close on foot."

Eric found a clump of shrubs big enough to conceal his pickup. They waited a few minutes, and the sound of another vehicle told them Dioko must be approaching. They waited a little longer, until Eric saw his brother's pickup almost next to his on the tracking app.

River and Eric got out. Dioko parked alongside them. Eric got a rifle out of the back of his pickup.

"Do you have a spare?" River asked as she was putting her cell phone in her pocket.

He looked a little surprised and then remembered.

"Ex-military," he said. "Yes. I have."

Dioko had taken his own rifle out of the back of his truck. Eric handed River a Winchester 70 and a box of .458 Winchester Magnums.

"I guess you know how to use one of these," he said.

River nodded. "I knew that rifle before I joined the Air Force. I saw it chambered with the .458s and used against charging animals. Dad didn't like the idea, but he got a Ruger 77 after he encountered a very angry buffalo once."

She picked up the Winchester and the ammunition with confidence. They loaded their weapons and were on their way. From now on, no one would speak; they would communicate only through hand signals. Dioko led the way, and Eric, for security, brought up the rear.

They walked through the bush for fifteen minutes, then Dioko lifted his hand, and they all stopped. He pointed in the direction of a clump of trees in the distance and took a small pair of binoculars out of his jacket pocket. He handed these to River. She brought the binoculars to her eyes, adjusted the focus, and scanned the terrain.

River instinctively dropped to one knee, and the two men followed suit, giving her a concerned look—had she spotted someone coming? She gave them a thumbs-up, and they relaxed a little. River stashed the binoculars in her pants pocket and looked around. She found a stick and started drawing a shape in the gravelly soil.

She drew a rectangle, then several circles, some with Xs, others with plus signs. She took the binoculars out of her pocket and then returned to observing the compound and its surroundings. Eric and Dioko paid attention to what River was doing and seemed to understand what she was trying to achieve.

Once she'd finished with the map, she took a picture of it with her cell phone. Dioko pointed in the direction of the compound, indicating they might be able to get closer. River thought for a moment, and then she nodded. They stood halfway up and proceeded to walk, hunched over, Dioko again leading the way. They went slowly, each looking for signs of movement around them.

And then River saw it—a small box that had been planted in the ground, most likely sending out a barely visible laser beam that would trigger an alarm back in Kruger's compound. She lunged and grabbed Dioko's shoulder, pulling him back. He lost his balance and fell backward, his legs shooting in the air in the direction of the trip wire. River wasn't sure his foot had missed it, so she simply whispered, "Invisible trip wire. Must go *now*."

They turned back and started to run, still hunched over, hoping they wouldn't displace the long grass so obviously as to attract attention. If they'd triggered the alarm, they'd know within moments. When Dioko and Eric felt they were far enough away, they stood up and ran hard to their trucks. No one spoke. The two men climbed into their respective pickups. River joined Eric, and they left the site fast.

They were well on their way to Masisi when Eric dialed Dioko's phone. "We need to pick up Reggie and his friends."

"We need to talk, too," Dioko replied.

"We do," River said, "and it's not good news."

River and Eric stayed silent until they reached the fork in the road. One way led to the Outpost, the other to the Mutele-Masisi Airfield.

"What do you want to do?" Eric asked.

It wasn't reasonable, but River asked anyway. "What's the chance of someone surveilling the airfield?"

"Very small but not zero."

River was torn. It would be so good to welcome her team.

"Let's get to the airfield," Eric suggested. "I'll give the terrain a good check. If I have any doubts, don't get out of the truck."

River smiled in agreement. "Let's do that."

Eric parked in the spot he'd selected the day before. He stepped out, raised his binoculars to his eyes, and walked around to the pickup's front bumper. He took his time to survey the perimeter around the airstrip. Dioko had already parked. He waited a moment, then Eric dropped the binoculars and nodded. River got out, and Dioko followed. He took some small bottles of mineral water out of a cooler he kept in the back of his pickup and handed them out. They took much-needed sips.

"Were you worried I'd triggered the compound's alarm?" Dioko asked.

River shook her head. "The property has a drone platform. They would have launched one on us if you had."

"You saw that?" he asked, surprised.

"That's part of my training," River said. "I might be a medic, but I used to be dropped in the middle of battlefields. I'm trained to detect any surveillance activity that may compromise my mission."

"I guess the compound is well protected," Eric said.

River let her body slump against the side of the truck as she said, "It's not a compound. It's a fortress—surveillance towers hidden in the trees, drone platforms, cameras peppered along the entire perimeter, and then laser trip wires. I reckon two to three security barriers organized in a circle around the building, possibly with different trigger ratios."

Dioko frowned.

"I mean the outer one might be triggered by large objects, to avoid, say, a snake or a bush baby triggering the sensor. Otherwise, there might be an alert overload, but then as you get closer to the building, the object that triggers the sensor gets smaller."

"Could we try to see inside the compound by looking at it from the air? I mean on Google Earth?" Eric asked.

"I tried that when I was still in the States, and I couldn't spot anything. There is a function on Google Maps that allows people to ask for their homes be blurred. I think Kruger did that. He didn't even need his contact in DC to help."

"That means we won't know how many men the compound can hold," Dioko said after finishing his water.

"That's correct," River said. "We won't know with a great deal of accuracy, but we know a couple of things that help. One, the buildings are almost certainly only a single story high. Their roofs don't show over the tree canopy. I'm not sure how easy it is to dig a basement, but the Limpopo River is close, so flooding would be an issue."

Eric and Dioko grunted in agreement.

"And two, the compound's circumference doesn't go beyond the trees, either."

The three of them fell silent, and then Eric ventured an estimate. "The compound needs space for a couple of storerooms—one for the weapons and one for the munitions. Then they need a room for surveillance, and as we know they have a kitchen and dining area. Kruger will get his own space. The rest can be rooms for the men. So I reckon a dozen guys or so—perhaps a few more, but not many."

River considered his assumptions. She remembered how the military encampments in Afghanistan were organized. There might also be a firing range, but she reckoned Kruger's men would simply go somewhere remote in the bush and shoot targets there.

"That sounds about right," she said. "I suspect he doesn't always have a full house, though. It would be too visible. The compound would need a large amount of supplies on a regular basis and would eventually be noticed by the locals. But it will be at full capacity after the armaments arrive and at its lowest capacity after the shipments are delivered to their ultimate destinations."

"What's Kruger's background?" Eric asked.

"I've got someone investigating that, but he's got to be military. He had that look about him."

Eric and Dioko exchanged a glance. "You've met the guy?" Dioko asked.

"I did, but when I turned up, he had a bullet in his thigh and wasn't much of a threat," she said, omitting a crucial fact: The bullet that hit Kruger had been delivered by one of Clery's men on the assumption that Clery had instructed him to shoot. But it was River who had cleverly conned the hit man into believing that his instructions came from his boss.

"If he is ex-military, you know what that means?" Eric asked. He didn't look scared by the prospect. He was just pointing out the facts.

"He'll be surrounded by ex-military or mercenaries with a similar background."

"Without a doubt," Eric said.

"Not all ex-military are quality personnel," River said.

"Still, they're trained, and that makes a difference to the way we approach things."

River was about to ask what Eric meant, but the distant sound of a plane engine interrupted them. They all turned toward the south, where the Cessna would be coming from. River hadn't returned the binoculars Dioko had handed her, so she fished them out of her pocket and adjusted the focus to get a clear view of the approaching aircraft.

The early morning thermals were gentle, and the plane hardly rocked. She thought about Reggie's cross-Atlantic experience and was grateful that this leg of the journey would have been kinder to him. Dioko stepped closer to her, and she returned the binoculars to him. She shielded her eyes with her hand and followed the Cessna's approach until it landed.

River suspected that Danny was the captain and on his own mission to impress Karen. The landing was impeccable. Hardly a bump as the Cessna touched down on the grass runway, with a hint of dust rising from the wheels when he applied the brakes. Despite the sobering news about the impregnability of Kruger's compound, River couldn't help but smile. Friends were arriving. She'd be able to discuss tactics with them and, more importantly, be surrounded by their warmth.

The plane came to a stop at the end of the airstrip, did a sharp U-turn, and stopped close to the trucks, its wings only a few feet away from Eric's pickup. Danny waved at River from the cockpit and switched the engines off. He then stood up and went to the door, opening it slowly and letting a set of steps slide down to the ground. River walked to it.

"Nice to see you, Danny. Good flight?"

"Hello, River," Danny said with a grin. "Strange to switch from a cargo plane to a Cessna. I kept looking for features I forgot don't exist on these small buzzers."

Karen appeared at Danny's elbow and waved. She climbed down the steps and gave River a bear hug. River hugged her back.

"Great to have you here," she said.

Reggie came down the steps, but instead of saying hello, he dropped to his knees and mock-kissed the ground. He raised a hand, seeking to stop any comments, and then stood up.

"I've crossed eighty-four hundred miles to come to this place. Tell me you know where the SOB is," Reggie said, looking pale and serious.

River hesitated. "I do, thanks to Eric and Dioko."

Reggie sprang up and gave River a hug. His cousins gathered around, slapped his back, and had a few words with him, all smiles.

Karen picked up on River's guarded response. "It's more complicated than you thought?"

A cloud obscured the sun, and River shivered. "Let's get to the Outpost. I'll call Orson, Mike Wilson's brother, and we can talk about what we found out this morning."

There was a rumble of agreement. Eric and Dioko helped Danny off-load everyone's luggage. Danny secured the Cessna, and they got into the trucks—Dioko, Reggie, and Danny in one, and Eric, Karen, and River in the other.

"What did you find?" Karen asked.

"Let me call Orson first, and then we'll chat."

River took her burner phone out of her pocket, found Orson's name, and pressed the Call button. He answered immediately. "I've got news."

"And I've got the team meeting at the Outpost in forty-five minutes."

"I'll be there. Whom should I ask for?"

"Ask for me," River said, and then, "What's your news?"

"Two aircraft are going to be landing at the airstrip next to my guesthouse the day after tomorrow. The date is now certain. The old boy who runs the place has also been told to make himself scarce."

"That's got to be strange."

"You bet. He makes sure there is nothing on the runway before the planes land, like an elephant or a herd of buffalo, and he usually stays there until they depart for the same reason—but not this time."

"So he must have been told exactly at what time they are due to land. Can you prod a little more?"

"Sure. I'll see what I can do."

Orson hung up, and River turned to Eric and Karen. Karen scooted forward and wrapped her arms around the back of the front seat so she could better see.

"We went for a little reconnaissance this morning," River said.

Eric nodded. "Never spotted the place before."

"The compound is well concealed and well guarded," River continued.

"Military grade?" Karen asked immediately.

"I couldn't get close enough, but from what I saw through the binoculars, I'd say 99 percent certain."

"Any idea of how many men the compound can hold and what's their external base defense?"

River couldn't help but smile. This is what she liked about Karen—no longer in the service but with the same sharp mind that had kept her alive when she was.

"A dozen, perhaps a few more, and as external security, a series of infrared trip wires and cameras, fortifications hidden by vegetation with surveillance towers and a drone platform."

Karen gave a low whistle.

"I know," River said. "Not what I was hoping for."

The three of them stayed silent until Eric said, "You're both connected to the military back in the United States. Don't you have someone there who can help with this? A special ops guy who's mounted missions before?"

Karen rolled her eyes, and River froze in her seat.

"I haven't known you long, Eric," Karen said, "but I like your ability to put a finger on where it hurts and press—hard."

"I'm not sure I get it," Eric remarked, wondering what could have been contentious about what he just said.

River took a deep breath and turned away from them. She stuck a hand through her hair and left it there for a moment.

They're right—I need Jason's expertise to pull this off.

River pushed the thought to the back of her mind. She wanted to have everyone in one room. Hear what they had to say. Get the latest intel from Orson and then decide. Her stomach churned. Perhaps she wouldn't get justice for her parents' death or get Angela out of Matondo's clutches after all.

Karen's hand on her shoulder made her jump.

"You haven't mentioned Ariana. So I guess we need to hear what her latest intel is, too. Then we'll have the full picture."

River turned once more to face Karen and Eric.

"I don't think what she tells us will make a difference," River said. "We're facing professionals who use intimidation and murder as a way of life. They're trained for it. I need to step back and think."

Chapter 14

River jumped out of Eric's pickup just as they reached the gate of the Outpost. She walked down the path that led to the gorge below her cabin and glanced back. Karen, Danny, and Reggie were at reception with Dioko and Eric helping. River reached the brook. The hippos seemed a little more sedate. She didn't stay to check and ran back up the path that led to her cabin.

She was about to open the door when her burner phone rang. She took it out of her pocket and looked at the name displayed on the screen. Ariana was calling at 3:00 a.m. DC time.

River answered and immediately heard Ariana's muffled voice. "I'm in trouble."

"Are you still in DC?"

"I am, but not at home. I'm at the office. It's the only place I feel safe, and even here I'm no longer sure. You need to help me."

Ariana had lost the composure River had known her to have ever since she met her. "I'm still in South Africa, so you need to tell me more before I can find the right help for you."

There was a long silence, and River thought she'd lost the connection, but then Ariana said, "I've been followed for the past day or so, and last night when I came home, I knew someone had been in my apartment. Nothing was missing, but certain things hadn't been put back in the right place, as if they wanted me to know—"

"I believe you," River said. "Is this because of what you found out about Kruger?"

"Yes and no. I found out that Kruger is ex-military. He was with the South African Defence Force. He joined in 1986, when South Africa was still under apartheid, and left in 1996, and then there is a gap in the intel, but I got enough to suggest that he'd become a mercenary for a while. He then resurfaced in 2001, after September eleventh, and got involved in arms deals in the Middle East. A lot of this file is redacted, but I think he started providing protection for large shipments that need to sail around Africa without being pirated. Then his business expanded, but that part is redacted, too."

Ariana stopped, as though out of breath.

"How did you manage to get hold of redacted documents?"

"That's the part that worries me," Ariana said, dropping her voice even further. "Documents are being added to Kruger's file, as I said previously, by whoever is on the team when they deem the intel worthy of attention. I didn't notice it to start with, but the file is being updated now very regularly. I mean daily, but I don't know why or by whom."

"You mean someone is feeding you the intel deliberately?"

"It feels that way, but the intel looks genuine."

"That person knows we're after Kruger, and they want to help?" River said.

"And in the world in which Kruger operates, there aren't many do-gooders."

"You feel threatened because you think these people are using you?"

"And when they've finished using me to transfer the intel, I'll be extraneous, if you know what I mean."

"Do you have a lot more information?"

"I do," Ariana said, doubt in her voice, "but I'm not saying more until I feel safe."

"Don't worry. I won't drop you after you've told me everything. I just need to think how best to protect you now."

Ariana remained silent for a moment but then, "I'm scared, River."

"I know, and I would be, too, in your place," River said, her mind racing. "I need to make some calls and will be in touch in the next hour. Call me back if you feel the threat is escalating."

River had barely noticed that she'd entered her room. She sat on the sofa, which faced the vast open space of the South African plains, laid her burner phone next to her, and thought about whom she could trust with Ariana's life.

Only one name popped into her head, and she let her body slump against the cushions.

Jason Wayne.

She cursed. She'd never wanted to be in a position of needing to ask for his help, but now here she was. She'd put her life on the line for him five months ago, but she didn't want to call on him for a return favor. They'd had had a difficult breakup, and for that she was willing to take the blame. But that was water under the bridge, although the lingering uncertainty of whether she would ever want to settle down—and with whom—kept gnawing at her.

She stood up and paced a few times. She should perhaps consult with the others, but she could predict what would happen if she asked—Reggie would want to go back to DC immediately, and he wasn't the right person to keep Ariana safe. Karen would give River her typical I-told-you-so look, and of course she would be right. Orson might offer to go to DC, too, but she needed a man who was willing to use a gun. Eric and Dioko would probably also offer to go, and although she was certain they'd have no qualms about using a gun, she needed them here to guide the team through the African bush.

Her burner phone rang. She rushed to the sofa and picked it up.

"We're almost settled," Karen said. "Where do you want us to meet?"

"Let's meet at my cabin. It's the most isolated one and can be accessed by a small path that runs parallel to the brook below. Give me half an hour, though. I have a call to make."

There was a short delay, then Karen said in a low voice, "Something's up?"

"Ariana is in trouble. I need to find a safe place for her so she can release the intel she's gathered on Kruger. We'll talk later."

"You know what this means," Karen said.

River gave a short exhale. "I'm about to make that call and hope he'll listen."

"He will," Karen said, then hung up.

River fetched her backpack and returned to the couch. She took her cell phone out and laid it on the large coffee table. Her mind was in turmoil. She wasn't concerned about apologizing or admitting she'd made a mistake.

All men make mistakes, but only wise men learn from them.

River remembered the Winston Churchill quotation and hoped she would be wise enough to be as transparent as she needed to be with Jason. Her fear resided not in his reaction. He might think she'd been a fool or be angry at not being told she was after the man who'd tried to frame him. Rather, her fear came from knowing he'd been one of the best Navy SEALs of his graduating class and that the wound he suffered in Afghanistan had robbed him of a career he was made for. He would never be operating at the level he had for the better part of ten years and would never be deployed in special ops again.

River couldn't help but think that the temptation to return to the field and see some action again would be extreme. She'd saved Jason's life in the mountains of Afghanistan. She wouldn't risk it in the plains of South Africa, yet she and Ariana needed him.

She rubbed her hands together, hesitated one final time, and picked up her cell phone. It was almost 3:30 a.m. in DC, but she was sure he would answer her call. She found his number in her contacts list and pressed the Call button.

The phone rang a few times. It almost tripped into voicemail when a sleepy voice said, "River?"

The first words stuck in her throat, but then she said, "Hey, Jason. I know it's early, but do you have a minute?" She cringed at the silliness of her words.

Jason took a moment to respond. "Where are you?"

"Not in DC," River said, "which is why I'm calling you." She fought the urge to hang up and continued. "Someone is in trouble, and I need your help."

"What sort of trouble?" Jason asked, this time fully awake.

"Before I tell you more about that, I need to come clean about what I've been up to in the past few months."

"Okay," Jason said, sounding more intrigued than surprised.

River closed her eyes and concentrated on telling him about Kruger, Clery, and the note she'd found on Clery's desk containing her parents' names. She expressed her doubts about their being collateral damage in a feud between warlords and her suspicion that they were the ultimate targets of the massacre. She told him that Kruger must be involved and that she managed to track him to South Africa despite his connections in the United States.

Jason listened, interrupting a few times just to let her know that he was still on the line. She then told him about the people who'd helped her find Kruger. She didn't mention Angela but talked about Karen, Reggie, and Ariana.

"And now Ariana is in danger," River finally said. She felt dreadful and amateurish.

"I am almost speechless, but not quite," Jason said. "Shit, River. You sure know how to go after the big guns in style."

"Except that now I'm stuck," River replied, shaking her head.

His response reminded her why she'd fallen in love with him—no recriminations, no I-know-better-than-you attitude. Just an open mind and the desire to make the best of any situation.

"I can get to Ariana and find a safe space for her, but I also want the full story from you. You said you tracked Kruger to a place he owns in South Africa. Where exactly is it, and, more important, where exactly are *you*?"

River wiggled on the sofa, but she couldn't lie. Jason knew her too well; he would figure it out, and she didn't want to damage the trust that had been rebuilt between them.

"Kruger's compound is near the border between South Africa and Zimbabwe as well as the border with Mozambique."

"Good for arms smuggling throughout the entire African continent," Jason said.

"That's right. And he's turned the compound into a fortress—built using the natural cover of bush and trees, with watchtowers, military-grade security, and a drone platform," River said, delaying the inevitable question of why she knew so much.

"And you know this because . . ." Jason said pointedly.

"I've seen it for myself."

The silence was deafening. She waited a moment and said, "I didn't know until Ariana told me that Kruger was ex-military."

She didn't know, but would it have stopped her? Of course not.

"Let me get this straight," Jason finally said. "You're in South Africa, scouting Kruger's compound in the middle of the bush, and are hell-bent on bringing him to justice. At least tell me you're not on your own there."

"I'm not. I've got two rangers helping me out."

"Trustworthy?"

"They're Reggie's cousins."

"Reggie is in South Africa?" River could hear the disbelief in his voice.

"That's right."

"How about Karen?"

"She's here, too."

"The A team from DC." But he wasn't being sarcastic; he seemed amazed at the sheer grit of it all. "Anyone else?"

"The rangers are fully in. They don't like arms traffickers because the traffickers supply poachers with heavy weapons used to hunt game in the national parks."

River omitted mentioning Orson. He'd been an asset so far, but it would mean talking about Angela's rescue, and River was short on time. She needed to call Ariana back.

"So you're going to storm Kruger's compound and force him to admit his crimes?" Jason asked.

River thought about telling him he was basically right, but Jason didn't leave her time for it.

"My God, Riv. That *is* exactly what you're going to do."

"Nope," she replied, one finger up in the air as though he could see her. "That is what I *was* going to do. I'm reconsidering."

"Right," Jason said. She could hear that he must have gotten out of bed and was walking around, almost certainly looking for his clothes. "I'm going to get Ariana and make sure she has somewhere safe to stay, and then let's talk some more. Kruger is also on my target list."

"She's still at her office in DC. The Department of Homeland Security, on 7th Street. I'll send you her cell phone number and warn her you're coming to get her."

"She works for the DHS? How did she get involved?" Jason asked, and then he added quickly, "Scratch that. We'll talk later. Just tell her I'm on my way."

River thought about telling him to be careful, but that would sound patronizing. He knew about risk and how to be as safe as he could. Jason hung up, and she turned to her burner phone.

Ariana answered after the first ring. "Someone came to my office and tried to get in. Thankfully, I changed the passcode this morning, but that means whoever is after me has access to the DHS database," she said in a low, shaky voice.

"I'm sending someone to collect you. He'll find a safe place for you to stay until this whole thing blows over."

"But can I really trust this person?" Ariana said, her voice still trembling.

"You can absolutely trust Jason Wayne. He—"

"The Navy SEAL Kruger tried to frame?"

"And the reason why Reggie got involved. I'm about to text you his cell number. He has the address of your offices, and he is on his way. Call him and follow his instructions. He knows who's after you, and he knows how dangerous the situation is."

"I've downloaded all the intel I got on Kruger onto a USB drive. I'll give that to him."

River hesitated before making her next request, but if she was right, she would flush out another man she was desperate to find.

"Before you leave your office, could you please send an email to yourself, using your work email? The email's subject line should be: "Message to Dexter Law from River Swift." The body of the email should simply say: We need to meet. You know where to find me," River said.

"Who is this guy?" Ariana asked.

"Almost certainly a CIA guy and the one who's having you followed. If he's after me, then it might distract him for a while. I'm sure his name isn't Dexter Law, but he knows why I know that name, and it will scare him like hell."

"I'm doing it now," Ariana said.

River thought about the USB drive. Jason would soon be privy to its contents, and this would drag him deeper into the mission.

"River?" Ariana asked, anxious.

"Sorry. Yes, give the thumb drive to Jase," River said. "And thank you for gathering all that intel."

"One last thing," Ariana said. "I'm almost sure someone wants Kruger dead."

"I think you're right, and the same Dexter Law might well have something to do with that. But for the time being, just call Jason."

River hung up and took a moment to gather her thoughts. She checked her watch and realized that her team was on its way to her cabin. She walked to the far side of the balcony, where it overlooked the brook below, and waited. A few moments later, Dioko appeared on the path. He raised a hand, and River waved back. Then, Karen, Danny, Reggie, and Eric appeared. They made their way to the front door of her cabin. She opened before Dioko knocked, and they all walked in.

Karen, Danny, and Reggie went out onto the balcony, and there was a wow moment when they took in the spectacle—the lush trees immediately below, and then as far as the eye could see, the tall grass of the savanna and then the bush.

Karen turned around and handed a device to River, tipping her head toward the inside of the cabin. River smiled and nodded. Karen and she moved around the room while everyone waited. No one spoke until both women had inspected every light fixture, electrical outlet, and smoke detector.

"All clear," Karen said.

There was a collective sigh of relief. Kruger hadn't yet had time to install listening devices in River's room.

"We're expecting one more person," River said as she invited people to sit.

The large sofa and chairs were enough to accommodate everyone. Eric was the first to sit and asked, "Who's that?"

The others found a seat, and River sat down, too.

"His name is Orson Wilson. His brother, who works for Doctors Without Borders, gave me his contact information, and he's the reason why Eric, Dioko, and I were able to find Kruger's compound."

Another intake of breath from the new arrivals, but this time, it wasn't the landscape that blew them away.

"Shit, Riv. When did you arrive in Masisi?" Danny said.

"We picked her up in the late afternoon yesterday," Eric said, with a hint of pride and a thumbs-up directed at his cousin Reggie.

Reggie was beaming. "You found the SOB. I now don't regret spending fourteen hours being tossed around like a ping-pong ball across the Atlantic."

River's burner phone rang, and she picked it up. Orson hadn't managed to escape the eagle eye of Sarah, the receptionist.

"There's a guy here called Orson who wants to see you," she said guardedly.

After last night's hair-raising encounter, Sarah had obviously decided to be extra careful.

"Thanks for being on the lookout for trouble," River said. "I'm expecting him."

"Who is he?"

"A priest friend of mine."

"Oh, good," Sarah replied, sounding relieved. "Nothing to do with . . . you know, looking for these . . . guys."

Lying is a sin, but River thought she'd have to do a lot more lying than that to complete her mission. "He's here to give me news of a mutual friend."

Sarah hung up, and a few moments later Orson knocked at the door. River opened it and ushered him in. He grinned when he saw the assembled crowd and said, "I'm glad to meet the A team."

River introduced everyone. They shook hands with Orson, and he sat down next to Reggie.

River should have been invigorated by the presence of her friends—old and new—but the weight of what was to come sobered her. Karen picked up on her mood and asked, "Tell us what type of security Kruger's got around his place."

"Good intro," River said. "The compound is a lot more secure than I anticipated. Military-grade equipment. We can't access an aerial view of the place, probably because he's activated a privacy tool that prevents the structure from being visible on Google Earth. I spotted several rings of infrared trip wires around the compound as well as what I think are cameras. I don't think there are any booby traps because of the animals that must cross the land all the time, but perhaps I'm wrong. There is also a drone platform and surveillance towers."

Karen crossed her arms and dropped her chin to her chest. Reggie looked around to gauge the mood of the others, and Orson chewed on his bottom lip.

Danny then ventured hesitantly, "I could fly over Kruger's compound with the Cessna, and someone could take pictures or a video while we're over it," he said.

"I knew you weren't just a pretty face," Karen said with a grin.

Danny chuckled, and everybody seemed to agree it was a good idea.

"I've brought a good camera with me," Orson said. "I can take aerial pictures of the place and make a bunch of them available to circulate."

"I'm not due to return to Johannesburg until late afternoon, and I'm happy to land there after dark," Danny said.

"Then if we're doing this," Orson said, "we'd better try this morning. The thermals will get more intense with the midday sun. The plane will be rocking around too much to take any decent images."

"Ready as soon as we've finished our war-room meeting," Danny said.

Reggie shifted next to Orson and then said, "I probably shouldn't say this, on account of my being a lawyer and technically trying to abide by the law, but how about guns? I mean, we're not going to get the intel we need from Kruger by asking nicely."

Orson raised his hands in mock surrender. "Can't help you there, guys. My order is open-minded when it comes to some of my activities, but I won't be going that far."

"I suppose you're not only talking about hunting rifles but also handguns, MP4s, and the like," Dioko said.

Danny and Karen exchanged a look, and she said, "We haven't come to the party completely unprepared."

"You smuggled weapons into South Africa?" Reggie asked, shocked.

"For starters, I'm clearly not the only one, and it's certainly not on Kruger's scale," she replied. "And anyway, we brought only a few Glocks and ammo and a few other pieces of tactical equipment—night-vision goggles, stab vests, body armor, a few balaclavas to cover our faces, and some camo face paint."

Danny looked proud. Dioko and Eric seemed intrigued. Orson looked serious, and Reggie piped up. "You could have said. I might have found a way of making all this equipment legal."

"True," Karen conceded, "but we didn't have the time, and Kruger might have gotten wind of it."

"A very valid point," Reggie said as he relaxed.

"So we still need more of the heavy stuff," Eric concluded.

River took a deep breath and said, "We're here because of one man who deserves more than just prison time, and I can't thank you enough for joining me in this fight. But we're now sliding fast into illegality. And some of us have been sliding into it quicker than others." River nodded at Karen. "So I need to ask the question. Are you sure you want to cross that bridge? It could cost some of you your jobs and possibly your lives."

Silence fell, and River added, "We will be in real danger if we get caught. Kruger and his men will make us pay dearly for our mistakes."

Karen looked around the room. "I'm speaking for myself, but I get the feeling I'm summing up what we all think. Kruger is a malevolent SOB who's killed, robbed, and trafficked for far too long with complete impunity. He's responsible for"—Karen stopped, locked eyes with River, and River nodded—"the death of River's parents and the kidnapping of Angela Graham. We need to put this right."

If Eric and Dioko were surprised by the additional information, they didn't show it. River was grateful they took it in without further questions.

Eric leaned forward. "I'll get the guns together, but it'll take a day or so. We don't want people talking about it in Masisi or the police knowing. We know that Kruger has contacts there."

"Would I be pushing my luck too far if I asked for explosives?" River said.

Eric raised an eyebrow. "I'll see what I can do, but that might be complicated. Do you really need them?"

"I've been thinking about options when it comes to Kruger's compound, and we won't have the people or the equipment to storm it, even with better weapons, so some explosives might come in handy."

Karen added, "Think about the combination of a munitions cache and a bar of Semtex—'explosive' doesn't even come close to describing what will happen when we detonate the Semtex."

There was a rumble of surprised realization around the room. This was a bold move. River scrutinized every face, and she couldn't detect any lack of commitment. She was expecting Orson to be more reserved, but he seemed to acknowledge that sometimes fire has to be fought with fire. He simply couldn't do the fighting himself, at least not directly.

River caught Karen looking at her questioningly, but she closed her eyes once. This wasn't yet the time to speak about Jason.

"I have one more request," River said. "Dioko mentioned that some San people live in the bush near the Limpopo River. I'd like to meet with them."

Dioko looked surprised but then said, "I can ask the clan and see whether they'd meet with you, but I need to tell them why. They'll discuss it among themselves and come to a decision. They're governed by group consensus, so they'll all have to agree to it. I need to explain."

"I might ask for their help," River said. "I'm sure they don't like poachers or the men who provide them with weapons, and they might be willing to help rid the bush of them."

"They don't use guns. You know that, right?" Dioko said.

"I do, and that's not at all what I have in mind, but I first need to meet them, and they need to get to know me before I ask anything from them."

The meeting was coming to a close, so River stood up and said, "I think we know what our next task is. Let's regroup later, when we're done with our allocated assignments."

Eric, Danny, and Orson were the first to leave—Orson through the cabin's front door and the other two by the path above the brook. They'd rendezvous at the airfield.

Karen and Reggie left after Karen said, "We're going to rent a couple of Jeeps." They, too, followed the path below River's cabin, and when they'd gone Dioko said to River, "You seem to know a lot more than I expected about South Africa."

"My parents and I lived in this country for a while. I liked it very much. It holds some wonderful memories, although the last time I came here and saw my parents, our meeting wasn't that happy."

Dioko said, "I'm sorry, but at least you're back."

"And I enjoyed meeting the San many years ago, so I'm looking forward to it again," River said. She wouldn't dwell on the disagreement with her mom and dad about her joining the military. It now felt irrelevant.

Chapter 15

The night had been long, and Kruger had gone to bed in the wee hours once more. Botha and he had been wrong about one thing: The mercenaries whom he used regularly to deliver the armaments across Africa knew about the location of the compound. He'd always kept the number of these mercenaries to a minimum, favoring the use of his own men, but he sometimes needed the extra manpower for deliveries to hot conflict zones.

He'd spent hours reviewing these men's profiles and still couldn't figure out whether one of them was more likely to have sold him out than another. They all looked solid, were paid way above average, and had been working for him for years. But mercenaries were just that—only in it for the money. They had little loyalty and focused solely on the size of the paycheck. He'd told them he would always match whatever offer a competitor made, but perhaps Davis had found ways of incentivizing them more creatively by dipping into their private lives. A little blackmail always went a long way.

Kruger hadn't slept for more than four hours, but he could still function well on that amount of sleep for a few days. He got dressed after a cold shower, which invigorated his tired body, and walked to the kitchen. The cook was busy with lunch, but stopped what he was doing when Kruger entered.

"Coffee?" he said, reaching for the coffeepot, which never seemed to be empty, day or night.

Kruger nodded, and the cook grabbed a mug that was hanging from underneath one of the kitchen cabinets and poured. He placed the mug in front of Kruger and returned to the meat he was preparing.

Kruger took a long sip and then asked, "You went to the grocery store?"

"Before the sun rose this morning," the man replied without taking his eyes from the lamb he was carving.

"Anything out of the ordinary?"

This time the cook stopped. He thought for a moment, as though following the trip to and from Masisi in his mind, and then he shook his head.

"Nothing, but I noticed that Ike, the owner, was a little rattled."

"Any idea why?"

"He's dating the sister of two of the national park rangers, and he thinks they don't like him. One of the rangers was in his store twice yesterday and bought very little each time."

Kruger took another sip, thinking.

"How well do you know this guy?"

"I don't get friendly with anyone," the cook said. Not defensive, just a statement of fact.

"But could you find out more about this ranger? His name, perhaps?" Kruger asked.

"I could, but it might seem a little odd."

"Do it," Kruger said as he pushed his cup forward.

The cook wiped his hands clean of the fat and blood that covered them, picked up the mug, and topped it off. "I'll ask when I go there next, in a couple of days."

"Make it tonight. Tell him you have some unexpected arrivals."

The cook looked a little taken aback but nodded.

Kruger walked out of the kitchen with his mug and went to his office. He heard Botha's voice in the distance. He was no doubt speaking to the men about the deliveries and what was expected of them. They knew the drill, but Botha was meticulous, and he liked to make sure that every single detail was checked and that the men understood.

The laptop that sat at the center of his desk had gone idle. Kruger ran his finger on the touch pad, and he logged in, still standing. He dragged his chair over, sat down, and checked his emails. Nothing from Davis. He'd called after the conversation he had with Botha, but Davis's burner phone rang without ever connecting. Kruger had only tried twice. He didn't want to arouse Davis's suspicions.

He then turned his attention to Matondo. The last conversation he'd had with him hadn't been as smooth as Kruger had expected. Now, he needed to have Angela Graham put on a flight to South Africa with one of his most trusted men. Kruger dialed Matondo's cell number. The phone rang for a while, and a cranky voice answered, "It's too early. You're gonna have to call back."

"It's almost lunchtime, and I need an answer. The shipments are arriving in the next few days."

Matondo yawned loudly. Kruger heard some background noise that sounded like a woman's voice, no doubt one of Matondo's many mistresses.

"I also want to discuss Angela Graham," Kruger said.

Another yawn and then, "Why don't you come to my place? We could have fun and then you can interrogate the old bag."

"Can't do that," Kruger said calmly. "Our friend in the United States has placed a tight timetable on delivery."

Mentioning Davis focused Matondo. "Did he mention the DRC?"

Kruger wondered why Davis would mention it, but he played to Matondo's ego.

"He did. He likes the way things are going. Notably with the coltan trade." Kruger let that hang, then continued, "Although it would be a shame if Angela Graham was to prove an issue when it comes to expanding the trade offer to more tech companies."

Complete and utter bullshit, of course.

There was a short silence, and then Matondo said, "So do I just kill the bitch or what?"

Kruger pressed his thumb and index finger against the bridge of his nose. Matondo was an animal he found increasingly hard to control. "I know someone in the States who'd like her to be kept in one piece. Let me deal with her, and you concentrate on the next arms shipment and the coltan deal," Kruger said.

The word "coltan" seemed to do the trick again. Matondo was thinking. "I'll send her when the second shipment arrives," he said.

Kruger's anger soared, and he barely managed to control his voice. "I need her *now.* I'm working on a deal with Davis, and I need the woman sent to me ASAP."

Matondo waited before replying. He, too, seemed to try to control himself, and Kruger realized that soon—very soon—he would have to deal with Matondo the way he'd dealt with all the other warlords he'd worked with before: a bullet to the head. He could also sense that Matondo was almost certainly entertaining the same idea. The happy days of collaboration were over, but Matondo still didn't seem to know where he stood with Davis.

"Fine," Matondo grumbled. "She's not worth the trouble anyway."

"I'll contact you again as soon as I have the flights scheduled," Kruger said, hoping he didn't sound too relieved.

Matondo grumbled something in French and hung up.

Kruger checked his watch—11:03 a.m., or 5:03 a.m. in Washington, DC. Kruger changed burner phones and didn't hesitate to place his call. Davis was an early riser, and Kruger didn't mind being his alarm clock. The phone kept ringing, and Kruger waited. There was no voicemail on the phone, and he never sent text messages. Davis finally picked up. "I hope this is worth it," he said, sounding fully awake.

"Speaking to Matondo directly isn't a good idea," Kruger said.

The long silence that followed told Kruger he was right.

"I thought you might be busy with the shipments," Davis said after clearing his throat.

"When has that ever stopped me from taking your calls?" Kruger's voice was cold, and Davis noticed.

"These shipments are important," Davis said. "You're the only one who can deliver in such a short period of time."

Kruger felt like punching the little shit for his nauseating attempt at flattery.

"Are you finally waking up to the fact that I am irreplaceable?" Kruger said with sarcasm. "I know Africa better than any of the goons you employ, Davis. You'd better remember that."

Davis seemed stunned into silence, so Kruger continued. "Matondo holds Angela Graham, and I need to speak to the woman.

I asked him to ship her to me with the first returning plane after the first arms delivery. Don't interfere with this."

Davis cleared his throat again. "If this has to do with the Swift woman—"

"What else?" Kruger demanded. "River Swift is in Masisi, and I want to know how she managed to discover where the compound is."

Another silence. Kruger had shaken Davis even more. Perhaps Davis had expected Kruger to stay silent about the location of his compound being blown. Or perhaps he wasn't yet ready to deal with Matondo directly, still assessing the man's potential.

"Keep me posted," was all Davis said at the end.

The last thing I plan to do.

"I'll call you when the shipments are delivered," Kruger said. He killed the call and pushed the chair away from the desk in anger. Davis was about to jettison him and his operation, which would allow him to burn the Masisi property and foster new alliances in the DRC. Kruger stood up and walked through the compound to try to find Botha.

The door to the munitions cache was shut, but the red light on the electronic panel fitted to the wall indicated that someone was inside. Kruger entered his passcode, and the door unlocked. He pushed it open and found Botha and one of his men taking an inventory of what they had and discussing how they would stock the arriving shipment. Botha raised his faded blue eyes to meet Kruger's, and he understood: His boss needed to talk. He left the other man to it, and he and Kruger walked out. They walked in silence to Kruger's office, got in, and sat in a corner reserved for conversations that should never be overheard.

"Davis is gonna screw us," Kruger said.

Botha leaned forward, elbows on knees, head dropped—thinking.

Botha swore in Afrikaans. "Naaier. How long have we got?"

"It depends on whether Matondo can control himself enough to let Davis believe he can replace us in the DRC."

Botha raised his head and couldn't hold back a bitter and scornful laugh. "Davis is a fucking idiot."

Kruger said, "You were right to doubt him. Now we know, and we can act accordingly."

Botha rose slowly and said, "I'll get ready to terminate our contract with Matondo. I'll get my team prepped."

Kruger got up, too. Botha then hesitated and asked, "How about the Swift woman?"

"I'm gonna let her come to us, as you suggested. She's resourceful. She'll find a way. She might already have found us, and then we'll be ready for her."

"If she's that smart, she won't be on her own."

Kruger shrugged. "True, but she won't be hiring mercenaries or have access to former special ops."

Botha considered this. "She's ex-military," he said, sounding dubious. "She might."

He walked out of Kruger's office, and Kruger returned to his desk. He sat down and pondered what Botha had just said.

River Swift didn't have the deep connections he and Botha had to the special ops pool of talents they recruited from, but her former partner, Jason Wayne, did. According to Kruger's sources, they hadn't spoken since the day he walked out of police custody. But perhaps Kruger should check again. If Swift didn't have the contacts, Wayne could provide her with names of men willing to help, and he had a good reason to want to help his former fiancée. Wayne would be fighting the man who sought to put him behind bars for a crime he didn't commit.

Kruger felt a chill blow through the room. He picked up the burner phone he used to call his US team and punched in the number of one of his best operatives.

Dioko stopped his pickup truck underneath a large tree that would provide shade as the sun rose to its midday zenith. River and he got out, and he went around to the bed.

"We'll do the rest on foot," he said.

He slung his rifle over his shoulder and led the way, advancing slowly yet confidently in the bush. River followed, her eyes and ears on high alert. She recalled that any animal confrontation was swift and unforgiving—bull elephant, buffalo, or lion. But you should never show fear.

Dioko slowed down and then stood still. He moved his head so that he could speak to River but kept his eyes fixed on the distance ahead.

"Gazelles grazing about five hundred feet away," he murmured. "We need to watch out for big cats."

They waited a little while longer, then Dioko started moving again. They walked for twenty minutes or so, then stopped once more. Now, River could see a few rudimentary huts shaped like cones gathered in a semicircle a hundred yards or so away. The familiarity of these struck her. She once visited the San people with her father because he'd been interested in the ways in which they use plants for medicine.

"They don't mind people dropping by, but we need to move into the open and then wait to be allowed in," Dioko said.

Simple good manners are called for everywhere in the world.

An older woman was sitting on a fallen tree trunk next to a hut on the far left. She raised her arm and beckoned them forward. As Dioko and River approached, she smiled and stood up slowly. Dioko waved back and said to River, "I know her well. She's one of the elders in the clan."

When Dioko arrived, they greeted each other with an elaborate handshake and exchanged a few words interspersed with clicks. River thought she recognized one word, *sawubona*—I see you.

River moved closer to the old woman. She didn't know how to perform the greeting ritual, so she simply said, "*Sawubona.*"

The woman's eyes widened, and she laughed, a welcoming, jovial laugh.

Dioko smiled, too. The woman spoke to Dioko, and he translated. "She greets us on behalf of her clan and asks if we'd like to sit with her."

River sat next to the old woman on the fallen tree, but Dioko preferred sitting on the ground. There was another exchange between the San woman and Dioko, and he translated.

"The men have gone hunting, and the women have gone to the water with their children."

"Do they hunt near the Limpopo?" River asked.

Dioko translated again, and the old woman shook her head and replied.

"They have gone to the west, and so have the women. She says that there are bad men who carry bad spirits in the east. They hunt with guns, and her people frown on that."

"The San still hunt with spears and bows. Now, that takes real skill," River said.

The woman nodded at the translation, and Dioko added, "They've been living like this for the past twenty thousand years, maybe more, but perhaps we should ask her about the men in the east."

"Do you think she means the Kruger compound?" River said. "I suppose when the compound is hardly occupied, then it becomes almost invisible, but when Kruger and his men are there, it ripples with bad energy."

Dioko got a little closer and started speaking to the old woman in a low voice. River wondered whether it was part of the belief that bad spirits shouldn't be invoked aloud. She understood why ancient people may not want to talk about the evils of the world.

"She's talking about Kruger's compound," Dioko said. "The San don't like the fact that the men shoot their rifles and sometimes bigger guns—she doesn't know what they are, but the men scare small game and even kill baboons for fun, not for meat."

River looked around at the number of huts. She could see ten of them. Some large, some small, but it seemed to her that the clan was large and successfully living off the land.

"Would her people like to get rid of the men in the east?" River asked.

Dioko looked puzzled, and then he understood and asked the old woman. Her response was animated, and River didn't need a translation.

"But she says the entire clan needs to agree."

"Then tell her that I might have a way and that I also might need their help."

The old woman listened to Dioko with keen interest. She looked at River more closely, touching lightly her forehead and then spoke, serious.

"You must lead the hunt," Dioko translated. "And only you. Then the shadow in your heart will disappear."

River felt a tremor run through her. She had seen it before—a wise man or woman telling you something about yourself you were trying to hide. Her father had always been skeptical about it until he had a conversation with a tribal elder in Rwanda. He never said what the old man had told him, but her father had stopped being skeptical there and then.

The old woman laid a kind hand on River's shoulder, as though she sensed that she'd created some disquiet. River managed a smile and then, remembering the San people's tradition of sharing, took the green bananas she'd stashed in her backpack and offered them to the old woman, who accepted the bunch with appreciation. Dioko winked his approval.

River and Dioko stood up, knowing the old woman would speak with the rest of the clan and that they would reach a conclusion as a group. But once they decided, they wouldn't reverse their decision.

River and Dioko bade the old woman goodbye and waved one last time before entering the bush again.

"I don't see how these people can help," Dioko said.

"They can make nature work for us," River said. She didn't have time to elaborate before Dioko put his finger to his lips and slung the rifle off his shoulder.

The long grass moved to their left, and a rhino took a few steps in their direction. Dioko eyed River with concern as he stood stock-still. River didn't move, either. She had once seen a rhino charge a Jeep and inflict serious damage to the vehicle. The ranger who had been driving walked away unharmed and shrugged off the encounter as bad luck. "Black rhinos are more aggressive than their white counterparts," he said. He didn't seem to care about his vehicle as long as the animal was fine.

His parting advice had been: You meet a rhino in the wild, you stay put; he may think you're a tree. That had sounded a little far-fetched at the time, but not so much now, when River was trying to be just that—as still as a tree.

The animal threw his enormous head to the side. He seemed as surprised as they were. He then turned around and disappeared into the long grass. They waited for a moment, and then Dioko relaxed and shouldered his rifle again.

"White rhino," he said, "much gentler than the black ones. Although when you see one, the rest of the group isn't far away."

"Better than a starving lion," River murmured.

"It's too hot now. The lions are asleep until dusk, then the pride will come out and hunt."

They walked in silence until they reached Dioko's pickup.

"You didn't lose your cool," Dioko said, impressed.

"Not my first time in the bush."

Dioko took his cell phone out of his pocket as they got into the truck. "Nothing from Eric."

"You've got Wi-Fi?" River asked.

Dioko opened the glove compartment and drew out a yellowing, dog-eared piece of paper. River looked carefully at the username and password and entered them on her burner phone and cell phone. The devices connected to Dioko's car's hotspot device, and the cell phone pinged immediately.

Call me. I'm at the DC airport. Ariana is safe.

"No," River cried. She bit her lip and held back the tears. What she feared the most was about to happen—Jason was on his way to South Africa. She ignored Dioko's concerned look and dialed Jason's number using the burner phone, hoping he would pick up.

"Jason Wayne," he said after a couple of rings.

"It's River," she managed to say. "You don't need to come to South Africa to tell me what's on that USB drive."

It sounded all wrong and ungrateful. She should have asked about Ariana first, even though Jason had told her she was safe. More important, she shouldn't give him the impression that she didn't want to see him. She bit her lip and added quickly, before he could reply, "I mean, what if I need more intel from the States?"

"Trust me," he said. "You've got everything you need on that drive."

"Then that's another worry," River said.

The line went quiet and then, "Meaning what? Too much information in one go sounds suspicious?"

River couldn't suppress a brief smile. Jason might have lost the full use of one of his limbs, but his mind was as sharp as ever. "Whoever is supporting Kruger is about to throw him to the lions."

She heard a chuckle. "Are you being literal?"

"Perhaps," River said, not so amused. And then she decided to be honest. "Jase, I don't want you here. I'm gonna be worried if you turn up in Masisi."

"I know," Jason said, "but you're going to have to get over it. I'm sure you've gathered a team of good people who are willing to help mete out justice to this SOB Kruger. But you don't have the knowledge to mount an operation against a guy like him. I've seen his file. He's the real deal, and he knows what he's doing."

"But do you have to come to Masisi to help us?"

The moment River said it, she knew she wouldn't win the argument.

"Are you serious?" Jason said, still calm. "I need to see the terrain. I need to talk to you and your team, and I need to know how good they are with weapons."

"We're not taking on the Taliban."

"Kruger's men are trained, and maybe they don't have the fanaticism the beardos had, but they'll shoot without hesitation, and if they capture any of you alive, you're going to wish they'd killed you in the first place."

"I don't intend to take them on in a full-blown assault," River shot back. "I'm not that stupid. I know we don't have the capacity, but even if you join us, it won't change the odds."

River's heart skipped a beat. Telling Jason he no longer was the operative he once was was brutal, and she felt the pain sear through her for having said so.

She heard a distant sound at the other end of the line. Perhaps a flight announcement; she wasn't sure. The line remained quiet for a little longer, and River thought Jason would kill the call.

Instead, he sighed. "I know you have my best interests at heart, but you need to let me do this. I, too, have a score to settle with Kruger, but I don't intend to get killed while settling it."

"Then you need to let me decide on some of the operational parts, too," River said. "You know the Middle East like the palm of your hand, but not Africa. And I do."

"I'm not coming to South Africa to tell you guys what to do but to help make sure we catch Kruger," Jason said.

"Except that you don't believe he's going to let us catch him, and neither do I."

Silence again, so River continued. "A full-blown assault is out of the question, but that doesn't mean there won't be a shoot-out. I can't imagine Kruger letting himself be caught—"

"And your next question is what?" Jason said. "Do I want to be the one pulling the trigger on Kruger? I can't deny that I'd love to, but I wanted to pull the trigger on a lot of people when I was deployed, despicable men who didn't deserve to live for what they did to their people and ours, and yet I didn't because it was the rule of engagement."

"This isn't a deployment, Jase. The only thing that will stop us from killing Kruger—or anyone else, for that matter—is our conscience."

"True, but more than Kruger, I also want the shitstains who are backing him up to pay."

"Did you get anything from the files Ariana handed over to you?"

"Nothing. I didn't have time to think it through properly, but I could see there are plenty of details about Kruger's operation."

"Enough to get an Interpol red notice slapped on him and enough for most of his clients to want him dead to avoid exposure?" River asked.

"Now that you mention it, that sounds about right."

"Then the people who were backing him up are cutting him loose," River said. "And I have my suspicions that someone is feeding Ariana the details she found."

"And now that she's served her purpose, they want her dead."

"That's my guess," River said.

And who else better to do the job than Dexter Law of the CIA?

River thought about mentioning the CIA to Jason and the message she'd asked Ariana to send, but she wasn't ready to do so in front of Dioko. He and his brother had been more supportive than she'd ever imaged, but the US intelligence agencies were powerful, and perhaps the less the brothers knew about it the better.

"Look," Jason said, "I've gotta get through customs. I'll call you later."

He hung up, and River slumped back in her seat. She had hardly noticed, but Dioko had driven off, and they were on their way back to the Outpost.

"I don't want to pry, but who was that? Someone else joining us?" Dioko said, glancing at River.

"He's the man I told you about. The one Kruger tried to frame back in DC."

Dioko shook his head. "He must be seriously pissed off. I would be."

"He is seriously pissed, and he's also a former Navy SEAL."

Dioko made a whooping sound and grinned. "Maybe I can get a few tips from him about dealing with poachers."

River, riding shotgun, turned toward Dioko. "What do you mean?"

"You know—more effective ways of getting them to tell us who they work for. That sort of thing."

River rolled her eyes.

The CIA would be better for that.

But then she saw the turn for the lodge coming up and said, "Let's not go to the Outpost just yet. Let's go to the Mutele-Masisi Airfield. Danny and Orson might be back."

Chapter 16

"Perfect timing," Dioko said as he parked the pickup at the far end of the landing strip.

The Cessna was already lining up for touchdown, rolling sideways under the influence of the midday thermals. Danny steadied the plane, and it landed in a cloud of dust and a few bumps. The aircraft slowed to a crawl and came to stop twenty feet or so from the pickup.

As soon as the propellers had stopped, Orson opened the Cessna's door, dropped the steps to the ground, and climbed down. He brandished his Nikon D7500 camera and said, "I got really good pictures of the compound."

River ran to him, and Danny stepped out of the plane, too. They huddled around Orson's camera as he scrolled through the images on the display screen. Dioko joined them, and they watched as the secrets of Kruger's compound were revealed.

"Do you mind?" River said, extending a hand.

Orson handed over the Nikon, and River flipped back through the photos more slowly. She enlarged them and took time to consider the details of the buildings. The place was as she expected—fortified, with low structures topped by flat roofs from which snipers could take up their positions. Her guess was that the walls were heavy-grade concrete composites and would shield the men from high-caliber munitions and rocket-propelled grenades.

Her attention was drawn to two smaller buildings that were separate from the main one and kept apart from each other. She guessed these were the places where Kruger kept the arms shipments he received—one for the ammunition, the other for the weapons themselves.

If the ammo goes up, the rest won't.

The group was silent while River finished reviewing the images. She returned the camera to Orson, aware of expectant faces waiting for her conclusion.

"It's as bad as I thought it might be," River said. "Kruger has managed to use what looks like military-grade construction without the South African military noticing."

A few shoulders slumped. River, too, felt deflated. She felt the sting of defeat, but pushed the feeling away.

"We were never going to get to Kruger by mounting an assault on the compound anyway," she said. "We need to play it smart and use the information and the assets we've gathered."

She wasn't yet committing them to action, and the thought reassured her somehow. Orson and Dioko nodded. Danny looked more reserved, and she picked up on it. He shrugged and then said, "I'm not an expert, but I'd say they watched the plane as we flew over the second time around."

River cursed inwardly. She should have told them to limit themselves to one pass.

"What makes you say that?" she asked Danny.

"I saw something glitter. Like a flash. I wondered whether someone was following us with binoculars and the sun reflected on the lens."

Orson added, "I saw it, too. I tried to use the camera to pinpoint whether there was someone watching us, but I couldn't see anyone."

"I presume there are very few planes that fly over this part of the Limpopo," River said to Dioko.

"Kruger's compound isn't near the national park, and the planes going in and out of the closest airstrip don't go over his property."

"Which is why Kruger chose his location in the first place," Danny said.

River leaned against the fuselage of the aircraft, her head bowed. She then straightened up, facing Danny.

"You need to go now," she said. "If one of Kruger's men has seen the plane, then Kruger will send someone to this airfield, and you don't want the Cessna tampered with before you take off this evening. You also don't want to be shot at."

Danny rubbed a hand over the back of his neck. He said, "I see your point, so maybe I should go right now, as you said."

"But don't plan your return flight to Kotzebue yet," River said. "Jason is on his way from DC. He'll be arriving early tomorrow morning in Jo'burg and could use a lift."

Danny gave a short, sharp military salute. "I guess you'll let me know where and when."

River nodded, and Orson, Dioko, and she walked away from the aircraft. It took Danny a couple of attempts to start the engines. He turned the plane around, took off, circled one time to say goodbye, and was on his way to Johannesburg. He'd contact the tower there to ask for permission to land, claiming an emergency.

"Jason is the person Kruger tried to frame for murder," River said before Orson could ask.

"Why ask him to join now?"

"Because he holds details that might be useful for us and because he has experience we are going to need."

Dioko started walking toward his pickup, and Orson and River fell behind.

"It still doesn't make sense," Orson said.

River thought she could fob off the question but decided against it. Orson needed to know, and she needed everyone to trust her and her judgment if they were going to win the battle against Kruger.

"We were due to get married, and then I got cold feet and called it off," she said, her gaze fixed past Dioko's pickup.

"It's tough to be honest, and even tougher to be honest with oneself," Orson said. Something in his voice told River that he might have struggled with some of these issues, too, and that he wasn't there to judge but to understand.

River's burner phone rang. She didn't recognize the number but had a pretty good idea who would be calling.

"I got a burner of my own," Jason said.

Orson kept going, and River stopped.

"Danny is on his way to Johannesburg with the Cessna that

brought the others in. He'll be at the gate for you when your plane lands," River said.

"I'm on South African Airways, landing at 6:30 a.m.," Jason said. "Will you deal with the accommodations?"

"I'll find a place," River said, a little curt. Jason wasn't sharing her cabin. It was stressful enough to have to mount the mission against Kruger and his men. She didn't need her head and her heart messed up by having her former fiancé sleeping in the same room as her.

"Got to go—we're boarding," Jason said. "I'll see you tomorrow and we can talk."

He hung up before she could add anything else, perhaps intent on showing that he, too, considered this trip strictly business. Dioko sounded the truck horn a couple of times. He might have picked up movement in the shrubs that surrounded the airfield. With this morning's rhino encounter, River didn't need to be told twice. She jogged to the vehicle and got in.

Orson was in the back of the pickup scrolling through the images he'd taken.

"Have you deleted any?" River asked as she sat down.

"Just a couple," Orson said.

"Then stop," River said. "You probably think some of your photos are bad, but an expert eye may see something that you wouldn't have noticed."

"Shall I send them all to you?" Orson asked.

"Please—and to this number, too." River gave Orson Jason's burner phone number.

"Who shall I say is sending the pictures?"

"On behalf of River. He'll understand."

Silence fell in the truck—Orson, busy with sending the photos; River, thinking about whether an alternative means of fighting Kruger would be enough to avoid casualties on her side.

Soon the Outpost's main entrance appeared in the distance, and Dioko slowed down his pickup.

"I can drive you close to the path that runs along the brook below your cabin. As long as the hippos aren't there, you'll be able to get there that way."

"Let's try," River said.

Dioko took a sharp right, and the truck rolled slowly down to the bank of the brook. Loud grunting and groaning told them that the hippos were around and jostling for the best patch in the cool, muddy water. Dioko cut the engine and let the vehicle roll along the soft incline without a sound.

None of the animals noticed to start with. River and Orson got out on the side away from the brook and started walking toward the path. Two large males were shoving each other, their mouths open, teeth bare, competing for dominance. They suddenly stopped and turned their attention to the intruders.

River and Orson noticed, too, and started to run up the path. Dioko started his truck and accelerated in the hippos' direction—a challenge. They turned with lightning speed toward his vehicle, preparing for a charge. Dioko managed a quick U-turn and drove the vehicle up the banks of the brook and away.

When they reached River's cabin's front door, River and Orson entered and rushed to the balcony. They spotted the back of Dioko's pickup disappearing in the distance, and the two disgruntled male hippos looking shortchanged by the lack of action.

"That was close," Orson said.

River shook her head. "The basics of what *not* to do in the presence of hippos. They look cute, but they're such meanies."

A few moments later, River's burner rang again, and she picked up.

"Got two Jeeps," Karen said, "and Eric is on his way to a place near the Zimbabwe border where he thinks he can get some proper guns."

"Jason is on a flight to Jo'burg, and Danny has taken the Cessna back there to bring him to Masisi. He'll be with us by 9:00 a.m."

River felt Karen take the information in and assess it. "Let's talk about the elephant in the room—thankfully not literally. How is that gonna work?"

"I've got a day to figure it out," River said, "but I did tell him he's got to listen to people who know the terrain better than he does."

"Jason never struck me as a guy who doesn't listen."

"Perhaps, but the dynamics are going to be very different here. He's been out of the military for more than three years. We'll be working closely together, and he's gonna want to settle scores with Kruger just as much as I do."

"So, what, you're gonna compete to see who's gonna stick a bullet in Kruger's skull first? This isn't the way this gig is gonna roll, Riv—"

"I get that. But we need Jason. He needs us. Although I'm not sure what he's going to make of the people I got together," River said.

"It's not the people. It's how we deliver this op. You said it yourself—unexpected, creative, but when the time comes, in their faces."

Orson had taken a seat on the balcony, not wishing to eavesdrop.

"But we also need to make sure we don't compromise our chances to rescue Angela," River said, lowering her voice.

"Has this guy Mike tried to contact you again?"

"I haven't heard anything, and neither has Orson."

"That doesn't sound very promising, does it?" Karen said.

"We can't give up on Angela. That's not what we do."

"Never been my intention to give up, but we've got to know what her chances of survival are, as we do with every patient."

Karen's words made River shiver. She turned toward Orson and saw him watching the landscape beyond the balcony. She marveled at his calm demeanor.

"It's almost lunchtime," River said. "Let's go to the main building and confirm that the other visitors have not returned from their morning safari. I heard that the crowd would be back around 1:00 p.m., so that gives us some time before they and their rangers return."

"Let's go."

River hung up and turned to Orson. "Let's get some food."

Orson stood up and said, "We should call Mike to check whether we have news."

Kruger had just finished his inspection of the two facilities his men would use to stock the armaments about to land at the airfield. The sound of a small aircraft approaching made Kruger raise his head to the sky. He'd never seen a plane fly over the area before, and his stomach tightened. He ran to his office in search of binoculars, found a pair, and ran out again.

The Cessna was on its way toward the Limpopo River, and for a moment Kruger's shoulders relaxed—tourists or smugglers crossing the border into Zimbabwe. But the plane banked left, and in a sharp turn, retraced its route over the compound. The aircraft was too high for him to see inside, and Kruger could only spot the registration number of the craft on its side. He memorized it and would check it as soon as the Cessna was out of view.

Kruger followed it until it became a small dot in the sky, but he was certain the Cessna was on its way back to the Mutele-Masisi Airfield. And that airfield was only a few miles away from the Outpost, where the Swift woman was staying.

"Fuck," Kruger spat as he lowered the binoculars.

The thought that popped through his mind enraged him—the compound was toast. Whether he eliminated Swift or not, she would have at least spoken to the pilot about the place, and he, too, would have seen it. Kruger had never thought about what the compound looked like from the air, but he was certain it didn't look like a tourist lodge—reinforced concrete, surveillance towers, a drone platform camouflaged among the trees.

One of his burner phones was ringing in his office, and Kruger turned back, reaching his desk in a few long steps.

"Monica," he said, checking the time—11:00 a.m. in South Africa, 5:00 a.m. in DC. "I have another assignment for you."

"And I have news for you," she said. Her voice sounded tired, and Kruger knew she must have been surveilling Reginald Cameron's apartment all night. "I don't think the guy is there. I know he's supposed to have caught COVID, according to my sources, but something's not right. His sister comes in once a day but never carries anything with her that looks like food. No other deliveries otherwise. The lights are switched on and off at the same time every day, so I guess they're on a timer. I decided to go to his front door and ring the bell—nothing. He could be dead, but I don't think so. I'll wait until his sister visits again to confirm, but he's not at home."

"What time does his sister come?"

"Around 7:30 a.m. Before she goes to work."

"After that I have another assignment for you. Equally urgent."

Monica took only a few seconds to reply.

"I'll nap in the car. Where do you need me?"

"I'll text you an address in DC. Jason Wayne. No need to be subtle. Go knock at his door and dream up an excuse if he answers."

"That's it?"

"For the time being. Keep me posted about Cameron as soon as you know."

Kruger killed the call, texted Jason's address to Monica, flung the burner in the top drawer of his desk, and sat down. The urge to take a gun, walk into the Outpost, and finish Swift off was overwhelming. He looked at the room around him. A place much less comfortable than the Johannesburg house and far less grand than the DC apartment he owned, yet this was the place where he felt most at home. All that was about to go. He'd known this moment would come one day, but he'd imagined his enemy would have been a lot mightier than a mere Air Force medic and her ex-military boyfriend.

He gave a bitter, angry laugh. Now, Reggie Cameron, the black junior lawyer who'd done so well for Wayne, had almost certainly joined the chase. The other Air Force medic would probably be here, too. He could eliminate them all, but even if he did, the compound was no longer the secure place it had to be for the business of arms trafficking he was in.

Rage coursed through him, and he hammered the desk hard with his fist. His laptop jumped, and so did the lamp next to it. A mug that contained some coffee rolled to the end of his desk and crashed to the floor. Kruger grabbed the desk with both hands and barely resisted the urge to throw it across the room. He inhaled and exhaled a few times. His revenge would be lethal and cruel, but for the time being he needed to make sure the arms consignments he was about to receive were delivered. He would then pay himself handsomely and sever links forever with Masisi and the team that had served him faithfully.

Davis's time would come, too, and he would do well to make sure he was on guard 24/7. Kruger never forgot or forgave. For now, he needed to keep his rage under control. He called the cook, asked him to clean up the mess on the floor, then asked for a fresh cup of coffee and a plate of cold meat. He would be working in his office until he heard from Monica again.

The burner phone rang from inside the top drawer of his desk. Kruger turned away from his laptop and opened the drawer with force to grab the phone.

"Cameron isn't at home," Monica said. "His sister has come and gone, no drama. I'll call you back as soon as I've checked on Wayne."

Kruger forced himself to go through the final details of the arms delivery he was about to make. His focus became absolute against the temptation to dwell on Jason Wayne. Almost an hour passed before his burner rang again.

"I rang his bell," Monica said without preamble. "I walked around the building. I can't see any lights on. I tried one more time, so unless this guy goes for an early morning jog, he's not around."

Kruger ran his hand through his buzz-cut hair and stuck his nails into his scalp. He paused to feel a little calmer before he spoke. "No need to stick around. I think you're right. These two have left DC."

"What now?"

Kruger thought about what his next move should be and yielded to his impatience. "I'm about to send you a third address. This is a much more complicated tail—"

"You know what that means?" Monica interjected.

"Price goes up," Kruger said. "Do this one right, and you'll be able to retire."

Monica seemed to think about it and then said, "Then I want a payment on account first."

Kruger took his time and then said, "Okay—10 percent up front."

"Twenty up front."

"Fifteen. I don't want you to disappear into the sunset without doing the job."

"That's not the way I work, but okay. I'll settle for fifteen."

"This is surveillance, too, but this man is in the game, as you'll find out."

"Anything else?"

"Just a tail for now."

Monica hung up, and Kruger opened an encrypted file and scrolled down until he found the name he was looking for. He then sent Monica Dexter Davis's address.

The SOB doesn't know I know where he lives.

Kruger settled back in his chair. He didn't want Davis to know he knew—not yet. It would precipitate matters prematurely. But he needed to have an idea of what Davis's movements were.

His attention turned to Matondo and Angela Graham. He wondered whether it was worth the effort to bring the woman to South Africa. He now assumed she knew what had happened to the Swifts fourteen years ago. Perhaps she even had evidence of the massacre.

Kruger also had to assume that if he disappeared, he would be one of the most wanted men on the planet. The thought didn't scare him, nor did it excite him. He would deal with it in his usual methodical and detached way; the same way he dealt with all the problems he'd ever faced.

He was in possession of enough information and intelligence for his former clients to want to leave him alone. And he knew how to protect himself, too. Still, Kruger hadn't been ready to give up the lifestyle. Nothing to do with fame or money, but the risk-taking. Doing all he did, despite the laws and the surveillance surrounding arms trafficking, made the job the only one worth doing.

The burner phone only Davis used rang. Kruger picked up after a couple of rings, trying to control his anger.

"The first shipment is on its way, ready for pickup at the location I'm about to send you. Your men should load it today so that it arrives at the compound tonight," Davis said.

Kruger refrained from telling Davis to fuck off and instead played it cool. "Will do. And we'll start dispatching tomorrow. Matondo is ready, too."

The slight hesitation in Davis's response told Kruger once more that he was right. Davis and Matondo now spoke directly.

"I'll call you when the dispatch is done," Kruger added. He killed the call and let his body slump into his chair. He rested his head against the headrest, eyes closed.

The burner phone buzzed with the arrival of the text Davis had promised, letting Kruger have the coordinates for the arms pickup.

Kruger didn't bother to open the message and instead thought about the steps he'd rehearsed in his head many times when he thought he'd been close to being caught or terminated by one of the secret services he'd worked for. Now the time for execution of that plan had finally come.

Nothing would be left of the compound and the files he kept safe there. He'd pay his men well. Not out of generosity but out of a sense of duty and a strong sense of self-preservation. He'd have enough assassins looking for him without adding his own men to the list. But he couldn't leave South Africa without settling the score with the woman who'd caused him more grief than anyone else in the past—River Swift. She had to pay, but Kruger wouldn't delegate the kill to someone else, as he did with her parents. He'd do the job himself, just the way he should have done fourteen years ago.

Someone knocked at the door and then entered. Botha walked to Kruger's desk and stopped dead. Kruger's face must have said it all, and Botha took a moment before asking, "What was that plane that flew over the compound?"

"Cessna," Kruger said. "By the time I got my binoculars out, it was too far for me to read the registration."

He hadn't yet decided what he would do with Botha. The deal had always been that if Kruger retired, Botha would follow. He'd been paid handsomely over the years, and Kruger was certain he had enough to live comfortably. But Botha may not yet be ready to concede that the compound was terminally compromised. Kruger would leave his options open until he further tested Botha on his views. He couldn't afford a massive disagreement with him on this, and he'd have to take the necessary measures if it came down to it.

Botha nodded a few times and said, "I'd say the plane was on its way to the Mutele-Masisi Airfield. I'll find out who landed there today."

Kruger forced himself to be open to the idea. "As you say, let's find out whether we need to be concerned about this aircraft. I've just spoken to Davis, and the consignment is on its way, ready to be shipped to us late this afternoon. You need to call the men in Jo'burg and organize the first crew to take possession at this location."

Kruger opened Davis's message, glanced through it, and handed over the burner phone to Botha. Botha picked up the phone, memorized the coordinates, and handed the phone back to Kruger.

"The men are ready. I've called a couple of mercenaries I've used in the past to make sure we're secure for both shipments."

"Do I know them?" Kruger asked.

"They were with us last time we visited the DRC."

Kruger remembered the last visit to Matondo's encampment. He and Botha had had their own men build a soft perimeter around the room laid out for them. Tension had become palpable as Kruger and Matondo were talking about the money split—Matondo wanting more, and Kruger not being swayed. They both compromised in the end, but Kruger could already tell that Matondo needed more cash to fuel his excesses and that one day he'd demand too much out of Kruger. Kruger had wanted to keep him alive to find out more about what happened to the Swifts, a mistake in retrospect.

"Good," Kruger said. "They'll know what to expect."

"Are you still wanting to talk to Angela Graham?" Botha asked. "I need to know whether we'll be expecting resistance."

"I think we can expect resistance from Matondo from now on. As we suspected, he and Davis have been speaking directly, and you and I know what this means."

"I'll prep the men," Botha said.

He turned around and walked to the door. He stopped before he opened it and said, half turning around, "Is this the end of the road?"

Kruger froze for an instant. He would never answer such an open question from Botha with a direct lie.

"It might well be," was the best he could say.

Chapter 17

River and Orson had seated themselves first, choosing a table as far away from the buffet as possible. Karen and Reggie arrived, looking as though they were lost and disoriented, and finally joined River's table as new guests. While they ate lunch, they caught up on where they were in the fight against Kruger. River did most of the talking, and the others asked questions when they needed clarification.

"Are you waiting to speak to Jason about how to best play our hand? Or do you have an idea?" Karen asked.

"I have an idea, but it depends on one more thing," River said.

"You said you visited the San people who live next to the Limpopo River. Anything to do with that?" Orson asked.

"Yes, but until the old woman I met with has spoken to the entire clan, I won't know."

Karen frowned. "How are you gonna get those guys involved?"

"I'm not intending to use them in any confrontation, but they know the terrain better than anyone else—and, more important, they know the animals."

Reggie put down his forkful of food and asked, "So what? The big five against a fortified compound full of special ops men armed to the teeth?"

Karen frowned again, and River translated: "The big five—lions, leopards, rhinos, elephants, and buffalo."

This time, Karen's eyes widened in mock disbelief. "You're gonna use a herd of elephants to trample Kruger's camp, and then they'll be backed up by the buffalo, while the lions are gonna wait to pick off his men as they flee for their lives? You gotta be kidding me."

River couldn't help but smile and said, "That sounds like a good idea."

Karen and Reggie exchanged a look. Orson bit his bottom lip to stifle a laugh.

"The animals haven't volunteered to help, though, have they?" Reggie said, only half joking.

River turned serious. "And that's why I don't intend to endanger any of them. But the San will know how we can work with them and keep them safe."

Reggie had just raised a questioning finger when Orson lifted his hand to quiet the others. He rose and walked to the edge of the building, then lifted his head toward the sky. He cupped his hands around his eyes, stayed there for a moment, and returned.

"A plane is flying toward the Exodus Guesthouse airfield," he said as he sat down at the table again.

River felt a shiver run down her spine. "You mean the first plane carrying armaments is about to land?"

"I can't be certain, but it tallies with what the old man Okomi, who looks after the guesthouse, said to me," Orson replied.

"Then what are we waiting for?" Karen said, already pushing away from the table.

"Jason," Reggie said, raising his finger again.

River shook her head. "No. We can't wait until tomorrow. We need to know exactly what they're transporting."

"Why?" Reggie asked.

"I want to know how much ammo they're transporting and what type," River said.

"What's the plan?" Orson asked. "We should be able to get close. The airfield is surrounded by trees and shrubs."

"And plenty of long grass?" River asked.

"Some of that, too. If you intend to sneak up on them, you'll need someone to watch your back. Most animals hunt at night, but we are in the bush, after all," Orson said.

River stood up. "I have a plan."

River was leading the way, driving one of the rented Jeeps. Karen and Reggie were following in the other. River left the main road and eased the vehicle onto a trail that seemed to head in the right direction. Orson was using the compass on his cell phone to direct her.

"We're close," he said.

River slowed to a stop, and Karen parked behind her. They left the Jeeps, and River handed Karen one of the Glocks she'd picked up when fighting Kruger's men. The other Glock was stuck in River's waistband against her back. The four of them huddled for a moment as River explained what she needed them to do.

"Karen and Reggie, you stay with the Jeeps and use the binoculars to scour the bush. It's hard to spot an animal if you're not used to it, but do your best. Orson and I can walk until we get as close as possible to the airplane," River said. She turned to Orson. "Time to use your camera again."

Orson rubbed his neatly trimmed beard and said, "I have a better idea."

He walked to his Jeep, opened the door, and seemed to be rummaging in a backpack. He took out a long piece of white plastic and returned to the others. Orson started to fit the white plastic around the neck of his shirt.

River, Karen, and Reggie stared at him as he transformed his ordinary collar into a clerical collar with just a few practiced moves. He made a *What do you think?* gesture with his hands, and they all nodded, impressed.

"This should do the trick," he said.

"Just because you're a priest doesn't mean they won't shoot you," Karen said.

Orson shrugged. "A risk I'm happy to take."

"So what now?" River asked. "You're going to walk up to them and ask them if you can help off-load the plane?"

"Something like that," Orson said to Reggie's horror. "Except I'll pretend I'm expecting a supply of medicine for the area and came here to collect it."

"I can be in your Jeep and sneak out when you distract them," River mused.

"I was thinking about doing this on my own," Orson said, now sounding concerned.

"Nope," River said. "You've never seen boxes of ammo before, and I need to take as close a look as possible."

"I know what a box of ammunition looks like," Orson protested.

"Do you know the difference between a 9mm round and a 5.56 NATO?" Karen asked.

Orson wiggled his nose.

"Right," River said. "I'm going."

She climbed into the back of the Jeep, took a pair of binoculars out of the backpack she'd dropped there earlier on, and hid in the footwell of the vehicle, throwing an old plastic sheet that lay on the back seat over her. The dust it shed over her made her sneeze, and she hoped she wouldn't need to sneeze again when they reached the airfield. She took her burner phone out of her pocket and checked Karen and Reggie's coordinates.

Orson climbed into the driver's seat and started the engine. "I'll stop the Jeep as close as I can to a shrub or long grass," he said.

"Sounds good," River said as she settled in for a hot and sticky ride. "If things go south, if they find me, you run like hell."

Orson chuckled. "Hell has never made me run."

River chuckled in turn. "But you know what I've got in mind."

"I do, and I'm still not running."

The vehicle started to wobble as Orson cut across some uneven terrain, then he joined a set of smoother trails. He pushed the speed and slowed again as River guessed they were approaching the airstrip. The vehicle came to a stop, and River heard Orson speak first.

"Good afternoon," he said. "I'm coming from the mission in Tshilamba. I've been expecting some medicine we urgently need."

"This isn't that sort of shipment, Father," an Afrikaner-sounding voice said, suspicious.

River slid to the other side of the vehicle and waited for Orson to open his door. He did, and the same voice said, a little more menacingly this time, "I told you. We're not carrying medicine, and this shipment is entirely allocated to one person."

River opened the back door and slid to the ground. She then closed the door silently and slithered into the bush. She crouched, taking in the scene, adjusting the binoculars. Two Humvees with their rear doors open were surrounding the aircraft. It was the type of cargo plane she'd seen a lot in Africa, with hardly any seating and a lot of space for transporting goods.

Men dressed in jungle khakis and tight shirts showing their powerful muscles were going in and out of the plane, off-loading large crates. River recognized the markings on them—5.56 NATO and then M202A1 FLASH, which she thought was a rocket-launcher type of weapon. More crates came out until one of the Humvees was fully loaded and ready to leave.

River dropped her binoculars to check on Orson. Another man—taller, beefier, and with the requisite square jaw—had turned up. He looked more composed than the first man Orson had spoken to, but his arms were crossed over his chest, and he didn't look like he was there for a chat, either. Orson opened the door of the Jeep and cast an eye in the direction he guessed River had gone. He had no choice but to leave her behind.

As soon as Orson's Jeep had reversed and left, one of the Humvees followed. River used the binoculars to see whether they might intercept him, but the Humvee overtook his vehicle and went on its way. She turned her attention again to the aircraft and the activity surrounding it. More crates, including ammunition and guns of various sizes and capabilities, were coming out. River was almost impressed by the quantity and the quality. Kruger must have some serious contacts to be able to deliver this sort of selection.

The tall man River had noticed was checking the second Humvee when something stopped him dead in his tracks. He turned his head in River's direction, and she ducked to the ground, flattening her body as much as she could in the long grass. A rustle next to her head froze her to the spot, and she waited a few seconds before belly-crawling to the nearest tree.

Tough choice. Bitten by a snake or gunned down by one of Kruger's men.

The sound of boots advancing toward her made River squeeze even harder against the tree. She would have to belly-crawl again to the next cluster of trees, but she didn't think she had enough time to do this without being spotted. She took a small rock that lay at her feet and threw it in the distance. It formed an arc and landed in the tall grass, displacing it in a wave.

The man stopped. River seized the opportunity and made her way in the opposite direction to another tree. She repeated the move and then risked a glance. The tall man had changed direction but hadn't entered the bush—cautious, as one should be—and River cursed herself. She would have to make slow progress to the place where Karen and Reggie were waiting if she wanted to avoid being detected. She would be exposed, and even with a gun, a lonely walk in the bush isn't a walk in the park.

River risked another look, and now the man was crouched, doing what any good scout would do—looking for prints. As he was bent down, River threw another stone in the tall grass. Soon, the man would see the displaced earth where she'd crawled and know someone had been observing them.

A crazy thought went through her mind. She'd done it before, many years ago, and had been surprisingly good at it.

River closed her eyes, took a deep breath, and visualized a hyena. And then she let out a long and loud whoop, and then another.

Seconds later, she heard the tall man run away, toward the Humvees. She doubted he was the type to flee; instead, she surmised, he was returning to the vehicle to pick up a rifle. River didn't loiter. She moved away as noiselessly and quickly as she could. She didn't look back until she thought she was in the clear. She then stopped, took her cell phone out of her pocket, and used the compass to get a fix on her coordinates.

"Shit," she muttered.

She had deviated a lot from the initial direction she was aiming for. Then a subtle sound focused her to concentrate on her immediate surroundings. She heard it again. In the distance, someone was walking in the bush, following tracks—hers. River turned and moved deliberately low and fast. She presumed the tall man had only been fooled briefly by her imitation.

Time seemed to stop as she pressed on, compass in hand, toward her goal. Perspiration started to run along her back and her forehead as she moved more recklessly, fighting the desire to run. She almost tripped and bit her lip so she wouldn't swear aloud.

Then a flash of metal in the distance gave her hope. At least one of the Jeeps was still there, waiting for her. She accelerated her pace, and a moment afterward, the discharge of a rifle and the whap of a bullet hitting a large shrub to her right got her to break into a run, zigzagging between trees.

The sound of a couple of vehicle engines starting, followed by another shot, pushed her to run harder. She barreled into the small clearing where Orson, Karen, and Reggie were waiting. One of the Jeeps had a door open. She darted into the vehicle, and it left in a flurry of dust, accelerating away. One more rifle shot hit the Jeep's trunk. Orson was focused on driving, hands clenching the wheel hard. Karen and Reggie were in front, leading the way.

As soon as the Jeeps reached the main road, they accelerated further. River picked up her burner and called Karen, switching the speakerphone on.

"What the fuck was that?" Karen said.

"A fiery introduction to one of Kruger's top men," River said. "This guy knows the bush, too, because he tracked me down to the cars."

"So now they know you're not alone," Reggie said.

"Unfortunately. He hasn't seen me, though, so he doesn't know who was snooping on him. It could be other traffickers looking to steal their cargo. And trust me: That shipment is worth a lot of cash."

"What have they got?" Karen asked.

"A lot of ammo—9mm rounds, 5.56 NATO, 66mm incendiary rockets—"

"They're selling rocket launchers and what else? Mortars?" Karen said.

"That, too. I think they're selling precision-guided shells, like the 120mm XM395 precision-guided mortar munition."

Karen whistled. "Serious stuff."

"Sorry to interrupt the pros here," Reggie said, "but why does it matter?"

"Because it's not guerrilla weaponry. These are proper assault armaments," River replied.

"You mean like in a coup, to topple a government?" Orson asked.

"Exactly right," Karen said, anger in her voice. "I wonder which civil war these SOBs are fueling."

"Or which new war is about to break out," River added.

River checked the rearview mirror. They hadn't been followed. Kruger's man had a full Humvee and no desire to chase one of these lighter vehicles.

"No one's following," she said.

"How did you manage to get away? The guy who almost shot us seemed freakishly switched on," Reggie asked before she hung up.

"I did something I haven't done for a very long time. I imitated the cackle of a hyena."

"No way," Reggie said.

"Yep. I can believe it," Karen said. "Riv is very good with animals. She gets along with my huskies back home, and not a lot of people do."

Orson shook his head. "How did you learn to do that?"

"My brother and I rescued a hyena when we were small. Dad wasn't best pleased, but Mom sided with us. Anyway, I learned a lot about hyenas then and used to imitate their call. It worked every time, because our hyena used to reply and run to me. And then one day, Dad and I went on a visit to one of the San camps. I can't recall why or how. Maybe he bragged about how I used to call Betsy—the hyena—and she replied. No one wanted to believe him. Just so you know, the San are incredibly gifted when it comes to imitating the sounds and the way animals move. I gave them a couple of whoops, and they started to laugh and nod. They thought I was good enough. I felt very proud."

"That's a hell of a story," Reggie said. "I've got to tell Eric and Dioko."

River smiled at the memory. Family moments she'd cherish forever.

The sound of a car horn made them jump, and Orson gave a worried look into the rearview mirror. River turned around to see a hand waving out the window of an old pickup. Eric was back from his trip to the border between South Africa and Zimbabwe—alive.

Eric drove his truck alongside Orson's Jeep on River's side and shouted through his window, "Got a good selection of rifles and plenty of ammo as well as your other special order."

River gave him a thumbs-up. "Let's get together again in my room. Orson and I have got something else to do beforehand. Let the others know."

Eric waved and drew up alongside Karen's Jeep.

"Do we have something we need to do?" Orson asked, intrigued.

"Did you tell the big guy who spoke to you at the airfield that you were staying at the Exodus Guesthouse?"

Orson nodded with what looked like a pang of remorse.

"Then you need to clear the room you're using there. I'm sure the big guy who almost caught me has put two and two together and recognized your vehicle when we fled."

"Shit," Orson said. "I hope old man Okomi, who told me about the planes, won't be in trouble."

"Let's go and find out."

Orson didn't bother to slow down as he U-turned the Jeep in a flurry of gravel. He accelerated, body hunched forward, as though it might help the Jeep move faster.

"What happens if we cross paths with the Humvees?" he asked, sounding more annoyed than scared.

"The compound is due north of the airfield. They'll be cutting through the bush and won't be driving on roads or established trails," River said.

Orson pushed the Jeep a little harder. Ten minutes later, he made a sharp left onto a badly maintained road that soon turned into a pothole-riddled trail. Orson kept going, and River clutched the grab handle to avoid being thrown around the shaking vehicle.

A few one-story buildings in need of maintenance appeared in the distance—the Exodus Guesthouse. Orson skidded to a stop in front of the reception area in the main building. He opened the Jeep door without closing it and ran inside. He called out a few times, but no one answered.

River left the Jeep more cautiously, scanning the area for the presence of humans or animals. She then walked into another building and called out. Still no answer. Orson was already searching the farthest building. He came out empty-handed, shoulders slumped.

"Someone trashed the place," he said, holding up the old travel bag he'd arrived with. "They tore some of my clothes. I'm glad I took my laptop and camera with me this morning as well as my backpack."

River returned to the reception area and checked thoroughly for blood but couldn't find any traces of it.

"He can't have gone far," Orson said, his voice trembling. "His old truck is still parked at the back."

River checked the backyard. It led straight into the bush, where the tall grass hadn't been cut back. She then walked around the small yard, bending a few times to inspect the ground. She took her cell phone out of her pocket and snapped a couple of pictures. When she stood up, Orson was at her side.

"What is it?"

"Tracks of a heavy vehicle. I'm not an expert, but it could be one of the Humvees."

She turned toward Orson to see his face draining of color. "You think one of Kruger's guys took the old man away?" he asked.

"I don't know," River said, then added, "I might be completely wrong, so let's not jump to conclusions."

Orson shook his head; his face clouded with anguish. He might have cost a man his life.

"We don't know yet," River said as she squeezed Orson's arm.

He gave a feeble nod and walked to the Jeep. They left the Exodus and remained silent throughout the journey back to the Outpost. When they got there, the sun was high in the sky, and the main building was teeming with people. A new group of visitors had arrived, and Orson went to park at the far end of the inner yard.

Sarah was welcoming the new arrivals. She must have spotted Orson's Jeep, because River saw her stop and wait to see who was getting out. She seemed to relax when she saw River and gave a quick wave in recognition. River waved back, indicating she'd come up to talk to Sarah later. Sarah nodded—she understood.

Both River and Orson walked to her cabin. She called Karen on the way, who agreed to meet them there. But when River entered her room, she saw a silhouette standing on the balcony and froze. She was about to take her Glock out when Eric called, "The hippos down below were otherwise engaged, so I took the path from the brook to your balcony and climbed my way in."

River managed a smile. "Not a good idea unless you want me to use you as target practice."

Eric smiled. "You're the kind who thinks before she shoots."

"Thanks for the vote of confidence, but I wouldn't want to put it to the test."

The three of them sat on the balcony, and a moment later, River heard a soft call from the path below. She went back to the door and opened it to Karen and Reggie.

"What was that all about?" Karen asked as she went to settle next to the others.

"I thought it might be a good idea to have Orson check out of the Exodus Guesthouse," River said. "As it turned out, we arrived too late to salvage his clothes, but more worryingly, the old man who runs the place seems to have disappeared."

Eric frowned. "Old Okomi? He never goes anywhere without his pickup."

Orson ran his hand over his face. "Those SOBs have taken him."

River was about to protest that they still didn't know, but he raised his hand. "Let's not kid ourselves. They took him to question him, and by now—"

Eric's cell phone rang. He picked up and mouthed "Dioko" to the others. He listened to what his brother was saying, his face turning pale, and then anger ripped through it like a flash of thunder. He hung up, paused, and then said, "Ike, the owner of the grocery store, has been mauled by lions."

The shock moved like a wave through the room, stunning everyone.

Reggie was the first to ask, "It's probably a stupid question, but how can that happen? I mean, the guy knows how to stay safe, right?"

Eric shook his head. "It *doesn't* just happen. Someone *made* it happen."

More heavy silence, and then it was River's turn. "Justice for my parents isn't supposed to cost more innocents their lives," she said, her voice shaking in anger.

Eric stood up slowly. "If you're thinking about quitting, don't. Even more so now. I can speak for Dioko, too: We want to see these bastards behind bars at a minimum."

"I know," River said, "but I can't make another mistake. You understand? I couldn't live with myself if I cost another person his life. I just need to think."

They all stood up to leave. Reggie turned to Orson and the others, saying, "Come and share my cabin. I don't think it matters anymore whether people realize that we're all together."

Orson nodded, and the room emptied slowly. When the last of them closed the door, River dropped on the sofa, her head in her hands, and swallowed a sob. She needed to do something she'd postponed until now—go through the images that Angela had sent to Mike and that were stored on her laptop. Images she knew would be dreadful. But she had to fully measure the extent of the savagery she was facing. Perhaps she hadn't wanted to know, or she feared it would weaken her resolve to see the mission through. After she looked through them, she would ask Reggie to be the guardian of the evidence they were accumulating.

The laptop was in the safe, so she retrieved it and sat on her bed. As she booted up the device and went through the log-in process, her stomach knotted. She navigated to the files she'd created to hold the evidence and chose the one titled "Angela Graham."

Her hand hovered over the touch pad for a moment, and then she opened the file. Images displayed immediately. She ignored the first ones. She'd gone through them already—burned houses and destroyed fields. Now, the cruelest images from the massacre were about to be displayed, and River braced herself. She needed to look at them. She owed it not only to her parents but also to the young girl who'd been brave enough to take these pictures.

As she anticipated, the details were horrific. Still, River went through the entire file—thirty-five pictures—and toward the end, she recognized the man she'd seen on Zoom the day Angela had been abducted. He looked younger, laughing among his troops. From the angle of the image, River guessed that the girl who'd snapped the picture did so while hiding behind the ruins of a house.

Then a thought she'd been grappling with took hold. It was impossible that her parents had escaped the savagery of the attack with a simple gunshot to the head.

River suddenly stood up, ran to the bathroom, and was sick. She remained kneeling for a moment, then rose slowly to rinse her mouth. She returned to the bedroom. Her laptop was still on her bed. She looked at the last image, of the man and his troops, and grabbed a pillow, screaming into it—rage and sorrow swirled inside her. She would never give up.

Ice-cold determination had replaced the small hesitation she'd felt earlier. She would take Kruger on, and then she'd track down the DRC monster and the CIA's Dexter. And she would show them no mercy.

She closed Angela's file. Checked her inbox to find the file that Ariana had assembled and Jason had sent.

As predicted, whoever had helped Ariana was targeting Kruger and no one else. River paid more attention to the details as she reread the file. A few names were recognizable, terrorists from the Middle East and Somalia, but there was very little about Kruger's sources or his ultimate clients. It was clever, she thought. A red cape to a bull, and a good way to convince her and anyone else reading the file that Kruger was dealing illegally. And yet the evidence looked shaky to her. She'd have Reggie look at the file later on.

The large clock on the wall indicated 4:30 p.m. Tomorrow morning, Jason would arrive. She still had mixed feelings about that, but not for the obvious reasons. Something he said as he was boarding his plane to South Africa troubled her. She closed her eyes and stayed still for a moment, creating a calm space within so that she could process her apprehension.

And then it came to her. If she was concerned about Jason no longer being able to operate as a SEAL, he must be concerned that she'd never had the training. Taking on a man like Kruger and his special ops men would sound like pure madness to him. She had said she didn't intend to mount a full-blown assault on the compound, but whatever River had in mind would seem almost certainly mad to a man who was used to having the best human and technological resources—as well as weaponry—at his disposal.

Just as important, she didn't want to get Jason killed. She was sure he didn't want to see her dead, either. Such were the ties that still bound them. She now feared they would enter a stalemate: He wouldn't consider her ideas good enough to execute, and she wouldn't consider his good enough to execute, either.

River stood up and walked to the edge of the balcony. She surveyed the grassland that spread as far as the eye could see. She reached for her burner phone inside her pocket and dialed Eric's number.

"I need something else from you, apart from the rifles," she said.

"I'll do my best to get it."

"I need a motorbike, cross-country if possible. I'll pay whatever it costs."

Eric thought for a moment and then said, "When?"

"Tonight. It's important."

"Give me a few hours."

River spent time putting down on paper all she knew about Kruger, the compound, and the resources her team had. She then called Dioko.

He picked up almost instantly, and instead of sounding deflated, he sounded angry.

"What can I do to help?"

"Have you spoken to the San?"

"Not yet. I'll go back to the bush now. It's a good time. They'll be all around, gathering for the night."

"Thank you. And I'm sorry," River said, not needing to elaborate.

"I know," Dioko said, his voice steady.

After he hung up, River returned to the written notes she'd assembled. She sat back and pondered the plan she'd been formulating for a while now. It sounded solid to her.

When she was done, she called Karen first. River still wanted her buy-in on some of the main steps of the plan.

"I need to have a quick chat with you, alone," she said as soon as Karen answered.

"On my way," Karen said.

"Don't bother to take the path by the brook. Kruger knows I'm not alone."

"Whatever. I'm still taking the path," Karen replied after a chuckle.

River shook her head with a smile as she hung up and waited for Karen. She and Reggie were only a few cabins away. River leaned against the frame of the main door to the outside. Karen waved as soon as she appeared, and River waved back.

"So you have a plan?" Karen said as she walked into River's room and onto the balcony.

"I've always had a plan," River said.

Karen went into the small kitchen and started to prepare two coffees.

"I mean a fully-fledged plan, with all the *t*'s crossed and *i*'s dotted."

"Reading me like a book?" River tried to make light of it, but she wondered how much Karen had guessed.

Karen returned with two mugs, handed one to River, and sat down.

"You've been giving a lot of instructions to the boys on the ground, Dioko and Eric. You've finally called on Jase, but you've always had a plan, as you said, and now I bet you're getting worried that Jase is going to trash it."

River wiggled her nose. She wasn't quite ready to admit to Karen that she was right.

They both drank in silence, and River eventually said, "I was going to keep this to myself, but perhaps I was wrong."

"What? The fact that you're worried about Jase disagreeing?" Karen said after taking a sip. "I'd be worried, too. In fact, that's the one thing that could backfire—Jase looking at all of us and throwing his hands up in the air."

River thought for a moment. "There is that, and to start with, that worried me the most, but now I fear a stalemate between the two of us."

Karen frowned, drank a little more coffee, and then said, "You're worried about him. He's worried about you. And then nothing happens because you each find holes in the other one's plan."

River nodded. She hoped that Karen wouldn't be as protective as Jason might be about the first phase of the mission.

Chapter 18

The sound of an aircraft interrupted Kruger's conversation with the men who were off-loading the Humvees. He glanced skyward and then at his watch. There wasn't any plane that had been authorized to land that evening, and he didn't think Swift would want to organize another reconnaissance mission now that the light was fading.

He left his men and walked toward the back of the compound to a room he used as a cell. Old man Okomi was sitting in the corner of the small space, looking terrified when Kruger opened the door. Kruger walked to him without bothering to close the cell door.

"Any plane supposed to land at the airfield next to the Exodus Guesthouse?" Kruger asked as he towered over his captive.

The old man shook his head. "No, sir. No one told me."

Kruger leaned forward, and the old man recoiled further against the wall. He lifted a protective arm, anticipating a blow. Kruger didn't need to use force. He could see it in the man's eyes. He wouldn't dare lie. Kruger walked out, locked the door, and went inside the main building in search of Botha.

He was talking to some of his men about the deliveries that would start filtering through Africa, mainly by air, when Kruger entered the prep room that stood next to the surveillance center. Botha must have seen it on Kruger's face. He stopped and just walked out of the room, closing the door behind him.

"Problem?"

"A plane has landed at the Exodus airstrip, unannounced," Kruger said, barely containing his anger. "There is only one asshole who would dare do that."

Botha's eyebrows shot up. "Matondo?"

"He's using Angela Graham as an excuse. At this point I can't tell whether Davis has given him orders or whether he's just being a stupid fuck."

Botha crossed his arms over his chest. "He's being overconfident, and perhaps he's gathering intelligence for a future confrontation. I don't think he would want to take us on, not on our own turf and not with the camp brimming with our own special ops men."

"Nonetheless," Krueger said, "get your guys to help the others empty the Humvees and store the armaments securely away."

Botha nodded and disappeared into the room. Kruger walked to the surveillance center, pressed his thumb to a pad on the wall, and entered a six-digit code. The door opened, and Kruger entered to find two of his men manning the screens. They didn't turn around but waited for Kruger to approach them. His instructions: Never take your eyes off the terrain you're surveying.

"Hendrik, launch a drone. Direction, the Exodus landing strip."

Hendrik's hands flew over the keyboard in front of him as he said, "On it."

A screen that had been dark came to life. The small camera flickered a couple of times. Kruger exhaled impatiently, but Hendrik steadied the flow of images, and the drone took off.

"It'll take the drone a little over five minutes to reach a position where we can see the airstrip well enough to ID who's on it," Hendrik said.

Kruger grunted and stood still, waiting for the images to start showing the plane and who had landed. He needn't have bothered. His burner phone rang. As soon as Kruger answered, Matondo's booming voice announced, "I've got a present for you."

"I hope Angela Graham is in good enough condition to talk," Kruger said.

"She's all patched up and ready for you," Matondo replied after another laugh. Kruger could hear it in his voice. The big man had pushed a few lines up his nose already.

"I've also come to pick up my shipment," he then said, now dead serious. "I wondered whether you could throw in a few extras."

The only thing Kruger felt like throwing at Dr. Death was a well-aimed grenade. Kruger would normally have told him in no uncertain terms that a delivery was a delivery, but this time, he relented. "I'll see what I can do."

Matondo seemed to have expected pushback, and he sounded pleased. "That's my man. Things are moving fast in the DRC. I might need more of the heavy weaponry we discussed last time you came to Kivu."

"The compound is in lockdown at the moment," Kruger said as the images of the Exodus airfield materialized on the screen. "You understand that I have other orders to fulfill."

Matondo went quiet, and then he said, "How do I deliver Angela Graham?"

The Pilatus PC-6 Porter was parked at the end of the runway, and six men had spread themselves across the airfield, forming a perimeter around it. They were all outfitted with top-of-the-line munitions, and Kruger realized that Matondo had been upgrading his men's equipment since he last saw him. There weren't enough of them to take Kruger's compound down, but it was a show of strength that sent a message—I have ambition. I am a major player now.

"There is a guesthouse half a mile from the airfield," Kruger said. "You and your men can settle there. Happy to treat you to dinner this evening."

"And we can start loading the plane," Matondo said.

"I'll ask for the shipment to be ready in an hour, and then I'll come to collect Angela Graham," Kruger replied.

He killed the call and turned to Hendrik. "Keep the drone as far away as possible. I don't want to lose track of those men, but I don't want to be noticed, either."

"I'll let you know if anything changes that's worth noting," Hendrik said.

Kruger left the room and hurried to the two secure storage facilities that housed the latest deliveries. Botha was there with his men. He stopped and walked to Kruger as soon as he saw him in the distance.

"Matondo has brought Angela Graham, as we suspected," Kruger said. "He also wants more Carl Gustaf 8.4."

"Where is he going to stay?" Botha asked.

"The Exodus Guesthouse is now empty. But I'll feed him tonight. He'll bring his bodyguards, but even if he brings six men, he won't be able to take us on."

"He could try to raid this facility," Botha said.

"If that was his intention, he would have brought many more men," Kruger replied.

Botha pursed his lips. "I think you're right. He might have set his sights on grabbing more power in the DRC, but he would be ill-advised to fight on two fronts at the same time."

"Davis may not have made his move, either," Kruger said, lowering his voice.

"But he will as soon as the deliveries are completed," Botha said, then added, "I'll start getting Matondo's armaments ready and check how many Carl Gustafs we can spare."

Kruger returned to his office, closed the door, and sat at his desk. Matondo had only been to the compound once, a long time ago, when he was still a young mercenary who spoke broken English but wasn't shy about making every effort to please the likes of Kruger and Davis. At the time, he'd landed at another airfield in Zimbabwe and had been driven across the Limpopo by Kruger's men.

Now Matondo would see inside Kruger's compound and know its exact location. Kruger shook his head. He was somehow glad he had already decided to sacrifice it, although there was still a big part of him that wanted to reverse that decision. And yet Kruger's much cooler self knew it was over. He had an hour to keep pushing forward with the exit strategy he'd formulated many years ago and refined over time.

He pulled a USB drive from the top pocket of his safari shirt and logged in to his laptop. He'd already downloaded a large number of the files he would use to blackmail his soon-to-be-former employer and clients, but he wasn't done yet.

A text interrupted his progress.

Second delivery this evening. Coordinates to follow in one hour. Get your men ready.

Davis was sending the second shipment out, as he'd told Kruger. Except that Matondo's aircraft was now in the way. Kruger almost smiled. Matondo hadn't informed Davis of his impromptu hop across the border to South Africa. And Davis hadn't yet pulled the plug on Kruger and his people.

The fear of being rushed made Kruger hesitate for a moment, but then he called Davis.

"What?" Davis answered, irritated.

"I'm delaying sending the new shipment to Masisi till tomorrow," Kruger said without further explanation.

Davis seemed stunned. Kruger never broke a delivery promise. "Unacceptable. I don't pay you to slack."

Correction . . . I pay you from the money I make in arms trafficking.

But Kruger bit his tongue and instead replied, "Then speak to Matondo. He's decided to pay me a visit to take his own shipment away—and that means his cargo aircraft is blocking the airstrip."

Davis's silence told Kruger it was as he suspected—Davis didn't know. But it was Davis himself who had made Matondo more ambitious and less controllable.

"I wonder why the sudden change in attitude," Kruger couldn't help but say. "Matondo's ambitions have grown all of a sudden."

Davis's mind seemed to be working overtime to deliver a response that didn't betray his double-dealing.

"Tell him to go back to the DRC," was all Davis could come up with as a suitable answer.

"No can do. It'll be dark soon, and these small airstrips don't have lights."

Davis's breath had become a little more labored as they spoke, and Kruger was enjoying the moment. Perhaps he had a little more time than he thought before the CIA man pulled the plug—time he would use wisely, not only to render the compound unusable but also to plot his revenge on Davis.

"How fast in the morning can you take delivery?" Davis asked, now working on damage control.

"The sun rises at 6:00 a.m. I'll get my men in Jo'burg to pick up the new shipment tonight and then fly it tomorrow as soon as Matondo has freed the airstrip."

"Keep me posted," Davis said before he hung up.

Kruger opened one of the drawers in his desk and threw the burner into it. He'd inform Davis when he was good and ready. The more pressing issue now was how to deal with Matondo. It was perhaps a unique opportunity to eliminate the SOB, but Kruger wasn't ready to face the domino effect his murder would set in motion. He'd have to indulge the miserable bastard for a little longer. His top priorities remained Angela Graham and River Swift.

The bike was ready to ride, and Eric had hidden it a hundred yards or so away from the Outpost. River and Karen used one of the Jeeps to get to it. River stopped the vehicle, and she killed the engine, as well as the headlights. They sat in darkness for a moment until their eyes got used to it. River was glad that Karen had forced her way into River's initial plan.

Karen dragged a bag out of the footwell and opened it. She handed River her gear and took out her own. Then they began equipping themselves—body armor, a shoulder harness, various pouches in which they could carry some of the equipment they needed, and night-vision goggles. Karen had brought a helmet of her own, and River would wear the motorbike helmet.

"How did you manage to get all that?" River said as she started to spread some camo makeup on her face. She might not need it with the full-face helmet, but she'd always enjoyed the ritual.

"Made a few calls before Danny and I left Kotzebue. There was a nice big parcel waiting for me at the airport in DC. I still have some contacts in the force, you know."

River grabbed her backpack, checking one more time that the Glock and spare clips were inside it. Eric had delivered ammo, as well as the other items River had put on her list. She'd been impressed by how resourceful Reggie's cousins had been, no doubt helped by Reggie's legal expertise.

River turned to Karen and checked her gear. Karen did the same for her, and they tested their wireless communication system. They'd rehearsed the steps needed to get the results River wanted, refining them for a few hours before deciding they were ready. River closed her eyes for a short moment, then nodded. Karen nodded back.

Time to deliver Phase 1.

River got out of the Jeep and got on the motorbike, a Honda CRF125F. She put her helmet on, secured the backpack on her shoulders, and fired up the engine. It gave a grunt that felt much louder than it was. River didn't rev the engine but instead gave the bike some time to come to life. It was midnight, and the people in the lodge were asleep, but she was certain that the rangers on duty would have heard the sound. She didn't wait to see whether they'd come to investigate, but instead moved forward onto the trail that led to Masisi, with Karen following.

The sky had clouded over, and it was almost impossible to ride without the headlight on, so River reluctantly had to use it. Karen could see well enough by using River's headlight, and both women got to Masisi without encountering anyone. They turned onto a rougher trail, and River slowed down, barely avoiding some of the potholes. They finally reached the clearing where Dioko, Eric, and River had gone the first time they investigated Kruger's compound. River stopped, killed the bike engine, and stepped off. Karen followed suit and came to stand alongside her.

"The compound is half a mile away," River murmured. She raised her wrist and pushed the dial of her watch to illuminate its face. She turned to Karen, and both women synchronized their chronographs, each programmed with a succession of alerts scheduled to go off at the precise intervals they'd plotted out.

Karen took out the first pieces of equipment she'd stashed in the pockets of her gear—incendiary devices and fire retardant. River took a pair of night-vision binoculars out of her backpack and brought them to her eyes. If the San people were going to help, they would have started working on the animals a few hours ago, and the gazelles would be arriving near Kruger's camp soon.

River surveyed the terrain. She spotted slow movement in the far distance, and she silently thanked Dioko and the old woman she'd visited during the day. Several gazelles were grazing, slowly moving toward the first circle of the invisible trip wires surrounding the camp.

"They're coming," River whispered.

Karen fitted her night-vision goggles on. "I see them," she murmured. "Let's wait a little longer."

Both women remained stock-still, watching the progress of the animals. They looked peaceful and relaxed, but they were about to give Kruger's surveillance system an alert overload. River smiled as a small flash told her that an infrared trip wire had been triggered and that the fun must have started in Kruger's surveillance center. She saw another and then another.

"We're in business," Karen said in a low voice. "Good luck, uuma."

"Same to you," River murmured. They bumped fists, and each went her own way—Karen through the long grass toward the grazing animals, River to her motorbike. She straddled it and checked that she had what she needed in her backpack—a torch she'd prepared, the accelerant she'd use to make sure it caught fire immediately, and the Zippo to light it.

Karen needed ten minutes to place the small incendiary devices around the perimeter of the compound. She would then douse the area surrounding them with fire retardant. The idea wasn't to fan a fire that would spread without control but to create panic in Kruger's compound. Nothing was as dangerous and terrifying as wildfire in the savanna.

River's watch buzzed lightly against her wrist – Phase 2 complete. Ten minutes gone. In the distance, small flames started to rise at regular intervals around the compound. River kick-started the bike and rode hard toward Kruger's compound. She stopped at one of the incendiary devices, whose flames had now grown into threatening blazes. She took the torch out of her backpack, doused it with accelerant, and struck the Zippo. The torch caught in a whoosh. Lights had started to go on in the compound.

With the torch held high, River rode the bike right to the wall of Kruger's fortress. She stopped in a flurry of dust and lifted the visor of her helmet, staring into the lens of a camera that had turned to focus on her.

"Kruger," she shouted. "Let's go to war!"

She threw the blazing torch with all her might over the compound wall, turned back, and rode fast toward the road. A searchlight beam illuminated the bush, moving around systematically to identify the intruder. River skidded to a stop next to a large shrub. Karen emerged from behind it. River dismounted; Karen replaced her, and they swapped backpacks. Karen took off without a word. River's watch buzzed lightly against her wrist again.

Phase 2 complete. Phase 3 to come . . .

River squatted and waited for Karen to disappear. The searchlight beam moved past River's position, trying to catch up with the bike rider. River duckwalked back toward the compound and stopped next to one of the dying incendiary devices. The fire retardant had done the trick, and she calculated that the surveillance system was still in data overload. She ran low toward the compound wall and disappeared behind the bushes that camouflaged it.

With one shoulder hugging the wall, River edged toward the back of the compound, where she would find the gate. The aerial footage Orson had taken yesterday had given River enough to know what she'd be expecting—a reinforced steel gate managed from inside. She stuck to the shadows and listened closely.

Kruger's men were on the move, and she imagined that Kruger would be leading the charge. A small pang of excitement popped in her stomach. The top man, the former special ops heavy hitter, was taking the bait. The sound of vehicle engines rumbling into action and the metal creak of an opening mechanism pushed River further into the shadows. Two Humvees dashed outside the gate, taking a sharp turn in pursuit of the bike.

Another buzz of her wristwatch told River that Karen should by now have abandoned the bike and gotten into the Jeep. She had ten minutes on her pursuers, and it might be just enough to maintain her advantage. The sound of the gate slowly closing refocused River. She made her next move, sliding to the corner of the wall. As the gate was about to seal the opening, River slipped inside the compound and ran toward the first building she could spot. She flattened against its wall, her heart pounding.

She spotted a camera mounted on the far side, facing the gate. It was fixed, and she judged that there must be a dead angle she'd exploit later. She checked the rest of the building and couldn't see any more cameras. She slid down its external wall, stopping a few times. She still couldn't spot any cameras and slowed down. Was she missing something?

Then River shrugged.

Too late to go back . . .

She reached the far side of the building without being stopped and paused. Two buildings stood separately from the main one. River dropped to one knee and opened the backpack Karen had given her. She took out the five blocks of Semtex and the electronic detonators she was going to use and assembled them. Her watch sent a low buzz through her wrist, telling River she had to start distributing the charges now.

She ran low to the first separate structure. The door looked impressively solid, with a digital keypad to one side. She applied two packs of Semtex to it, waited a moment, and ran low to the other structure. She repeated the process and then heard voices in the distance. She looked around for a place to hide and darted back to the shadows of the bigger building.

The Semtex was stuck low enough to the ground to be inconspicuous. People would walk past without noticing it unless they strode directly to the door.

"There is damage to the drone platform," one of the men said. "I'll repair it now, and we'll be able to launch again in a few hours. I asked more men to station themselves at the watchtowers next to it."

"Good, but I want to see it for myself."

River recognized the voice of the big man who had spoken to Orson yesterday. Both men moved past her and walked to the far end of the complex. River waited a moment. The two men had come from the other side of the building—the doors must be on that side.

She stood at the corner for a few seconds and darted across to the other corner. She dashed down the side of the building the men had come from. If more men came, she would be spotted immediately. She could still detonate the charges, but her chances of surviving the blast would be close to zero.

She noticed a long room that looked like a refectory and then a solid wall, and finally a room fitted with a sliding glass door, its curtain half drawn. She stopped and took a peek inside. The light in the room was low and directed at a desk, a laptop open on top of it. She pushed the sliding glass door, expecting resistance, but it just slid open with a soft sigh.

River stepped inside and closed the door behind her. When she turned around, she slammed a hand over her mouth to muffle a cry. Angela Graham was slumped in a chair in the middle of the room, handcuffs securing her to the armrest. River's stomach clenched at the sight of the woman she'd only met as an adult on Zoom but who'd put herself at so much risk to help River in her quest for justice.

Angela's eyes were closed, but she must have felt that someone was observing her. She woke from her slumber with a jerk, fear etched on her face. She didn't recognize River at first, but when River came to kneel next to her, fear was replaced by amazement.

"You?" Angela murmured, her mouth bruised, hardly able to get the words out.

"I'll get you out of here," River said. "Do you know where the keys for the cuffs are?"

Angela shook her head. "Too late," she said, slowly raising her free hand to her shirt and painfully undoing a button. River undid a few more and this time, couldn't stop a cry. Angela's body was a sea of bruises, all of them the result of inhumane brutality. River closed the shirt, and her head dropped for a moment, incapable of taking in the implication of what she saw. But Angela was a medic, and so was River. They both knew that the chances of surviving several days of onslaught at Matondo's hands were almost nil.

"Check the laptop," Angela murmured.

River stood up and stepped over to what she now realized must be Kruger's desk. A USB drive was still stuck in the device, and the laptop hadn't timed out yet. Kruger was transferring a large amount of data onto the drive. The transfer was consuming most of the laptop's resources, preventing its time-out function from triggering.

River left the drive inside the laptop and opened the drawers of Kruger's desk. She found an identical USB drive as well as the keys to Angela's cuffs.

The loading bar seemed suddenly to accelerate, and the download completed. River moved the trackpad to prevent the laptop from locking. She opened one of the files that had been downloaded at random and gasped. The name of the man was well-known—a member of the US Congress, and the list of bribes was as impressive as his position. River understood. Kruger was downloading the intelligence he'd gathered over years and was preparing to cut loose.

A small vibration on her wrist told her that she should have already placed the fifth Semtex load and prepared to activate the devices. Instead, she searched for a first name: Dexter. A couple of names popped up, and one Dexter Davis stood out—CIA employee, head of a unit dedicated to central Africa's surveillance. River clicked the file to start the upload, but the flash drive indicated that the Davis file had been uploaded already.

River pocketed the USB drive, stuck the new one in the laptop, and went back to Angela. She unlocked the cuffs, but Angela shook her head.

"Save the girl," she said.

River shook her head in turn.

"I might be former military, but I still don't leave anyone behind."

She helped Angela stand up, and Angela yelped in agony, making to sit down again.

"Orson is at my lodge. He's helping set you free," River said.

A flash of hope crossed Angela's eyes. She bit her lower lip and leaned on River. Both women walked to the sliding glass door. River and Angela retraced River's steps. They had to stop a few times, with River now carrying most of Angela's weight. When they reached the gate, River sat Angela on the ground and went to install a much smaller piece of Semtex against the control pad. She spotted what she was looking for in the parking lot, a Jeep that looked old and ratty—the sort of vehicle the owner might not bother to secure, especially inside the compound. River returned to Angela. A buzz, this time, in her headpiece told her Karen was calling.

"You're now ten minutes late," Karen said.

"I have Angela, and the fireworks are about to start." River killed the call, took her burner phone out of her pocket and pressed the Call button, dialing a number she'd entered the night before.

The first detonation shook the ground underneath them, but the one that followed was terrifying. The flash emitted by the munitions depot explosion made it look as though it was broad daylight. Pieces of the two buildings that had been blown up by the Semtex, as well as part of the main building flew over River and Angela's heads. The main gate's control box was gone.

The blast would have taken down the systems in the control room. She ran to the gate and pushed. The heavy slab of steel didn't move, so River applied all her weight against it. It budged a little. Rivulets of sweat had started to gather along River's back. She gave the gate a massive shove, and it finally budged. She pushed it open and then ran to the Jeep. As predicted, it was open, with the keys in the ignition. River started the engine and drove it to the place where Angela was waiting.

She lifted her from the ground. Angela couldn't help another cry of pain. And then she muttered, "Old man in the cell."

Angela managed to tip her head toward a door that was facing the compound wall. River helped Angela onto the front seat, walked to the door, and, taking the Glock out of its holster, discharged the weapon into the lock. She slammed her foot into it, and the door banged open. An old man was sitting on the floor.

"We're going," River said to him.

He looked dazed and stood up slowly. River grabbed his hand and dragged him out. She opened the back door of the Jeep. He understood he was being rescued and got in. River climbed into the driver's seat and drove off to the sound of men shouting. No one on the drone platform had survived the blast, River was certain, but men who'd been located deep enough into the main building would have. She floored the accelerator and left Kruger's compound behind, decimated.

Chapter 19

Someone was shaking Kruger hard, and he pushed back, grunting, before he realized he needed to wake up and get out of bed. The evening with Matondo had been heavy—too much food and too much booze. Matondo had complained that there weren't any women, but Kruger placated him. This was a compound to house armaments, not a brothel.

"Don't see why you can't have both," Matondo had grumbled, almost certainly referring to his own encampment.

"Fire near the compound," Hendrik kept saying.

Kruger sat up with a jolt. "Wildfire?"

A ripple of fear coursed down his spine. This was the only thing that Kruger dreaded the most in the bush.

"No," Hendrik replied as Kruger dressed quickly. "It looks as though someone has lit incendiary devices around the periphery of the compound."

Kruger slid quickly into a pair of pants and shirt, and grabbed the Glock that never left his bedside table. He slid it into his waistband. "Show me."

They ran across the compound and arrived at one of the surveillance platforms, quickly climbing to the top. Botha was already there, looking through binoculars. "Someone's created a ring of fire around the compound," he said. He handed over the binoculars to Kruger, who slowly surveyed the flames.

"Didn't the trip wire around the perimeter flash a warning?"

"The system went into overload. A small herd of gazelles walked across the trip-wire field," Botha said.

"And then the fires were lit?" Kruger asked.

"Yes—that's what it looks like."

Kruger didn't believe in coincidence, but he couldn't reconcile the two events. The only people he knew who could summon the animals were the San, but he'd made sure he and his men left them alone. Yet he was also sure they would never have created fires in such an orderly fashion. They feared fire as much as Kruger did, and they only used it to cook what they killed.

"We need to take a look," Kruger said.

He and Botha were already at the bottom of the tower when they heard the distinct sound of a motorbike. Hendrik had replaced them up on the platform, and was scanning the terrain around the camp. He remained silent, and Kruger asked, irritated, "What do you see?"

Kruger ran back up the steps to the top of the tower as Hendrik said, "Someone's on a motorbike, riding toward the compound with"—the words seemed to fail him—"a torch in his hand."

Kruger stuck the binoculars to his eyes just as the figure stopped the motorbike around 150 feet away from the walls of the compound and yelled, "Kruger, let's go to war!" The voice was muffled by the helmet, but he knew who was calling him out.

River Swift threw the torch she was holding in a perfect arc, and it landed on the drone platform in a flurry of sparks. The men there looked helpless for a moment, but one of them took his shirt and tried to smother the fire with it. The shirt caught fire instead. Hendrik climbed down the watchtower and darted to its side. He returned with a fire extinguisher, climbed to the top of the drone platform, and doused the fire with foam. A strange fizzing sound indicated that the fire was out, yet the platform was damaged.

Kruger had drawn his Glock, but it was too late. He used all his willpower to hold back. He'd been challenged in front of his men. He wouldn't want to miss his target in front of them as well. He climbed the steps down two at a time. Botha was waiting for him at the bottom.

"I'm taking the Humvees with three men. I'm going after her," Kruger said in a low voice that shook with rage.

Botha's face showed disbelief, and then he said, still unsure, "It was the Swift—" But he stopped himself short. It wouldn't do to tell the men who were around them that Kruger had been challenged by a woman.

Kruger just nodded and then shouted, "Hendrik, with me in the Humvee. Get Gerrie and Hannes in the other. Tell them to follow us."

Hendrik ran toward the main building, and Kruger turned toward Botha. "The compound is under lockdown until I return with the head of this bitch," Kruger said through gritted teeth.

Botha nodded, but Kruger could tell he wasn't happy.

"What?" Kruger asked.

"She is taunting you," Botha said.

"I know," Kruger said, "but I can't let that happen in front of the men."

Botha ran a hand over his face. Kruger had to chase and defeat his challenger. He couldn't be caught on his back foot, even more so with Matondo around—loyalty could be fickle among mercenaries, and he needed his men to deliver the arms shipments.

Kruger reached his office, where Angela Graham had been left handcuffed to an armchair. She looked very pale, and Kruger wondered whether he would get any more out of her. He'd revisit the question when he got back. He grabbed an AR-15 from the gun rack that stood behind his desk along with a box of ammunition. He pocketed three more clips for the Glock and ran to the gate, where the Humvees were waiting for him. As the gate opened, he dived into the first one.

The gate was slow, and Kruger's anger grew. He closed his eyes briefly. This is what Swift wanted: to replace calm with anger and force him to make a mistake. Kruger refocused. He needed to find her fast and get rid of her, even if it meant getting into the Outpost and gunning her down there.

Hendrik followed the light that seemed to move toward the main trail that led to Masisi. The Humvee crushed through the long grass and then the bush. Unexpectedly, the motorbike light went out.

"Faster," Kruger shouted. Swift must be switching her bike for something else. Hendrik pushed the Humvee harder, but the beast wasn't made for speed, and it took ten minutes to reach the main trail. They stopped, and Kruger got out. It wasn't difficult to follow the tracks of the bike to a nearby bush and then identify the tracks of a vehicle, probably a Jeep, going in the direction of Masisi.

"They're going to Masisi," Kruger said as he sat back in the Humvee. Hendrik turned and floored the accelerator. The heavy vehicle started to shake, and both men were thrown around, but neither complained.

"I can't see any headlights," Hendrik said.

"They'll be navigating by the moonlight," Kruger answered. Despite his anger, he'd calmed his mind down. River Swift had been successful at outsmarting everyone so far. It was time her luck ran out.

Botha's warning kept coming back to him. Perhaps Kruger wouldn't kill her immediately, and he might instead indulge in an interrogation session. There was always something that people feared the most. It was a question of finding out what it was and then pressing on that tender spot with brutal determination.

"I see something," Hendrik said.

Kruger leaned forward and grabbed the AR-15. It was too bad that the armored Humvee's side windows couldn't be rolled down. He was confident he could have shot the Jeep even from this far away. But the distance between the Jeep and the Humvee was closing. A few more minutes, and they would ram the vehicle off the road.

"How many men in there?" Hendrik asked, jerking his head forward.

Kruger was about to answer, and then he paused. What if . . .

The shock wave of the double blast spread across the African savanna and made the Humvee shake. Kruger shouted, "Stop!" and Hendrik skidded the Humvee to a halt. They both turned around to check whether the other Humvee had been hit by a rocket-propelled grenade, but the vehicle was intact.

Kruger flung the door open as a cold sweat covered his body. He turned in the direction of the compound. Dark smoke was billowing into the air, and Kruger knew—the munitions storehouses had just been blown up.

Rage choked Kruger, and for a moment, his mind went numb with it. He grabbed the AR-15 from inside the Humvee and lined up the Jeep in its sights from the hood of the vehicle. But Kruger had lost the advantage. Swift's vehicle was now moving quickly away from the farthest point at which Kruger knew he would hit his target. He took the shot anyway and pulled back without checking the result in his scope.

The urgency was the compound.

Kruger knew what to expect. What he didn't know was how many of his men would still be alive after the detonation. When the Humvee turned the corner that led to the compound, Kruger heard Hendrik gasp. Kruger felt the shock of devastation hit him, too, even though he'd prepared for it. The entire front of the compound had collapsed, and so had parts of the main building. The heavy blocks of concrete had decapitated most of the trees, and though the sprinkler system had prevented the fire from spreading on the ground, everything was now soaked in water.

When the Humvee reached the open gate, it stopped, and Kruger got out. He stood for a moment. Rage had been replaced by something even more potent—the need to survive. He walked slowly into the space that was once one of the most strictly guarded compounds in southern Africa. He heard the distinct sound of a gun being racked and took cover, calling out, "It's Kruger."

"Boss," a voice he barely recognized replied, "they're all gone."

Kruger's jaw clenched so hard he felt his teeth grind against one another.

"Botha, too?" Kruger asked. He had once considered what he would do if the man had been reluctant to follow Kruger's decision to eliminate all witnesses once he decided to unwind his operation in Masisi. Now that Botha was gone, Kruger felt robbed. Robbed of the decision to keep Botha alive.

"Yes," the other man replied, his voice trembling.

The man rounded the building, face drawn, and Kruger recognized Willem, the youngest of the team. Kruger squeezed his shoulder as he came close and nodded his head toward the two Humvees that still stood outside the gate.

"Go tell the others. I'll be with you all in a few minutes."

Kruger didn't bother to check how bad the devastation was. He went straight to his office. The reinforced glass had fractured into a spiderweb, and the sliding glass door was jammed open. Kruger stood outside. He used the flashlight on his cell phone to first check the integrity of the structure. It would hold. He stepped inside and found that his laptop was still there. Angela had disappeared, but he was past caring. He snapped the USB drive from its socket, pocketed it, and closed the laptop with a swift slap. He went to the weapons rack, took the MP4 out, and stuffed his pants pockets with all the ammo they could hold. He picked up the laptop and left.

The four operatives—the only ones still alive out of his entire team—stood outside the gate, looking haggard and lost.

"Go back to the second armory. Take all the equipment you can carry. We need to catch a plane," Kruger said.

Hendrik frowned, and Kruger simply said, "Matondo came on an aircraft that is now parked at the Exodus airstrip. That is our ticket out of this mess."

Kruger witnessed a renewed sense of purpose among his men. His own ticket might look a little different, but he wasn't going to tell them that.

As soon as River reached the main trail that led to Masisi, she turned away from the small town. Angela had dropped into a deep slumber, and even in the dark, River could see that she needed immediate medical attention. But River couldn't risk being caught by Kruger as he was returning to his ravaged camp. Eric had told River of another route back to the Outpost. So she'd turned away from Masisi and toward the Mozambique border. Two miles out, she would follow another trail that led to the back of the lodge.

The sun would be rising in two hours, but there still wasn't enough light to help her navigate. She concentrated hard on the trail, keeping an eye on the odometer. She hadn't turned the headlights on because they would make the Jeep instantly noticeable. She slowed down when the two-mile mark approached, looking for a trail that would dip to the right. She stopped as soon as she noticed the bush thinning, but this trail looked like a path used by elephants rather than vehicles. River kept going, hesitated a few more times, and grew more impatient each time until someone put a hand on her shoulder and said, "A little farther down."

The old man Okomi had made himself unobtrusive, still shocked by the treatment he'd received at the hands of Kruger's men. River had forgotten about him and was startled by his voice. She then glanced in the rearview mirror and asked, "Do you drive down there sometimes?"

"Sometimes."

"I need you to guide me so that I don't use the Jeep's headlights."

Okomi stuck his head between the two front seats and directed River through the thick bush for the next forty-five minutes. The trail became clearer and easier to use as they approached the Outpost. River checked her watch as soon as the lodge was in sight. Breakfast for the guests would soon be served, so they could make their first outing into the bush as the sun rose.

The communications between her and Karen hadn't been turned off, although Karen had only contacted her once. River called Karen, hoping the radio silence wasn't a bad sign.

"River here. Are you back at base?"

"Yup," Karen said. "The fucker had a crack at me, but I guess the fireworks at his compound shattered his nerves."

"He tried to shoot you down?" River said. "He was that close?"

The thought made her shudder, but Karen didn't leave her time for self-recrimination.

"But you came through, Riv, and I must say . . . man, that was a hell of a display."

Karen was right, and River concentrated on giving Karen the details that mattered. "And I found Angela and Okomi, both alive, although Angela needs medical attention right now."

River glanced at Angela once more and then said, "Find Orson and get ready. I'm only a few minutes away."

"You mean she needs a priest?" Karen said, anguished.

"She needs a friend above all," River said.

River switched the headlights of the Jeep on and increased the speed. The vehicle bounced around a little more, and Angela moaned. River cursed. It was a fine line between getting Angela to the lodge quickly and making her injuries worse by driving too fast.

The main building of the Outpost had its lights on, and the staff was preparing the tables for a 5:00 a.m. breakfast. River drove past the building, spotting Sarah among the staff. Sarah stopped what she was doing and, for a moment, froze. River drove the Jeep to Karen's cabin, stopped the vehicle, and got out. She waved at Sarah. The other woman waved back—nothing to worry about.

Orson and Reggie were walking down the path when River opened the passenger door. Orson sprinted to the Jeep. River tried to slow him down to warn him, but he just pushed past her and leaned into the vehicle. Orson's knees buckled, and he grabbed the seat to support himself. He bit his bottom lip to stop himself from crying. Then he softly pushed Angela's hair away from her face, and his touch made her open her eyes.

Angela recognized him instantly. She tried to speak but only mumbled a couple of words. Karen appeared at Orson's elbow and laid a friendly hand over his shoulder.

"We need to move her inside my cabin."

Orson put an arm around Angela's shoulders and one underneath her knees, and then slowly lifted her. She yelped in pain, and he froze.

"It's going to hurt even if you're cautious," River said.

Orson straightened out of the Jeep, careful with Angela. Karen opened the door and went in. River turned to Reggie and Okomi.

"She's bad," Okomi murmured.

River took a quick breath. "She is."

Reggie stuck his hand in his hair, and the three of them stayed silent for a moment.

River shook off the numbness that came over her when she knew there was little she could do to save a life. She returned her focus to what she could do.

"Reggie, I collected some intel from Kruger's laptop. There is a name that strikes me as of more interest than the others—Dexter Davis."

Reggie took the USB drive River had taken out of her pocket.

"I'll take a look and see what else I can find about him. I've transferred all the data you held on your laptop onto mine and have started organizing it. Ariana is not gonna believe it. Your laptop is back in your safe."

"We're not ready to talk to her yet," River said.

"I get it. And I won't call her until we agree," Reggie replied, a little put out.

River then turned to Okomi and asked, "Do you know when the next plane from Jo'burg is due to arrive?"

"I thought this morning, but men came into my cell to take my keys to the guest rooms. I guess it must have flown in earlier."

"Did they hit you?" Reggie asked, outraged at the thought that anyone could mistreat old man Okomi.

"They shook me a bit and then threw me into the cell," Okomi said, and then he lowered his voice. "I thought they were going to kill me, but then they brought the woman into the cell, too. I tried to help, but I had nothing—"

A cry of despair erupted from Karen's cabin, and River, Reggie, and Okomi ran to it. When they got in, Karen was performing CPR on Angela, and Orson was looking on in horror. Angela gasped. Her eyes opened wide, and River darted to the bed. Orson took Angela's hand in his and pressed it against his heart. "Stay with me."

But Angela looked restless until she saw River. She opened her mouth, but the words were inaudible. River leaned over her, her ear almost touching Angela's mouth.

"Josefina Bofane," Angela struggled to articulate. "Photos . . . Katuba."

River understood. The person who'd taken the photos of the Katuba massacre was still alive.

"I'll find her and make sure she's safe," River murmured, her lips close to Angela's ear.

Angela closed her eyes briefly to show she'd understood. The expression on her face changed. She looked suddenly peaceful. Her eyes opened once more, looking for Orson. He squeezed her hand even tighter and then brought it to his lips.

River and Karen stepped out the door, knowing the time had come. Angela and Orson deserved to have a final moment alone. Reggie and Okomi had stayed outside. No one spoke.

The soft sobs that came from inside the cabin told them that it was over. River was the first one to go back in. Orson was kneeling next to the bed on which Angela lay, still holding her hand. River shivered as she approached, and then anger punched her in the stomach. She'd just started with Kruger and hadn't even begun with Davis and Matondo. Angela's death wouldn't be in vain.

Karen walked in, too, and then whispered into River's ear, "Let me deal with this. I didn't have time to tell you, but Danny called me. He's managed to take off from Johannesburg earlier than he thought. He and Jase will be landing at the Mutele-Masisi Airfield just after daybreak."

Another punch in the stomach, and this time, it was one of anxiety. River would have to explain to Jason why she'd started the operation before he arrived, and she feared it might not go down well. She walked out again, knowing that the time when she could tell Orson how sorry she was about Angela would have to come later.

"Let's go to my cabin," River said.

Reggie and old man Okomi followed. She opened the door with caution and then let the two men in.

"If I give you a piece of paper, will you be able to draw the layout of the Exodus Guesthouse for me?" River asked Okomi.

Okomi nodded, then walked to the sofa and coffee table. River handed over what he needed, and he started to draw. The details were precise, and he added directions and distances—to Masisi, to the Limpopo River, and from there to the border with Zimbabwe, and then to Mozambique. He drew the Exodus landing strip, took a final look at his handiwork, and gave the sheet of paper back to River.

Reggie took his burner phone out and said, "Do I need to call Eric and Dioko?"

"Please," River said. "And let them know that Danny and Jase are landing in about an hour."

Reggie walked to the balcony to make his call. River thought for a moment and then asked, "You think this unannounced airplane was carrying Angela?"

Okomi scratched his chin and then said, "When they opened the door to bring the woman in, I heard a lot of people talking together. Perhaps it was the people from the plane."

River thought a little more. "Were they from South Africa?"

Okomi shook his head. "No, and I can't even tell you where they *were* from."

River's heart started racing. Was it possible that Matondo was also in Masisi, only a few miles away from the Outpost? Her plan had always been to go after Kruger once his compound had been destroyed, even if it meant crossing the Limpopo into Zimbabwe. But this new piece of intelligence could change everything.

Reggie interrupted her thoughts. "Eric and Dioko are on their way."

"Matondo is almost certainly in Masisi," River said.

Reggie looked puzzled.

"He's the one who was holding Angela prisoner. He brought her here; I guess at Kruger's request."

"Or one of his lieutenants did," Reggie said.

It was a good point. River went to the safe, took her laptop out, booted it up, and logged in. She scrolled through a series of images she saved to a file titled "Katuba" and then turned the screen toward Okomi.

"Did you see that man?"

The old man took some time and then closed his eyes. He shook his head. "I can't be sure."

River then asked, "Did anyone mention the name Dr. Death?"

Okomi's face darkened. "One of the guards who brought the woman in joked about it."

"In what way?" Reggie asked.

"The woman was still alive despite being on the same plane as Dr. Death."

River frowned, and then Okomi said in a low voice, "He has a reputation across the whole of Africa. He likes to throw people out of his plane to get rid of them."

River and Reggie looked at each other, amazed. Matondo had landed a few hours ago and was staying at the Exodus Guesthouse.

Someone knocked at the door and then entered. Karen looked sad. She'd witnessed a lot of deaths, but River knew that each of them left a small scar on Karen's heart, just as it did on River's. Karen walked to the room where they were all sitting.

"I spoke to Eric. He and Dioko are on their way to the Mutele-Masisi Airfield. Eric will help with Angela, and Dioko will go to the landing strip," she said.

"I'll speak to Sarah, the manager at the lodge," River said after a long silence.

Okomi raised a hand. "I can speak to her if you'd like. I've known her a long time. Just let me know what you'd like me to reveal."

Reggie sighed. "I'll come with you."

Both men left the cabin, leaving Karen and River on their own.

"In less than an hour, Jason and Danny will be landing," River said as her eyes fell on the large wooden clock that hung on the wall.

Karen sat next to River and gave her a quick hug. "You did the right thing this morning. If Jason gets pissed at you, I'll tell him myself."

"Thanks for the vote of confidence," River said, "but now we need to get to Kruger before he disappears completely, and that means we haven't got much time."

"He can't just flee like that. He's got men he needs to pay off before he cuts and runs."

"But now we also have an additional target. Matondo is in Masisi." River let that hang.

Karen flopped back into the sofa. "Shit. How're we gonna get the two in one go?"

"That's where Jase shows us what it means to run an op like a SEAL."

Chapter 20

The pale face of Angela kept haunting River as she drove to the Mutele-Masisi Airfield. The windows of the Jeep were open, and she breathed in the soft air that brushed the African plains as the sun rose.

She'd rehearsed a hundred times what she would say to Jason in an effort to convince him that she'd been right to start the operation without him, but her arguments sounded hollow, even to her own ears.

The sound of a turboprop engine made River floor the accelerator. The Jeep rocked hard, and the steering wheel almost got out of control, but she steadied the vehicle and stopped at the top of the runway just as Danny flew over to check that it was free of animals.

He lined up the Cessna and once more performed a perfect landing, hardly producing any dust. Dioko had already arrived. River got out of her Jeep and jogged to his side.

"This guy's really good," Dioko said. "Shame he lives on the other side of the world."

River nodded.

"I'm sorry about Angela Graham," Dioko said, picking up on River's mood.

"But now we have Matondo here in Masisi to deal with," River said, focusing on the task ahead.

"I heard that, too," Dioko said as he waved at the taxiing Cessna. "I'm not sure what your friend Jason will make of Eric and me, but we're in all the way."

"He'll be grateful," River said. Of that she was sure. She'd seen how Jason worked effortlessly with every ally in an operation, Navy

SEAL or not. After all, he sustained his injury when he was on a mission to support some of the locals who'd helped American forces in their fight against the Taliban.

The door of the aircraft opened, and River recognized the bulk of Jason's body—the solid physique of a man who trained every day despite his leg injury. His dark hair was still cut short, and he was shielding his blue eyes from the sun with an old pair of Gatorz glasses. River waved, and Jason waved back. He dropped the Cessna steps to the ground. Danny appeared next to him. He, too, waved, and Jason got out.

He negotiated the steps sideways, careful of his damaged leg. River felt a pang of regret at the sight, but she pushed it away. Jason had gone past resentment and anger. He was doing something different with his life.

Danny handed Jason his backpack. River reached him just as he let it drop to the ground, and they hugged each other. River held back a sob as she leaned a little more into his arms. She then pulled back, looking flustered.

"What happened?" Jason asked.

River blinked back the tears. "We lost Angela."

Anger flew over Jason's face. He hugged River again for a moment and said, "We'll get this SOB."

Danny finished securing the Cessna, then he retraced his steps back to River and Jason. He shouldered his own backpack, ready to go, but didn't ask for an update. Dioko was waiting next to his truck, and they all walked to it. River introduced Dioko to Jason, and they both exchanged a warm handshake. Danny jumped into Dioko's pickup, and River and Jason got into her Jeep.

"What's the update?" Jason asked.

River was glad he got straight to business, but then she needed to deliver her explosive news.

"Karen and I completed phase 1 of the operation," River said, hands tight on the wheel and looking straight ahead.

The atmosphere in the Jeep dropped by a few degrees. Jason turned in his seat and then said, "I should have taken the bet with Danny: I would have won."

River glanced at him, shocked. It wasn't the reaction she was expecting. Her head swam for a few seconds. All the arguments she'd rehearsed on the way to the airfield went away with a pop.

"Let me guess," Jason said. "If you know Angela is dead, it's because you managed to get into Kruger's compound and achieve whatever you needed to achieve there."

River cleared her throat. "But that means that Kruger and his men will soon be leaving the compound."

Jason's eyebrows shot up.

"I blew up the munitions storehouses inside the compound."

She didn't need to elaborate. Jason knew exactly what that meant. She could see his eyes widening and then a smile forming on his lips.

"Now, I was not expecting that." Jason shook his head.

River shook her head, too.

I wasn't expecting that, either.

Then he asked, "What did you use—Semtex? C-4? Dynamite?"

"Semtex, five packs in all."

"How did you get in in the first place?" Jason asked, his smile broadening.

She spent the entire journey to the Outpost telling Jason about phase 1. She gave him as many details as she could while emphasizing what mattered—the compound was no longer viable. Kruger lost several of his men, and the ammunition, as well as the armaments he stored in the two buildings, were gone. But he would almost certainly know about the existence of the young woman who took photos of the Katuba massacre.

Jason asked a few questions but mainly listened with complete focus. River could feel the weight of his attention, but she also sensed it wasn't critical in nature. He was absorbing intelligence, preparing to get ready for the next phase of the op.

"So Matondo felt he needed to pay a visit to Kruger," Jason said as they approached the Outpost. "Why do you think it is?"

"I think Kruger was about to be cut loose by the CIA."

"And you think the guy there is Dexter Davis. The man whose name you spotted in Kruger's files."

"We'll soon know," River said, a little more relaxed about telling

Jason about another of her decisions. "I asked Ariana to send herself an email asking Davis to call me."

"Wow—the more the merrier," Jason said. "Let's have a party. What if he turns up, too?"

"Kruger is his key asset in Africa, and I can't imagine Davis having other assets as senior as Kruger is. Kruger wouldn't tolerate it. I know Davis is CIA, but it's not a good idea to double-cross Kruger or to fail him. Remember what happened to Clery."

Jason straightened up as the Jeep entered the Outpost. River parked next to her cabin, and they got out of the vehicle. Then River took the Glock she'd stored in the glove compartment and walked to the door, cautious. It wouldn't do to drop her guard now that Kruger had become a wounded animal, more dangerous than ever. She cracked the door open and then pushed it hard with her foot. It banged open on an empty room.

Jason shouldered his backpack and followed River inside. He closed the door and said, "Kruger isn't an idiot. He must have known that Davis was no longer playing ball. Sending a couple of shipments one after the other isn't very clever, and Kruger would have taken the hint. Then Matondo turning up would have confirmed that suspicion."

River started preparing coffee. Jason continued, "You found the USB drive because Kruger was going to cut himself loose before Davis did. It's a race to the bottom. He must have a fallback plan—a way to get out of South Africa unnoticed and then disappear in Africa or somewhere else. But his immediate problem is the men he has with him. They are ex-military or mercenaries, and he doesn't want to piss them off."

River returned with two cups of coffee.

"Okay. So he pays them off," River said.

"Or he gets rid of them just the way he did Clery."

River was about to hand a cup to Jason, but stopped in midair. "They haven't betrayed him," she protested.

"I don't think a man like Kruger cares. He needs to make himself untraceable, and he might have spotted an opportunity to do so," Jason said, taking his coffee.

"How?"

"Matondo flew in, which means that there is an aircraft sitting on an airstrip not far from Kruger's devastated compound. But Matondo has come with his own men. If Kruger and his men want the aircraft, they're gonna have to battle it out with Matondo. And what better opportunity to eliminate his own men than in a gunfight with Matondo's troops?"

River sat down and said, "I was about to say that we haven't got much time before Kruger starts making a move, which means that we need to hurry back to his compound. But you're now suggesting that the action will be at the Exodus Guesthouse airstrip."

"I can't be sure, of course," Jason said after he took a sip of coffee.

River's burner rang, and she picked up.

"Eric is on his way to the lodge," Dioko said. "Orson and Okomi are dealing with Angela's remains. Orson is contacting her family."

River gave a heavy sigh, then said, "Come to my cabin. We need to discuss our next move."

River turned to Jason, now grimacing an apology. She perhaps should have asked. But Jason gave her a thumbs-up. He, too, wanted to move fast.

"Before we call everyone in, let's run through how you see phase 2," Jason said.

River was taken aback, and Jason smiled at her surprise.

"A good leader knows how to listen, too."

River sipped some coffee to mask her emotions—relief, anguish, and a little guilt at thinking that Jason would have wanted to stop her from making up her own mind. When had he ever done that, anyway? She cleared her throat and told him how she envisioned catching Kruger and bringing him to justice.

When they were done, River called Karen and Reggie to tell them about the meeting. They turned up within minutes, Danny in tow.

They all found a seat. River made more coffee and handed over cups to the team. She then sat down. Eric arrived last. He knocked at the door, and Karen went to open it, casting an eye through the side window before she did.

He entered carrying a large item wrapped in paper in one hand and a box in the other. It looked bulky but not heavy. Eric walked into the room and nodded a hello to the people he hadn't seen in the last few hours. Jason stood up and went to shake his hand. Eric smiled as he unwrapped the item he'd laid on the floor.

"This is a surveillance drone. It's light and has a good range," he said.

Jason examined the drone. "That will save us a lot of time we don't have."

River stood up and said, "We have a plan."

Reggie and Danny were the first ones to leave. Reggie had been a little miffed that he was going to miss some of the action, but he understood why he needed to. River had entrusted her laptop to him again, and he had used it to store all the intelligence the team had gathered since the beginning of the mission—he'd become the guardian of the evidence. And River's instructions were clear. If the rest of the team didn't make it, he and Danny were to leave, return to the United States, and make use of the damning evidence they'd assembled.

He was also tasked with drawing Davis further out, and he'd be using River's laptop to do so. Ariana had sent a text in the early hours of the morning to Reggie. Dexter Davis had replied to River's email suggesting that River wanted to talk, and he was offering a call.

Eric left shortly after. He'd be manning the drone and was on his way to Kruger's compound. He would only go as close as he needed to to operate the drone, confirming whether the property was empty and whether Kruger had decided to cross the Limpopo into Zimbabwe.

River, Jason, Karen, and Dioko went out last. They carried the equipment Karen and Eric had assembled for the hardest part of the operation. The four of them would gear up after leaving the Outpost, on their way to the Exodus airstrip.

Dioko and Karen jumped in his pickup, and River and Jason got into her Jeep. Dioko went first, and they drove out of the lodge. It was early, but the animals would still be active around the bush and the savanna. They drove for around twenty minutes, and then Dioko turned onto a small trail that led them deep into dense shrubs. They stopped their vehicles, and Dioko got out, rifle in hand. He stood still for a moment, then crouched to look for animal tracks. When he stood up, he said, "We're good."

River, Jason, and Karen got out, and the four of them started gearing up: body armor, backpacks for ammunition, Gerber multi-tool kits, hydration bladders, GPS, helmets, and communications gear. Dioko got some help from Jason, then Karen opened the long bag that held the most important pieces—four AR-15s, three Glock 19s, and a SIG P320.

Jason grinned at the choice of equipment.

"It's a pretty decent choice, considering you guys aren't military anymore," he said as he finished gearing up.

"Hey, I still have contacts, you know," Karen said.

"And Eric knows where the poachers get their gear from," Dioko said as he picked up one of the AR-15s. "The bastards now use heavy weapons to kill the animals they seek. It's a disgrace."

The slight buzz of a cell phone silenced everyone. Dioko picked up, listened, and then turned around to Jason.

"You were right. Kruger's compound is empty. They're all gone."

"Can Eric redirect the drone toward the Exodus airstrip?" Jason asked.

Dioko relayed the instructions, listened again, and then hung up.

"Eric is on his way to a place in the bush where he can redirect the drone. It'll take another ten minutes."

"Okay," River said. "Let's check our equipment and go. We'll drive to the airstrip and stop half a mile away, at the place where we did our last reconnaissance."

Dioko led the way again, through narrow trails only rangers would know existed. But less than ten minutes into the drive, he signaled with his brake lights that they should stop. As they did, the distant sound of gunfire told them that Kruger and his men had already engaged Matondo's troops.

"I presume you have Dioko's number on your burner," Jason said. River fetched it from her pocket and handed it over.

Jason dialed and said, "How quickly can Eric get to us?"

Jason listened to the answer, thought for a few seconds, and then said, "Let's meet a mile out. I need to see where the shooting is taking place."

Dioko stretched his arm through his truck's open window and gave Jason a thumbs-up. They resumed their progress, and as they did, the sound of gunshots and bursts of machine-gun fire grew louder. River cast an eye toward Jason. His entire focus was on the exchange. Her throat tightened. She couldn't imagine he would stay behind despite his limp.

Movement on the right-hand side of the vehicle drew his attention. Jason picked up the AR-15 that he'd placed muzzle-down against his thigh. He trained it toward the disturbance, but Dioko waved him down through the window. Eric's pickup appeared, and the three vehicles stopped.

Eric stepped out of his truck first, drone control in hand. Everyone else got out, and Jason was the first one to reach him. Eric handed over the control and the screen that came with it. Jason stared at it for a moment and then said, "I presume that the men inside the Exodus Guesthouse are Matondo's and that the men outside are Kruger's. I can already see that one of Kruger's men is down. But the shooting is coming from only one building, which I think is the main one."

"They're surrounded?" Karen asked.

"Which means they're not going to last long."

"How many men are around the main building?" River asked.

"Four."

Nervously, River pulled the scrunchie from her hair and retied it around her ponytail. "I've been to the Exodus Guesthouse. There's a pickup at the back that belongs to Okomi, unless someone has taken it already."

"The backyard has a trail that leads straight to the airstrip," Eric said.

Jason scrutinized the screen again. He drew in a sharp breath and said, "One more down, three to go. Matondo's troops will try for a breakout and run to the plane. We need to go now. Eric, come with us in the Jeep. I need to use the drone to determine our approach."

Eric stepped into River's Jeep. This time, River took the lead and followed Eric's direction toward the guesthouse. The gunfire exchange increased in frequency but dropped in intensity. More of Matondo's men had gone down.

"How far?" Jason asked.

"Five hundred yards," Eric said.

Jason maneuvered the drone. "I can see our Jeep. Let's stop."

He extended his hand out the window to ask Dioko to stop. River came to a halt just as two men darted out of the Exodus's main building and ran toward Okomi's pickup.

"Let's go," Jason said as he stepped out.

Everyone was ready.

"From now on, we're only using hand signals or the comms," Jason said.

River, Dioko, and Karen tested their equipment and got ready to move.

"Eric, take the Jeep and go to the airstrip. Yours is the only call we'll take. Tell us when the aircraft is ready to go. You're our fallback guy in case the drone goes down."

Eric hurried to the Jeep and was gone.

The other three huddled around Jason. "Karen and Dioko, right flank. River and I take the left one."

Jason strapped the drone control to his body armor, and the two pairs deployed in silence. River stepped forward, taking the lead, and simply said, "I know where I'm going."

The bush got a little less dense as they moved forward. The sound of gunfire was more sporadic, and it altogether stopped on the left flank. Two down, two to go. Jason put a hand on River's shoulder to tell her to stop. Someone was moving from left to right, leaving the left flank completely open.

Jason activated his comms and said in a murmur, "One hostile coming your way."

The sound of gunfire moved to the right flank. River and Jason started running, but then River could hear it from his grunts: Jason wouldn't be able to keep up.

"Cover me when I get into the main building," she said.

They exchanged a glance full of regret and fear. Jason nodded. "I'll be right behind you."

River got within a few yards of the building as another burst of gunfire erupted from inside. The exchange was taking place far enough away from her so she could run all the way to the closest cabin.

Another shot came from the bush, and then silence. River gritted her teeth. She had to know. She pressed her comms and asked in a low voice, "Karen, do you read?"

"Three down, one to go," Karen said, and then she added, anticipating River's question, "not Kruger."

The sight of a man running toward the main building startled River. She now felt Jason at her side and murmured, "Someone's run toward the main building."

A series of gunshots rang out from inside the property, and then there was complete silence. Jason looked at the drone screen and said, "Someone's running due north."

"That man is running toward the Limpopo River. He'll cross it into Zimbabwe."

"River, Jase," Karen said on the comms system, "we've just checked the two men who died in the bush on our side . . . they both have a bullet to the head, and as far as I can see, those bullets were fired at close range."

Jason shook his head in disgust. "He's terminated his own men."

"Then it must be Kruger, trying to cross the Limpopo," River said.

Her burner phone vibrated. Eric was calling.

"I drove the pickup right in front of Matondo's plane and removed the truck's spark plug," he said as soon as River answered.

"Have they arrived?"

"Just now, and they look seriously pissed off."

"Stay put. Don't engage yet," River said.

Jason called Karen and Dioko. They arrived just as River turned around to relay what she'd learned from Eric.

"Matondo is at the airfield with one of his men. Eric has immobilized his pickup in front of the aircraft."

"Is Matondo going to try to cross the river?" Karen asked.

"No," Jason said. "He doesn't know the terrain. Kruger is out there, and he doesn't know about Kruger's men. Matondo wants to go back to safety, and safety for him is the DRC. He needs a plane."

"Then we need to go after Kruger first," River said, restless. "Once he crosses into Zimbabwe, he'll have a route planned that will be difficult to track, and we'll lose him."

"There is only one safe place to cross the river because of crocodiles and moving sands. He's got around five miles before he gets there," Dioko said.

River and Jason exchanged a look. She didn't want to have to say it, but she doubted Jason was going to be able to follow Kruger. His limp seemed to have gotten worse, and if he had to run . . .

Jason took off the lanyard holding the drone screen and the control from around his neck and handed it over to River. "As much as I would like to finish off this SOB, this one is yours, Riv."

River stood speechless for a moment. She was about to grab the screen when Dioko stopped her.

"The drone won't be enough. We need to track this Kruger guy. He knows the bush, and he'll move fast. I'm coming with you."

River shook her head, but Dioko grabbed the screen and handed it over to Jason.

"Jason can follow us with the drone and tell us what he sees using our comms."

Jason hung the lanyard around his neck again. "Karen and I also need to keep Matondo and his man busy."

"Okay," River said, checking her watch. "Let's go. Kruger has almost fifteen minutes on us."

Dioko led the way and moved fast. River turned back once before they disappeared into the bush. Jason turned back, too, and gave her a nod of encouragement. River gave him a quick smile and then kept going, hiding the sadness that she knew would have crept over her face. Jason would always be fair, no matter what.

River and Dioko walked in silence. He stopped a couple of times, checking the ground for tracks and the shrubs for broken branches that could indicate a recent passage. He picked up a twig and rubbed it between his fingers. He didn't stop as he said to River, "It's blood. He's wounded, probably in the arm."

They walked for twenty minutes, and then Dioko came to an abrupt halt. He crouched, surveyed the ground closely, and murmured, "Lionesses are on the hunt."

He pointed at several sets of tracks. River glanced at her watch. It was still early morning, and given an opportunity, the lionesses would try to take down a prey. Their comms crackled, and Jason came through.

"The bush is not as dense now. I see someone moving ahead of you at one o'clock."

"Copy all," River said. Her mind momentarily drifted to the airstrip and Matondo, but she blinked back into focus. Dioko stood up and whispered, "He's using an old poacher's trail. We can cut the route by walking through the bush, but—"

"The lionesses might spot us," River murmured. She was about to suggest that she would take the risk if he would, but Dioko shook his head.

"They're ahead of us, and the wind is blowing away from us. They won't smell us."

River's heart started to race at the implication, and she said, "Kruger?"

Dioko nodded. "He's bleeding."

River then said, "Let's cut through the bush and get to him before the lionesses do."

The bush became a little denser again, making their progress slower than they'd like. Both River and Dioko carried their rifles at the ready. They stopped a couple of times, and then the bush thinned down to a point where they could see way ahead.

Someone was walking at a fair pace, yet looking around. His camo shirt was torn, and blood had now dried around an entry wound in the left shoulder. River indicated to Dioko that they must stop. She placed a knee to the ground and trained her rifle on Kruger's back. She had a clear line of sight. She would get him if he tried to run. Dioko stood behind her, watching for the lionesses.

"Kruger," she shouted. "If you try to run, I'll get you. Or the lionesses that are hunting today in the area will."

Kruger froze. His gun was drawn, but he didn't try to turn around and shoot. Neither, however, did he raise his hands in submission.

"You won't shoot me in the back," Kruger shouted.

"You made a lot of assumptions about me that turned out to be very wrong," River replied.

Kruger's head dropped, and when he lifted it he said, after a bitter laugh, "How does the English proverb go? Hell hath no fury—"

"Like a woman scorned," River finished. "And the murder of my parents was more than just scorn."

River felt her entire body tremble with rage. She'd moved her index finger to the trigger, and the desire to shoot was overwhelming.

"You don't want to do that," Dioko said calmly.

"So what's it gonna be?" Kruger asked.

River swallowed her anger. Dioko was right. She wouldn't stoop to Kruger's level.

"Even if you make it to Zimbabwe, you'll be hunted by your pal Dexter Davis, who's about to cut you loose."

Mentioning Dexter whipped Kruger up straight. "I know, and I intend to bring him down with me if I fall."

"I saw the file. But he'll claim it's all fabricated." River wasn't sure why she was going down this route, but a hunch told her she was right.

Kruger dug his hand into his pants pocket without caring about the consequences and took a cell phone out of it. He fiddled with it for a few seconds and then said, "Not if you've got that." He waved the phone a few times. He bent down to place the phone on the ground.

"And now, if you don't mind, I'm going to take a chance with those lionesses," he said.

Kruger started running, and River took aim.

But Dioko deflected the weapon before she could shoot. "You don't need to."

The tall grass ahead of them to their left started moving. Kruger must have noticed, and he half turned back, raising his gun, but he never had a chance to get off a shot. The rush of an animal in full flight was a magnificent sight, and the alpha female took him down in one go.

Kruger didn't cry out. He collapsed under the weight of the huntress, his neck crushed with a single bite. Two other lionesses turned up, and Dioko dragged River slowly away from the scene. Nature had been judge and jury.

The sound of a vehicle in the distance startled them. River's burner phone buzzed. Eric had sent a text.

Saw the lionesses. On my way.

River and Dioko stepped into a clear patch of savanna. Eric sped toward them, then came to an abrupt stop. They both climbed into the pickup.

"Don't drive off just yet," River said before Eric could turn the truck around. "I need to pick up Kruger's cell phone."

Eric didn't ask why, and he drove toward the place where Kruger had been downed by the lionesses. When they arrived, there was nothing there but a smudge of blood that led into the tall grasses. Eric slowed to a crawl, and then Dioko extended a hand to tell Eric to stop.

"I see it."

He scanned the area for a few seconds then dashed out, picked up the cell phone, and jumped back into the truck. He handed the device to River as Eric turned the truck around. She pocketed the phone, her mind now on her next target.

"Is Matondo still here?"

Eric nodded. "We've been trading gunfire with these guys ever since you left. They've got a lot more ammunition than we have, though. Jason and Karen are running low, and I'm completely out."

River turned her attention to the cell phone Kruger had left behind: If he was going to get revenge on Davis, what better way to do that than giving River even more intel? And as Kruger had learned—to his detriment—River always delivered the justice bad men deserved.

To her surprise, Kruger had removed the password protection from his burner phone. She wondered whether there was a trick she should be wary of. The roar of a plane engine stopped her in her tracks. Eric accelerated, and they reached the side of the airfield, where Karen and Jason were positioned. Jason had stuck his hand in his hair, looking upset. Karen still had one knee on the ground, her rifle lying next to her.

"Shit," Eric said. "They ran completely out ammo."

He skidded the pickup to a halt next to them and got out, the engine still running, followed by Dioko, both carrying spare ammunition. The plane had reached the end of the runway and was about to start its takeoff sequence.

River jumped into the driver's seat and floored the accelerator. The vehicle hit some heavy branches but pushed onto the runway. She steadied the pickup and, driving with one hand, took the Glock out of her waistband.

The pickup gained on the aircraft as it accelerated. River took aim at the engine compartment behind the propeller from her open window. She discharged the entire clip. The plane took off, barely avoiding the trees at the end of the runway. But River couldn't stop in time and braced for impact with the dense brush.

Chapter 21

She felt someone lifting her body as her head screamed in pain. Voices faded in and out. River forced herself to open her eyes. Karen was checking her vitals. Jason must have carried her into the shade of one of the trees surrounding the airstrip as the sun grew stronger. Her throat felt tight, and it took her a couple of attempts before she could speak.

"Did I get it?" she mumbled.

Jason took her hand. "I'm sure you hit the plane, but it still took off."

River squeezed her eyes tight. She couldn't bear it. She wanted to yell at the injustice and tried to sit up, but Karen's hand firmly pinned her to the spot.

"You ain't getting up, uuma, until I've made sure you're all in one piece."

"I'm in one piece," River protested, her head still swimming.

"I'll be the judge of that," Karen said in the bossy voice she used when she had a difficult patient.

"Matondo is getting away," River cried, tears in her eyes. She shook the hand Jason was holding free and tried to stand up again.

Karen nodded, and Jason helped River rise to her feet.

"You told me about the young girl who took images of Katuba fourteen years ago. She's the priority now," Jason said softly.

River swayed and gripped Jason's arm. How could she have forgotten? Josefina Bofane was still in Katuba, where Angela had found her. If Matondo knew of her, he would be heading for the village as soon as he reached the DRC. And this time, he would raze Katuba to the ground. The horrific images Josefina had taken came back to her mind, and River felt sick.

Eric had pulled the truck out of the thick shrubs into which it had crashed. The pickup looked intact except for a few scratches, and Eric opened the passenger door.

"There's nothing left for us here. We should regroup. I'll call the Masisi cops when we reach the Outpost."

River took her seat in the back, with Jason next to her. Karen would drive River's Jeep, and Dioko would take his own pickup. River stayed silent for the entire journey.

Kruger was gone. But Matondo was still alive, and Davis was secure back in the States. It didn't feel like the justice she'd dreamed of for her parents.

Eric slowed down as they reached the entrance to the Outpost.

"We don't need to hide any longer," River said. "Sarah knows enough by now, and we won't be here for long."

Eric drove the pickup past reception and parked it where a few other Jeeps were lined up. Karen and Dioko followed. They all got out and made their way to River's cabin.

Karen caught up with River before entering and said, "I spoke to Danny and Reggie. They're on their way. Reggie says you got a message from Davis."

The news sent a surge of energy through River's body. "Davis is taking the bait?"

"Reggie sounded mighty pleased, so I'd say Davis has swallowed it hook, line, and sinker," Karen said. "Speaking of which, we, too, need something to eat. I'm gonna speak to Sarah."

River squeezed Karen's shoulder and went into her cabin. Eric and Dioko sat down, and Jason went to make some coffee. A moment later, Reggie and Danny knocked at the door. River opened it, and they both hugged her, then sat down.

Jason put the tray full of mugs of fresh coffee on the coffee table. Everyone took one, and they sipped in silence. Karen came in and told them that food was coming.

"What's up with Davis?" River asked as Karen was picking up the last mug on the tray.

Reggie gave a grin that lit the whole room up.

"Davis is shitting himself," Reggie said, sipping a little coffee before he continued, keeping his audience in suspense.

"I sent him a couple of images taken in Katuba fourteen years ago. I told him there is a witness and that Kruger's file on him is now in our possession. He wants to talk."

There was a murmur of approval around the room.

"By what medium?" Jason asked.

"The telephone."

River shook her head. "Tell him that if he wants to talk, we need to meet face-to-face in Johannesburg."

Everyone went quiet, and River continued, "We need to get him to try to leave the United States. Make it look as though he's escaping."

Reggie picked up on River's idea. "And if we happen by chance to have the right contact at the DHS, that contact *might* grab him just before he leaves."

"Surely Davis has informants or backers at the DHS," Danny said.

"But there is a point at which too much evidence makes it impossible to back someone. Davis was about to throw Kruger to the lions. He doesn't know Kruger is dead. He's got to cut a deal with me before he can safely deal with Kruger, and this is what I'm counting on," River said.

"Kruger was thrown to the lions, all right," Dioko murmured.

Reggie didn't pick up on it. Instead, he said, "And if the DHS doesn't budge, I'll make sure all this information is sent to every major media outlet in America."

"Then call Ariana. This is the moment she's been waiting for—Davis is hers. I'd say this is an even bigger catch than Kruger," River said.

"And if she doesn't want to be looking over her shoulder for the next twenty years, she better get Davis for sure," Karen added.

Reggie got his laptop out and started booting it up.

"We have another urgent task. Josefina Bofane is the young woman who took the images I just mentioned. She still leaves in Katuba, in the DRC, and we need to get her out," River said as she took her own laptop out of Reggie's backpack.

She opened the laptop, logged in, and brought a map of southern Africa up on the screen. She turned it toward Danny and Jason, and they both leaned forward to take a better look. Someone knocked at the door. River got up and went to answer it, and Karen followed. She lifted the curtain that shielded the window next to the door. Sarah and another staff member were waiting with trays full of food.

River opened the door. "That's so kind," she said as she picked up a tray. Sarah held on to it, bent forward, and whispered, "Did you get them?"

River nodded, and Sarah let go of the tray. "Good," she murmured with a satisfied smile. "I hope eventually you'll tell me more."

River smiled back. She owed Sarah the conversation she'd promised her.

Karen took the other tray, and they laid the food on the coffee table.

Danny was frowning, and Jason was on his cell phone, typing.

"We can't do this trip in one go. Katuba is eighteen hundred miles from here, and the Cessna can only fly nine hundred miles without refueling."

"Then we either refuel, as you say, or someone brings Josefina halfway," Jason said.

"But we need to find someone we can trust in the DRC," Karen said before she helped herself to some food.

The aroma of brunch reminded them all how hungry they were. They all dug in and started eating. River took a couple of bites of the roast beef sandwich she'd chosen. She put it down, wiped her mouth with a napkin, and said, "I know who we need."

She walked to the farthest spot of the cabin's balcony and took her burner phone out of her pocket. Orson's phone rang a few times, and then he answered.

"Are you all safe?" he asked.

"We are, and Kruger is dead."

Orson sighed. "I know I shouldn't be, but I can't deny that part of me is pleased he's gone. Time to answer for what he's done."

"But Matondo has managed to escape," River said, anger flaring.

"Does that put someone else in danger?"

"I'm glad you asked," River said. "Yes, it does, and I need your help."

River told Orson about Josefina Bofane. That Angela, as she lay dying, had given River the name of the young woman and that the Cessna wouldn't be able to fly to the DRC without a refuel.

Orson listened without interrupting. He thought for a moment and then said, "Get the Cessna ready. I have contacts in the DRC, reliable missionaries who will assist. They'll help her cross the border into another country or even bring her halfway. If they can do it, they will. I'll call you in an hour."

Orson hung up, and River returned to the room. Everyone stopped eating, and she said, "Orson is going to contact missionaries he knows in the DRC and ask them to help Josefina."

"How soon?" Danny asked.

"He said to get the Cessna ready."

"Can his contact bring her to Malawi? Lilongwe's airport is almost exactly halfway between Masisi and Katuba," Jason said, pointing at the map on the laptop screen.

Eric stood up. "I'll get the Jet A truck to come to the airfield so that you can refuel."

Danny stood up, too. "Now, I don't want to be a pain, but we gonna have to limit the weight. More weight, more fuel, and I want to make sure we can make Malawi without me calling a Mayday."

"Then it's gonna be River and Orson," Jason said.

River gave Jason a quick smile. He tipped his head in acknowledgment. She'd done a good job so far.

Reggie looked up from his food and his laptop. "I've contacted Ariana, and I'll stir up Davis some more."

River took the cell phone she'd picked up from Kruger and handed it over to Reggie. He raised an eyebrow.

"Kruger's phone, unlocked. His parting gift. I guess he wants Davis to go to hell, too."

"You never said what happened to Kruger," Reggie said as he took the phone.

"Dioko can give you all the details you need," she said. "I had a quick look at the contents of his phone. There is a call log, and I think a lot of them are between him and the United States."

"I'll speak to Ariana. Burners are more difficult to track down, but she'll have the tools to triangulate positions," Reggie said.

Karen had stood up and was about to leave with Danny so she could give him a lift to the airfield. River was about to leave, too, when her burner rang again. She mouthed "Orson" to the group and answered the phone.

"Pete Bosh is the missionary who will be helping. He's already on his way and waiting to hear where he and Josefina need to go."

"Malawi," River said.

"Lilongwe has a good airport. I know that some of the planes that bring supplies to the region commute from there. I'll let Pete know."

"It might a good idea if you joined him," River said. "I don't know this man, and I don't know Josefina."

Orson only hesitated a second. "I'll be on my way to the airfield as soon as I've spoken to Pete again."

He hung up, and River turned around. "A missionary called Pete Bosh is on his way to collect Josefina. Orson will call him again and check whether Father Bosh can take her to Lilongwe."

"We'll call as soon as the refueling is done and the Cessna is ready," Karen said.

River finally sat down, and her body protested in pain. She hadn't slept for twenty-four hours. She could still feel the force of the crash into the bush coursing through every muscle of her body, and yet she needed to be alert—at least until she'd brought Josefina to South Africa and then to the United States.

Jason came to sit alongside her with two fresh mugs of coffee.

"You need more food, and you need more of that," he said, pushing the coffee in front of her.

She chose another sandwich—bacon, egg, and tomato—and tucked into it. After two mouthfuls and a sip of coffee, she said, "You didn't mention sleep."

"That, too, but the moment you close your eyes you'll be replaying this morning's scenes in your head," Jason said, taken a sip of his own coffee. "It takes time to wind down when you're in the middle of a mission. But then you know that."

"This feels different," River admitted. "I guess when I was deployed the target was clear: Save the guys in the field and get them out. It was about deciding quickly on the best medical intervention."

River's burner phone rang again, and she picked up.

"Pete can get to Lilongwe on the plane that just came to deliver medical supplies to the DRC. The pilot has agreed to delay the flight by an hour. I'm on my way to the airfield."

"Me, too," River said.

She hung up and turned to Jason. "We're good to go for Lilongwe."

They both stood up and hugged each other a little awkwardly. When they separated, Jason handed her backpack to her and said, "No guns. You don't want to be stopped in Malawi."

She took the second Glock out of her backpack, handed it over to Jason, and pressed her fingers on his shoulder.

"You're the right person for the job, Riv."

She pressed her fingers harder and then picked up the backpack. Time to prove Jason was right. Someone knocked at the door, cracked it open, and stuck his head through the gap.

Dioko said, "The Cessna is refueled. Danny'll be ready to go in half an hour. Do you need a lift?"

River left the cabin without turning back. She didn't know what to say to Jason. They needed to talk, yet she couldn't untangle her thoughts.

By the time she and Dioko reached the airfield, Orson had already arrived. He looked gaunt and tired, but he managed a smile. River noticed that he was wearing his clerical collar and looked more priestly than she'd ever seen him look.

"Danny is an ace," he said. "We have a plan to land at Lilongwe in five hours."

Danny popped his head out of the Cessna's open door. "I'm ready to roll whenever you are."

Karen appeared at his side and pouted in mock annoyance. "I'm tempted to sneak on board, but the captain tells me he can't afford the extra weight. I'm glad *I* don't care so much about my size."

Danny rolled his eyes as Karen stepped out of the Cessna. She hugged River for a moment but didn't need to say anything. She would be thinking about her friend.

Karen and Dioko waved goodbye, and Dioko said, "Eric called me. He's helping the local police, who are completely in the dark about what happened near the Exodus airstrip. I'm going to go help him manage our side of the story."

"What are you gonna say?" Orson asked.

"It's a poaching incident," River replied firmly.

"That's exactly right," Dioko said after a chuckle. He waved again and then walked back to his pickup.

River and Orson boarded the plane. Danny secured the steps inside the Cessna and locked the door. He returned to the cockpit, put his headset on, and exchanged a few words with the nearest air traffic controllers. He gave River and Orson a thumbs-up and started the engine. The aircraft taxied to the top of the runway, and Danny pushed the throttle down. The Cessna bounced off the compacted earth a few times, and they were airborne within moments.

River had chosen a window seat, and she watched as the plane banked right and then gained altitude. Soon they would be flying over the Exodus airfield. The memory of Matondo's escape made her angry once more, but she pushed the feeling away. Her next focus was Josefina.

She turned to Orson, who was sitting across the aisle from her, and asked, "Have you spoken to Pete again?"

"He was close to Katuba when we last spoke. The road is dangerous, but he's lived in the DRC for a long time. He knows we'll be in Lilongwe by 3:00 p.m."

"I just hope Josefina will trust him."

"I told him to mention Angela."

Orson's eyes welled and he quickly used his thumb to wipe away the tears. River stretched out her hand and squeezed his arm.

"I know that I should rejoice and that if anyone deserves paradise, Angela does. But some events in life really test my faith," Orson said.

"Isn't doubt part of what makes us stronger and more certain?" River asked.

He turned toward her. "Mark 15:34, 'My God, my God—'"

"Why hast thou forsaken me?" River finished.

"Doubt makes us better people and gives us renewed strength, but boy, it's hard when it hits."

Orson settled into his seat and closed his eyes. River reached in front of her, where a large bag containing beverages and snacks had been stored. She wasn't sure whether she should interrupt Orson. His face looked troubled, and a frown hadn't left his brow since they boarded the plane. He must have felt River's attention, and he opened his eyes.

"Angela and I loved each other, but I made the choice to dedicate myself to something I thought was bigger—the church, the message of Christ. But now she's gone." Orson's voice trembled, and he stopped.

"I, too, pushed away someone I loved," River said, feeling his pain. "Jason is back in my life, but I can't figure out what that means."

"Talk to each other more, with candid honesty. I didn't do nearly enough of that with Angela—or with Mike, for that matter."

River's reply was interrupted by Danny, who shouted from the cockpit, "Any chance of a coffee? You don't want me to fall asleep midflight."

"Aye, aye, Captain," River shouted back.

She felt glad for the interruption. Although she was certain he didn't mean to, Orson had pressed on a tender spot, and it would have been painful to finish the conversation. River opened the bag and found some cups and a large Thermos of coffee. She poured two cups and handed one to Orson. She unbuckled her seat belt and went to the cockpit to hand Danny his coffee.

"How close are we?" she asked.

Danny slid one of the headphones off his ear. "Another three and a half hours, perhaps a little less. We've got good tailwinds."

River nodded and returned to her seat. Orson had placed his coffee in the cupholder at the side of his seat and fallen asleep. Like all of them, he hadn't had a rest for a long while. River sat down, buckled her seat belt, and poured herself a coffee. She pondered what Orson had said and suddenly understood: Mike must have been in love with Angela, too. Life felt sometimes too complicated to figure out. River finished her coffee and let her head sink into the headrest.

Danny's voice calling her name and Orson's woke her up. She wasn't sure where she was for a moment and then remembered—the plane; Lilongwe; Josefina.

"We'll be landing in fifteen," Danny shouted again.

River rubbed her eyes and stretched. Orson looked exhausted despite the rest, and she dreaded to think how she looked. Not awful enough to scare Josefina, she hoped. Orson hid a yawn behind his hand and turned to River.

"As soon as we land, I'll call Pete."

Danny excelled once more, executing a near-perfect landing, and they were soon taxiing along the Lilongwe airport runway toward one of the gates. Orson switched on his cell phone. He had received one voicemail message. He listened to it and smiled.

"Pete's found Josefina. They're on their way—they should be here in half an hour."

Danny parked the plane. He unbuckled his five-point seat belt and walked back into the cabin. "If they're flying another Cessna, it'll park somewhere close."

"Pete didn't say, but I guess it's got to be a small hopper, too."

Danny released the door, let the steps down, and went back to the cockpit to pick up a handful of documents.

"I need to complete some paperwork for the landing and then the return journey. I'll ask a few questions about flight activity at the airport," he said as he left.

River and Orson unbuckled their seat belts and stood up. They stepped out onto the tarmac. Kamuzu International Airport was quieter than River had anticipated. There was another small Cessna parked a few yards away from them, and a large Boeing 737 was about to take off. Danny came running back to the plane and said as soon as he thought they could hear him, "They're on the approach."

The three of them walked toward the tail of the Cessna, and Danny pointed at a dot in the sky. They shielded their eyes against the afternoon sun to follow the plane's progress. The dot grew bigger until the Cessna came in full view. It lined up with the runway, and the plane landed effortlessly. It slowed down and took a turn toward the gates and the airport building, where River, Orson, and Danny were waiting.

The aircraft parked alongside their Cessna, and the pilot killed the turboprop engine. Orson was the first to approach the plane when the pilot opened the door and let the steps down. River and Danny exchanged a quick glance. She suddenly regretted not taking her Glock with her.

A small, wiry man appeared in the frame of the open door and waved at Orson. He climbed down, rushed toward him, and clasped his hand, looking relieved.

"I am so glad you're safe," he said. "We heard that a small aircraft had crashed in Zimbabwe near the border with South Africa. I thought it might be you."

River walked closer, and Orson introduced her. "Do you have details about the occupants?"

Pete Bosh shook his head. "It'll take time before help can get there. I fear the worst."

River felt her knees buckle. Was it Matondo's plane? She was sure she'd hit the engine compartment.

"Not someone you know, I hope," Pete added, concern returning to his face.

River hesitated, and Orson stepped in. "Someone I don't know. But the most important thing is that we are all here. Thank you for helping us find Josefina."

River was grateful. Orson was right: He didn't know Matondo. He knew *of* him. Danny had disappeared to check what the next takeoff slot would be.

"Of course, I don't need to know why you want her safe, but Kivu is such a terrifying place for young girls and women. I'm glad she was able to leave and I was able to help."

Pete stepped back inside the aircraft. When he came out, a young woman, slim and neatly dressed, appeared at his side. Her hair was tied in a bun, and she looked much younger than River had guessed her to be. He climbed down the stairs, and then she followed. River went forward first. Josefina looked worried, and she advanced with caution.

River tried a smile, and when she was close enough, said, "Angela Graham sent me to fetch you. My name is River Swift, and I think my mother might have given you her camera when . . ." And then she faltered for words.

Josefina took out a very old Polaroid camera from her bag. "Is this the one?" she said, handing it over to River.

River nodded, and then Josefina hugged River. "Thank you for coming for me. Angela promised I would be safe."

Danny called from a distance. "We have a takeoff slot in twenty. Just enough time to refuel and do the preflight checks. It'll be dark when we land, but Eric said he would lay lights down on the airstrip."

"Okay, then," Pete said. "Be safe, all of you, and God bless."

He shook Orson's hand and then River's. Josefina gave him a brief hug.

Pete walked to his own aircraft and went to speak to the pilot.

"Time for a comfort break," Danny said.

They all walked into the airport building to find the restroom. River and Josefina exchanged a few words about the next part of the journey, knowing they'd be able to speak more freely inside the Cessna.

When they returned, Danny had already completed the preflight checks. The last of the fuel was being loaded, and when the pipe came out of the tank, they all stepped onto the aircraft.

Orson lifted the steps and secured them. Danny closed the door and checked that it was safely sealed. He stepped into the cockpit, settled himself into the captain's seat, and prepped the plane for takeoff.

"We're good to go," he said after a to-and-fro with air traffic control.

They took off due south, and River felt a weight lift off her shoulders. She hadn't noticed until now, but she suspected she'd been carrying it for a very long time. Josefina had chosen to sit right next to her, and Orson was sitting in the row behind them.

"Pete told me about Angela," Josefina murmured with a tremor in her voice. "I hope I can help make those monsters pay."

"Some of them already have," River said, "but there is one more left."

Josefina took River's hand and said, "I was very young when your parents came to Katuba, and I only knew them for a short while. But they were generous people who only wanted to help. Matondo and his men, they only wanted to help themselves and arm people. Everyone I knew perished fourteen years ago. If you are building a case and need me to testify, I will."

"Your offer is courageous, and yes, I think your testimony will make a difference."

Both women fell silent. River sank back into her seat. She was almost done.

Chapter 22

A sudden jolt woke River up. She must have drifted into a deep sleep, because the turbulence hadn't disturbed her until this point. Josefina looked worried, and Orson had settled himself next to Danny to help with the navigation.

"The weather has turned," Josefina said. "It's the beginning of the rainy season, and thunderstorms are becoming more frequent."

Another flash of lightning smashed through the sky, and thermals sent the Cessna lurching left and right. River checked her watch. They had another hour to go before they reached Masisi.

"Can you divert the plane?" Orson shouted. He was using the split screen on the dashboard to scan the radar. "The weather system is straight ahead of us."

"I won't have enough fuel to divert way out, and it's darker outside than normal because of the weather. Even with Eric and Dioko placing lights along the airstrip, we need to land before it rains and the deluge prevents me from spotting the lights," Danny shouted back.

River gripped the armrest of her seat and swore. She couldn't fail now, but the outcome no longer was in her hands. She looked at Josefina, and the anguish must have shown on her face.

"We'll get through it. I don't believe I'll be allowed to die today," she said.

Another thunderbolt tearing open the sky made River jump. She wasn't as sure as Josefina was, but she sat back in her seat. She thought about her friends and family and then about Jason. What was she so frightened of?

"I'll fly to the edge of the storm," Danny shouted. "It's our best chance."

The plane banked left, but it kept being thrown about. Darkness was all around, and rain lashed at the windows. A small glimmer of light appeared in the distance, and Danny banked left a little more. The light grew stronger, and the wind that had been beating the Cessna for almost an hour subsided.

"We're out of the brunt of the storm," Orson said, relieved.

"But by the time we reach Masisi, we'll be low on fuel," Danny said, killing the sense of relief. "I hope Dioko and Eric will have cleared the airstrip of any animals, too, because I won't have the luxury of implementing bush-pilot best practices."

"I'll text them," River said.

"Why not?" Danny replied. "I'm throwing the flying manual out the window, so you might as well."

River took her burner phone out, switched it on, and messaged Eric.

Low on fuel, need an emergency landing.

She pressed Send and hoped that somehow it would reach its destination. The tension was now palpable in the cockpit. Dusk was turning into night; the sky was cloudy, with very few stars and a feeble moon. There was no sign of a human presence on the ground, and Danny and Orson were scanning the terrain below for signs of the airstrip. River and Josefina were doing their best, too.

"Come on, come on, come on," Danny kept repeating.

"Here," Josefina pointed to a spot in the distance.

Danny banked left and shouted, "I see it."

He corrected the course of the Cessna once more and said, "We're almost in the red."

People on the ground must have heard the sound of the engine, because the lights that lined the airstrip grew brighter.

"Almost there, baby," Danny pleaded with the Cessna. "Don't let me down now."

He lined up the plane with the runway, then the engine spluttered and died as they touched the ground. Danny pressed hard on the brakes. The Cessna came to a stop, and he collapsed over the controls. River, Josefina, and Orson clapped and cheered.

"Shit, guys. This is the scariest landing of my entire career, and I fly in the Arctic."

Someone was knocking at the door, and River went to open it. Dioko and Eric stood there, looking relieved.

"What happened?" Eric asked.

Danny stood up. He lowered the steps to the ground and said, "I'll tell you over a beer, but for now, I'm gonna go and get sick somewhere where I can't be eaten by a lion."

He stepped down, but didn't go very far. He was sick next to plane's propeller.

Orson stepped out and handed Danny a bottle of water. River was the next one to disembark, followed by Josefina. River introduced her to Dioko and Eric.

"Let's keep you all safe and get out of here," Dioko said.

Eric and Orson offered to help Danny secure the Cessna and stayed behind.

When they reached River's cabin, everyone was waiting for them. Jason, Karen, and Reggie were on the balcony. They all went inside, and River introduced Josefina once more. As they reached the living room, Josefina cleared her throat and said, her voice trembling, "I just want you to know that I'll do whatever it takes to bring the last man to justice."

"And I offer you my legal services free of charge," Reggie said. "I won't lie to you: It will be hard, but we can do it."

"It will never be as hard as what I've been through in Katuba," Josefina replied.

A knock at the door interrupted them. Danny and Eric let themselves in.

"Where is Orson?" River asked.

"He went back to Masisi," Eric said.

He didn't need to elaborate. Orson would want to remain at Angela's vigil.

"What's next?" Dioko asked.

"We need to get to Johannesburg and then DC, but the timing depends on Ariana."

"She still can't believe the amount and quality of intel we sent her. She's gone over the head of her boss," Reggie said, "and her boss's boss. But anyway, she likes our plan very much."

"I've checked the timing," Jason said. "If we leave here at 8:00 a.m. for Jo'burg, we can catch a flight at noon and arrive in Dulles at 6:00 a.m. DC time the next day."

Danny stuck his hand in his hair. "When are you proposing we leave?"

Jason grinned. "Tomorrow morning. A little birdie told me you had a bit of a tough landing. But don't worry—the weather is fine all the way to Jo'burg, and you won't be flying the big plane across the Atlantic."

"Good news travels fast," Danny grumbled.

"The more we wait, the worse the weather's gonna be," Karen added.

"But is Davis ready?" River asked.

"He needs a final small push," Reggie said.

River thought for a moment and then said, "Why don't you all get a table in the dining room for our last dinner at the lodge? Reggie and I need to make things clear to Davis."

"I'd like to stay," Josefina said.

River stretched her arm. "Please, come sit next to me."

"I'll book the flight after your final push," Jason said.

"You're right. Better not jinx it," River said in agreement.

"Oh, I'm not worried about jinxing it. Davis is gonna come running. I just need the laptop you're about to use to do the booking," Jason said. He turned around to join the others.

Reggie had already booted up River's laptop and opened her email account. River sat down and read the last series of email exchanges with Davis. In addition to knowing about the Katuba photos and the file Kruger had on him, he'd been told about the phone call lists and recordings on Kruger's phone.

But he didn't know about Josefina. And he didn't know that Matondo and Kruger were dead. She thought for a moment and then started typing.

I now have a witness who will put Kruger and Matondo at the scene of the Katuba massacre. Kruger and Matondo are not going to like this very much. Kruger won't like the fact that you've tried to double-cross him. Matondo won't like the fact that you've not been able to prevent all this from coming out. If you don't want to spend your life looking over your shoulder or wondering when it will all be revealed, you'll be on the 8:40 a.m. United flight from DC to Johannesburg tomorrow. This is your last chance.

She read the email once more, pressed the Send button, and closed the laptop.

"Let's join the others at dinner."

Eric and Dioko fetched River and her team from the Outpost the following morning. Sarah had hugged River when she settled her bill and invited her to come back for a more *relaxed* visit. The Cessna was refueled and ready, and Orson was waiting for them near the Masisi airstrip. He shook hands with Danny, Reggie, and Jason. He hugged Karen, River, and Josefina. Eric and Dioko followed his example.

"Don't be strangers," they said, "especially you, cousin Reggie."

Reggie grinned. "Next time, we're stalking the poachers."

While the others were boarding, River stayed behind.

"Mike is coming for Angela's funeral. We'll spread her ashes over the grassland in the national park," Orson said.

"She loved Africa," River replied.

"This is what she wanted."

River gently squeezed his shoulder and made her way to the Cessna.

"Don't forget to have that conversation," Orson said as he waved.

River waved back. Jason took the steps up and secured the door. Danny announced takeoff, and they were airborne in minutes.

The tension of the last few days weighed on everyone. Karen went to the cockpit to make sure Danny was holding it together for the two-and-a-half-hour flight duration. Then they touched down as planned, made their way to the terminal at Tambo International Airport, and arrived at the gate of the South African Airways flight to DC.

Reggie checked a couple of times, but Davis hadn't replied. River didn't admit it, but she feared she'd overplayed her hand. Jason and Karen remained optimistic.

They took their seats just as the gate attendant was giving the last call to board. As soon as the plane was in the air, they all fell asleep. River was sitting between Jason and Josefina. She woke up a couple of times to sip some water and move her legs and feet. Whatever the result turned out to be, she felt privileged that her friends had chosen to trust her and grateful that she'd brought everyone home.

The announcement that the plane would be landing in half an hour woke River. She looked around to see that the team was as startled as she was. They made themselves ready for landing. Danny stretched in the row ahead of River and said, "For the first time ever, I'm glad I don't have to land a plane."

Everyone chuckled.

The plane touched down and taxied to its allocated gate, and the passengers started to disembark. Reggie and River were the first ones to switch their phones back on, but there was no message from Ariana. The lines through customs were light, and their luggage came through quickly. They'd just walked out of customs when a message came through on Reggie's phone.

"We're on," he said, waving his phone in the air.

He started running toward the escalators and in the direction of the departure gates. The others followed, and they arrived just in time to witness a SWAT team of heavily armed police officers surrounding a man with his arms in the air. He dropped to the ground facedown. One of the policemen started to handcuff the man just as Ariana walked toward him. Dexter Davis wouldn't be going anywhere.

River's team stopped, but River kept walking, and as she got closer, one of the SWAT team went to stop her. But Ariana lifted a commanding hand, and the man retreated. She gave a quick nod of acknowledgment to River, and River reciprocated. For the briefest of moments, Davis and River exchanged a look. Then she knew he recognized her. It was enough. She didn't need to gloat. She wasn't that sort of person.

As she walked back to the team, Jason and Karen gave her a quick military salute. Reggie and Danny did a good job at imitating the others, and then River smiled. Josefina had taken the old camera out of her backpack and was snapping photos. River joined them for the final shot. Nothing trumped the power of a strong team—certainly not human greed.

Coming Soon from Freddie P Peters

Also Featuring River Swift

Life Saver (spring 2026)
Arctic Fire (fall 2026)

Dear Reader . . .

I hope you enjoyed reading *Trip Wire* as much as I enjoyed writing it!

If you'd like to follow River in her new adventures, the next book, *Arctic Fire*, is available for preorder. Check it out on the link below.

https://geni.us/ARCFIRE

Perhaps you would like to know about my other series. If so, check out the Nancy Wu Smart Woman Crime Thrillers at https://mybook.to/NWCT and the Henry Crowne Paying the Price Thrillers, also featuring Nancy, at https://mybook.to/HCPTP.

On my website, you can gain access to the backstories that underpin the Henry Crowne series and learn about my creative process and how the books are conceived. You can also read the opening chapters of each book as well as the prequel to the Henry Crowne series, *Insurgent*. Just go to https://freddieppeters.com/ and join Freddie's Book Club today.

And now it's time for me to ask you for a small favor. Please take a few minutes to leave a review on Amazon, Goodreads, or BookBub. Reviews are incredibly important to authors like me. They help readers decide whether they might enjoy my books and increase my books' visibility among those who do enjoy them. So if you'd like to spread the word, get writing or leave a star rating. Thank you so very much.

I look forward to connecting with you!

Freddie

Acknowledgments

It takes many people to write and publish a book, and for their generosity and support I want to say thank you to the following individuals:

Barbara Clark, my editor, for her immense knowledge of good language and of what makes a good story great; Lizzie Gardiner, for her expertise in design and for producing a book cover no reader can ignore; Danny Lyle, for his proficiency in typesetting and knowing what it means to work with kindness under pressure; and Jean Durbin, for her precise proofreading.

Appreciation also goes to the friends who have patiently read, reread, and advised on all matters connected with my book, including the team at MIDAS public relations in London, especially Maddie Dunne-Kirby, who's been a tremendous help in marketing the River Swift series; Kathy Vanderhook, my most wonderful supporter, on whom I can test my storylines; and, of course, my very cool ARC team.

Printed in Dunstable, United Kingdom

79503265R00167